LAWLESS
and the
HOUSE
of
ELECTRICITY

D0870377

LAWLESS and the HOUSE of ELECTRICITY

WILLIAM SUTTON

TITAN BOOKS

Lawless and the House of Electricity
Print edition ISBN: 9781785650130
E-book ISBN: 9781785650147

Published by Titan Books
A division of Titan Publishing Group Ltd
144 Southwark Street, London SE1 0UP

First Titan edition: August 2017
10 9 8 7 6 5 4 3 2 1

Names, places and incidents are either products of the author's imagination or are
used fictitiously. Any resemblance to actual persons, living or dead (except for
satirical purposes), is entirely coincidental.

William Sutton asserts the moral right to be
identified as the author of this work.

Map illustrations by William Sutton.
Map design by Rebecca Lea Williams.

A CIP catalogue record for this title is available from the British Library.

Printed and bound in the United States.

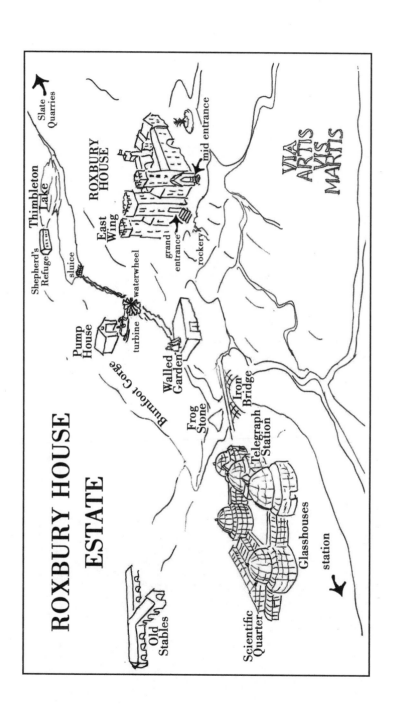

ROXBURY HOUSE ESTATE

Slate Quarries

Thimbleton Lake

Shepherd's Refuge

sluice

ROXBURY HOUSE

East Wing

grand entrance

rockery

mid entrance

waterwheel

Pump House

turbine

Burnfoot Gorge

Walled Garden

Frog Stone

Iron Bridge

Telegraph Station

Scientific Quarter

Glasshouses

station

VIA ARTIS MARTIS

Old Stables

BOOK I
BODIES IMPOLITIC

EAST END PROLOGUE: BODIES & SECRETS, PART THE FIRST [SERGEANT CAMPBELL LAWLESS]

Knife in the heart, knife in the throat. Each holding the weapon that did for the other. On the table, money, in two piles.

I shook my head. "Gambling men, were they?"

"Some folk can't resist a bet," said Molly, "even if it kills 'em."

"What happened?"

"Ain't it plain enough?"

"I'm asking you."

"You're the sleuthhound. Earn your crust, why don't you?"

I sighed. I checked the men were both dead.

Molly was huddled on the bed in the corner. Nowhere near the two bodies. At first, she'd said not a word, which was unlike her, though she gave me a look to make my soul shiver. Both men were dead, and she was glad. They may not have recognised her, but she knew them. And so did I.

They had killed a friend of ours, a little star of Molly's Oddbody Theatricals theatre troupe. They had done it maliciously and cruelly. They were under orders, true, employed by a distant paymaster who remained unpunished; yet they were culpable. I would find it hard to mourn them.

Blood soaked into my trousers as I knelt beside them.

Credible enough that they had killed each other. Still, I would need Dr Simpson to examine the wounds, so he could corroborate whatever tale Moll was about to tell me. Whatever our history, I could not let her go free if she had any part in their death. It is a dictum of police work—and my personal belief—that every man deserves equal treatment in the eyes of the law, and every woman too. Even these blackguards deserved justice, in life and in death.

"Are you all right?"

"I'm alive. They're dead. Preferable to the other way around." She was curled up against the bedpost. Her bottom lip jutted out from a face like brooding thunder. Was this what Molly looked like, afraid? Her clothes were ruffled, but not torn; there was a spatter of blood on her face, but it was their blood, not hers.

I'd been afraid for her since the final days of my previous case, during which Molly made inspired contributions—and formidable enemies. I had worried enough to seek out an escape from London for her. I'd persuaded Molly to accept lessons in polite manners from our friend Ruth Villiers. Over recent weeks, they'd worked on everything from her accent to her underwear in order to transform her from East End urchin into a well-mannered young woman. Maybe not transform: her natural style was irrepressible. Miss Villiers was at least equipping Molly to pass as a decent citizen. I'd been seeking a position for her as a drawing mistress in the further reaches of the kingdom, far from recriminations such as this. I'd finally found one that would serve well, and had all but sealed her employment; but—foolish girl!—too late.

Or was it?

Her hands were behind her back. Only now, as I drew nearer, did I see that she was trussed to the bedstead.

"Well, I never." I clapped in wonderment; inappropriate,

I know, but I was so relieved. "All this is nothing to do with you, eh, Moll?"

"I was talking to the gentlemen, I admit." She sniffed. "The gentlemen as is now deceased. I invited them back for a drink. I suggested a wager or two. Is that a crime?"

"You didn't kill anyone?"

She looked at me, lips pressed together in indignation, and tugged at the ropes.

"Yes, Moll, but I'm asking what you did."

"You police." She rolled her eyes. "Always the woman's fault, ain't it?"

"Did you incite them to violence?"

"No incitements needed, with these two. As you yourself can testify from their previous crimes."

"And I shall have to testify," I said, "when the coroner is puzzling over these deaths."

I looked at her. If she had done no wrong, nothing legally culpable, I might still spirit her away to safety. Her sniffs were eloquent of distress, rather than prevarication. Molly was a liar, but she wasn't lying now. At least, she'd better not be. Nor was her clothing of her usual fashion. She had the look of an apprentice tart. Not the style Miss Villiers had counselled, it was apt enough for this threadbare backroom in Madam Jo Black's tuppenny brothel off the Ratcliffe Highway, but far from her yobbish garb as impresario of the theatrical urchins.

I gestured for her to lean forward and let me at the ropes. "I see why you haven't scarpered."

"Sent for Lilly Law because I preferred you see for yourself, Watchman."

Her friend Numpty had roused me from my bed in Scotland Yard in the dead of night. It was not the first time Molly had requested help; but I owed her, and I had come at once.

"Lest you drew unfortunate conclusions." She coughed.

"Lest you heard reports that I'd been consorting with these gents, now deceased."

"Consorting? Ha!" I looked back at the men. Now that I thought about it, she must have sent Numpty to fetch me before the fatal blows were dealt.

"Besides, Numpty ain't so good with knots. Summon the old crocus, will you?" She gave me a look, tugging at the ropes. "I'd like to see 'em certified dead, then be on my way."

"Keep your drawers on, young lady." I puzzled at the knots on her wrists. "By the time we remove these bodies, you'll be far from this hovel and on a train from King's Cross, bound for the shires, where Miss Villiers and I have secured you a position."

"Exile?" She sniffed. "To the frozen north?"

"You wee southern jessie." I laughed. Coming from Edinburgh, as I do, Roxbury House hardly seemed the north. "Questions will be asked at the inquest. If you are telling the truth, these two oafs have slain each other. If their injuries are consistent with that narrative, according to the doctors, I shall state that they were quarrelling over a bet in a brothel. Over whom they quarrelled will be inconsequential."

One whore is as faithless as another, to the coroner. But Molly was no harlot: her guileful answers were as like to incriminate as exonerate her.

I had no doubt that her wit unsheathed the weapons. She wished them dead, but so did I, and wishes are not forbidden.

"No harm in quitting London a while, I suppose." She wriggled against her bonds. "Lean pickings in the countryside, though."

"Where I'm sending you, young Molly, you'll survive." My recent induction into the Home Office had set me a challenge. Molly was a liar, it's true, but I trusted her. I needed an ally for a mission of surveillance. Could I trust her with such a task, and kill two birds with one jagged rock? I screwed up my eyes. This was not the send-off I had imagined. I tapped on her wrists, to give her the all clear. "Besides, this is work."

"Ta kindly, Watchman." She shrugged off the ropes, all melodrama and sniffles, as she rubbed at her wrists. "But no thanks. I'll find my own hidey-hole, and my own employ."

"It's not a request, Moll. I have a task for you. You'd be wise to accept."

"Or else what?" She raised an eyebrow, and her laughter faltered as I held up the ropes, which had slipped off her wrists with suspicious ease.

"Or the coroner may find it odd that I didn't need to undo these knots."

PILLS FOR THE PALE AND PARALYSED

Dr Williams' Pink Pills for Pale People. They cure:

paralysis	**weakness**
locomotor ataxy	**scrofula**
anaemia	**sundry ailments.**

2s/3d per box. Beware of imitations.

BODIES & SECRETS, PART THE SECOND [LAWLESS]

Bodies are found at the London docks all the time. Jeffcoat thought this one different, but then we rarely agreed on anything.

I handed Molly over to Miss Villiers, by good fortune in town early. Ruth would pack Molly on to the train to the north, give her a talking to, and send her out of danger. I wired Roxbury House, to request we bring forward Molly's employment somewhat abruptly. I received forthwith a short but friendly reply in the affirmative. I was barely arrived back at Scotland Yard, when Numpty appeared again. He delivered the note into my hands before I had time to worry further over Molly's departure. A summons back to the East End. It was terse, typical of my friend, Sergeant Solomon Jeffcoat. Solly and I had worked closely through the spring on the Brodie case, so closely I often felt he knew what I was thinking before I thought it, and I wasted no time in setting off.

He had something he wanted me to see: a corpse secreted in a lifeboat.

Secrets will out, my father told me daily. "All your filthy secrets, laddie, are seen by God and, in the end, by man." Five years at Scotland Yard has taught me otherwise—at least as far as man is concerned—but my father meant that I must tell him everything. Punishment would be swifter and juster if I confessed, before I was found out. For example, when I botched the mainspring of the procurator fiscal, grandmaster of father's guild of watchmakers. (I was apprenticed to my father, hence Molly's moniker for me of Watchman.)

"All your secrets are visible to Him, you wee devil, and shall be to me."

As every honest parent knows, chastising a child for lying will not teach him to tell the truth, but to lie brilliantly. The best liars I've known share one thing, beyond their differences social and temperamental. All had a childhood where discovery meant punishment. I therefore thank my father for my talent in dissembling, useful in my profession, essential to this case in particular. Yet I wonder if it was not just in reaction to my old man that I learned to lie, but in imitation of him. When he died, I stowed his papers away; now that I have the courage to leaf through them, I have found hints of father's own lies and inclinations that make my wrongdoings look angelic.

* * *

Lies lay striated through the House of Roxbury—or must I style it the House of Electricity, as the newspapers did? The house was built on a lodestone of lies, though none could discern them. Nor could I have guessed what lay in its deeper foundations: love. Reckless love, ready to sacrifice anything. Money. Integrity. Souls. Oh, it was on a bloodstained altar this love was sanctified; and there was no ghost, holy or otherwise, to offer a sacrificial reprieve.

Am I harsh? Judge for yourself. Or, rather, judge from the reports and correspondence of that articulate guide, my friend Molly, the urchin, or rather erstwhile urchin, whom I sent into this lions' den, from the frying pan into a furnace where souls were smelted in the service of... well, in whose service such harms were done, you must judge for yourself.

Molly won our hearts long ago. She fell ill, when just a little tyke among her urchin brothers. I was reassessing my naive notions of London, of the rich, the poor, and the malevolent. When Molly took ill, the Hospital for Sick Children had saved her; but it was Ruth nursed her back to health. Since then, I daresay, we have looked out for each other. Her clandestine networks saved my bacon more than once: solving the insoluble, finding the unfindable. She and her brother even saved my life once or twice. Thus bound to them, I could overlook certain illicit activities.

These murders were different, though. I took the decision gravely: I would pack her off to safety. She was doubly beholden to me, and she knew it.

I was charged to find out what was wrong in the House of Roxbury. I was just starting my investigations in the south. I could not waste time in unproductive visits, when they might easily hide any irregularities. Better to place a spy in the north, and an unimpeachable one at that.

To learn what she discovered, let us turn to her own

accounts, both the brief reports she encoded for me and the hyperbolic letters to Miss Villiers which betray a richer story of her fears and hopes and successes.

TO FORGET [MOLLY]

My dear blue-bellied Captain Clocky, Sergeant Lawless, that is, Watchman, old friend,

Safely arrived.

Nothing to report.

Molly

Dear Miss Villiers,

Sometimes a girl wants to forget. And we all know the best way to forget. I am the kind of person who seeks love in all the wrong places. Blame my upbringing if you will, or lack of it, among the Euston Square Worms; though I rather think I benefited from such a particular education.

"Miss Molly, is it?" hollered the lad, a bronzed Adonis.

I've never been met by a private carriage at a railway station before. The statuesque farm hand stood tall at the end of the platform. He gestured to our sturdy carriage. "You'll be the new drawing mistress, if I han't bin much mistook."

Quite a trip. Speedily packed off, after my East End contretemps. Final confab with your good self, Miss Villiers. Changed into suitable attire. The luxurious train. The branch line. Out I stepped to find the air chilled, despite the sunshine. It may have been the second-best phaeton, and driven by the stable boy, but I took no snub from that; besides, Jem was not hard on the eye. Belgravia drawing mistresses may expect better; but this wilderness is not Belgravia, and I am no drawing mistress, if truth be told.

I should be more disciplined: I shall not write such incriminating things.

I stood on the platform, gawping at the thickets and copses as far as the eye could see. As if Hampstead Heath had grown monstrously overnight, obscuring all civilisation, but for stone walls and flocks across the hillsides, the horizon altogether unfamiliar, what with no St Paul's dome, no fog, no stink, nothing to make one feel at home.

"Kindly step up, ma'am."

I recalled your stern injunctions that a lady drawing mistress must not heft her own luggage. Up I stepped into his chariot of the sun.

Jem Stables loaded on my bags and my new drawing case, with its stencil declaring it FRAGILE. He stroked the mare's mane, leapt up, checked I was ready, with a guttural utterance, and set out into the wilds. Of his bare arms directing the reins, I took little note: the loose shirt, the waistcoat a nod to propriety, flaxen locks strewn beneath his cap, smile on his lips. I am no stranger to stares, yet something in the glance of this rustic unnerved me. It was these fine clothes you coaxed me into: his glance bore through my crinoline to these lacy unmentionables. I blushed. Could he see through me? Could he see me for the street Arab I am? I was angry with myself, though you always say blushes flatter my Boadicean skin. Yet it was the first time I've felt a man was looking at me not lest I swindle him, but because I was beautiful.

Damnable nonsense.

Start again.

Roxbury's towers loomed over the valley. Cobbled streets gave way to dirt tracks. An avenue of trees.

Fervid stream, placid lake. Surmounting the bend we saw it. Jem chuckled to hear me gasp. Nothing like the forbidding manors engraved in those gothic phantasies you lend me. This was a mansion of the gods, where I was unworthy to set foot. As safe as the Tower of London, as buttressed as Westminster Abbey. Bumpy, lumpy and broad-shouldered, stretching its elbows up the hillside, and gazing down at the glasshouses shimmering by the Burnfoot Stream, where a melancholic orange monkey sat nibbling the nettles in company with its friend, a strange-looking hare.

Roxbury House.

Dash it all. I promised I wouldn't write such overblown nonsense.

Start again, and keep it simple.

REPORTS AND CORRESPONDENCE [LAWLESS]

Such was Molly's first impression. Yet of the above lines, all that Molly sent to me was the abrupt message at the beginning. This she inscribed on a card, then re-used the paper of her melodramatic letter (so as not to be wasteful) for the letter to Miss Villiers that follows. The overblown drama of the scenes above remained, lightly scored out, on the reverse of the pages. Whether Ruth was meant to read them or not, who can tell?

Molly's reports to me were always businesslike and brief. But the generous letters to Ruth in which she wrapped them were uneven, discursive as her speech, pocked with exclamations, derailed by tangents, and sparkling with injudicious revelations (often encoded, which I reproduce here deciphered).

The excitement of her first arrival we noted with relief.

Despite the brevity of Molly's encoded reports to me, Ruth deemed her letters suitable for my perusal, mostly. We chuckled over her hotchpotch of self-doubt, showing off and scandalmongering. As you may judge for yourself, Molly is a compulsively honest narrator, mostly, if overenthusiastic. Of this gallimaufry, however, how was I to know what was relevant, what was distraction? For instance, in the revised letter that follows, Molly recounts a series of faux pas on her part. This put the wind up me: if my spy in the north was dismissed as a fraud, it would be a personal embarrassment and a professional disaster.

"Don't be an oaf," Miss Villiers reassured me. "She's establishing herself."

I looked at her doubtfully.

"I'll drop Roxbury a line, if you wish." Ruth brandished the letter at me in scorn. The earl had been a friend of her father, and he'd listen to her. "She's just trying to amuse me, as usual, by belittling her considerable abilities."

ROXBURY HOUSE, REVISED [MOLLY]

I saw movement at the window in the east wing. As the carriage swept around the meander of Burnfoot Gorge and up past the main steps, I saw it and I thought nothing of it.

A heavy floral curtain, pulled tentatively aside, to look down at the Walled Garden, and beyond, toward the botanical greenhouses, where scientists bustled over the advances that underpinned Roxbury Industries.

I found myself stood alone at a middling sort of door set in the corner tower. Jem vanished round the back. I fought back the urge to run after my bags. (In London, I wouldn't let them out of my grasp.)

I studied the door. I decided it wasn't the door for me. Jem, hastening back to work, must have overlooked my station. I took myself down the steps and strode across the gravel— tricky terrain in these boots you've foisted on me in place of my trusty old muckers.

Up the main steps, I lost no time in ringing the bell. I gazed up at the doorway, feeling like a sprite in a cathedral. Etiquette, I told myself, etiquette. I know the way of such places: follow the etiquette.

I heard a cough behind me.

I kept my eyes intent on the door. Nothing so important as first impressions, you said. I smoothed down my skirt. I checked my bonnet on my noggin. I reached for the bell again.

I hesitated. In a great house, as we discussed, the butler may have a distance to cover before reaching the door, and there's no insult in that.

Again, the cough, and a face peering round the corner, stage right, from the door where Jem had dropped me. I extemporised a little ditty to myself.

Lo, upon the steps I spy
A lordly figure standing spry.
His pigging cough suggests: "Clear off!"
His stare would make you cry.

"If you please, miss?" One of them questions that ain't a question. I made a point of holding my tongue.

Again, the cough. My resolve wavered. Could this be the lord of the manor? The fellow descended in chagrin. A tall, solid type, his jacket cuffs as weary as his frown, he approached, with the deliberate plod of the manservant. The butler, for sure.

"Miss, if you will please to step this way, I may show Miss...?" He waited for me to fill in the gap in his sentence, eager to shoo me off his front steps before I sullied them.

"You may show Miss what?" Which sounds pert but wasn't

meant thus. Seeing as you'd cabled ahead, I wouldn't brook disrespect for my station.

"I am asking your name."

"None of your sentences has ended with a question mark, rightly."

His lips whitened. "What, pray, is your name, miss?"

"That's a question, I grant you. My name is Molly."

"Miss Molly...?"

"That's right." I revised my posture to a more ladylike stance. "Miss Molly."

"Begging your pardon." He gritted his teeth. "That, I do believe, is your Christian name."

"Not much Christian about it, so help me God." From his look of horror, I judged I'd better create some further nomenclature; we never discussed names in our lessons. "That is, the children are to call me Miss Molly."

Again the cough. "But your family name, for the servants' purposes?"

"Oddbody," I burst out.

His face struggled between disbelief and disdain.

"Terrible name. Miss Oddbody will just not do. Not for children, not for servants. I insist on being Miss Molly." I restrained myself from cursing the pigging door, and smiled, recalling your guidelines on how to treat servants. "Open the door, won't you?"

"If 'Miss Molly' would kindly come around the mid entrance."

"I amn't a servant, you know." Not to make a scene, mind, but I was anxious to get off on the right footing.

He stared. "I know. I employ the servants, and I should never employ you."

I stared back. "Why invite me round the servants' entrance, then?"

"The low entrance is at the rear arch, miss, facing the Pump

House. This mid entrance welcomes artisans and unexpected callers. The grand door is only opened for functions, for aristocracy and for royalty. The housekeeper will show you your quarters, where you shall, I'm sure, be wanting to recover from your journey." He gave me a look up and down, as if to suggest my clothes were flecked with rainwater and my hair soaked in mud.

That was me told.

TRAINING THE URCHIN [RUTH VILLIERS]

Could Molly inspire in her countryside retreat the same devotion Sergeant Lawless and I felt for her?

She is a quick learner. But to make this street Arab into a young lady—a young woman, at least—seemed as tall an order as converting a jack-in-the-box into a person. Molly's bulletins to Campbell suggested I'd succeeded; her letters to me, however, described gaffes and improprieties to make me cringe. Which were true? We could not be sure until I paid her a visit.

That she believed she was continually bungling was a measure of the high standards I had set her. When finally I did visit, it was clear she had made a decent impression after all; she was already part of the fabric of the house.

To reassure Campbell, I described the stringent lessons I had given Molly to prepare her for country house life.

I chose, for Molly's mnemonic acronym, the word CHAOS.

"C for Clothes."

"Nothing wrong with my clothes," Molly had said.

I jabbed at her blotchy waistcoat. "If you're going to protest every step of the way—"

"Gravy, that'll be." Molly rubbed at it with her thumb, then licked the thumb clean. "Meat pie. Spitalfields."

"It's not the foodstuffs in your clothing that worry me, Molly. It's the style."

"Latest styles, Miss V. I picks 'em up for a song off a chap down Covent Garden."

"A chap?" I sighed. "There's the rub. There comes an age when every tomboy's innate charms can no longer be repressed. Her youthful vigour irradiates through her frumpish disguise. Her head may be turned. Or she may notice nothing, and encourage admirers and suitors, willy-nilly. Try these."

Her disgust redoubled. "What's these when they're at home?"

"Drawers."

She rolled her eyes.

"They're the fashion. Else, servants will think you common and maltreat you."

Our lessons proceeded.

"H is for Holding," said I. "How one comports oneself."

"Do you mean not putting my feet on an armchair?"

"Never decorous." I laughed. "Especially with those boots."

A was for Accent. Knowing thespians aplenty, Molly responded to this challenge. She squeezed her lowly London tones towards more refined elocution, though her diction will always be injudicious.

O for Obeisance. Women are obedient. Women are faithful, moral, and passive. If they should hazard any show of defiance, faithlessness, or aggression (palpably masculine traits), they are shunned, ruined, or incarcerated.

Finally, S for Servants.

"Everyone," I said, "must develop their own style with servants. Overfamiliarity is never wise. Lack of acknowledgement is equally risky. Be kind, but be entitled. And, Molly, never carry your own bags."

BODY OVERBOARD [LAWLESS]

"Who's been and moved this body?" I growled.

The harbour master stood in his office, staring at a length of tarpaulin, rolled up and crumpled at one end. Bodies at the docks are no surprise, as I said. There is a world of difference, however, between a sailor drowned after a dust-up with his wife's other husband, sad as that may be, and a passenger on a luxury liner despatched en route between Indonesia and the Isle of Dogs.

"I said, who brought this body in?"

The harbour master did not bother to muster an excuse. A short, sweaty man in a jacket of indeterminate colour, he walked past me to survey his domain, the East India Docks. Scotland Yard had jurisdiction only over Her Majesty's Naval Dockyards, not over the merchant fleet arriving at the Thames. He knew it. I knew it. To these commercial monsters, questions of evidence mattered nothing. Get the ships out to sea, get the profits rolling in. Engravings of the Eastern Steam Navigation Company's vessels lined the wall. Beneath lay this bizarre exhibit, like equipment to be rolled out for a marquee.

"Ugh." Raising the tarpaulin, I flinched away. The aroma was not so strong, but vile, the remnants of putridity mixed with rancid brine. I forced myself to peer beneath. Only the head had been unwound; the rest was still wrapped. I glimpsed the face, or should I say the skull? A gossamer residue of skin clung across one cheek, like a blister soaked in soda: no fresh corpse. "Where's Sergeant Jeffcoat?"

The harbour master gestured to the lifeboat, raised on blocks by the warehouse wall, not far from the water. If he gave me an adieu, it was drowned out by the strident machinery.

The lifeboat sat askew against the warehouses. Behind it loomed the vast bulk of the *SS Great Eastern*, being refitted to rescue the transatlantic cable. Wonderful venture: we'd soon catch up on the latest news of Lincoln's cats over our morning coffee.

Jeffcoat popped his head out, in response to my halloa. There was always something sublime in the diabolical machinations of the dockside: he seemed etched in miniature against the leviathan, like a bible story illustrating man's puny stature before the godhead.

"Trouble boiling your porridge, Watchman, you good-for-nothing haggis-muncher?"

"I've been at it since cockcrow, Sergeant Lazybones." I would leave it till later to explain Molly's evacuation, our plans having come to a sudden head—indeed, two heads. "While you were clutching your hot water bottle."

Jeffcoat ignored my jibes. He was examining the boat up and down, gunwales to rowlocks, or whatever. I watched intently: why pay such attention to the boat, while the corpse lay still wrapped? If it were a simple drowning, he would not have called me, nor if the fellow had perished from cold or drink. That he had, abruptly, meant a mystery.

Jeffcoat pressed his knifeblade nose to the flaking paint of the aft seat. "Dints," he muttered.

"Why have you called me?" I frowned. "Just another unfortunate stowaway."

"What, on this lifeboat?" He ducked under the seats, checking every recess. "Never afloat."

"So he snuck on to the liner. Came in on its coat-tails. Didn't survive the trip."

"He was only found when the ship was being refitted. Not even then. They said the old lifeboats stank. Swapped them for newer models, and sailed off."

"Sailed off?" I blinked up at the *Great Eastern*. "The ship's right behind you, dunderhead."

"Our body is two months old, at least. Dunderpate." Emerging from his searches, he tapped on the lifeboat's prow,

the liner's name emblazoned in white on the red edging: SS
GREAT BRITAIN. "The *Great Britain* came in from Australia, via
the Cape, two months back. In and out in a fortnight. Other
lifeboats were sold off. Nobody wanted this one. It's sat here
ever since, with him in it." Jeffcoat jumped down. "They
thought it was oars wrapped in the tarpaulin."

"Two months? He's been dead longer, I'd say. Haven't you
looked?"

We headed back to the office, past towering cranes and
clanging repair shops. Jeffcoat brushed off his hands on his
police trousers. "How did nobody smell him?"

I hadn't smelt him until I moved the tarpaulin. "He was
wrapped so tightly, I suppose."

"Wrapped? So he didn't climb in himself."

"I'd say the body was put there, already dead."

Jeffcoat narrowed his eyes. "Or did it fall in?"

"Fall?" I glanced back at the *Great Eastern*. The lifeboats were
visible, lined up, midway atop the great upper deck. "Slap bang
in the middle of the first-class deck?"

We strolled into the office, ignoring the harbour master's
glare. The smell was permeating the room now, like the
recollection of decay. Jeffcoat turned away from the body to
study the engravings.

"I can think of smarter places," I said, "to hide a body."

Jeffcoat tapped at a picture: a liner at sea. "Look." The
lifeboats were slung from the sides of the upper deck. He
glanced at the tarpaulin and took a pencil stub from his pocket.
Grinning, he rolled it over the engraving, as if it were rolling
off the deck, and made a whistling sound to signify it tumbling
into the lifeboat hanging there. "Where are the lifeboats kept,
when they're at sea?"

The harbour master gave us a dirty look. For Board of Trade
inspections, he grumbled, they must be brought on deck; but
at sea, they hung down port and starboard sides. He mopped

his brow, warming to his theme, and began boasting of their promenade decks as broad as Piccadilly, incalculably strong, and buoyant as a life-preserver—

"Didn't preserve this fellow's life." I batted away a fly, as I gently stripped back the tarpaulin. I was pleased to see Jeffcoat grimace as much as I had.

Remnant of a face, withered down to bone, sinews, vestiges of hair. Impossible to tell age, lineage, or even gender. These traces had been weathered to a skeletal pallor by his ensconcement under the flaking gunwales, as the lifeboat dangled in the rains of Cape Finisterre. Prominent teeth: put me in mind of a rabbit.

The skeleton seemed restful. Clothes long disintegrated. Around the wrist, strips of leather: a kind of amulet. Broad leather belt, still in place, though the trousers were long gone. Leather sandals, of uncouth style. At his feet, a basket, woven of bark strips with a type of bamboo, and filled with stones.

Of what he had died, I could not tell, but I would make damn sure Simpson told us.

"You know what Wardle would say?" Jeffcoat elbowed me. He emulated our erstwhile inspector's Yorkshire accents. "Eee, lad, leave well alone."

"He's dead," I continued in the same tones. "He's unmourned. Why dig up t'past and ruin more lives on top of his?"

I'd idolised old Wardle, in my first tender days at the Yard. Now I was grown cynical, his maxims sounded hollow. Jeffcoat had looked up to the old scoundrel too. His ignominious departure had left us both rudderless, until we overcame our differences: a touch of envy here, prejudice there. As a team, we were as good as any detectives in Scotland Yard; in the country, God damn it.

"Aye," he went on, unable to acknowledge the superiority of my impersonation. "Schoolchildren study history, and so they should, but not the finest minds on the force. Out on them streets. Catch me some lowlifes and ne'er-do-wells. Leave bygone crimes to lesser minds."

We looked at each other and laughed.

"Inspector," I addressed our absent inspector, "we think differently. History has come alive, and no more evidence of that is needed than our late orders from—"

Jeffcoat touched my shoulder. His glance toward the harbour master shut me up. He was right: I should know better than to spout in public of our briefing at the War Office.

We knelt to examine the corpse, disturbing as little as possible.

"Fair hair." At my touch, the strand disintegrated. "Germanic, or Nordic."

"Maybe." Jeffcoat never agreed with me. "Or bleached by time."

"The chin," I mused. "That certain weakness common among the upper classes."

Jeffcoat shook his head, unconvinced. The strip of skin drawn against the skull was waxy and emaciated.

"Prominent forehead speaks of ill health," I hazarded. "Curvature of the neck. Bony shoulders. Looks ill nourished."

"Skeletons will look out of sorts." He clicked his teeth. "Odd shoes, though."

I nodded. "From the colonies? Queensland? The Transvaal?"

"I don't know."

"But someone may. Casual-looking. But the stitching is rough. Not a working man's shoes."

"Cultural differences, though." Jeffcoat was a terrific one for his cultural differences, which can make mock of such surmises. Our continual disagreements he wrote off to our disparate heritage: my Caledonian artisan stock (father a watchmaker, mother from island weavers); he from rough Kentish Men mixed with unspeakable Men of Kent (a mongrel breed if ever there was one).

As I touched the strange basket, its reeds friable, the waft of decay caught in my throat. Nothing inured you to that. Yet this was not the stench of fresh death, with its oozing juices and bloating flesh.

"No obvious injury." Jeffcoat was still examining the bones.

I frowned. "Simpson is never going to give a date of death."

"Nor cause." He cocked his head and pointed, squinting. True enough, one shoulder was out of kilter, as if from an impact. The left hip, beneath it, bore an indentation. Jeffcoat drew back, that look of connection in his eye. He drew his palm sideways, then sharply down to bang the floor. "Ka-donk. He fell from the deck."

"Pushed."

"Pushed, then, wrapped up tight. Fell—what?—fifteen feet. Got jammed under the boat's aftmost seat. Invisible from deck."

"Just a tarpaulin. Why would you notice it?" I pushed at the basket, heavy with stones. "And the weight intended to drag him to the bottom of the sea—"

"Simply dinted the boat." He stuck out his lip. "Strange that nobody looked for him. Nobody noticed him gone."

"Maybe they did. We'll check the records." I thought a moment. "Who knows how long he'd been there?"

"Simpson, though?"

I laughed. "Simpson will say—"

"You fearful gendarmes." Dr Simpson stood in the door of the harbour master's office, obscuring the daylight. "What inarticulate tripe are you attributing to my tender lips?"

THE UNIVERSITY DOCTOR [LAWLESS]

Our medic, for all his corpulent frame and bombastic style, had sneaked up on us, absorbed in our deductions. Neither of us held out a hand of welcome.

Jeffcoat's lip twisted into a smile. "You're about to tell us, I've no doubt."

We stepped back to make way for his Falstaffian bulk. To my surprise, Simpson lost no time getting down on his knees to peer at the skeleton.

"Oh, dear," he murmured. "No, no, no. Look, you've gone and let the flies in. This would have been a lovely set of remains for my students. Hermetically sealed. How long dead?"

"We were rather hoping," I said, "you might tell us that."

Jeffcoat and I looked at each other. "You're doubtless about to say that inside that tarpaulin, damp, salty, shielded from the sea, this fellow may have been dead a week, may have been dead a year. Which will stymie our ever identifying him."

Simpson smiled smugly. "My, my, Jeffcoat. What a lot you have picked up under my tutelage." He lost no time prodding the nasal cavities, poking at the teeth. He frowned at the strips of emaciated skin, picking at them, as if disappointed with his dinner. He felt the ribs, frowned again at the basket, sniffed, blinked, and called for a lamp. "Long dead, all right. Soft tissue almost totally decomposed, bar the odd sinew. In the absence of the usual carrion insects, the body has eaten itself, as it were. Yet the absence of putrefaction is surprising. Six to eight months, at least. Possibly years."

"Doctor," I groaned. "Don't be messing us about."

He touched the skin, sniffed at his fingers, and looked puzzled. "I couldn't be sure without taking it for further analysis."

I stared at him.

"Lawless," Simpson snapped, "you whisky-addled Celt, I'm not obfuscating, merely refusing to rule out possibilities you may subsequently discover to be true."

"Take it for analysis, then," said Jeffcoat.

"You're the detectives." He began to get up. "Plenty more you can dig up about him, I'm sure."

Jeffcoat placed a hand on his shoulder, preventing him

from rising. "You can do better than that, Doc."

"Come along, boys." A desperate look came into his eyes. "Does it matter? Johnny Foreigner lays down his knife and fork out on the high—"

"How do you know he's foreign?" Jeffcoat let go his grip. He hauled the doctor up on his feet.

"His bloody shoes, man. And this Hottentot pot, whatever it is." Simpson took his chance to step away from us, looking for his exit. "Look, the fellow was tubercular. Angular kyphosis in the thoracic and lumbar region. See? Touch of ankylosis below the neck—"

I blocked his way. "Did it kill him?"

Jeffcoat stood shoulder to shoulder with me. "You don't see signs of foul play? The shoulder here—"

"Could be. Could be any old injury. Pointless worrying over it." He saw that we were not going to yield so easily. He rolled his eyes. "Maybe he died of consumption. Let's say, the ship's doctor was reluctant to keep him in the sanatorium. I'd be the same. Some halfwit porter found a place to stow the bugger, and they clean forgot."

Jeffcoat puffed. "A likely story."

"Are you sure," I said, "he died of consumption?"

"For heaven's sake," Simpson groaned. "I can't tell."

"You can," Jeffcoat said.

"Not by looking."

Jeffcoat smiled. "You'd need tests?"

"So you can tell." I smiled too. "And you will."

"We wouldn't want to turn nasty."

"Speak with our friends in the medical council."

Jeffcoat gripped Simpson by the arm. "Or your friends at the newspapers."

Simpson rocked unsteadily. "Ho, there, must you—!" He noticed the harbour master observing our contretemps. That quieted his complaints. There were scandals aplenty about doctors, and a secret sold to the papers might garner a nice fee.

"Are you sure," said I, "he was dead before he was wrapped up?"

"Are you sure," said Jeffcoat, "he wasn't poisoned?"

"He may have been." Simpson lowered his voice to a rapid rattle. "He may have died of Drugs. Poison. Might account for the inconsistent preservation of the soft tissue."

"But you'd know," said I, "once you'd taken in the body for analysis?"

Simpson looked at me.

"Come off it, you fearful crocus." I wasn't going to let him wriggle out of it; he could roll his eyes all he liked.

He turned, teeth clenched, and barked at the harbour master. "Have the body brought out, will you? I'll drive it up to University College Hospital myself, before you let every fly in the dockyard lay in him."

"Him, eh?" Jeffcoat nodded satisfied.

Simpson replied testily. "Almost certainly."

"Still discernible, poisons and the like, after such a time?"

"Most likely. If any diagnostic tools can discern them, ours can." He huffed to the doorway. "I'll bring up my carriage. The shoes you may send for, if you wish, but take the blasted pot yourselves."

The harbour master welcomed our further queries as a mother-in-law welcomes her son's wife.

How could we check on passengers gone missing? We must have the SS *Great Britain*'s itinerary, stoppages, moorings, passenger lists; how strictly the passengers' comings and goings were enumerated; likewise, traders en route. Unlikely this was a Bombay spice merchant, yet one might have done away with him.

The harbour master demurred. Such a load of copying work would take weeks.

I shook my head. My librarian friend Miss Villiers would do the job at triple speed; she did not enjoy the Yard's measly copyist rates, but she loved a mystery. He should send the papers to the Yard. The glimpse of a ten-bob note sweetened his look; I toyed with it a moment, running through any last doubts. Might the body have been secreted there after the lifeboat was deposited ashore?

Unlikely. The docks were busy day and night. A corpse couldn't be lumbered around without drawing notice.

We would not delay Simpson's analysis. I left the tip squarely in front of him.

"Jeffcoat, any point in getting a drawing—"

"To see if anyone recognises the skull?" Jeffcoat laughed. "Why not?"

"Of the basket. See if any museum johnny can tell us where it's from?"

Jeffcoat reconsidered. "Send for your friend Molly. She's our best artist. True to life, and discreet, mostly."

"Ah, yes. Molly. Jeffcoat, there's something I've been meaning to tell you."

POST MORTEM [LAWLESS]

The Erith explosion took us by surprise. That it happened the next day was pure coincidence, I was sure, but it was a coincidence that cost us dear: it was months before I connected our tubercular skeleton and the terrors which loomed over London that summer.

We heard the boom as we were driving up to the University College mortuary. All London heard it. We should have done something about it straightaway, but Londoners ignore anything that doesn't stop the traffic around them.

We'd gleaned all we could from the harbour master the

previous day. We harassed Simpson, to make sure he attended to the post mortem. We sent for Molly's minion, Numpty, to sketch the basket. I sent word to Miss Villiers about the copying job; what might be turgid to others would to her be delightful prying.

Simpson tried to shoo us off. We would have none of it. He was an evasive wretch at the best of times; but this was not the best of times. To identify this lone corpse, with his rabbit-like face, was a long shot, no doubt, but we must know if it was foul play or not. Customs were alerted to suspicious imports around the country docks. An isolated death might point to a larger warren of plots.

Simpson worked in silence, ignoring our brooding presence. He took samples of the remnants of skin and hair. He annotated the dental patterns. He examined the skin minutely. Since arsenic poisoning hit the headlines, doctors were anxious not to be caught out; if their certified as natural deaths later proved accidental, or criminal, they could lose their licence.

Simpson found that the disjointed shoulder and damaged hip bone Jeffcoat had spotted were not the only signs of a fall. Checking the ribs, he declared two fractured. Consonant with falling from a height—or being rolled off deck. His skeletal frame made a pitiful corpse. There were no glands left to analyse for consumption, but, along with the tubercular joints, the brittle bones showed signs of starvation. "He is long enough dead to make diagnosis difficult. There remains some skin for the Marsh test, to check for arsenic. I warn you, though, foreigners have strange ways. No Register of Poisons. Many consider arsenic an aphrodisiac. Any murderer you accuse may claim the Styrian defence, saying the fellow took arsenic of his own free will. I will seek the usual things." Alcohol, poisons, narcotics, opiates. "Given his quaint shoes, I shall cast the net wider. There could be peculiar herbs at work. The analysis will take time. You're fortunate to have access to my laboratory." Taking hold of the skull, he stared into the eye sockets. "I'd adjudge him what we now call Caucasian."

"Is that a kind of Russian?" said Jeffcoat.

"No, Sergeant." Simpson laughed, and he never laughed kindly. He leant his corpulent bulk towards us and whispered, "That means, he's one of us."

I ignored his leer. "How did he die? That's the thing. Where in the world is he from? Where did he live? The clothes surely give some clue."

Simpson gestured to a pile on the next workbench and carried on with his work. We examined the material closely. The leather was good quality, though worn; the stitching was rough, without the pinpoint work we expect today, finished by dextrous children indentured at low wages (a scandal, to be sure, but clothes must be stitched).

Jeffcoat found the secret pocket, inside the belt loop, for travellers fearful of robbery. Rolled in that little tuck, Jeffcoat found, secured by a twist of paper, a ten-shilling note. He frowned. "My father always said: ten bob in your pocket and you ain't destitute, my son."

It was as if the dead man was refunding my tip to the harbour master. "Pay your way across the river of death, at least." I spotted pale ink on the twist of paper Jeffcoat handed me, one word faded by time: ROXBURY.

I dropped it in astonishment.

"Something wrong, Watchman?"

I looked at Jeffcoat. Molly would be on her way right now, despatched as far as possible from the double murder. Before I could explain, in burst Molly's little chap, Numpty, his urgency beyond the appropriate.

Simpson grunted in reproach, as the boy tugged at my arm.

"Calm yourself, Numpty. As you're here, you can sketch the basket. But it's not rushing anywhere, nor are we."

"I ain't, Sergeant, but you two 'ave to." He drew breath and declared with all the gravity he could muster, "There 'as been a hexplosion."

CONTRAPTIONS & RENOVATIONS [MOLLY]

Dear Miss Villiers,

The butler, Birtle, loomed in the doorway. He stepped aside to usher me in with all the hospitality of a vampyre considering his dinner.

My first steps inside Roxbury House. Before I'd gone two paces, Birtle coughed his pigging cough again. I hadn't realised: I was still clutching my drawing case. Ladies never carry their own bags; contrary to life on the London streets, you impressed upon me that a country manor rarely threatens a body with theft.

Birtle bade me leave it on the step. "It will be brought up forthwith."

A fearful blunder.

I strolled into the back hall, nonchalantly gazing about, polite and inquisitive like.

"Miss? Follow me." He gave me a dirty look.

He has me down as a thief.

I did gawp, I suppose. I ain't never seen a place so beautifully situated as Roxbury House, stowed up a valley amid the crags, streams caressing the rockery, forests tickling the ramparts.

I expected to find the interior dilapidated. I've seen inside many a house more lavisher and grandiose in London, Bucks Palace by no means the grandiosest. Imagine my flabbergastery to find it jammed to the rafters with contraptions and contrivances I've never seen before. As I followed Birtle down the back corridor, he rang one of the servants' bells, only it didn't ring: it buzzed, like a bumblebee.

Clunk, clank.

Before my very eyes, a sort of cage descended from the ceiling; a porter emerged through the metal grate and went to get my bags. He gave me a friendly tip of the hat, with a sideways look to check Birtle hadn't seen.

A clock struck the half-hour, only it didn't just strike: it played a musical quartet.

After the chill northern air, I couldn't understand how it was so warm. As we crossed the threshold of the central hall, an updraft of heat fluttered my unmentionables, emanating from the floor; no sign of a fireplace.

Whoosh. Thud. A metallic shake, and up through an opening in the marble floor rattled a foursquare trunk, bumping to a stop beside us. Birtle turned to it, with a sigh. He raised a finger, to bid me pause. He pulled at the clasps, his distaste apparent. The lid sprang open, nearly fetching him a nasty blow on the chin.

I leapt back, expecting a leopard to jump out. It was the afternoon post, sent up from the glasshouses by pneumatic railcar, including a package marked FRAGILE: ELECTRIC. How many passageways are secreted in these interstices? I'd better watch what I say, for who knows how room is interlinked to room?

The grand entrance was in a state of upheaval. Scaffolding. Dust sheets. Decorators at three levels. The top fellow painstakingly brushed the wall, as if restoring the Mona Lisa; the mid-level workman was delicately removing plaster; at the bottom, a woman mixed paints, daring the occasional daub.

"Renovations." Birtle coughed, uncomfortable. "Lady Roxbury had wanted it repainted, but of course…" He took the package, with a glance aloft, then shooed me up the stairs: he couldn't wait to hand me over to the housekeeper.

* * *

Roxbury House is a topsy-turvy world. We climbed two storeys from the entrance and were still at ground level, the hill behind being so steep. We reached the kitchens, with the housekeeper's quarters adjacent, atop the butler's flat. The servants' quarters fanned out from this hub of power, clambering up the craggy hillside. All this too up the rear of the household, leaving the front for drawing and reception rooms, libraries and bedrooms, with wondrous views.

Birtle's brows, thunderous black, made it clear he thinks me as tagrag as a Dutch button. But I hadn't never heard of a mid entrance. I thought you had me well prepared. If I can navigate Catherine Wheel Alley of a late evening, evading flimps, filchers and hedge creepers—

Damnation take it, I meant to steer clear of costermongers' argot to pass muster, if not as a lady, then at least as a lady's drawing mistress.

DEAR WATCHMAN,
CONTRAPTIONS APLENTY.
FURTHER REPORTS AS I FATHOM THE ELECTRICALITIES.
MOLLY

LIES AND EXAGGERATIONS, PART THE FIRST [LAWLESS]

What a correspondent Molly was. To her first arrival she devoted a series of letters. More followed daily. I had asked her to note the goings-on in the house and grounds. No more than that. I alluded vaguely to the nation's security, but this was just to give her a sense of purpose. She would be too loyal to wander off and let me down. I didn't expect her to discover much; I gave her first missives little attention.

With the growing national panic, though, her surveillance became important. I needed more from her terse reports, more than the wide-eyed wonderment of her letters to Miss Villiers (which she knew Ruth would give me to read, if I were so inclined). We did not need to know of Skirtle's bosomy voice, like warmed milk, or Birtle's, as insistent as a door-knocker. Her wide-eyed wonderment was winning, but distracting, even as she tried to focus on the contraptions, and the machinations animal and mineral. Molly loved subterfuge. From the start, she concealed my reports within these letters to Ruth. There could be nothing suspicious in correspondence with her sponsor, whereas notes to Scotland Yard might attract attention.

Once I made it clear that her reportage might be vital to the nation (and diabolically useful to our enemies), she encrypted as if her life depended upon it. She wrote in invisible ink, she wrote in abstruse vocabulary, she wrote in forgotten slangs. She did this partly to annoy me, partly to spice up her bourgeois position, but mainly so I'd need help from Ruth. Miss Ruth Villiers, erstwhile British Museum librarian, now freelance scrivener, notary, and researcher. My raven-haired Ruth had shrugged off her dowdy library clothes for dresses, once her Aunt Lexie had rescued her wardrobe from her home—which she refused to visit, due to a tiff with her father. Of Miss Villiers, more anon.

I can scarcely think of anyone with a more realistic grasp of the world than Molly. Yet in her letters to Ruth she did overwrite. Those gaffes upon first arrival she overstated; even if Birtle did think her indecorous, they had orders from Roxbury to overlook teething problems. Molly had to make everything wilder. Consider this, in which Jem took her to view the greenhouses:

Through trees tall as Nelson's Column, my flaxen-haired Jem named the buildings we pass: Pump House, by the gorge; Shepherd's Refuge on the crags above; Walled Garden; glasshouses, encompassing the scientific quarter. Below, the menagerie, where his favourite orang-utan gave us a wave; behind, tropical trees rose through a steamy haze; two storeys up, gardeners on the balcony, busy as bees, collected botanicals in the pale northern sun.

Everything, to Molly, is pale and northern.

She painted a pastoral idyll, with sublime peaks neath inclement skies. I shall not reproduce her glowing manuscripts in full; and I shall supply missing information, from other contributors and things we learned later through guesswork and guile.

Ruth knew, though I did not, how Molly edited her cast of characters. I am a lazy reader of fiction: a volume with a family tree I will quickly close; I prefer a map. She met all the servants, the gardeners, the scientists, but mentioned precious few. She told of butler, but no underbutler; she told of Skirtle, but mentioned none of the staff of maids, except Patience Tarn, the deaf-mute girl; she told of Jem's work in the glasshouses, but not of the researchers who directed him.

I later accosted her over this. "What the hell were you thinking?"

"Narrative economy, Watchman, my friend. Mr Dickens advises reducing the dramatis personae for clarity's sake."

"But, Molly, this is no shilling shocker; these are investigative reports. You needn't follow the dictates of novelists."

Economy and clarity indeed. Still, I took her point. No reader can absorb a panoply of characters all at once; they must be introduced singly, and memorably. She excised Lodestar's scientists, and gave us Jem the stable boy; and memorable he was.

Even Skirtle was not actually Skirtle. The irrepressible

Northumbrian housekeeper was in fact Mrs Soutar. Her pseudonym derived from the Roxbury children's efforts at saying Soutar as toddlers, and everyone at Roxbury House still called her so.

And Birtle, the butler—heaven forfend—was not truly Birtle. The previous butler, long ago, rejoiced in the name of Edward Butler. The earl could not bring himself to call out "Butler!" It sounded too imperious. Nor could he call "Edward," as that was his own given name, by which Lady Elodie was wont to call him. Thus the original Butler was rechristened Birtwell, after a university friend of Lady Elodie's. The later butler graciously accepted this title, deciding that sounded better than his own name.

It was Molly who transmogrified this into Birtle, or simply misheard it, by analogy with Skirtle. I will not correct it, for that was how we learned of him, but it caused us no end of embarrassment when we arrived and got it wrong.

Thus Skirtle. Thus Birtle.

Roxbury House presented challenges beyond Molly's ken. Her reports of the earl evoked a simplistic portrait. I suppose I saw the picture I wanted to: a jovial gentleman, withdrawn from the tussles of business to his rural sanctuary; thence Lodestar emerged, a young man with the hunger to keep Roxbury Industries where the empire needed them, at the forefront of power.

The exaggerations in her letters were all "in the interest of the narrative" (as she later protested). These I shall unravel as we go; but Molly was no fantasist. After all, her literary models were penny dreadfuls, Spring-heeled Jack and the gothic nonsense lent her by Miss Villiers. Though these led her to exaggerate blunders, such as her quarrel with Birtle, she made little of other things, such as her falling in love.

* * *

SKIRTLE [MOLLY]

"The new drawing mistress?" said Skirtle, the housekeeper, her accent outlandishly northern. She ogled me, judging whether I was a delicate orchid or a dung heap in the doorway. She reproached Birtle. "This wee slip of a thing? But they'll eat her for breakfast, the feral wee rapscallious unthinking excuses for bairns. Think how they gulled the last tutor, and him an Oxtobrian gradient with a masterly degree of scientography."

I looked to Birtle for a reply.

He had slipped away soundlessly.

Skirtle buzzed at a button by a hatchway. She tugged me into her lair, hurled me on to a chair and furnished me with cup and saucer. The hatchway buzzed back, and up surged a copious tea tray: it was the dumb waiter. She mashed the pot, eyeing me thoughtfully, and poured my tea: steaming hot, splash of milk, no mention of sugar.

Skirtle gazed into the broad mirror above the window, distracted. Whatever was she looking at? I craned my neck: a view across the Burnfoot Gorge—that view, with the sun setting golden on the peaks! Yet these rooms were at the rear of the house, the crags rising sheer in front of us. Ingenious mirrors, reflecting via a spyhole above her door the view from the upper drawing room's bow window.

Skirtle was a-muttering, half to me, half to herself. "See what you done? What you done is you made an enemy of Birtle. Already! Before you're halfway in the door, like. Swift work. Grand door's Birtle's. Mid door's mine, dear. You would have to ring the wrong 'un." On went the monologue, with an invention that would have earned her a living extemporising at Wilton's Music Hall.

I took my chance to study her.

Skirtle wore a tweed jacket, speckled oatmeal brown,

barely buttoned around her middle. Forest green taffeta draped her bumpy terrain demurely, but fell short of concealing her ankles. Shoes in need of a stitch. She resembled nothing so much as a lovely fruitcake, in which the mix was poured right to the brim, with no thought how much would spill over in the baking. She was fruity and delicious. I think a slice of Skirtle, whatever my troubles, will make the world a good and kindly place.

OMISSIONS [LAWLESS]

Thus Molly on Skirtle. Molly revelled in showing Ruth round through her letters. She illustrated for us the rumbling world of Roxbury House. There was always calm; there was always activity. There were great events; there were quiet evenings. There was Thimbleton Reservoir; there were the Burnfoot cascades. Whether well-born or lowly, tentative or tenacious, you could find a place at Roxbury.

Her feelings, though, as Miss Villiers pointed out, were discernible more through omissions: that Birtle was a prig, Skirtle a font of energy, Jem kind, and Lodestar—well, we are coming to Lodestar.

Explosion [*Erith Evening Reporter*]

The gunpowder explosion this morning was heard all over London and felt fifty miles away.

At 7 o'clock, two barges were being loaded with gunpowder from a magazine on the Erith marshes. One barge exploded. The second barge exploded.

Thereupon the magazine exploded. A column of black smoke rose to the heavens, visible for miles.

No trace of the barges was found. By the time the area was approachable, bricks and timber from the magazine and nearby houses were scattered over a wide area. Scientific instruments at the Royal Observatory showed sixty undulations in the five seconds the explosions lasted.

Still more alarming was the destruction of three hundred feet of river wall. Flooding of the marshes was threatened, an irreparable disaster.

By good fortune, it was low tide. Officers from Scotland Yard called at once for support. In an unusual spirit of cooperation, Woolwich Barracks sent 1,500 soldiers, who plugged the gap with patriotic fervour.

Nobody saw how the explosion began. The causes are under investigation. The quantity of gunpowder is estimated at 750 barrels in the depot and 200 in the barges, each barrel containing 100lb. The sufferers number seventeen. Of these ten are dead (five reckoned as missing, but surely blown to smithereens). Seven of the sufferers are doing well at Guy's Hospital, with one exception.

The effect upon domesticated animals has been remarkable. Thousands of pets succumbed with fright, the mortality to canaries being especially severe.

TERROR ON THE THAMES [LAWLESS]

"I thought the end of the world had come," a gentle old lady kept saying to all who would listen, as we tried to steer her away from the dangers of the rubble, the repairs and the river. "I thought it was the end, and I'd soon be reunited with my Harold."

I need not add my description of the Erith explosion to those published at the time, by press, pamphleteers, victims, rescuers and busybodies. Jeffcoat and I arrived in time to be of use. We cleared the area of bystanders. I tackled the self-appointed moral guardians voicing their unwanted opinions on the state of the nation, while people lay in pain:

"How have you let it come to this?"

"Slipped through the net, did they? I'm appalled, but not surprised."

"Immigrants, ain't it?"

"Please," I said, ready to give them my plain opinion of how it had come to this. But there were more urgent tasks. "Let us get to the injured."

We stanched wounds. We tied tourniquets. We sent the wounded to hospital. We removed the dead, or what was left of them. A local fisherman spoke quietly of the danger posed by the river: it could kill a hundred times more than the blasts. We took stock of the damage, and wired Ripon at the Home Office.

The soldiers arrived before lunchtime. They worked tirelessly. The river wall was redeemed: a temporary job, but sufficient for now. How lucky we were that the tide was out. Floods would have engulfed a huge area. Was that the intention? To cause untold damage and deaths? Was there an intention? Or was it accidental? I found myself wondering: whoever perpetrated this, did they stay around to see the terror? Were they watching me now, among those vociferous bystanders, laughing at our efforts?

Jeffcoat and I attended the disaster not just as Yard officers responding to the crisis, but as officers deputed by the Home Office to investigate subversion, intimidation and anti-British activity. Could someone have planned this? What kind of organisation would dream up such a scheme?

We lost no time in contacting perennial culprits. The Chartists denied it. Not that they styled themselves Chartists any more. They were essentially the same folk agitating for the same goals demanded throughout the thirties and forties: reform the Poor Laws, universal education, universal suffrage (at least, broader suffrage; let us not be ridiculous). But these days, they had learned to couch their moral goals in economical arguments, which made Tories and Liberals tangle to pick up their policies in search of the popular vote.

The Fenians neither claimed it nor denied it.

There were other groups and sects, but none so organised, nor so polemical.

Someone circulated the rumour, and the satirical papers picked it up: it was the French.

NAPOLEONIC MURMURINGS [LAWLESS]

"Gentlemen, you have saved London's most powerless and unprotected," said George Frederick Samuel Robinson, Marquis of Ripon, stroking his beard, "and now you are going to save the nation."

Before these explosions, and the fracas in Guernsey which followed, I would have sworn there was no threat from France. Any sane person would. This was when everything changed: not just my opinion, but the approach of the governmental department to which we had been seconded.

Jeffcoat and I had been summoned to the Home Office just three weeks before, in June. In our late investigations of Brodie's business empire, we had made enemies. I had expected recriminations: our investigations implicated policemen, press, priesthood, charity workers and businessmen; not to mention politicians, right up to the Prime Minister. I was expecting the worst. At best, we might be reprimanded: we'd be relegated to the bureaucratic hinterland, and spend our careers in menial duties in the back offices of Scotland Yard. At worst, I foresaw us sacked and publicly shamed.

Jeffcoat told me to stop worrying.

I was sure they would accuse us of things we knew nothing of, by way of retribution. There had been threats aplenty before the cases came to court. I was exhausted by it all. The late nights, the aftermath, the human complications, with rescued women who had no place to go, and we had to find them lodging wherever we could. I imagined our enemies would accuse us of the very crimes we'd been investigating; they were powerful and without scruple. That was the meeting we steeled ourselves to appear at.

"Let's wait," said Jeffcoat, "and hear what Ripon has to say."

"Save the nation?" Jeffcoat smiled at Ripon uncomprehendingly. "Delighted to. How?"

Ripon enlarged upon his hyperbolic declaration until we almost believed him. He was newly appointed Secretary of State for War, to general astonishment. For he was a bluffer. An intellect, no doubt, and of schooling so private nobody knew where. He was prone to inflammatory buffoonery. That is all very well at the Hounds Club; when enacted on the diplomatic stage, it tends to start wars. He allied himself with Gabriel Mauve, MP, in a hawkish anti-French stance (that is, the late Gabriel Mauve, MP). But they fell out over an interpretation of Homer, or a cravat, or something. Ripon was truly one of those floating liberals whose political views shift with the times— or indeed with *The Times*, to which he contributed scurrilous articles demeaning his opponents' dress sense.

"Murmurs have been overheard in Parisian circles," Ripon began, "about Louis Napoleon III's ambitions. Cross-Channel ambitions." He poured drinks. "Five years ago, I grant, these would have scarcely seemed credible. The British Navy without equal. Dominating any port we chose. Hence our nice trade arrangements. The Chinese buying our opium. Garibaldi safeguarding our lovely Marsala."

I frowned. Louis Napoleon was our friend, I thought. He'd proven it in the Crimea.

"He stood by us against the Russian bear." Ripon nodded. "Stood close enough to notice our antiquated guns. Relics of Waterloo. Cumbersome muskets. Ships powerless when the Tsar barricaded Kronstadt Harbour. When we've wrought-iron commercial wonders like the *Great Eastern*, why are our warships rickety and slow?"

Jeffcoat gave a quiet whistle. "So he built *La Gloire*." He always took an interest in France.

Together they explained to me the glory of *La Gloire*: the first ocean-going ironclad naval vessel could not be sunk. Not by seaborne guns, not by emplacements in the Channel. Her hull, twenty inches of armour-plated timber, could resist a 68-pounder over twenty yards. She could sail right up the Thames. If Portsmouth Harbour, home of our great navy, was vulnerable, "Britannia rules the waves" was obsolete nonsense.

"You follow?" Ripon tugged his beard, as if to make it longer. His mouth slanted downward, but his eyes were broad and kindly. "We are no longer safe in our beds at night. If this concerns you, as much as it does me, I shall pour another drink and bring you on into our inner office. Work out how we counteract this threat."

"Are you joshing us, sir?" Jeffcoat said. "I mean, your Lordship?"

Ripon gave him a glum look.

This induction into the Home Office opened our eyes. Crimes were no longer isolated. The security of the nation was a constant concern. It required attention to patterns of crimes, to unexplained deaths, to suspect disasters, and vulnerable thresholds. Panic over immigration had been the province of bigots and xenophobes. Now it was echoed in the corridors of power.

Within two hours, we were fully apprised of the Royal Commission on the Defence of the United Kingdom of 1859:

depositions from senior navy and army boffins; proposals for barriers and batteries to protect harbours such as Portsmouth (initially rejected); the parliamentary debates which slashed the funds for the extraordinary ring of newfangled forts, latterly caricatured as Palmerston's Follies.

Thus the importance of Roxbury. Roxbury Industries were already central to our national defences as weapons innovators. For the completion of these defences, Roxbury was essential: for the guns, the hydraulics, for the brickwork.

But the earl had changed. This was the concern for Ripon and the Home Office. Roxbury stopped coming to the House of Lords. Only last year, sick of the government's vacillations, he had ended the government's exclusive deal with Roxbury Industries and begun pursuing international contracts. Thus our first charge: find out what was wrong in the House of Roxbury. We needed a spy in the north.

I thought at once of Molly. Whenever I needed help, I liked to offer Molly employment. She would be perfect for elucidating Roxbury's withdrawal. But there were drawbacks. Molly was not quite an appropriate employee for such a house. Miss Villiers would have made a suitable governess, but I had no wish to send her to the ends of the kingdom. Molly, on the other hand, was young and malleable. She could draw, she needed the work, and she needed to get out of London. Why couldn't she be a drawing mistress? It was too beautiful a chance to spurn.

Jeffcoat and I discussed the urchin's strengths. He was unsure; I thought her perfect. I swayed the day. We decided to withhold the details from Ripon; we simply referred to her as "our eyes in the north". Molly was a professional trickster, after all. She could be headstrong, she could be errant, but spies require a complex cocktail of characteristics. Above all, I trusted her. I would need to trust her ever more in the coming months, if the nation was to be safeguarded.

As of this first meeting, in June 1864, Palmerston's Follies stood uncompleted.

After Erith, the groundswell of support began rising, and then more after Camden. After Guernsey, it was beyond contention.

OF THE OLD EARL, PART THE FIRST [LAWLESS]

The earl had a favourable notion of Molly before I sent her north. They had even met, briefly, at the Commons Enquiry in the spring, where Jeffcoat and I uncoiled the secrets of the aristocracy in public. Roxbury had attended the enquiry, and Molly had given expert testimony on the subject of misdirection, dear to her heart and her pocket.

The earl mentioned his admiration to me. "Nice to see such verbal acumen in a youngster."

"You should see her drawings," I said. For Molly was making sketches of the scandalous courtroom proceedings, for which the illustrated press paid well.

From then on, he observed her closely. She sketched witnesses with unerring accuracy, capturing not their exact likeness, but a fluid essence: she laid bare their soul.

"I could use such an artist on my estate," the earl told me in passing. He seemed admirably unconcerned by Molly's eccentric style.

I thought nothing of it at the time. Molly had never thought of venturing north of Finsbury Park. Now that I recalled that invitation, it felt right to send her as our agent. Molly was in danger anyway. When she engineered her revenge on those men, I seized my chance.

Molly was not grateful. She was sixteen, or fifteen, or thereabouts—nobody knew rightly—and ripe for trouble. Removing her to —shire was a wise precaution. She took some persuading, not to say blackmailing, but she soon began to make her observations: the brief version to me, the elaborate to Ruth.

OF THE OLD EARL, PART THE SECOND [MOLLY]

WATCHMAN, MY OLD CHUCKABOO,
YET TO BE PRESENTED TO THE EARL.
HIS EXPERIMENTS KEEP HIM OCCUPIED.
YOUR NORTHERN EARWIG

Dear Miss Villiers,
Of the old earl, I yet know little.

Disappointed to report little progress. My first researches involved nosing around, getting under Skirtle's feet as she was overseeing the house cleaning.

"Oh, the earl used to busy himself in town," said Skirtle proudly. "Made his name in hydraulics. Toured his manufacticaries all round the kingdom. There in't a theatre in London dun't use hydraulic safety curtains, nor a self-respecting hotel without Roxbury lifts. The docks use 'em. The locks use 'em. From this acorn grew the oak of Roxbury Industries, crowned by all this."

She gestured to the grandeur all about us: the oak panels of the lower drawing room, the wild rockery outside, and the shimmering greenhouses. In Skirtle's halcyon tales, the earl was as likely to be up north, overseeing ironclads, out west with army artillery, or down south at the brick quarries. The brickworks come from his wife's family, taken over when her father died. Once I'd got Skirtle going, she recounted the potted history warmly.

"The queen made him an earl. Respected both sides of the House. No wonder they turned to Roxbury Industries to fortify our island." She hesitated. "There was a hiccough, though, back in the late fifties."

"What?" My ears pricked up. "What happened?"

"Some funny business over a bomb in Paris." She turned her attention to the floor, adjusting the grates through which heat arises so magically. "That's all forgotten now. Now the navy wants their wooden wall plated in steel. Who does England turn to but Roxbury?"

"Nothing wrong, is there?" I refrained from asking if the country could still count on Roxbury Industries. Mustn't blow my cover. "The earl no longer busies himself in town?"

"No." Skirtle bustled around the lamps. She couldn't keep the tone of regret from her voice. "Nor with his industries neither."

"I've barely seen him. I haven't done anything wrong, have I?"

She ignored me, holding each lamp up to check the wick and content herself the glass was clean. "Well, he's distracted, you might say." She mustered a kind look for me. "Don't worry your pretty head over it."

I rather thought I'd have the lowdown for you by now. I imagined I'd be presented to him forthwith, prior to embarking on the children's drawing lessons on Monday.

I caught Birtle tidying the lower drawing room. "Will I be meeting with the earl soon?"

He snorted. "No, no. His Lordship is occupied."

"Occupied how?"

He glared, as if this were the rudest question he'd ever heard.

"How?" I repeated. "How is he occupied, then?"

"Well, he has business," he blustered. "Down the scientific quarter."

"The glasshouses, you mean?" I gestured down the hill with my thumb. "What's going on there that's so important?"

"The earl's business is not my concern." Birtle harrumphed. "Nor is it yours. He has his plants. His animals. His machines. His electrical experiments."

"You consider his work important, Birtle?"

"Of course I do, you pipsqueak." His black eyebrows worked in astonishment, like a caterpillar quadrille. "But it's none of my business whether it is important or trivial. I am here to facilitate his work, without interruption from the world, the estate, or upstart employees such as you."

"Experiments?"

"I'm sorry?"

"You mentioned experiments." I stepped nearer, to unsettle him. "What experiments?"

"I don't know, blast you." His eyes blazed. He blinked in horror, as he realised what he had said. "You have made me do something that never happens: I have lost my temper." His eyebrows arched for the skies, and he muttered reluctantly, "For that I am sorry."

"I haven't made you do anything. Nor have you answered my question." I smiled. "If the earl is neglecting his wider affairs, tied up with these experiments, where are his sons? Why don't they step in?"

"The eldest, Wilfred, Marquis of Burnfoot, is soon to return from his tour of India and China, training for the Dragoon Guards. The second son, Nicodemus, only yesterday took five wickets for Harrow in the match. He returns tonight. In the morning you shall be teaching him along with his sisters, as he takes a special interest in drawing."

"Not much use in industry, then?"

"The earl has Mr Lodestar for that."

I nodded, for I've heard this name Lodestar bandied about, but Birtle offered no further account. "And the earl's wife?"

"His wife?" He looked at me. "His wife is…" And Birtle turned away, his voice constricted. "She is departed from us."

I regretted my question, which had apparently unmanned him.

"Miss Molly, it's advisable that you restrain your inquisitive nature, at least until you have understood the ways of such a house as this. You are keeping me from my duties. I bid you good day."

With that, off he went. I watched him pretending to busy himself, checking the buff on the servants' buzzers in the hallway.

Next I meet the children, and then the larks begin.

Roxbury's experiments keep him busy. That is all I can say for now.

CORRESPONDING WITH ROXBURY [LAWLESS]

Why should the name Roxbury be in the secret pocket of a dead man's trousers arrived from the other side of the world? The body at the docks dropped swiftly down my list of priorities after Erith; further after Camden; and after Guernsey, I disappeared down a governmental rabbit hole, as we began not just to solve crime but to anticipate it.

We'd done all the checks we could think of. The few passengers who'd died on board were all accounted for. They listed the victuals supplied at every dock, the menu for top table, the staff and passengers and their coming and goings. Nothing stood out. Crew came and went at every stop, of course, but never was a passenger noted as missing. We scoured the records for inconsistencies and incidents. If such a man vanished without vestige, he was unlikely to be a passenger. We gave up hope of identifying him. We informed

Simpson the body could be buried in the police graveyard in Moorfields. But not before I'd written a courteous note to Roxbury himself, enquiring if he might have known any passenger arriving on the *Great Britain* over the last few years.

Nor did I forget the men who had ostensibly tied Molly up and then killed each other. Too easy to write them off as the kind of men nobody would mourn.

I tracked down their next of kin. I informed them plainly that these men had been killed in the line of duty. No need to mention their dishonourable duties, or brand them as criminals. Soldiers of fortune, they died as they lived, by the knife, in the slums. Seeing as there were no culprits to be arraigned, the coroner reported death by misadventure, for simplicity: the paperwork for murders is tremendous.

One wife wrote to request a pauper's burial. The other sent no reply. To think how the men's shadowy labours had been rewarded gave me a pang. Whatever Brodie had gifted to them, they had paid for it with their immortal souls.

Roxbury's answer came not from the earl himself, but from this elusive Lodestar whom Molly had mentioned. He replied by telegram, verbosely, from the wire station in the greenhouse scientific quarter. An expensive communication, this paid excessive respect to an enquiry from Scotland Yard, while demonstrating that Lodestar considered his own time too important to waste on detailed correspondence. He wrote as follows:

WE ARE CURRENCY. ANY NUMBER OF REASONS
FOR NAME IN POCKET. WE SELL ENGINES AROUND
WORLD, ARMS, AND SHIPS. THERE IS STATION IN
BRAZIL WHERE EVERY NUT AND BOLT IS ROXBURY
MANUFACTURED. EXCUSE EARL IF CANNOT FATHOM
WHY IMMIGRANT SHOULD HAVE HIS NAME IN
POCKET. NO LESS USUAL TO FIND COIN WITH QUEEN'S
NAME ON IT.

"We are currency." Well, well.

I replied, by letter, trying to diffuse any ill-feeling, as I felt Lodestar's message brusque, if not rude. But businessmen will be busy, and telegrams terse. I thought no more upon it, until I started working in earnest with Miss Villiers.

THE NORPHANS PRACTICKLY [MOLLY]

WATCHMAN,
LESSONS DULY COMMENCED.
MOLLY

"Miss Molly, oh—how—delightful." Peggy, the middle child, curtseyed carelessly and sat down at the puzzle. "Welcome to our pale and insignificant world, to which we beg you to bring colour, else, lost in the phantasmagoria of our woe-begotten dreams, we shall kill ourselves."

I'd been forewarned that she, the plainest of the three, was the pertest, and a deceitful traitress; but I've encountered many supposedly evil folk in my days and found them personable enough.

"Yes, we shall kill ourselves. With promptitude." She scratched her eyebrow, eyeing me sidelong. "We are the Norphans Practickly. I am Margaret, known as Peggy. This is Mary Catherine, known as Kitty. The fool dressed as a London dandy there is Nicodemus, El Nico, the diablo of Burnfoot Gorge."

The other two, without looking up from their puzzle, gave an apathetic bow. All three sported discreet items from Jay's Mourning Warehouse on Regent Street: the girls wore jet rings, and Nico a cravat in the mauve of half-mourning.

I have met many youngsters full of bluff and flam in my time, but never a one from the higher echelons of society so full of it; fuller than I was at her age. (You'll object that I'm scarcely older than Peggy, but I seem older, with my city savvy; let us hope the Roxbury children never twig they've been palmed off on an apprentice.) I bit back a smile to think how rude they were aiming to be, and how pale were their efforts against my Oddbody dunces.

I blinked. "Norphans, did you say?"

Young Kitty prodded her brother's arm. "Ah-ha-ha! Nico said it wrong," she chanted, "Nico said it wrong."

Nico looked up from the puzzle. They tell me there's always a puzzle on the go in the art room; this was a view of London. Nico's brows angled as steeply as the Palace of Westminster, where one day he may scorn the opposition as he scorned his sister. "If I may explain the history," he said drolly. "As a child, with Fa always working and mother obsessed with good deeds, I once complained to Skirtle, saying, in my childish voice, 'Skirtle, I am a norphan, practically.' Skirtle found this so hilarious she had me repeat it to my mother, then to Fa; they reeled me out at parties, when the quality visited, as they did in their droves—no more, alas— to repeat my plaint: 'I am a norphan, practically.' My diction caused such hilarity that our parents took to calling me the Norphan Practickly, an appellation my fool sisters, lacking in invention, have greedily adopted."

Giggles from the girls. They turned back to their puzzle, rather insolently, as if to deem my reaction insufficiently entertaining.

"Is this," said I, "where our drawing lessons are to be held?"

Peggy frowned, as if at a plate of boiled cabbage. "Drawing?"

Nico picked up a piece of the puzzle, huffed confidently, and forced it in, on the lower right of the map, tapping it insolently down.

I squinted at it. "I don't think so."

He rounded on me with as much disrespect as his undeveloped vocal style could muster. "What do you know about it?"

"I know the statue of Nelson." I removed it to the correct spot, mid picture. "I know it stands not on London Bridge but atop of Nelson's Column. As any good Englander knows."

Kitty, obligingly, laughed at him.

"Perhaps not." I did not smirk; disdain was enough. "Not here in the countryside."

My insult hit the mark. Nico tugged at his dandified collar, gnashing his teeth. To a would-be swell, nothing hurts more than being revealed as a rustic.

"Sadly," said Peggy, allying herself to him, "drawing must wait till the completion of this mighty puzzle. There is no other table."

I looked at her. This was a lie. A spiteful lie. I considered laying down the puzzle cloth that Skirtle had provided for this very scenario.

I did nothing. I did not dole out the pencils and paper. I would not force upon them the lesson I had planned so brilliantly with your help, and the advice of old Mr Lear, the filthy landscape painter.

I picked up my drawing case and walked to the window. On the side table stood a daguerreotype of the family, five years old perhaps. To one side, the earl and his wife, a fine-looking woman, bright-eyed and kindly; to the other, the children; beyond my three terrors stood a fourth, staring out with a haughty bearing. Between the four children and their parents, a gap.

I sat myself down, at the end of the table, where the light was good. I glanced up at the three children, endeavouring to ignore me, though little Kitty was poorly rehearsed and kept peeking.

I took out my sketchbook. I laid it on my lap, not the table, so they would not see what I was drawing. I took out my favourite charcoal stick, and chalks. I pursed my lips. I drew.

My sketch of Nico was outlined within minutes. Chalk marks captured the sneer, charcoal shadowed the haughty eyes. I blew off the excess, and laid the drawing on the table, at an angle, so they might see I had drawn something but not exactly what.

For Peggy, my caricature centred on her mouth, fussily pronouncing so many lies. It was not my kindest drawing. This I laid to the other side. Not only Kitty but Nico too gave in to the urge to peek at it sideways.

Kitty's portrait was less unkind, but lively, with her hilarious mop of hair falling over catlike cheeks and sleepy eyes.

With the three of them skewered, I nodded in satisfaction. "If you wish to take up the drawing lesson offered you," I said, "kindly come down this end of the table, where the light is better, and try drawing this bowl of apples."

None moved. After a polite interval, I shrugged.

I turned my back on them. I gazed upon the ravishing view which fell dramatically from the window, flung across the hillside with an abandon that belittles all the Royal Academy landscapes I've seen. I am not fanatical for formal gardens: Hampton Court's cold, Regent's Park is straight; Hyde Park retains a bit of wildness. But this was another realm.

Rocky peaks rose to both sides, heathers and gorses struggling to hold on. Vast trees—don't ask me the variety, Miss V, but big ones, straight and true, and bushy ones, gnarled and ancient—lined the Burnfoot Gorge. Below, an iron pedestrian bridge arched over the river churning through the valley. I felt electrified by the energies of nature, so gloriously untamed across Roxbury's lands. Would my abilities as an artist be up to a landscape so fine?

I laid out paints, mixing jar, cleansing jar. I stared and stared, measuring the scene in my mind. The contours and outlines I sketched in haste. Pencil lines always in haste: it gives a vivacity to the line. The children kept puzzling in this interval. Kitty was only restrained from looking at my caricatures by her siblings' stringent stares. I heard Nico's huffings as he tapped pieces into place, doubtless setting St Paul's dome upon the British Museum Library. Peggy resisted; she was the ringleader of their japes.

Lucky I had befriended Skirtle, else I would not have been forewarned of the Roxbury children's form.

I began to paint. When I paint, time flows by. It is the only time an enemy might sneak up and do for me.

After an hour of lacing cotton ball clouds over the brooding distance, fading the crags to floating backdrops, dabbing the trees greener, and deepening the nearer boughs, I sat back to survey my efforts. Art brings renewal, and my frustration was forgotten. As my senses returned, I felt eyes over my shoulder and smelt Kitty's perfume.

"Ho, now," called Nico, "you blundering zounderkite."

I turned to see him clutch Kitty's wrist and tug her back to her place. Peggy tutted, planning repercussions for this disloyalty. But I saw the little one's eyes dancing with mirth, for she had viewed my caricatures. She could see that my ability to sketch them so damningly gave me power over them. Careless of her siblings' wrath, she desired that power.

The clock trilled and warbled.

Skirtle popped her head in. "How lovely." She looked astonished to find a pacific scene, as if she was expecting to find my head on a platter. "Lunch, my little ducks."

The children rose as one. They bolted past her without a word in my direction. How completely children fail to conceive their elders as humans, with feelings of our own. On the bell of lunch, I was relegated from drawing mistress and foe to employee and invisible.

"Must I eat with the ingrates?"

"Oh, love." Skirtle could see behind my forced jollity. "You've lasted till lunch."

"Oh, I'll last."

"Come and take a bite with me, won't you, pet?" She linked arms with me, and I noted the scratch of the crepe trimming on her sleeve, over the dull fabric of her dress; subtler than the children's, these were her signs of mourning.

HARNESS'S ELECTROPATHIC BELT

The first and only effectual application of Electricity to Suffering, by mild and imperceptible currents, instantaneous and lasting. All in search of health should wear Harness's Electropathic Belt. Thousands of unsolicited testimonials received. Beautifully designed. Scientifically constructed. Comfortable to wear. A boon to sufferers. Never fails.

The "very thing" for Ladies. Try one and you will never wear any other kind. For health, comfort and elegance. Don't delay, send at once. No woman should be without one. These beautiful designed corsets cure

**WEAK BACK
BILIOUSNESS
INDIGESTION
FEMALE IRREGULARITIES
ALL NERVOUS, MUSCULAR, FUNCTIONAL AND
ORGANIC COMPLAINTS.**

Ladies residing in the country, and those unable to call and inspect these corsets, have only to send waist measurement with postal orders, and they will obtain by return of post the prettiest, best-fitting corset they have ever worn. Its high-class style and beautiful finish, combined with marvellous health-giving properties, have won the highest reputation among the leaders of fashion.

*Also available:
Harness's Xylonite Truss, Gentleman's Belt.*

TERROR IN CAMDEN [LAWLESS]

The Camden Road train blast, two weeks later, has also been well documented. Jeffcoat and I were quicker to the scene, but not quick enough to save lives.

It could have been worse. The Fuse Wire Bomber, as the press dubbed him, surely imagined that his "mule" would set the thing off at peak hours. Instead, the costermonger slept in. His donkey was just pulling the cart into its habitual position, at the end of Platform One, when it set off the explosion. Fortunately, the coster escaped with minor injuries; that was a miracle, and not proof of complicity, as the press intimated. Unfortunately, the costermonger's donkey and cart were what protected him.

Over his poor animal, he was inconsolable. He spoke barely a word of sense. Jeffcoat and I could testify to that. But this senselessness predated the explosion. As a candidate for subversion by whatever radical organisation planned the shebang, he was unlikely.

Who did plan it? On behalf of the Home Office's investigations, we pieced together the sequence of events.

A porter was coupling two sets of carriages together. The guard stood, whistle in hand, waiting for the signal. The engine driver awaited the guard's whistle. As he opened his regulator, the report resounded across North London.

The station was enveloped in steam. The engine was no longer on the viaduct.

It had fallen twenty feet, into the road below. They would carry out a formal rail investigation, but this was no accident, we were confident of that, nor even a defective boiler. It was intended to be worse. Half an hour before would have been carnage.

The Fuse Wire Bomber, indeed. We found copper wires, dislodged by the coster cart from its nook by the waiting room.

What explosives were used was a mystery. A wooden crate lay smashed across the platform. Its glass sides were blown out, more wires were strewn around, and the platform beneath tinged yellow. The coster swore he had never seen it before. To what purpose the wires, none could tell us.

This was not Chartist style. Too advanced for the Fenians, unless they had made swift developments with explosives.

After the casualties were cleared, Jeffcoat made me comb the area with him. We found, where the blasted cart had been, the remains of a mechanism: bits of iron; a strange ball, pocked and scorched, neither wooden nor rubber. Whatever it was had fallen to the platform, knocked by the cart, and ignited upon impact.

A FENIAN DENIAL [LAWLESS]

I brought in O'Leary, purely for questioning, without charge. When I showed to him what was left of this contraption, his eyes bulged.

"What's that, now, when it's at home?" he said.

"We hoped," said Jeffcoat, "London's top-ranking Fenian might be able to tell us."

"And so he might. But I can't. Interested to know, though, if you catch 'em." His envy was such, I felt sure he had no part in it. "On a scientific basis, you understand. It's not fulminate of mercury, is it now?"

"No." I examined him. "And yet your Fenians claim they did this."

"Do they now, Watchman?" He lathered on the scepticism. "Would you be meaning the Irish Republican Brotherhood? Or could you be referring to the Phoenix National and Literary Society?"

Jeffcoat groaned. "And they're not Fenians?"

"Not necessarily. These laudable sodalities remain at

loggerheads with your government over Irish independence." He leaned forward. "But we don't exterminate donkeys."

I stared at the card in the file in front of me, received by *The Times* just hours after the explosion: OURSELVES ALONE. "Ourselves Alone" being the translation of Sinn Fein, of course, the Fenians' slogan.

O'Leary tapped the table. "Show us it, then."

I looked to Jeffcoat, but he shook his head. He was right: it might complicate a prosecution, if he'd seen the evidence.

"Read us it then, ye daft Gardai." He shook his head when I read it aloud. Now he could not keep the indignation from his voice. "Pah! Now, that's interesting, I'll grant you. The International Brotherhood is based in Manchester, I needn't remind you. They managed to hear the news, write the card and deliver it within hours of the explosion. Wouldn't you grant that's interesting?"

"Easy enough, if it was planned." I gave a sardonic nod. Besides, the Brotherhood had circles in every city in England, with cloak-twitchers aplenty to deliver such notes.

"It wasn't."

"It couldn't be the work of some renegade?" said Jeffcoat.

"Like Dolan the Red?" He shook his head, thoughtful. "Never."

Jeffcoat rounded on him. "Why not?"

"The thing is," O'Leary scratched his ear with maddening lugubriousness, "Dolan and such are fools, but they're not likely to forget the *Gaeilge* now."

I looked at him.

"The Gaelic, Sergeant. Their own Irish tongue as they were brought up with."

Jeffcoat snatched up the card. "This supposed mistake being?"

"Can you not see it?" He tutted, impudent. "And you, Lawless, a Gael, of a sort."

I made no answer.

"'Ourselves alone', indeed! Sure, isn't that the common mistranslation? There's no 'alone' in the Irish. 'Sinn Féin' means 'ourselves'. At a push 'we ourselves'."

"You're pushing your luck," said Jeffcoat.

"False witness." O'Leary fixed him right in the eye. "If an Irishman's identifying himself to the world as the author of such an event, which the IRB deplores, by the way, this is exactly how he would not do it." He thrust his chair aside. "Bloody libellous. If you catch him, add that to his crimes, and I'll back you up in court."

Out he walked. Jeffcoat and I looked at each other.

We reported it to Ripon. Who else could it be? He said it had to be the French.

AGE OF WONDERS [LAWLESS]

The rail disaster caused vast disturbance in Camden, yet from it we only recovered the fuse wire, the iron, and the broken crate—which told us nothing. We had the pocked remnant of a ball analysed. It took them a while: nitrocellulose, some new wonder material. A sharp-eyed constable, packing up the remains of the broken crate, examined the metal attached to the crate panels more closely: three shards of it. Thank goodness he did, for we should have spotted them, and they might prove telltale in the end.

O'Leary's eyes had bulged at the sight of these remnants, and I believed him when he claimed he knew nothing. These were times of swift change in armaments. Britain remained at peace (bar a few brawling New Zealanders). Other nations warmongered merrily, hungry for fresh methods of annihilation. The French spatted with the Austrians, the Austrians with Prussians and patriotic Italians. Russia crushed the Circassians; the samurai troubled the Japs. Paraguay wrestled its neighbours. Revolutions, wherever you cared to look, joyfully stoked the north of England's furnaces. When the Americans fell out over slavery, it was to England they turned for weaponry.

Roxbury had armed the British since the Crimea—aside from that public disgrace in the fifties which Skirtle alluded to. For that spell, Joseph Whitworth of Manchester snuck into favour.

Today Roxbury armed the United States of America and the Confederate States of America. Both sides. Why not? Their dollars were as green. Yes, slavery was frowned upon in enlightened England (conveniently forgetting how it built the Empire); but the Confederate States struggled not for slavery, but the sovereign freedom to decide their own laws.

Arms meant money. No wonder Roxbury Industries and Whitworth Enterprises competed over the latest scientific developments. Newfangled fuels: paraffin or kerosene, whale oil, guano from Pacific atolls, peat from Irish bogs. Ironclad ships. Roxbury's breech-loading guns saved our army, Bessemer's steel our navy. This was the age of wonders.

Three shards of iron, fuse wire, and a ball: all that we had to work from. On two shards, no distinguishing feature. On the third, sliced crosswise, the remnants of words:

JO
TWO
CHE

DIVERGENCES [LAWLESS]

Molly told me of her discoveries, as yet limited.

To Ruth she explained her struggles in the role of drawing mistress with equanimity. If she suffered from the children's maltreatment, she did not say it outright; at least Skirtle had given her to understand the little devils' history of rank behaviour.

"She is exaggerating," Ruth said, "I'm sure."

"Sure?"

"More or less sure."

"Let us hope you are right," I said. "If she is doing as badly as she presents it, Roxbury will throw her out, I will have learnt nothing, and Ripon will extract my guts to restring his violin."

The trajectory of Molly's lessons we learned later.

The initial lessons proceeded similarly. The Roxbury children had not so much freedom that they could refuse to attend; besides, they enjoyed the challenge of leaving Molly to draw alone while they struggled with their blasted puzzle picture. So, little by little, one by one, Molly took on the challenge, reporting each stage to Ruth. She won them, as she wins everyone, sooner or later.

AN ART MISTRESS [MOLLY]

WATCHMAN, YOU OLD CHARPERING FEINTER,
LESSONS SATIS.
EARL REMAINS ELUSIVE.
MOLLY

Dear Miss V,

Kitty has succumbed. You may but guess at my sense of triumph.

I left my caricatures out for the taking. If the older two thought of destroying them, they did not wish to be seen to care.

Kitty secreted them away.

Over recent days, I secretly furnished her with paper and chalks. She studied the rudiments of copying with me. First, we copied my versions of her siblings, simplistic and remorseless, which was motivation enough. She has been sketching and re-sketching these wheresoever she goes, at all times of day, all over the house. Her school notebooks are adorned with gargoyle versions of her whole family— mother excluded—and the older two, I am sure, have remarked and are inwardly digesting...

Peggy I won over with my air of knowingness.

The thought of London is thrilling to her. Our acquaintance with the famous intoxicates her youthful brain. In their heyday, of course, the Earl and Lady Roxbury entertained the most celebrated in the land, but the children were small. Peggy was only ever presented and packed off to bed; she was never allowed to present a play, being a dilatory student; never allowed to converse. This has built up such individuals to an unattainable glory in her mind. I know Watchman's scribbler friends, of course, Mayhew and Dickens and Wilkie Collins; I've supped with the editor of *Punch*, worked for Bazalgette, entertained the prince and his wife. I've witnessed crimes and assisted investigations. Such accomplishments tally awkwardly with being a drawing mistress, I know. I've merely hinted. Enough to hook young Peggy.

Peggy is dying to know life, which I do. Peggy is making plans to escape this pale northern prison; and escape's my forte. Thus, after initial hostilities, Peggy has decided to sue for an alliance.

Peggy began by drawing. Badly.

I told her straight, it would impress me more if she tried to be civil. What at last won me over was her knowledge of life at Roxbury House. Current duties aside—you know what I mean—I am an inveterate snoop.

Two pupils conquered and willing to participate. One to go. Nico has fallen last. Nico has fallen hardest.

Nicodemus is an arrogant child. He first had a letter published in *The Times* at the age of fourteen. Don't ask him, or you'll get a lecture on it: a complaint about the nation's rotten bread, demanding government reform and imprisonment for bakers adulterating our foodstuff. This gained him notoriety at school, amused his parents' friends, and gave him a puffed-up notion of his own importance.

Nico liked to sit, insolently tapping the puzzle pieces into place, ignoring my lessons. He makes an affectation of reading *The Times* every afternoon—so late is it delivered in those remote parts—in order to express outrageous opinions. These opinions he first tries on his sisters, at mealtimes. When I began dining with the Norphans, he tried them on me too.

"These striking factory workers." He wiped the fat from his chops in satisfaction. "They should be marched down to the sea and shot. Don't you think, Miss Molly, my dear?"

Kitty stayed silent.

Peggy didn't dare challenge Nico's politics.

"I'm not your dear," I said. "And I'm afraid your views seem somewhat foolish."

Nico huffed. "The strikers are the fools."

I continued with my lunch. "Girls, what do you imagine the strikers want? No, first: what do their bosses want?"

"Money." Peggy was keen to earn my favour. "Profit. That's what Fa wants. Production increased, profit doubled."

"And shooting the workers." I caught Nico scowling at us. "What will that achieve?"

Kitty was round-eyed. "Who would work Fa's machines?"

"Production stymied," Peggy declared, like a newspaper hawker. "Profit slashed."

"Perhaps the bosses," I teased, "will work the machines themselves."

Nico could not resist. "There are workers all over the Continent who'd gladly take the jobs these strikers complain of, for half the wage."

"Oh, yes." I nodded, raising an eyebrow to Peggy.

She couldn't resist. "You mean those immigrant workers you were complaining of last week."

"Telling us to deport them," Kitty agreed.

"Because they keep blowing up factories."

Nico's face was turning scarlet. "Yielding to ridiculous demands only encourages more strikes."

"You're welcome to your opinion," I replied.

"But?"

I grinned. "You think activists naive, but your thoughts lead to bad decisions in the long term."

"How so?"

"Grant an extra shilling, they go back to work. Safe workplace, you boost their confidence. Fewer accidents. Fewer illnesses. A sense of purpose. Collaboration. Willingness to meet deadlines. All for an extra shilling."

"Cheap, I'd say," chimed in Kitty obligingly.

Nico regarded me with loathing. "You're utterly village."

"Meaning what?" I laughed.

He drew himself up to his full height. "Not of the House."

"Oxford slang," Peggy translated, with a snort. "He got it from Wilfred."

"Christchurch College is the House." Nico was pleased with his knowledge. "Anything else is village.

That is: of the lower echelons, pitiful."

"I see." I poured myself a glass of wine, particularly enjoyable as Nico is not allowed it.

Peggy tutted. "A rather snobbish expression."

"For a snobbish boy," Kitty crowed.

I couldn't help smiling. "This debate is more robust than you are used to in school."

"I'm head of the debating society, I'll have you know."

I blinked. "Oh dear."

"You're not head," said Peggy, "you're treasurer. But you'll probably steal Miss Molly's logic to become head."

OF THE OLD EARL, PART THE THIRD [MOLLY]

WATCHMAN, YOU SHRINKING LILLY LAW,
NEARER TO MEETING EARL.
MOLLY

Dear Miss V,

I will confess, I had expected to be introduced formally, before I started teaching. I said as much to Birtle this morning.

"When will the earl himself interview me?"

"Interview?" Birtle stared. "You? The earl employs you to occupy his children's time, not his own."

"He keeps his distance, doesn't he?"

"He doesn't suffer fools gladly." Birtle enjoyed his insult. "And why ever should he?"

I could not answer. If I suggested he ought to check I'm a suitable tutor for his brood, that might prompt suspicions that I ain't, suspicions Birtle clearly harbours already. "Only that is how I have previously been employed. In the south."

"In the south?" Birtle made no attempt to conceal his mirth, as any London butler with a semblance of manners might. He turned and walked away, muttering. "In the south, she says."

MYSTERIES [LAWLESS]

JO TWO CHE. We racked our brains in search of the solution to the mystery. We studied the metal shard. We made notes, compared copious ideas.

"We might find," I suggested, "a blacksmith called John Twomey in Cheshire."

Jeffcoat shook his head. "More likely, a Josiah living at a Number Two Cheyne Walk."

"Or in Chester-le-Street."

We ransacked the Yard's list of criminals. Nothing.

It could refer to the second job done by a specific chemist.

Or the Book of Job, Chapter II, the verse where God shows off to Satan about his servant Job who escheweth evil.

The transpositions, permutations, peregrinations were endless.

Solutions? Solutions we could not find.

I noted another coincidence that week: a fire at the East India docks, where we had found that forgotten body. Jeffcoat went along to investigate, but arson was frequent enough. When goods from the Indies proved unpopular, they redeemed the expense by burning them and claiming the sum insured.

The harbour master's office was burnt down, he told me, along with a building for shipping records. It was unnerving. "Still, what does it matter? We've taken copies of everything. Besides, the chances of finding out who it was were astronomical."

I nodded. "You've given up hope?"

He laughed. "Haven't you?"

"Well, I may have." I opened my palms. "But Miss Villiers is very persistent."

Simpson's final report on the body was equally unsatisfactory. Sent, after typical delay, it featured his typical bombast. Still, noting our threats, he was more conclusive than usual.

He could not rule out foul play, but the tubercular decay suggested the most likely cause of death. Advanced consumption often causes paroxysms; the disjointed shoulder might be evidence of this, or of an impact. Equally there was malnutrition, likely as not due to tuberculosis.

Amid the indiscriminate matter within the tarpaulin, Simpson was surprised to find minimal signs of discharge from the orifices. There were, however, soap traces soaked into the tarpaulin. This might suggest the body was deceased some time before being wrapped, and carefully cleaned at the last, as if for burial. Traces of arsenic lingered on the skin fragments, but no more than arsenical soap would leave. Close examination of these fragments suggested skin fair and freckled, the type that often uses the damnable stuff. Simpson hazarded that death took place in the winter, at sea: in sweaty port towns there are so many species to prey on a cadaver. If insects had got to it, there would be no trace of soft tissue left; but the tarpaulin was wrapped tight, and the body showed only signs of self-destruction (that is, a kind of fermentation, or digestion by its own bacteria).

Yet he had come up with a suggestion as to how long ago the man died. The basket was made of corn husks and armature of cane: an African doctor of his acquaintance recognised the materials. How lucky we were that he was a university man! By examining the growth of mould inside the basket, he declared the man dead at least four years, and more likely five.

Five years. We had searched through the *Great Britain*'s records only three. Wasted effort. How far back should we have gone? How can you excavate the past? Too late now. The fire at the docks saved us that trouble.

I showed Simpson's report to Miss Villiers. "Consumption, most like. He died on board, was cleaned and wrapped for burial at sea."

"But they were in haste." She frowned. "Acting furtively. At night, perhaps. They wouldn't know the lifeboat was hanging there."

I could picture it. In the darkness, they roll the body over the edge and duck away, not knowing they have tumbled him into the lifeboat. "Simpson's revised the date of the death."

She rolled her eyes. "I'm to read more records, am I?"

I sighed. "How many immigrants have died trying to get here, to the promised land? Some poor soul died far from home. Does his name matter?"

"But this isn't some lonely stowaway." She wrinkled her nose in thought. "Somebody was with him. Cared for him. And then—"

"And then dumped him overboard, unreported. Anyway, no further researches possible." I told her about the fire at the docks.

"Oh, but Antony Gibbs Shipping has everything copied in their office on Oxford Street."

I smiled. "Nothing to be gained, I think. It'll remain a mystery."

Ruth didn't like that at all. "Let me know if you change your mind. I can't bear a mystery unsolved."

DR FOULD'S ARSENICAL SOAP
[*ENGLISHWOMAN'S DOMESTIC MAGAZINE*]

Dear Dr Fould,
I adore Fould's Arsenical Soap, and shall be devoted to it
till the day I die.

Respectable citizens must shine with morality from every
pore. In my youth, I suffered diabolical disfigurements:
blotches, blemishes, freckles, pimples and pustulance. To
overcome these handicaps, I determined to eradicate dirt.

Oh, the trials I endured, with endless carbolics and
caustics, each slogan more lurid than the next. My skin
became as tough as the dragon's hide, as leporous as Job's.
Until, at length, I discovered your patent soap. Ah, the
aromatic joy. I pronounce Fould's Arsenical Soap the
only efficacious remedy.

Yours, forever indebted,
Mrs AH Brown and family,
New Malden

Warranted to give satisfaction or money refunded. Also
available: Fould's Arsenic Complexion Wafers, and
Fould's Medicated Complexion Soap.

Beware of imitators. 2s 6d per cake.

Not to be used with prussic acid.

LODESTAR COMETH [MOLLY]

WATCHMAN,
ROXY'S NO. 2, LODESTAR,
AN AFTERNOONIFIED COVE
WORTH WATCHING.
MOLLY

Dear Miss V,
Cometh the hour, cometh Mr Lodestar, of whom I have
heard so much.

I was teaching above—the Norphans practising their
caricatures—when I heard a fashionable fleet-wheeled
phaeton rumbling up the driveway. In its wake rode Jem.

Through the broad art room windows, I viewed the
vehicle sweep wildly round the rockery. With careless
ease, the driver called the horses to stop square in front of
the grand entrance, below my nose. Removing his hat, he
wiped his brow languidly, and descended as if he owned
the whole kingdom. He snapped his fingers. There was no
arrogance in it, just efficiency: time of the essence; work to
be done. Jem, appealingly disarrayed, leapt down to tend
the horses, but the new arrival took all our interest.

"Who is this," I said, "in the courtyard?"

The girls set their scrawls aside and crowded round, for
they loved a distraction.

"Oh, that," said Kitty. "That'll be Lodestar."

"Fa's devilish right-hand man, you know." Nico
declined to look up from his composition. "Who steals all
his blasted time from us."

"And his interest and his affections," said Peggy. "A
deadly important fellow."

I glanced at Peggy's page and gave some spurious
advice on delineation, so as not to appear too interested.

"Lodestar," I mused. "Strange name."

"Strange chap," said Nico. "African. Odd manners. Big opinion of himself."

"And so he should have," Peggy said. "He runs the company now."

"Gadsbudlikins, Peg," said Nico. "He does not. Fa runs the company."

"And relies upon Nathan Lodestar to redeem all his gaffes." Peggy's eyes flashed. To rile Nico, she said to me, "He'll doubtless run the whole show, soon enough. A job that should have been Wilfred's, if he had a modicum of aptitude, or Nico's."

"I like that." Nico held up his sketch: Peggy, in the form of a monkey.

Peggy beat her fists against his shoulder. "You vinomadified lickspittle."

He took no notice, swiftly adding a setting to the image: the pneumatic railway connecting the house with the scientific glasshouses, down which, giving chase to the monkey, was Lodestar.

Peggy wailed. Ah, the joys of siblinghood.

"Birtle," said Lodestar. "Good day."

The children dragged me from our lessons to the landing on the stairs, where we cowered to witness the hurricane that was Lodestar's arrival.

Birtle just opened the grand entrance in time. Lodestar tossed him his coat. He stretched, catlike, to shake off the journey. His dark brow lightened, flashing with mirth, to see Skirtle descend all aflutter from her housekeeper's domain.

"O-ho, there, Skirtle, what fine health your complexion speaks of, as the spring days grow warmer."

She looked flustered. "Sir."

"Now, I am only passing through, like the camel through the eye of the needle. This evening I must away, as soon as I have talked to his Lordship. There is business to be done seeing off our wily competitors in the west, the vile Whitworths—" Upon pronouncing the name, he pretended to spit: the feigned impoliteness drew howls from Skirtle and a wry smile even from Birtle. "During these meagre hours, I propose that you twice feed me, as I tire of London fodder, that my shirts be sent down to me starched, for the Hounds Club laundress is a sluggard, and that Jem clean my phaeton and refresh the horses. They brought me swift from town, skipping that botheration with the branch line, and I would hence with the same pair."

"Very well, sir." Skirtle attempted a curtsey, quite unlike herself, as if the *Great Eastern* were to trying to dock in a canal lock. "Will you be visiting—" she lowered her voice, "—the glasshouses, sir?"

"Why, yes." He smiled darkly. "Send lunch to me there, will you? I'll be in my office, experimenting with this new material. Then to the slate quarry. We should be blasting by two. I know you hate the noise, Skirtle, but the stables must have roofs. What else?"

Birtle stepped forward. I'd rarely seen him and Skirtle in the same room; they go to lengths not to tread on each other's domains. But the whirl of Lodestar's arrival in his phaeton had set the household spinning.

"Sir?" said Birtle, as broad an offer as he could make.

Lodestar sized him up. The children bristled with excitement, and Kitty nudged me to watch closely. Lodestar pursed his lips, full and red. His waistcoat fell trim from broad shoulders. His dark locks are too long for a gentleman, but somehow fit this wild uncompromising chap, as if to suggest he plays fast with the rules of business, and his brooding gaze brooks no opposition to the march of progress. He leaned toward Birtle, thinking, and placed a finger on the butler's midriff. It was a gesture outside decorum, somehow typical of Lodestar's style. Yes, that's it. Lodestar is outside decorum. A visitor from another realm, with alien manners and alien demands. Some might thus be criticised, but he is cherished for it. A natural zest oozes from him, lighting up our visages, as we scurry to do his bidding. "Have you the best paper? And the Indian ink? Good man." The tiny tap that Lodestar gave Birtle's midriff many would not have noticed; but I am a devotee of close-up magic, and I saw him palm the coin into his fingers and thence into Birtle's waistcoat pocket. A considerable tip—though the tippee knew nothing about it. He would discover it later, and bless Lodestar's liberality.

Lodestar is plainly pleased with Birtle, whom he has bewitched exactly as I have failed to. Birtle renders him special service, which he affords to no other household members, nor any of the visitors to Roxbury House. Nobody treats Birtle with such freedom; even Roxbury is reverential to the gloomy butler. Yet Lodestar's mysterious magic needed no gasp from its audience; it just worked.

I decided I ought to be presented to this fellow, such an important cog in the Roxbury machine. I shooed the children away. (They looked on, egging me on through the banisters.) I descended, as if by happenstance, to the great hall. Birtle did not present me; Skirtle did not notice me. I was on the point of coughing for attention, when Lodestar sensed me behind.

He bestowed that dazzling smile upon me. "Why, look ahoy!"

I felt a peculiar quiver run through me.

"You are no chambermaid, nor housemaid, I warrant.

But maid you are, and made to feel welcome, I hope."
He extended his hand, which I took, uncertainly, having
never been introduced in my new station in life. This
chicanery of etiquette I find harder than circumnavigating
Hyde Park Corner on a highly strung pony dragging a
dozen milk churns. With the barest effort, he raised my
hand to his lips. "Enchanted, mademoiselle."

Birtle, as if sprung from a spell, came to his senses.
"Mademoiselle Molly, sir. I mean, Miss Molly, the
children's latest drawing mistress," he said, as if I
would not last the month. "May I present Mr Nathaniel
Lodestar?"

Lodestar wafted him aside. "Nathan. Please call me
Nathan. If we be members of the same household, I hate
to stand on ceremony. Don't you?"

I opened my mouth, thinking this one of those
questions not requiring an answer, bit my lip, looked up
at him—he was a foot and half taller than me, a dazzling
animal, his shoulders twice as broad—and heard myself
blurt out the following balderdash:

"Ceremonials, sir, whether funerals or matrimonials,
are a frippery of society I'd rather see tossed in the sea,
from Battersea to the Southern Sea. Mercy me." I put
my hand to my mouth. "My apology, I prithee, for my
parlyaree spree."

I blushed so bad it gave me cheekache.

Skirtle giggled.

Birtle looked away.

On the stairs, the Norphans Practickly held their breath.
Nico stared thunderously, Peggy was amused, and Kitty
mortified on my behalf.

Lodestar's eyebrows rose, arching over his brown,
brown eyes. He smiled. "I feel exactly the same,
Miss Molly. *Au revoir.*" And he swept from the room,

scattering Skirtle and Birtle in his wake.

Mid-afternoon, I heard the explosions in the slate quarry; beyond that, we heard and saw no more of him.

Lodestar flew in like a comet blazing its trail across an empty sky.

Lodestar's appearance has lit a fuse. The busy world is ignited by forces far afield. The explosives that shape dockyards and shake mines must be prepared somewhere. Where better than England's forgotten backwaters? We hear of Parliament placating the rest of the country: oh, we're raising capital for the shires; ah, we're powering the north, sending the fruits of Empire for the yokels to lavish their dreary hours upon, spinning, weaving, looming, those things that northern folk still know, while we southern swells are too modern for drudgery, so they do the work, which we invest with fashionable value.

Before Lodestar, I thought Roxbury House a haven of tranquillity, nestled in these wastelands of the north, far from the city's bustle (which I considered real life). Henceforth I shall seek interconnections north and south, rich and poor, straight and circuitous.

BOOK II
REPORTS AND REPERCUSSIONS

Credulous Days
[*Penny Satirical*, a London gazette]

"Boom. Bang."

Louis Napoleon III clicks his fingers and lo, there springs forth a dark figure, bounding across the roofs of London: Spring-Heeled Jacques.

"Danger. Beware. Fire!"

Will he spout fire over England's defences? Eat our navy for breakfast? Neither Spring-Heeled Jacques, nor his master Louis, adhere to a plan. He is conjured up to disturb us, trouble our dreams, and drive us deranged—as he drove certain ladies of Barnes mad back in the credulous thirties.

"Bombs! Explosives! Run!"

Are you laughing? Those days of credulity have returned. We are to believe not that some roof-leaping monster has returned, but that the French are hatching gunpowder plots on every street corner. South London might as well be Lyon or Lourdes, it is so filled with Frenchies, foreigners, and folderol-frothers. Expel all émigrés. Throw them in the Thames, before these Frogs kiss our lovelorn princesses, else trouble will be spawned.

CONSTANT VIGILANCE: GUERNSEY [LAWLESS]

The trouble with the Guernsey explosion was that nobody could say exactly what had happened. Nobody saw it, nobody was hurt. Was it intended to kill passers-by? Was it aimed at Victor Hugo, novelist in exile from Napoleon's Paris?

We could not discover for sure. Yet the information we gathered from that satchel under the sea wall changed everything.

Early evening, August 8, a boom was heard all over St Peter Port, principal town of the island of Guernsey. Some reported a flash, some a cracking sound. The sea wall was damaged by a strange blast below Hauteville, Hugo's house. The news was wired direct to Scotland Yard.

I caught the late train to Portsmouth. Awaiting the ferry, I spent the early hours of the morning talking with Ellie, a barmaid at the Fortitude Tap. I asked her what sights were worth seeing in Portsmouth. She poured me a pint of Long's Stout.

It was a one-sided conversation, though I was glad of the company. She told of her fourteen children. With the navy's new ironclads being built up north, her husband's hours at the dockyard were so reduced she had to support them all.

We docked at St Peter Port at lunchtime. Inspector De Nesle, chief of police, insisted on visiting a restaurant before he took me back to the station. He filled me in over a repast of garlic and shellfish, his report as copious as the French wine, and likewise accented.

"That is the hour when Monsieur Hugo normally takes his promenade. The attack was aimed at him, it is sure." He crossed himself. "*Grâce à Dieu*, our literary lion was dining at Sausmarez Manor. How I see it, the traitor sets the explosives. He is disturbed. In his incompetence, he sets off the blast. He escapes with his life, worse luck. He flees."

Nobody was seen departing the scene. Nobody was injured. But something was found near the rubble. Under a jacket of deplorable condition—how activists cultivate this deadbeat image—lay an old satchel, full of documents.

What an array: letters, telegrams, maps, from the 1780s to a few weeks ago. Beyond belief, beyond our fears: orders, munitions, shipping military and mercantile, diagrams. One document bore dates for the coming year; other annotations ran to the end of the century. And all in French.

Having riffled through the papers, De Nesle had taken a decision. "I have invited Monsieur Hugo to be our police translator. The fee will be nominal, but I have assured him the gratitude of the British nation."

Guernsey is a mess of contradictions. Many of the denizens are French, French-descended, and French-speaking. They love French food, French cheese, French wine.

On the other hand, so close to this warlike neighbour, they are xenophobes. They will demand that Westminster invade Normandy at the drop of a pin. This bomb was just such an occasion, and De Nesle hoped their parliament would kick up a stink about it.

"This is military information," I said, "and you'll show it to nobody." I would take the papers back to the mainland. I excoriated him for the liberty of summoning Hugo. "In the current climate, given the papers' nature, I'm astonished you've whispered a word to anyone. The Royal Commission on defence is reconvening this week. I may summon you in front of them, and see how you like that."

"In our bailiwick, Monsieur Scotland, British bureaucracy feels far distant. Your convoluted cogs turn too slow. History has shown us we must be our own protection. Constant vigilance. This is our only safety." De Nesle gave a continental snort. "Besides, I am answerable not to your parliament, but to my own, blast you *au diable*."

I paid for lunch, as amends for my outburst, eager to see this satchel. "But why Monsieur Hugo? Have you not French speakers among your trusted comrades?"

"But of course," he said. His own French was fluent; he was entirely capable of reading it himself. He put his arm around my shoulder, his manner uncomfortably informal. "Certain abbreviations are opaque to me. Slang. Military jargon." He shrugged. "Besides, who writes as well as Monsieur Hugo?"

At the station, Hugo was at work in the inner room, sitting at the chief's own desk. De Nesle's chest puffed with pride, as if a work of genius were being composed before our eyes. "The translation will be superb. You have read *Les Misérables*?"

"De Nesle, can we rely on Hugo's confidentiality? Given that he is, in fact, French."

De Nesle looked puzzled.

I did not spell it out: if Hugo communicated military secrets to French colleagues on high, any advantage this discovery offered was lost; De Nesle was like an archaeologist, unaware his diggers might sell off the treasures he sought. "Never mind."

"Bof! You know nothing of Monsieur Hugo's history." He spoke of Hugo's protests upon Louis Napoleon's grisly transition from elected premier to *soi-disant* emperor; of Hugo's exile from France and loyalty to Guernsey.

Ignoring his prattlings, I watched Hugo at work. The great author was absorbed, scanning, sifting, and annotating: getting the measure of his task.

I knocked and went in, shutting De Nesle out. I introduced myself brusquely.

"Thank heaven you have come." Hugo dragged his attention from the papers, like an opium addict emerging from the swoon. He was ashen-faced, and he spoke beautiful

English, gravelly with cigar smoke. "The things I must show you, Sergeant. The historic plots of De Béville and De Guines are reignited: the Portsmouth Plan. You must know of it?"

He unfolded an extraordinary map of the Channel.

"If this only were fiction, one would make of it a beautiful story. Such a beautiful story! It would take London by storm." He put his hand to his brow, every inch the Shakespearean hero, and fixed me with a piercing eye. "But it is no fiction. This makes the effort of 1779 seem the prank of the schoolboy."

I tore my eyes from him to study the map: the English Channel was annotated thickly, numbered arrows pointing ashore either side of Portsmouth, then sweeping round, all the way to the naval dockyards, the mainstay of our sea power, the heart of our empire.

Inscribed above, the puzzling phrase: UN GIBRALTAR FRANÇAIS

REPERCUSSIONS [LAWLESS]

"Military intelligence?" Miss Villiers said. We were walking over Waterloo Bridge, and in the dazzling sunlight I could not gauge her expression. "Sounds unlikely."

I laughed. For six weeks now I had been working on matters of national importance. We would meet at Waterloo Station. I accompanied her into town, where she was attending courses and meetings and job interviews, ever since losing her librarian post at the British Museum. We had a habit of discussing my work. She was ever intrigued by puzzles; our early acquaintance was spent cracking codes in Museum Street tearooms.

On my return from Guernsey, she sensed my anxiety—and my reticence.

"I understand." She looked askance. "A woman, of course, cannot be trusted."

Useless to insist that I was forbidden to trust anybody but Jeffcoat. Useless to deny it was anything to do with her being a woman.

We were already buried in paperwork. Jeffcoat chased round, gleaning facts, figures and names from anyone near the Erith disaster; I the same with Camden, quizzing the train companies and the costermonger's donkey's second cousin. While I sifted this mountain of minutiae, the Royal Commission awaited our report. After my days in Guernsey, we were further behind than ever. The satchel dossier was overwhelming, in volume and gravity.

I racked my brains for a solution. I went to Ripon. I confessed that we could not cover all the material; and I needed to check Hugo's work. Would he accept my employing a translator I had trusted with confidential documents in the past?

Ripon stroked his beard. "Trust him with your life, would you?"

"I'd trust her to the ends of the earth, sir."

He noted my pronoun with a raised brow. "If I were to vet every single secretary or bookbinder or mapmaker who worked for our department, Lawless, we would still be fighting the Hundred Years' War. The reason you are working for us—and working well—is that we trust your judgement."

The next day, as Miss Villiers and I crossed the river, I briefly feigned further qualms over sharing military intelligence, but I could not wait to hear her thoughts. By the time we reached the Strand, I had offered her the job. I apprised her of the task, its scope and gravity.

She gave a whoop. "I shall put off my return to the country. I must go to an interview just now. But I could join you afterwards, if that's appropriate?" She bit her lip.

"I'll be at Scotland Yard. Tell them at the desk I'm expecting you."

She ended up staying several nights at her aunt's club, at the expense of the Home Office. We discussed the papers over dinner. My admiration for Miss Villiers' intellect grew with every day we worked together. She had such a grasp of perspective. One moment she was gauging our whole strategy, the next dealing with the subtleties of translation.

The deadline was impossible; the work was troubling; but I loved these sunlit days, every moment, and so, I think, did she.

ROYAL COMMISSION [LAWLESS]

Miss Villiers pronounced Hugo's translation accurate. She picked up a dozen details he had missed in his haste. Like him, she grasped at once the intent of this Portsmouth Plan.

Armed with these discoveries, I went to the Royal Commission with a heavy heart, but determined. I had to sway the politicians. We had to resume at once the network of Portsmouth forts. These coastal fortifications, begun in 1860, had been delayed by continual debates and amendments. Typical that the press dubbed them Palmerston's Follies, when it was the press who bayed for protection against the French; but then newspapers denounce spending in peacetime, only to jeer at government imprudence when war looms.

Huge responsibility fell upon Roxbury Industries. Thrust back into the spotlight, they must arm the Solent forts against attack: they would not only make the artillery, but complete the forts in the middle of the sea, relying on Roxbury hydraulic pumps never used mid-ocean. On my way from Portsmouth to Guernsey, I had passed the incipient works, like Saxon forts rising amid the glistering waves. Now the forts would be completed with bricks from his Loth Brickworks, the papers fell over themselves to lament Roxbury's ill-treatment during that hiatus in the fifties, and canonise his return to national favour.

As soon as Miss Villiers had gathered the implications, she wrote to Molly. She frequently wrote to Molly, lest the correspondence seem one-sided. She did not encode her letters, lest that attract suspicion as Molly perused them over breakfast, but Ruth orchestrated the beginning of lines with acrostic messages. Using this subterfuge, we refined Molly's mission.

Focus on Roxbury's state of mind. Could we rely on him, on his wellbeing and health? Did he retain oversight of his business? Or was his withdrawal from London society the mark of some deeper malaise?

HALCYON DAYS [LAWLESS]

The Norphans Practickly were always at extremes. They laughed, they wept. Nico leapt for the moon because of an obscure judgement in the House of Lords and wrote scathing letters for upwards of a week. Peggy was downcast that anti-French sentiment might frustrate her escape plan crossing into Calais. Kitty won their brilliant game: "How Long Can You Hide Silently in a Box?" Poor girl missed a day's lessons, and meals. The others admitted they never went near their boxes.

"After such treatment," Kitty declared, "by those who profess to love me best, I henceforth dedicate myself to evil."

The Norphans expressed everything in superlatives. Their emotions were tumultuous as the crags that overhung the valley.

The earl too, Molly gathered from his visage, was subject to extremes of sentiment. Some days, with new contraptions delivered from distant manufactories, the sun beamed from his brow. More often, the shadow of depression dogged his features, though he spoke not of it.

Molly portrayed these as halcyon days. She taught, or feigned to teach. The Norphans' creative flair outdid her Oddbody Theatricals, for they could write plays, stage operas, hang exhibits, for which Roxbury House was the perfect venue. Molly loved it all, with a wild abandon—even as she failed to be loved.

Let me expand: from her first letter, we knew she had taken a fancy to Jem. She soon learnt he had a sweetheart in the village. She waited to get the measure of her rival. Did she figure her city charms would win him over in the end?

The royal road to unhappiness lies in urging the world to do one's bidding, and complaining when it does not. Molly, raised among the disempowered, knew this. She had patience. She knew how to suggest and divert. In this lay her power.

Lodestar, with his dramatic look and his unfettered energies, passed through again. He inspired devotion from Birtle, commotion from Skirtle, gawping from the Norphans, and clockwork efficacy among the glasshouse scientists.

They would deliver to him any number of items, with proofs, measurements and projections. Elsewise they seemed a disorganised shower, heads in the clouds, devising and imagining and inventing. For Lodestar, however, they met deadlines, completed documents, delivered devices to order, ahead of schedule—or else they were thrown out.

Oh yes, Lodestar dismissed staff with alarming regularity. To work at Roxbury was the peak of the engineering mountain. Lodestar had no time for shirkers and refreshed the staff regularly. Trainees were always arriving, fresh from laboratories, universities and botanical gardens around the kingdom.

New animals kept arriving at the menagerie. Jem would often stay overnight, tending the latest sickly arrival. His special friend, the orang-utan, was often poorly; he attended her on evenings when she couldn't keep from crying for whatever mysterious sorrow.

Chemicals were concocted, experiments framed, devices tested. Blasting was heard from the slate quarry over the hill. The roof of the old stables was swiftly replaced with fresh slates, converting it to staff quarters; but the blasts continued.

As far as Molly could report, Roxbury Industries was thriving.

Molly was at that age: her imagination ready for love, bold but uncertain. She yet knew not the havoc her blossoming youth might kindle.

Was she deserving of love? Oh, she was, she surely was, with her wicked tongue and handsome verve. Jem was yet to be swayed; but in her longing for Jem, was she blind to young Nico falling for her?

But we knew nothing of that, until Miss Villiers' visit.

As she settled, Molly began to describe Roxbury in more detail. The house she explored, under Skirtle's benign guidance: the earl's enigmatic laboratory atop Roxbury's central tower; studies, libraries, morning rooms; the kitchens' gurgling innards, hydraulic revolving spit and cauldron that washed dishes. The basement furnace, burning wood instead of coal. This not only provided hot water, but heated sauna, Turkish baths, and hydro-therapeutic appliances night and day; without need for fireplaces, it heated the whole house, through pipes that rose through its interstices, giving on to apertures secreted in every doorway.

The wild hillsides she explored herself. The clambering rockery. The glasshouses and menagerie glinting inscrutably down below, like an inverse reflection of the house. Miles of carriage drives, ten thousand trees buffeted by summer rains. Thimbleton Reservoir on the hills above. Burnfoot Gorge. And the Pump House, where she liked to lurk, looking back at the house across the gorge, listening to the village church bell as it tolled the quarter hour.

Molly asked Jem to explain the grounds' complexities, a canny way to spend some time in his company. He showed her how the reservoirs above were dammed above the Burnfoot Falls. As well as siphoning the waters off into the house, the stream was channelled on to a waterwheel at the Pump House, driving an industrial piston: this automated power was distributed through ingenious gears and cables to drive woodsaws, the kitchen spit, and the dumb waiter. There was no limit to the machines it might run, saving on manpower and steam engines. All through harnessing hydraulic power; no electricity required.

But there was electricity too.

Molly loved the buzzers that sounded around the house.

"Annunciators." Birtle was disdainful of innovations. "Not blasted buzzers."

She studied the wiring in fascination. When someone pressed a button (say, Roxbury, in his laboratory), the electrical circuit, powered by a battery, was completed. A coil on the servants' board was thus magnetised, pulling a tiny metal arm on to the bell: bing. That movement broke the circuit, releasing the arm, which completed the circuit, and the arm struck again: bing. Released, struck again, fifty times in a second: buzz, buzz.

Jem showed how this electricity was generated: the old millhouse, lower down the Burnfoot Stream, was reinvented as the Pump House, powering the scientific quarter. Before its antique walls stood a shiny new turbine, yet under development; behind it, discarded contraptions. Beside these, stacked wooden crates, plated with glass sides and full of strange chemicals: a poetic history of batteries, from Daniell cells and voltaic piles, through Grove cells, Poggendorff cells, gravity cells, and the mighty Leyden jars, to the latest Siemens prototypes, ready to be tested; all charged by the flow of water, modulated by Roxbury's system of levers, rails, dams, and outlets. Jem boasted it was a system more powerful than steam engines, more elegant than clocks. And he didn't understand it.

When Jem showed her round the glasshouses, she shared his company with the orang-utan. Staying clear of the inner quadrangle of laboratories, they saw trees from Brazil and fruits from Bali, geckos from the Galapagos and monkeys from Mauritius. Jem liked Molly to see the animals he was nursing back to health. For example, the strange hare Molly had seen on her first arrival was in fact a Patagonian mara, thriving now in this chilly domain and a favourite of the orang-utan.

Why so many ailing creatures? Lady Roxbury had protested it was wrong to kidnap wild beasts from their native lands. So the earl collected his menagerie from unwanted beasts already in captivity. This had the benefit of making the collection academically unique: zoologists and biologists nationwide signed up to spend a term examining these oddballs. Besides, Jem hadn't much to do down the stables. The Roxburys weren't hunting types, and had so few visitors these days. Jem had an inclination toward these sick and lonely creatures. She often saw him petting the mara and keeping the orang-utan company.

Where was the heart of this Arcadia? Jem spoke little of Lodestar; it was to the earl himself that he paid obeisance. Was it Roxbury pushing these levers, flicking switches, and ever enlarging his designs to bend the wildness of nature to his technological will?

ADAPTATIONS [LAWLESS]

After Guernsey, with the Royal Commission's decision on the forts, Roxbury Industries was paramount. Alongside our labours on the Guernsey dossier, Miss Villiers and I devoted time to Molly every week. I lamented my slipshod approach to Molly's correspondence. We pored over her missives as they arrived.

Now that Miss Villiers was approved to work beside me in Scotland Yard, her aunt's club seemed unsuitable for discussing weighty affairs. Yet the Yard was not always conducive to thought, with everyone bleating over the explosions, and what progress we'd made, and where would the next attack come. To avoid this scrutiny, I sometimes took a private room at the Rising Sun, the Yard's nearest hostelry. It was quiet and cheap, if a little inappropriate, but it brought a lovely intimacy to our work; Miss Villiers seemed determined to bring *Revelations of a Lady Detective* from the world of fiction into real life.

She decoded Molly's bulletin to me: all well and good. But after reading of melancholic explorations, she sighed. "Do you think our poor spy is struggling?"

I did not. As Miss Villiers explained to me what I was failing to read, I had to call for a fresh pot of tea. Ruth did not think Molly was hiding anything, just that her tendency towards novelistic flair disguised her unease. "I should visit Molly, and soon." She wrote to Roxbury, there and then. She explained that she was travelling to Edinburgh, and asked if she might stop in for a visit.

I read over what she had written. "Edinburgh, eh?"

She shrugged and explained no further, and I knew better than to press her.

OF THE OLD EARL, PART THE FOURTH [MOLLY]

WATCHMAN,
EARL BEFRIENDED.
MOLLY

Dear Miss V,

"I suppose we ought to have a chat," said the Earl of

Roxbury. He stumbled across me one morning as I was standing in the hall, pondering the old murals they'd uncovered during the renovations of the great hall.

"I suppose we ought, Your Lordship."

The earl's face was pinched and white. More drawn than I remembered him, back in London, at the Select Committee hearings. Look as I might, I could not see that he wore any mark of mourning, as the children did.

"Stuff and balderdash, young lady. Don't bother with that Your Lordship nonsense, not here."

"Right-o." I hesitated. "Your earl-y-ness."

He grinned. "I would take it as the most enormous compliment if you treated Roxbury House as your own house. No standing on ceremony. Slouch around. Help yourself and that."

I liked this familiarity. There was a northern flair to his intonation, making his speech ever so pleasant. I could listen to that voice all day, as pleasant as a stream burbling over rocks. I eyed him closely. "I won't treat it quite as my own home, sir, for you haven't seen my stablemates, troughers of the messiest kind, and terrible hoarders too, for they think that a found object may someday be the key to the kingdom of heaven, though it lie unused in a cupboard for a decade."

He laughed. "I am a terrible hoarder too."

"I doubt that." I frowned. "Do you mean those contraptions in the Pump House?"

"Wait till you see the dreadful accumulation of pistons and levers and tubes I have in the scientific quarter. Not to mention the electrical gadgets in my laboratory. Oh, give me a battery and a copper coil, and I shall squirrel it away. But then I should not be here if I did not store away the good things of life up here." He tapped his head. "Nor should this house."

He explained. He had visited these same crags as a child. He spent many an hour gazing at the Burnfoot Gorge, where I so loved to ramble. That established his lifelong devotion to energy and power, especially the untold powers of water. When he made his fortune, from hydraulic engines, he considered no other location for his lordly retreat. Today, this was the source of the invention that ever bubbled through the house.

"Anyway, forget Your Lordship. Call me Roxbury, why don't you, or something along those lines."

"Very well, Mr Roxy." I never could resist eliding a syllable. "I must go about my lessons, or your children will stay savage and untaught."

"Can't have that." He smiled. "I'm delighted you're offering them so much."

I sensed he did not mean my painting skills.

"I believe you have much to teach all of us, young lady. I've seen your skills at work." By which he meant not just my drawing at the Select Committee, but the sleight of hand with which I demonstrated subterfuges to the court. "I give you permission to instruct my lot in whatsoever subjects you choose!" He touched me lightly on the arm, as if we were old friends. Then he walked off in a direction quite the opposite to where he had been headed.

Only as I turned to go up to my lessons did I sense eyes upon me.

There, in the shadows of the butler's pantry, lurked Birtle, eyeing me as if I was a traitor.

REINTERPRETING MOLLY [LAWLESS]

Thus did Molly win free rein over the three Roxbury children. The Norphans Practickly were practically begging her to teach them more anyway, beyond their drawing lessons. Accepting that caricatures could not contain their mischief, Molly consented. By early August, they had developed a week-long roster of lessons:

—juggling

—puppetry

—prestidigitation

—ventriloquism

—slang, mainly argot and backslang, for conducting secret dialogues under the noses of straight people (Birtle, Skirtle and their father), requisite to any kind of secret society

—and twenty subjects improvised on the job, covering whatever Molly considered a reasonable addition to a young person's education.

She entertained them royally. And this led to Molly dining at the earl's table.

Miss Villiers and I loved the notion of our street urchin instilling her irrepressible verve into this aristocratic brood. Molly gave them more fun in those eight weeks than throughout the grind of their private (and expensive) education.

They conjugated parlyaree to the penny whistle. They learned the bite of satire, the shiver of gothic horror, the grandeur of tragedy. They imagined themselves Cleopatras, Boadiceas and Joan of Arcs, their kingdoms wrenched away and ruined. Molly was of old a devotee of theatre, museums and lectures, her memory cavernous and unpredictable.

Even Nico's respect for Molly blossomed.

Picture Molly, at the window of the art room. The sun steals through the forest to cast dappled light on the wood panels. It gilds the page; it sets Molly's chestnut hair aglow.

Picture, all the while, Nico sitting obstinately at the other end of the table, filling in puzzle pieces for as long as he could bear it. Then his sisters abandoned him. They asked for lessons;

they loved their lessons, which Molly made more hilarious day by day.

No wonder he fell for her. (Molly was not even aware, but Ruth discerned it, between the lines.) A schoolboy crush. He had tired of playing up. He was vociferous as his sisters, but the snobbishness was gone.

Absorbed in my investigations, I never considered how draining her lessons must be. Molly was used to coming and going. She preferred to rely on her own wit. To have responsive pupils, with wit of their own, was satisfying, once they stopped playing up and became devoted to her, but it was exhausting.

Still, once the children left for school, Molly would be quite bereft. I must warn her about that. Having never been to school, she knew nothing of the approaching school term, which would whisk her charges summarily away.

DINING DOWN [RUTH]

My dear Sergeant, or (if I may?) Campbell,
Molly had not yet been promoted to the earl's table, when I visited.

As a friend of the family, I am considered a lady; no question but that I would dine down, with the earl. The children were obliged to join us, which inhibited their fun, as Roxbury and I get on well (despite him having been friends with my father) and sit nattering idly. The moment the children finished dessert, they asked to be excused.

Last night, I accepted this as normal. When it happened again tonight, I asked why.

"Oh," said Kitty, "but Miss Molly is upstairs, with

our sketching pads, and puzzle."

Roxbury smiled. "Why should you hurry to her?"

"Because, Fa," said Nico, "she is so droll."

"Enlivening," said Kitty.

"Whereas you, Fa," said Peggy, "are dull as Burnfoot ditchwater."

"Should we summon your friend?" Roxbury looked amused. "Birtwell, bring the puzzle too. We shall have a night of it."

"Is Molly's style appropriate?" I hesitated. "For the table?"

Molly was summoned. Placed at the end of the table, Molly ogled our assembled company as if she'd been asked to dance naked in front of the empress of Japan. You know as well as I, Molly has met princes, actors and novelists, uncowed. She has given evidence to your parliamentary select committee; at inquests, indeed.

I attempted a rescue. "What games do you play upstairs?"

Molly searched for an apposite lie.

"Why," said Peggy, "we extemporise limericks about members of the household."

Molly winced.

"Molly, Molly, take the floor," Nico said. "Do one of your ones about Fa."

Kitty clapped. "No! About Birtwell."

Molly failed to conceal her horror.

"Gentle, now," said Roxbury. "You derail our guest's energies."

"Come, children," I said. "Why don't you begin? Show us how you've been taught."

Before Molly could stop her pupils, Nico plunged in, eyeing his sisters. "When residing at Roxbury House—"

[*Kitty*] "One must creep round quiet as a mouse—"

[*Peggy*] "Sneaking tidbits from Skirtle, tiptoeing past Birtwell—"

"Whose stare tramps one down, like a louse." [Molly, unable to help herself.]

Applause from Roxbury, applause from me, laughter all round. Then I noticed Molly's pained face. She was looking to the doorway, where the butler—whatever his damnable name is— stood, quietly looking daggers at her.

My visit was a success. Molly's friendship with the earl was cemented. I think it will grow, now that she is dining down. I imagine her having walks with him, and quiet evening chats.

I was desperate not to be too inquisitive—mustn't give the game away—but I asked Roxbury if he would consider opening his house again, as in old times. The aristocratic houses of England endure an unending round of visitors each summer, but I checked the guest book, and Roxbury has curtailed such visits since his wife's passing.

I have alerted Molly to oddities of the house she had not noticed. She's been willing, yet circumspect. There are rooms unfound and corridors unexplored. She doesn't know the way to the towers, or the furnace, nor has she investigated the scientists' laboratories and electrical innovations. "What, Moll, have you no curiosity?"

"Curiosity I have aplenty, Miss V," she said, "but it's killed molls greater than I."

Molly has no notions of how a house normally runs, but I have. I consider Birtle's sullen conduct a dereliction of butlerdom, and Skirtle's house management little better. Call me demanding, call me pampered and southern, but I cannot believe northern servants must be so obstructive.

These are subtleties beyond Molly's ken. And all offer insights into the earl's state of mind.

APPRAISALS [LAWLESS]

Miss Villiers' report on her visit surprised me. On her return from the north, we shared a meal at the Rising Sun. She filled in the broad brushstrokes of her letter with colourful undertones. So much that I had taken for granted as true in Molly's reports was, if not false, more complicated.

The earl was by no means idle; he was industrious—but working at what? Molly did not yet know, and Miss Villiers could not work it out.

The enigmatic Lodestar had become *de facto* manager running Roxbury Industries.

Birtle was not a useless butler, in Ruth's demanding eyes, but tiresome, and Skirtle an adequate housekeeper, but no more. The children, to her ears, were nightmarish.

And Molly was unhappy.

Roxbury House, she concurred, was a place of magic. Miss Villiers' descriptions enriched Molly's labyrinthine palace.

The earl Miss Villiers found likeable. "Not at all the brusque man of business the press used to portray him as. He has no time for public affairs, for standing on ceremony; no wish to brag of business affairs, like most men. His mind is always soaring like a buzzard, seeking the idea scurrying far below to feed his brood."

Miss Villiers wanted to know what I knew of this Lodestar.

"Nothing much. Why?"

"Worthy of notice, I'd think. If you're concerned for Roxbury and his Industries, that's where I'd start; it's Lodestar that runs them. I barely saw the man." She described how the staff deferred to him, and Roxbury signed off his suggestions, happy to leave the day-to-day running of the business in his hands. "Molly seemed taken with him, though."

"Surely not; she's devoted to Jem." We had been enjoying the developing drama of Molly's admiration of the stable boy. "And you? Did you find him so captivating?"

She strove to mask her aversion. I was relieved to see her distaste. Miss Villiers is younger than I am; I harboured a fear that some nimbler fellow would charm her away. "I wouldn't wish to prejudice you. I'd prefer that you come to your own conclusion. Can you cook up a reason to meet with him?"

"What, here?" I laughed. "Come to London often, does he?"

"All the time. He's all over the country. Newcastle, Portsmouth, Liverpool, Erith—"

I gave her an inquisitive look, my hand upon hers.

She shrugged it off. "Anywhere Roxbury Industries has business. Which is everywhere. Nothing untoward about it. He's one of these empire-building engineers, extending their domain, checking, cajoling, pursuing payments, haranguing slowcoaches. The company lives in fear of him, Molly tells me. But they try to impress, which keeps the whole caboodle at top speed. You can see why the earl would love him."

There was a reservation in her voice.

I poured fresh tea. I knew not to interrupt her in full flow.

She walked to the window. "The earl seems to love him like a son. More than he loves his own children. Them he barely seems to notice, and their mother gone. They are growing up wild. Skirtle mothered them when they were tots, but she hasn't the will nor energy to control them now they're filthy youths. Their schools evidently train them more in savagery than civilisation."

"England's public schools. When they say Waterloo was won on the playing fields of Eton—"

"They're not talking of fair play and decency, no. Witness

the backstabbing that enlivens the Tory party daily."

I laughed. "Have we dumped Molly well and truly in it?"

"She went as a drawing mistress. She teaches them street arithmetic and bad manners. A street urchin schooling an earl's brood makes me laugh. And she contrives to do it brilliantly, disguising her lessons. Mathematics she has turned into gambling. (She lets the boy win, else he would strop and stay an ignoramus.) They approach literature through comic poetry, which they compose daily to their amusement, extemporising at the expense of the household. In art, she hooked them through caricatures; they now depict the secrets of country life in Hogarthian triptychs. By this means, she digs out secrets the children know and should keep secret, of the household and neighbouring village: who hates whom, who has affairs, who is rumoured illegitimate, and worse. She is brilliant."

"But she is unhappy, you say?"

Miss Villiers sighed. "She spends many lonely hours wandering."

Molly had taken to exploring the grounds, in search of solitude, perhaps because so many doors of the house were shut to her. Indeed, Miss Villiers reported that the whole east wing was closed up, ever since the demise of Lady Elodie, the earl's wife, of whom nobody ever spoke. Yet the renovation in the hall was her idea: to brighten guests' first impression. When they found old paintings beneath the plaster, rather than paint over them, they decided to restore. They dated back to the old lady who lived there long before: Mad Wifey, she was known as. The tumbledown ruin was still known as Mad Wifey's when Roxbury bought it in the forties and began converting it into Roxbury House. All that remained of Mad Wifey's was the hall, with surrounding rooms and interstices; the rest of the wild gothic confection was Roxbury's design.

I had imagined it an ancient manorial pile. So it looked,

in the engravings. Yet Roxbury was as new a house as you might find in England, more appealing than Osborne House, more likeable than Blenheim Palace, more breathtaking than St Paul's.

"Molly's used to the city. She misses that aloneness. Noise and bustle, schemes and plots. There, she can be anonymous, snooping and watching over all. Here, simply to turn up in one corner of the house where she is not invited—*quel faux pas*. Birtwell spies on her, she says, waiting for a slip and thinking evil of her." She sighed. "I've arranged that we go up again in a few weeks."

"We?"

Miss Villiers' plan was even better than that. She had put into Roxbury's head the notion of a weekend visit, as of old. It was too soon, perhaps, to invite a sprinkling of artistic fellows, but she might return, with me at her side, if I dared.

LIES AND EXAGGERATIONS, PART THE SECOND [LAWLESS]

Why hadn't Molly found out more?

Her investigations were full of verve, as I had hoped, and acumen and insight. But they were strangely incomplete. She had barely described the hive of activity that was the glasshouses. Bee house, butterfly house, entemologicon, arachnidarium. Scientists on two levels, outer and inner. Outer houses brightly lit, open to see, full of life and the fruits of activity; inner cloister a place of sequestered study, darkened, papery, and academic.

Why such striking gaps? Molly was our "eyes in the north". She was surely curious about these secretive realms. I would have expected her to peek and peer, to report and surmise; but if she had, she neither reported on it, nor mentioned it on Ruth's visit.

Only later, when she befriended Lodestar, did he himself

induct her into the botanical and industrial mysteries, the chemicals, the botanicals, the herbs and homeopathics, the electrical experimentation.

DOG DAYS [LAWLESS]

In the heat of August, everybody left town; everybody who could afford to. There were no explosions, for that brief season. Jeffcoat and I sat down to fathom three things.

How immediate was the threat outlined in the Guernsey papers?

What could we learn from the blasts in Erith, Camden and Guernsey?

Could we anticipate future attacks? Could we not prevent them?

I set about harrying the Royal Commission. I co-opted the upper echelons of the military: they considered the Guernsey papers an urgent awakening.

I checked the progress of the defences recommended to the commission, so we could make their current shortcomings clear before Parliament voted on them again.

We asked ourselves who had the ability to design such bombs. If even O'Leary the Fenian was impressed, these activists must have specialised knowledge. They were not isolated cranks. Industrial workers? Researchers? We drew up a list of institutions and companies to visit.

We sketched out likely sites for attacks. Erith, on the Thames, was the gateway into London, Camden on the mainline train, Guernsey a staging post if the French ever invaded. Where next? Ports? Emblematic London sites? Somewhere to shock the nation.

I would visit learned institutions around London, Jeffcoat

construction companies. We kept up our interviews; we harangued local forces to keep an ear out. We sought allies we could trust. We circulated the notion of constant vigilance. Notice anything odd? About a colleague or a project, about the development of materials or the use of equipment? Let us know. We peddled the motto "See, share, secure."

This call for vigilance reached police forces all over. If they heard rumours, if they noted unruly gatherings, if criminals vanished from view or employed a new modus operandi, they should let us know.

The letters began arriving.

Miss Villiers hated an unsolved puzzle.

She could not forget the body on the SS *Great Britain* lifeboat. A fruitless quest, I told her. I was overwhelmed with the Guernsey paperwork; now letters poured in, full of dread warnings, which must be sifted through.

"Your Mr Lodestar is a bit of an optimist, isn't he, Campbell?" It was a quiet moment at the Yard, and she had dug out the *Great Britain* file. She was astounded that the name Roxbury had been in the dead man's pocket. "And Lodestar dismisses it as altogether ordinary?"

"As it is. Everybody's heard of Roxbury."

"There's a darker interpretation."

I set aside my work and gave her my attention.

"You're anxious about Roxbury's capabilities to defend the nation. The papers are crowing about malign French influence. What if this fellow was sent to attack Roxbury? What if he slipped aboard in Cadiz, say, planning some mischief?"

"To the ship?"

"To Roxbury."

I put my hand to my mouth. "But he didn't survive stowing away."

"He fell out with his accomplice, and they did for him.

These anarchists are famously argumentative."

"And ill-nourished. And tubercular."

She ignored me. "He intended to find a Roxbury crane, and blow it up. Or the new guns for your Portsmouth forts. In order to discredit Roxbury Industries."

I nodded. "Possible."

"And his friends are still at work." She grimaced. "Put that to your Mr Lodestar, and see if he's so sanguine."

Miss Villiers admitted that, since Simpson's revised estimate of how long the man had been dead—four years, or five—she was paying occasional visits to Antony Gibbs Shipping. Having lost so much in the dockyard fire, they would not let her take records away. So she was spending odd afternoons working, little by little, through their SS *Great Britain* lists in search of the unfortunate man.

Antony Gibbs's office on Oxford Street was sandwiched between the Princess's Theatre and a dingy alley, Adam and Eve Court. Not knowing what she was looking for, she was often distracted by music from the theatre. Through the summer evenings, the theatres struggled to lure audiences; gone was the spring mania for *Mazeppa* at the Astley with the American actress naked on horseback. They trumpeted moderate prices for *Perseus and Andromeda*, starring Mrs Ellen Ternan, frequently understudied (so the gossip went) for her visits to the coast at Mr Dickens's expense.

Then there was the fire.

THE HOUNDS [LAWLESS]

I took up the suggestion to enquire about Lodestar.

I learned that he was liked. Admired. A capital fellow. An old-style member of the club—though no drinker. He paid his dues, bought his rounds, joked with the right people and avoided the wrong sorts, dressed nattily, spoke succinctly, listened much, and judged when the evening was headed downhill in time to escape the debauchery. He was revered for his trick shots at billiards, and a bosom pal of Julian Overend, a young banker currently doing rather well.

I happened to intercept young Overend as he left work, heading for the Hounds Club, on St Martin's Lane. A highly strung fellow, he looked terrified when I said I was from Scotland Yard. I reassured him my intention was to protect his friend's interests. I bought him a drink, and he calmed down. "I'm told you're friendly with Lodestar."

"Terrific chappy." Overend was enthused to the point of devotion. "Such a grasp of finance. Stocks, bonds." Julian Overend was heir to the fortune of Overend and Gurney, the bank on everyone's lips due to their fabulous interest rates. "Lodestar's been a tremendous advocate for us. All over the country. The fellow gets around, don't you know."

"So I hear."

"They think nothing of such distances where he grew up. Four days on a camel through the savannah. That's just how it is there. Ten thousand acres his father had. Should have come to him, were it not for his father's dissipation. Inheritance tied up." Overend gabbled away, a sheen of sweat on his forehead. "And debts. Frightful debts."

Lodestar, he told me, was the son of Sir Chichester Lodestar, British consul to Mozambique and the Interior. Our Lodestar came to London when his father died, just a few years back, aiming to sort out the inheritance and return home. On discovering his fortune had been frittered away on his father's vast debauches and dissolute investments, he had no alternative but to stay in London and make his own fortune. His father had friends enough back in the day. People helped him out. Who had sent him to Roxbury, Overend had no idea. He had some notion Lodestar Senior had been at Oxford with Roxbury. The two men went their different ways: Roxbury into engineering, transforming British industry; Lodestar Senior into the Foreign Service, one of their more difficult postings, outwith the Empire, where he established a vast estate in the African interior.

There he imposed his stamp rigorously. As the years passed, he spent less and less time on governmental business. He acquired a reputation as one of the hard men of Africa, quashing tribal disputes with something of the iron fist.

"They say Nathan is the spitting image of the old goat. But a harder worker you won't find, nor a nicer chap. He's in town tomorrow. Come and meet him at the club, why don't you? Set you up with an offshore account while we're at it, eh? All the smart money's going there." He gave me his card.

I confess myself enchanted by his account of Lodestar. The wandering heir, arriving in the great city, surely dazzled by its vastness and variety, deprived of his dues and thrown back upon his own devices. Why not befriend bankers such as Overend? Why not make yourself well liked at gentlemen's clubs? How else to get an introduction to a job as steady as Roxbury's right-hand man? How better to make his way in Roxbury Industries? So much so that he was taking an engineering diploma, Roxbury's endorsement releasing him from turgid requirements of essays and lectures. What better way to thrive than to be brilliant at his job? Perhaps his father had been a libertine—I should be wary of touching upon what must be a tender subject—but young Lodestar was clearly both likeable and industrious.

* * *

MAGNETIC MANAGER [LAWLESS]

Lodestar met me in New Slaughter's Coffee House, adjacent to the club on St Martin's Lane. I had suggested a public house. He replied that he preferred a pot of Ethiopian than a jar of ale; the coffee in London was execrable, but New Slaughter's at least roasted their own beans.

I was early. I like to see my prey before they see me. Lodestar spotted me through the bow window. He swept in, his bright eyes fixing me, that broad brow fringed by his mop of jet-black hair. He had a vitality, unquenchable and winning. As he held out his hand to me, I felt as if I were reuniting with an old friend.

Lodestar held nothing back. Yes, his travels around the country were unpredictable and incessant. Roxbury Industries had more work than ever these last years. It was all he could do to keep it up. How Roxbury himself had it in the old days he could scarcely imagine.

I was glad I had caught up with him. Lodestar put me at ease, establishing a bond between us, as of men of the world. He talked of how we were both called back and forth to deal with trifles others should have dealt with; and yet we must stay alert, ready for that one serious call, where our attentions were needed to solve a crisis or avert disaster. I was flattered that a man running one of the largest businesses in the country should consider my labours as demanding as his own. We all think our efforts unnoticed, I suppose, and our struggles greater than others'.

I reminded him of our previous correspondence, concerning the body. I explained Miss Villiers' theory that the dead man may have planned mischief against Roxbury.

Lodestar shrugged. "But you never discovered who he was?"

"No. My colleague was hunting through the shipping lists. But there was a fire at the docks."

"I heard mention of it." He gave me a quizzical look. "Strange, how Londoners surround themselves with flammables. I have chemists developing safer materials. I'll show you the new billiard balls I've produced."

"I've been forewarned. Don't challenge me to a game."

He laughed. "Wood, gas, coal, paper. Fuels in the waiting."

"And we live on top of it all." I shook my head. "As if we're inviting disasters."

"In Africa, we have bushfires and accidents, but nowhere this density of population. I have seen violence, even on my father's cosseted estates, but I have never seen a place as vulnerable for apocalypse as London. Your Great Fires of London fascinated me as a child: in the fire of 1212, thousands died on London Bridge alone. Frightful. And expensive! In business, we try to foresee dangers. Prevention is cheap. You police must be moving that way. What a lot of bother would be saved if you could head off fires and explosions, eh?"

I smiled to think of him as a child in the bushveldt, studying histories of faraway England. "But as I was saying, we've found further records at the shipping company offices."

"You determined fellows. Bravo!" He smiled and called for fresh coffee.

I could not find it in me to decline, though my heart was already thumping and skipping. It was time for business. I asked him about Roxbury munitions works. Were they prepared for the demands of the Palmerston fortifications? And the brick factories? Was it within their capacity?

"Are they going ahead?" His dark brows lifted in amusement. "They have been ceased long enough with legal delays and political whatnot. I had the impression the commission was minded to cancel the whole plan."

I was permitted to make discreet enquiries, without

revealing official secrets; indeed, I was obliged to, on Ripon's say-so. It would not do for the government to make a grand announcement giving the go-ahead to such vast expenditure, crucial to the nation's safety, only for the private contractor to admit that they were not up to the job. That would advertise the nation's lack of defences. "The commission met. The plan isn't cancelled. You'll hear officially within the next week. Will that be acceptable to Roxbury Industries?"

"Acceptable?" He grinned, and poured more coffee, despite my protestations. "Oh yes, my friend, I'd say it's acceptable." Lodestar's accent had that clipped African overlay to its upper-class English vowels, and behind it a wild energy that spoke of vast confidence, a confidence that would sweep away objections and make the impossible possible, make the unimaginable within reach, make the future present.

I was emboldened to ask him how he came to know Roxbury, for I was fascinated that he had so quickly risen in eminence.

"Two sad tales," he said, "and one happy one."

His old father in Africa had dwindled away. He was a difficult man, toughened by years of toil, but devoted to his homeland and proud to have established a British protectorate in the interior. As he died, he packed off his son to London to seek his fortune. He had not explained that said fortune would come not as inheritance, but through merit and work.

Lodestar laughed to recall his own rude awakening. What his father had given him, however, was the introduction to Edward, Earl of Roxbury. Yes, they played rugby together at Oxford, when Roxbury was an ambitious engineering student, and Lodestar Senior a dissolute graduate, playing endless sports until his civil service posting came through.

The second sad story: after the early debacles in the Crimea, Roxbury was called upon to help his country. He set aside commercial enterprises, which supplied hydraulics across the world, to consider guns. What advances the French had made since Waterloo. We had ignored them pig-headedly; even the Russian weaponry was better than ours. In two months, Roxbury had designed, developed and tested a breech-loading artillery gun. This reached the Crimea just in time to make a difference. The British forces across the world were poised to adopt them.

In 1858, an unexpected reversal. A bomb at the Paris Opéra nearly killed Louis Napoleon III and Empress Eugénie. Policemen and passers-by died; hundreds were injured. Only by a whisker did the emperor and his wife escape. In the aftermath, the French unravelled the manufacture of the bomb. It had been finished by a Birmingham gun maker, who protested he knew nothing of its radical intention. But it had been tested in the north of England—where exactly was never proven.

Suspicion fell upon both great industrial manufacturing companies of the north: Roxbury Industries, which dominated the east coast, and their rival in the west, Whitworth Enterprises of Manchester. Diplomatic relations between France and Britain became strained (our government toppled promoting the Conspiracy to Murder Bill).

Whitworth pronounced that the technical achievements of the bomb—or its remnants—were beyond his company's capabilities.

Roxbury declined to investigate, absorbed in improvements in the British Navy's ordnance. This rebounded badly upon him. The press suggested that Roxbury may have, if not sanctioned, at least winked at the plottings, knowing that mischief done to France could only profit his company, inextricably bound with British armaments. In a spiral of suspicion and adverse publicity, Roxbury was vilified, and so soon after being lionised for his inventions. To his astonishment, the new government saw fit to withdraw their contracts, claiming pressure from the electorate. The government even went back on his technical advances, reverting to Whitworth's trusty old muzzle-loaders.

Roxbury was left with contracts broken, research wasted, and military sales slashed. He was stung and scolded.

He reacted in two ways. Reluctantly, he offered his commercial services around the globe. He soon found his wares in greater demand than ever, now that he looked beyond parochial Britain. The Brazilian army took him up; the Japanese bought warships; the Italians bought artillery; Union and Confederates armed themselves to the teeth with Roxbury guns—making that fruitless conflict more gruesome.

Personally, he withdrew from public duties. He only appeared in the House of Lords on occasions of the utmost gravity (such as the Fairchild Commission, where Molly had encountered him). He withdrew from his civic commitments up north. He broke off his habitual contact with the managers of subsidiary companies. And, though he never gave up his research, he looked to appoint a manager for Roxbury Industries.

Enter Lodestar.

NORPHANS' HIGH JINKS [LAWLESS/MOLLY]

Between Miss Villiers' visit and the sudden evanishment of the children passed several weeks. These proved quietly fruitful. Now Miss Villiers had galvanised her to get the measure of the scientific quarters, and the house's secrets.

Molly offered us glimpses of teaching the Norphans, the sport and the stramash. They sat in each other's places; they spat in each other's faces; they stole each other's napkin rings; they sowed cress in each other's bedsprings; they stole dessert; they denied stealing; they endured their punishments stoically.

"Molly?" said Kitty one morning. "After this lesson, remind me to kill myself."

"I'm sorry?"

"To kill myself. I've dedicated myself to anarchy and nihilism. Though, in consorting with the likes of Fa, I betray the cause."

Meanwhile, Peggy's escape fund was not flourishing. Peggy was continually selling her worldly goods, to squirrel away funds for running away. Her ambition was to join a gold rush to Australia or South America; failing that, to become arch ruffian of a gang of thieves. She longed for her birthday, and possessions she might sell. She got little from her siblings, but the odd treasure from an aunt in Portland; though opportunities for commerce were limited among staff and residents of Roxbury. She constantly reckoned up her savings to the nearest farthing, converting the total into so many days on the run: a miraculous effort, as she was the worst at sums.

Nico divided his time between correspondence with parliamentarians and posting mischievous signs around the house:

VISITORS ARE REQUESTED TO REFRAIN
FROM HOOTING AND TRUMPETING BETWEEN
THE HOURS OF MIDNIGHT AND 6AM.

When the "hide in a box" game lost its currency, the older two invented more games to torture Kitty:

—Who can make the highest chalk mark on the wall? (Never Kitty.)

—Who can steal Skirtle's teacakes? (Never Kitty.)

—Who will go nearest the Walled Garden without trepidation? (Kitty never got near. Quite why the Walled Garden was so trepidatious Molly could not get them to say.)

—Who can hit the Frog Stone? (Kitty had at least a chance.)

The Frog Stone was a great boulder mid-river, upstream from the Iron Bridge, at the confluence of the Burnfoot and

River Dally. To please the children, in younger days, Roxbury had painted it with a frog face; they loved to throw stones from the bridge, the scoring complex, with premiums for hitting eyes, nose and mouth.

VISITORS ARE POLITELY REQUESTED TO REFRAIN
FROM DRINKING THE TURKISH BATH WATER
DUE TO AN UNIDENTIFIED CORPSE IN THE GORGE.
IF THEY MUST SLAKE THEIR THIRSTS, THEY WILL FIND
THAT FOULD'S ARSENICAL SOAP ADDS FLAVOUR.

They sketched self-portraits on envelopes and sent them to school friends. A few brave souls sent back a daguerreotype, only to have the Norphans caricature their looks cruelly by return post.

In the evenings, they played fearsome parlour games, requiring feats of ingenuity. Molly's favourite was "When I embark on Auntie Mildred's ship", in which each child added yet more poetic items to the list for embarkation on an imaginary voyage. Where Molly chose apples, cake and books, Kitty would demand "a prince to save my heart from woe" and Nico "a bottle of the widow" (which meant, of course, champagne).

Molly shared with the Norphans a sense of unreality about her residency. Too perfect, it could not last. Kitty copied one of Molly's lovely sketches to her best friend, a view from the house over the valley, with herself and Peggy outlined, like sylvan dryads playing some Arcadian ball game.

"It's so beautiful," Kitty wrote. "I wish I was here."

I did not understand what Miss Villiers already intuited: that Molly was retelling her story in the guise of a romantic novel, precisely because she was not experiencing it so. Molly had lived always by her wits. To be the voice of authority jarred. She was used to bargaining over everything, always looking for the profit, the margin, even in her closest friendships. We are all parasites, she liked to say. To have livelihood and lodgings guaranteed confused her *raison d'être*.

On Nico's bedroom door:

No ruminators allowed.

BOOK III
MOLLIFICATION

A Fuel in Waiting [The Globe]

Horror at the Princess's Theatre on Oxford Street.

The ballerinas were thrilling the audience with their skill and beauty in the Friday pantomime performance. But joy turned to horror during their spectacular routine. A spark from the stage lights, it is believed, set fire to a dancer's dress.

Anne Huntleigh was engulfed in flames, to the sound of explosions onstage and gasps off. Fellow dancer, Sarah Smithereen, rushed to help. As she tried to smother the stricken girl, her dress too went up in flames.

Theatre staff ushered the horrified audience out on to the street.

The stage manager courageously extinguished the dresses using his cloak, though the fire had spread to the scenery. The backstage properties were alight. The fire was already engulfing neighbouring offices, where innumerable paper files provided ample kindling. The theatre blaze was soon under control and extinguished. The offices, where some say the blaze originated, are burnt down entirely.

Our wooden auditoria are a fuel in the waiting. When the modern thirst for lighting effects collides with cheap flammable materials, who will guard us against fires? We shall be reporting on such disasters weekly. Our houses are worse, with straw mattresses and linen coverlets, twill curtains and woollen socks, hung up to dry over a flaming range. London's housing is a disaster ready to happen. When will the authorities take up their mantle of responsibility? Who will regulate for our safety?

Huntleigh and Smithereen were taken to the Middlesex Hospital. Both are being treated for extensive burns. Huntleigh is badly scarred, but responding well.

Smithereen is unlikely to survive her ordeal.

MR SANDS IS IN THE BUILDING [LAWLESS]

When I heard that the Princess's Theatre was ablaze, I had no reason to think of Miss Villiers. Only on my way there did I realise: she had slunk away from the Yard early; she might well have popped up to Oxford Street without telling me. I'd made it clear I thought her efforts wasted.

I arrived in time to comfort the wretched audience, for whom Perrault's *Riquet with the Tuft* would be a nightmarish memory. They had thought the fire was part of the show. The ballerinas pirouetted so imaginatively, as the fire took hold. The stage and backstage of the theatre were still on fire. The theatre manager was beside himself. That everyone escaped was due to the staff's efforts, crying out the theatrical code: "Mr Sands is in the building."

The shipping office was all but burnt down. The theatre manager admitted the fire had started there, though he couldn't fathom how it had burned through an adjoining wall, setting light to the theatre curtains, unnoticed by the audience dazzled with lights and deafened by drumming.

But was the office cleared of people?

I ran to the door with my heart in my mouth.

Ruth was there on the street. My heart leapt to see her. She was attending to people, calming them. I ran to her, ready to shout with relief, ready to snatch her in my arms.

"Do your duty, Campbell, whatever it might be." She waved away my attentions. She was poised and beautiful, with black soot marks on her cheeks. She saw my concern and relief, and put her hand to her mouth, realising from my reaction what might have happened. She turned away to help others.

Both buildings were still thick with smoke.

The shipping fellow had ceased caring. I wanted to go in and gather evidence: where did the blaze start? How? The office manager shook his head, exhausted. Lamps on every desk. So many lamps. So much paper. It could have happened any day. And who would burn their offices on purpose?

I directed passers-by away from the incident. The theatre staff tended to the injured and shocked who remained. I overheard an audience member complaining about the smoke damaging their clothes; another bemoaned the shortage of taxis. We are vile creatures, and selfish, when we are frightened.

I found Miss Villiers again. She was searching, wild-eyed, for her bag. The panic she had contained in the crisis threatened to erupt from this trifle. But I found the bag, in the gutter, stuffed full of documents she had grabbed as the fire spread. She had come out to find the injured dancers, still screaming.

I have seen men dying, the aftermath of explosions and crashes, but Ruth's horror was palpable as she described it to me. Poor women, beautiful lithe girls, dresses ablaze and all their years of training no use to them. They could climb vertical ropes, they could execute a *pas de deux*, they could juggle burning clubs; but they could not put out their tulle dresses. These damnable wooden theatres, illuminated with gas.

Lodestar was right: we surround ourselves with flammables. Was he also right about the police? Should we not just apprehend criminals but anticipate crimes? Woe to the force's commissioner on that day. Already the detective shares with the popular novelist the obligation to imagine horrors. Not only must we expect the worst, we must tease out the dire possibilities of the menace that surrounds us. For shame, sir, if you do not curb your reading of yellow-covered novels, you may be a rapist. You, miss, with your mania for reading at night will set the house afire, incinerating not just your family but the whole street.

Sarah Smithereen never recovered; she died from her injuries a week later. Ruth—who was sure the blaze began in the offices—still talks about her elegant shape.

PUZZLES [LAWLESS]

Jeffcoat and I went over and over everything we knew about the explosions. Frustrating to make so little headway. We'd examined the minutiae of the blasts. We interviewed dozens of people in the vicinity of Erith, hundreds around Camden. I traipsed round London and Jeffcoat the whole country, questioning experts in explosives, but in vain.

With Guernsey, the dossier absorbed my attention at first. Now I turned to De Nesle's reports. He sent us lists of visitors to the island for the week before the blast, gathering from ferry companies and hostelries. He had combed through them, he had interviewed tourists and immigrants, but to no avail.

"Typical," said Jeffcoat, "that he rules out the possibility of a homegrown activist."

"Still, there was that wire." I screwed up my eyes. From my inspection of the blast site on Guernsey, I had learned little. The tides had washed away the debris, but I did find strands of copper, melted to the sea wall. "Suggests a common perpetrator."

"And our one solid piece of evidence." Jeffcoat took out the metallic shard from the Camden disaster: JO TWO CHE. This still had us flummoxed.

I copied out the letters on to a sheet of paper. We scribbled, rearranged, turned them upside down and back to front. Nothing.

NORPHANS' DEPARTURE [MOLLY]

WATCHMAN,
CESSATION OF EMPLOYMENT IMMINENT, I FEAR.
CONSIDERING APPLYING TO WORK AS A MAID.
THOUGHTS? PLEASE PUT IN A GOOD WORD.
MOLLY

Dear Miss V,
The departure of the Norphans Practickly has come upon me as lightning from a blue sky. I knew nothing of school terms. I came downstairs this morning to find the kitchen in uproar and Skirtle at capacity. She was directing maids, stacking laundered clothes into piles by trunks with names stencilled on:

NICODEMUS L ROXBURY

MARGARET V ROXBURY

MARY CATHERINE E ROXBURY

And, strange to say, a further pile.

"Pray who, Mrs Skirtle," I said, "is the mysterious fourth?"

"Out my way, young Moll. I've eight thousand chores, and you've none, so come on out of it."

I examined a shirt atop the fourth pile, peeker that I am. I found a label sewn into the collar, the style in schools to prevent careless boys from losing shirts: WILFRED E ROXBURY.

"The eldest?" I said. "How has Wilfred clothes to be washed when he's abroad?"

Skirtle barked an order into the kitchen, whence rose an herbaceous steam redolent of venison and bacon. Knives clattered. Broth bubbled in vats. Sandwiches were wrapped in brown paper, and laid into hampers. "In such houses as this," she said, smelling the piles, "damp cannot be kept off, neither with the new hentral seating, or whatever he calls it, nor God's own sunshine. Clothes unworn must be washed again before wearing. The likes of you and I—" She gave me a glance. "I don't mean to scorn you, Molly, rather to compliment your good sense— we would air them by wearing them out in the fresh air. Those who've grown up spoiled expect the world to revolve around 'em, as you may attest. The things they do in some houses: every fork named and washed separate; dinner approved with thermymometers; beds warmed with special irons. Not that the earl is that way. But, oh, he has spoiled his children."

"I thought Wilfred was abroad with the army."

"He is returned." Skirtle sighed. "Back from India, worse luck, to complete his studies at the House, in Oxford." She pronounced the word "studies" to suggest Wilfred's studies were centred more on the public house and the bawdy house. "Whether he'll deign to grace us with his educated Oxtabridgean presence, I don't know. The little 'uns are up to high doh about it, you can imagine."

As if on cue, Kitty popped her head round the door.

Skirtle snatched a feather duster to repel her.

Kitty ducked expertly. "Any sign?"

"Away out of it, and ready for your final supper."

"Supper," I said, "in the morning?"

"Aye, and they'll be asleep by noon, in the coach."

"Coach?" I began to feel unsettled. "Where do they go?"

"School, young Moll."

I blinked. "Are they not well enough schooled here with me?"

"Pah." She snorted. "Don't be messing."

"What, all three?"

"September brings Michaelmas term, everyone knows that. Don't you remember your own schooling, dear?"

I managed not to laugh.

Skirtle realised, for all my joking, I was knocked back. She laid a hand on my shoulder. "Don't be disconsolable, dear. You've done wonders enough with these reprehensibates. But away they must, to the corners of the kingdom, and avail themselves of the finest education money can buy." With a roll of the eyes, she began doling out fresh tea towels to set the maids polishing the plates. "What they learn there I cannot say, for they return more ill-mannered every holiday; but that is the way of the world. The earl has not made his fortune fifty times over to let them rot at home, not when there are lessons in Latin and trigamonetary to be suffered in Eton, Cheltenham and High Dudgeon, or wherever it is Peggy is sent."

The flagstones under my feet were falling away. "And they will return?"

"At Christmas, aye."

"Christmas." How many weeks off is that? On the balmy September morning, it seems an improbable dream. "It's a long term for them."

"Don't fret from their point of view, now. There's exeat weekends. October half-holiday." Skirtle smiled. "Though our three are popular brats, and get invites round the seaside resorts."

I made no answer. I was floating up into the eaves of the great hall.

"The earl must've spoken of your returning next holidays,

an't he?" She bustled past, directing the picnic baskets outside. "He'll engage you again, for sure."

I certainly did not know the earl well enough to guess his mind.

"I imagined your Miss Villiers has work lined up, has she not? All those letters of yours…"

I remained silent. I had known, I suppose. I knew this was imminent, but I had put it from my mind and ignored any mention of school.

"We'll miss you, mind. You know I will." She spotted a forgotten tray, laden with sandwiches, and hefted it up; I offered to take it. "Would you, pet? Out on the lawns. It's usually too brisk this time of year, but the earl loves an outdoor feast, so he does. Birtle's setting the tables. I'll bring drinks now in a minute. They call it their last supper."

BREAKFAST ON THE GRASS, PART THE FIRST [MOLLY]

The children were in high spirits. I found them smoothing picnic blankets and tarpaulin rugs before the house, beyond the point where the gravel gave way and the grass sloped down toward the rockery. It was the best view, but not the easiest place to eat.

They didn't care. They wanted to eat up as much as possible of Roxbury House—to gorge themselves on home-cooked meats, venison from the spit, bacon on the range, home-churned cream with preserves made with fruits from the hothouse, laden on to Skirtle's own scones, cooked at dawn, before the kitchens were busy.

Nico sat surveying the gorge, like a Roman emperor contemplating his kingdoms' riches, with no thought for the slaves labouring to bring him such comforts. Peggy was totting up her pocket book: she never had enough to run away, but next month, next year. Kitty was chasing the luridly coloured butterflies. (I prefer London's pallid moths.)

A peculiar screech from below. Nobody remarked upon it: one of Jem's menagerie invalids. We were awaiting the earl's arrival. It was rare for the children to see him outside dinner times; or rather, they saw him from afar, heading for the glasshouses, or Pump House, or reservoirs. His days he spent in the grounds, marshalling culverts and pipes and laying of cables; his evenings, in his laboratory. If, in his industrial prime, he poured the same energy into directing Roxbury Industries, he must have been a magician, popping up at dockyards, factories and grand openings, at parliamentary committees, at the Institute of Civil Engineers, at the Royal Society, to support the weapons and warships rolling off the production lines, exemplars of the latest techniques in design, engineering, and power, always power.

"Picnicking in September?" said the earl. He tucked his shirt-tails back into his work trousers, as he appeared from the rockery bushes. Skirtle would have sent him to change, but she was too aware that he might head for his dressing room and end up in his laboratory, and she wished the children to enjoy this rare time with him. "Remarkable."

Nico cleared his throat. "Indeed, sir, fortunate climes. Auspicious for the school year."

The earl looked at him in astonishment.

Nico hesitated. "Was that not what you meant, sir?"

"I meant," said the earl, "that industrial emissions are raising the average temperatures."

Nico laughed, pleased to hear his father joking. "Peggy, Kitty, you fiends, sit down."

The girls were gallivanting atop the rockery, catching falling leaves. Kitty had her pockets stuffed with conkers. She insisted on garnishing everyone's plates. "We will have a contest after," she said, "and I shall be champion."

"I shall be champion," said Peggy.

Nico's roar came simultaneous. "I shall be champion, you monkeys."

The earl stared at the chattering children, amazed that such creatures could be related to him. The children fell silent, conscious that the high spirits of our lessons were ill suited for family occasions.

"We shall let Miss Molly be champion." Peggy reached out and squeezed my hand. "If we must bid you farewell."

I peered around, at this mention of departures. I looked to the earl. He neither confirmed nor denied it. I wanted to ask him, but it was always the wrong moment. We were barely finished our starters when Kitty stood up, waving.

BREAKFAST ON THE GRASS, PART THE SECOND [MOLLY]

"Someone is coming." Kitty was bouncing on the gravel. "Someone is coming."

Somehow, above the wind and the roar of the gorge, she could hear the clunk of wheels on the cattle grid at the Iron Bridge. Into view swept the fleet phaeton.

"My goodness," said Skirtle. "If it isn't our Wilfred."

The vehicle whooshed past, a surly caped figure leaning out over the running board. Lodestar drew it to a stop up at the grand entrance. He leapt down from the driver's seat, as Wilfred clambered, unsteadily, down from the cabin, brandishing a cheroot. Birtle stepped forward, but Lodestar bade him stand at ease.

"I'll not tarry, Birtle. Just dropping off some riffraff I bumped into at King's Cross. Can't have Her Majesty's finest soldiery trudging up the Burnfoot like a common footpad."

Wilfred loafed towards us, sneering, as if disgusted to have accepted anything from Lodestar. All in a flash, I saw it: Wilfred was the heir to Roxbury Industries and the estate. Yet there he was, gallivanting off to India then back to his studies. In waltzes this upstart Lodestar, from darkest Africa's nether regions, takes up the slack left by the earl, and sets to the task with a will.

"Where there is a Wilf," said the earl. He shook his eldest son's hand manfully, then stepped aside to let the girls attach themselves to Wilfred's sides like limpets.

The earl excused himself, asking Lodestar if they might have a word. Lodestar tossed down a bag on the steps. With an ironic glance at Wilfred, he saluted us broadly, helped the earl up, and drove off toward the glasshouses.

As soon as his father was gone, Wilfred slouched on the rug. "Nico, you old fox," he said. He lit himself another cheroot from a silver case, oozing with wheedling satisfaction. "Slather some chicken liver on an oatcake for me, could you? I'm fresh in from Lahore and the Great Northern catering ain't what it was."

This set the celebrations off into a new frenzy. I kept my peace, while the family had exchanged quips and quibbles: who had not written, what angry words were left unrepented, how cruel to arrive on the instant they were departing when he knew they were eating their hearts out to see him.

Wilfred was staring at me as a magpie eyes a trinket. "Who is this firebrand in the shadows?"

"None of your cheek now, Mr Wilfred." Skirtle

wagged a finger; there was no real reproach in it, yet she seemed to have sway over him. She told him my name and my position.

He drew himself up, like the military man he is, to greet me properly.

Kitty rescued us from discomfort, distributing conkers and demanding the contest. Nico and Peggy kept the tone light-hearted, challenging Wilfred to duels. Their brother tried to enter into the jollity. He volunteered to pierce the toughest chestnuts for battle. We spent a half hour laughing and cracking each other on the knuckles.

Yet disappointment had entered the party. Wilfred could not help shooting dark looks down the hill. He was brooding on the usurper Lodestar and his intimacy with the earl, inspecting the glasshouses central to his father's business. He lit another cheroot; he smoked unconvincingly, as if holding it for someone else. "Smoke, Kitty, Peggy?" He showed off the engraved silver case to his sisters. "Clears the lungs."

When Birtle announced that the coaches were imminent to deliver the children to their respective stations, the complaints I was expecting melted away. They retired to put on their travelling clothes; even Kitty went peaceably. Birtle busied himself with the trunks; Skirtle was at the girls' toilet. On a sudden, I was left with Wilfred.

Wilfred asked me to pass the mustard. He grasped my hand and pulled me roughly towards him. "Give us a kiss, you saucy bit of chutney," he said.

I almost let him, such was my surprise. I scrambled to my feet.

There were no witnesses.

Wilfred eyed me insolently. "Nico told me you were a saucepot. How on earth did my old fool of a father engage someone like you, when I had dragon-faced Visigoths to tutor me?" He leaned towards me, mustard smeared on his chops.

I looked about for assistance. The phaeton, thank goodness, swept back into the courtyard. Lodestar leapt down, and the earl beside him.

"Ready?" said the earl. "We've time. Let's whisk the girls down to their station. Wilfy, why don't you drive Nico?"

Wilfred was ladling mustard onto his beef sandwiches, as if he had said nothing, done nothing. Yet, as Nico came out, Wilfred leapt up and put his arm around his brother, exchanging scurrilous words. Five minutes later they were all gone. As his coach pulled away, I saw Nico gazing back at me, as if ashamed on my behalf.

PROPOSALS [LAWLESS]

I met Miss Villiers, as always, at Waterloo, off the Petersfield train. My heart was singing.

Her smile as she descended, the perfection of her neck, the tilt of her head as she peered over the crowds from the carriage step; the way her skirts fell from her hips; the rasp of her voice as she hailed me, all set me a-thrill; and her hair, her gorgeous black hair, which she swept aside from her eye as she reached out to allow me—unheard of concession—to help her down.

She had no idea that I planned to go down on one knee. She had not the slightest idea that I'd made the clandestine trip to meet her father (from whom she was estranged). I was determined to ask his permission, an old-fashioned notion which she would disdain. Anyone may fall out with their kin, nothing more natural; I hoped to construct bridges into the divide separating her from her past. I did not care overmuch. Colonel Villiers might say whatever he liked; I was ready to ask, with or without his permission. But I got his permission, and along with it, I received Colonel Villiers' opinion of the Palmerston fortifications, an opinion I had not sought; but he was a military type, and his forceful views did not surprise. Indeed, I surprised myself by listening to such codswallop without making a retort which might dampen my marital prospects. He liked me. He wished us well. He thought it unlikely he would attend the ceremony—did he really say "unlikely"? No explanation of how Ruth came to leave home and throw herself on the mercy of her famed Aunt Lexie, with whom she still resided.

To survey the south bank of the Thames, with the height of summer upon us, was worth the risk, though the streets around the station were filthy. Hawkers squawked their puppets and jack-in-the-boxes; women eyed up passers-by, as they draped washing across the insalubrious alleyways behind the rails.

On Waterloo Bridge, we floated in sunlight. The river gleamed, teeming with boats passing under the bridges; to the left, the golden stripes of the clock tower of Westminster, to the right St Paul's dome radiant in the sunshine. Is there anywhere grander than London?

After the morning rush, the city seemed void of people. If I had felt weary of my Home Office researches, today I was reinvigorated. If I had found London tiresome, today I was restored to faith. Of course, the water beneath the surface was anything but clear. How many leap from this very spot on foggy nights, despairing of their future? This morass of humanity threatened to drag us all into its mire; but I rose above, soaring into a cloudless sky.

Ruth was in good humour. She could be impatient with dawdling pedestrians, but not today. I should have suspected a motive for such sweetness.

"Are you happy?" She tugged me to the side of the bridge. "In London, I mean?"

"Happy? Why do you ask?" Ridiculous question, today, with her, in this glorious late summer sun. The Guernsey papers were a headache, but the work was worthwhile and intriguing. With Molly's fair reports from the north, and Jeffcoat a dynamo of a partner, what had I to complain of? "Are you not happy, too?"

She pulled at my arm. We looked out over this city that had beguiled and bedevilled us. She had enjoyed living in London: theatre and opera, the British Museum Library, attending lectures at Bedford College. But her studies had gone awry. My fault, in part, for Molly had fallen ill, and Ruth had set aside her own obligations to nurse her back to health, all the while assisting my investigations with her talent for codes and ciphers—she could not resist the tickle of mystery. She lost her job at the library, over a request for an unsuitable book, and retreated to her Aunt Lexie's in the countryside. She spread her hands, as if to disclose a secret. "The Law Faculty of Edinburgh are seeking a librarian. The Advocates Library is in a state of crisis."

Edinburgh? Edinburgh was my home. My old home, where my mother died, leaving my father to bring me up, a puritanical watchmaker, from whom I escaped south, from the clock trade for the police force. It was not three years since my father died. The Clockmakers' Guild tidied up his affairs, letting out the Bruntsfield flat to graduates, which gave me a useful supplement to my police sergeant's income.

"Only I sometimes feel you have a yen," Ruth was saying, "to live there again. And I..." She hesitated, tongue-tied, which was not like her. She was enquiring of my plans for the future, without wishing to seem indelicate. Might our dreams be somehow entwined?

I reached for her hand, overtaken by a flood of feeling. Now was the moment. The sun, the cloudless sky, the gleaming river, and we two—just we! What place more perfect? (Except for the strange old man lurking, as if to ask money of us.) I felt in my pocket for the ring. There it was. It was only the old man made me hesitate—

"I don't intend that—" She flushed. "I wouldn't wish to presume upon your friendship." She looked at me beseechingly. She saw in my eyes that I had caught the import of her words, yet I held back. She bit her lip. She tried to turn and walk on.

I held my fingers interlocked with hers. (The old man—at last!—moved away.)

She struggled to pull free. "Oh," she said. "Forget that I— Won't you let me go?"

I would not release her. When at last she turned to lambast me, her face lustrous with anger, she saw that I had gone down on one knee.

PIGGOTT'S GALVANIC BELT [*THE TIMES*]

Piggott's Galvanic Belt, without acids or saturation, for
the cure of nervous diseases and irregularities of the
system produced by want of electricity.
Medical galvanic apparatus, without the aid of fluids,
always ready for use, with the current in one direction,
to be had of the inventor and patentee,

Mr WP Piggott, medical galvanist,
523 Oxford Street, Bloomsbury.
Treatise on the above, with testimonials, gratis.

LIMBO [MOLLY]

[NO NOTE FOR WATCHMAN, I'M AFRAID,
AS I'VE NOTHING TO REPORT,
AND THIS MAY BE MY LAST.
MOLLY]

Dear Miss V,
I was indulging my melancholic mood after the children's
departure, when I was reminded of my investigations yet
incomplete.

My room, in the western turret, rejoices in dramatic
views. I was packing my bags. I had not much to pack.
Freed from lessons, I whiled away the afternoon in folding
and refolding my clothes, so carefully chosen by your good
self, so carefully laundered under Skirtle's watchful eye.
Every hem brimmed with nostalgia for the summer I had
enjoyed, not realising its days were numbered.

I found myself drawn to the window. I reached for my sketchbook, to strive one last time for that dramatic perspective London never offered. It was the most fabulous view.

Or perhaps the second most fabulous. The east wing's turret must give views up to the crags, across to the Pump House and the Burnfoot Falls, and right down the gorge into the valley. I had not known—that first day, when the curtain twitched—that the east wing was shut up, and has been since the passing of Lady Elodie.

I craned my neck, staring across at the turret. As I stared, a shadow shifted at the curtain. My heart lurched. Or had I imagined it?

Nobody pulled them aside; nobody looked out, as they had done on my arrival; but then that could have been anyone, a maid or the under-butler. I thought back: who was the figure I had seen then? To pull back the curtains and gaze out seemed now to me so evocative of Roxbury's elusive magic.

The curtains hung immobile.

Who was allowed up there? It must be cleaned, I supposed, even if dormant. Now that my employment was to end, I felt ashamed that I'd barely begun to unravel the place's secrets. Was I too immersed in those gothic romances and penny dreadfuls? (I'm sure you regret lending me them now.) The heroine of *Revelations of a Lady Detective* overcomes all odds to tease out mysteries that defeat all London's detective policemen.

I stared until my eyes smarted. As I was about to give up, and return to my desultory packing case, the floral curtains were thrown aside. The window glinted, obscuring my view, as it too was thrown open. Breathing in the soft autumn day, Patience Tarn leaned out, the picture of prettiness, oblivious to my prying eyes.

LIES AND EXAGGERATIONS, PART THE THIRD [LAWLESS]

Why didn't Molly investigate the east wing sooner? At the time, I thought nothing of it; since, I have chided her and extracted the following, which are reasons, if not excuses.

Molly was not architecturally savvy. She was unused to such grand residences and bamboozled by the abundance of rooms—morning rooms, drawing rooms, galleries and boudoirs; brush room, shoe room, saucery, spicery; bakehouse, brewhouse, bamboo room, gun room; fish store, lamp room, game larder, chandry—so she simply did not know there was so much of the house she had never seen. (There was even a room for ironing the newspaper, though it was only ever used when Nico was home.)

Every house is several houses under one roof, just as every city is many cities superposed. Molly in London had leapt boundaries. She was one of the rare beasts visible to rich and poor, on speaking terms with law lords, landlords and layabouts. But Miss Villiers' lessons impeded that irrepressible curiosity, forbidding her to hobnob or lurk.

To fulfil her role was so demanding, no wonder she forgot that twitch of the curtain on her first arrival. Consequently, she never thought that exploring those closed rooms might have led her to the east wing turret. By the time she overcame that reticence, our investigation was drawing to a close.

PAX INTERRUPTA [MOLLY]

"Does Miss Molly require assistance?"

I jumped three feet in the air to find Birtle standing in the doorway of my room. His glowering brow skipped between me and the window.

He knew I was gazing at the turret.

I would ask him. He knew what I had been looking at. There was no space for dissembling. "Birtle, that eastern turret—"

"But, Miss Molly." He gestured at my half-filled case. "Wherever are you going?"

"Why, old cove, you know as well as I that with the children gone my employment must be ending."

A smile came to his lips, and it was not the smile I expected. Not triumphant, nor exultant, but wry. "No, no, no, I hardly think the earl could do without you."

I looked at him. "He has said nothing to me."

"Nothing about your leaving, I rather think."

"Nothing about continuing."

His smile became kinder, almost repentant. "Shall I endeavour to secure you an interview with him, as soon as he is back?"

"Back?"

"He is called away to Yorkshire, on private business. Let me take the liberty to issue you interim instructions. Consider yourself at leisure for the weekend." And with that, he took himself away, as was his wont, silently and without any attempt to answer my query.

REFUGE [LAWLESS]

While Wilfred was in residence, Molly went walking daily. Thimbleton Reservoir offered tranquil respite from her anxieties. She found a route up around the calm of the reservoir, into the hills above the house, and back down through the gorge.

The Norphans had shown her the Shepherd's Refuge. This was an old railway carriage that Roxbury had deposited as a hut for watching wildlife, amid the wild flowers and brambles above the gorge. From there, she looked across the valley, watching birds wheel over the house. A falcon hovered, ready to pounce; up flapped a disorderly crow to harass him. The larger bird eased away; but the crow flapped after, pecking at the bird of prey. The crow, she understood, was protecting its young; for that day, at least, it won the battle.

Excellent vantage point for spying. She could watch Roxbury fribbling around the Walled Garden. At the menagerie, Jem would carry his latest invalid rodent on a stroll, in company of the orang-utan; sometimes he rode to the village to show his dairymaid sweetheart. Lodestar headed past the Shepherd's Refuge, unaware of her, as he crossed over to the slate quarry for the blasting tests that so annoyed Skirtle.

The shadowed path down into the gorge made her feel secure from prying eyes. Wilfred often went away into town or hunting with friends. She would descend by the Pump House, where the ancient waterwheel jutted out into the Burnfoot Falls, the dam above controlling the water flow that powered the newfangled turbine. The river's roar was louder than any part of the Thames. The mist thrown from the turbulent rocks gave her a sense of magical repose. From here were channelled the healing streams that provided the house with ambrosial water and worked its contraptions.

A powerful sanctuary.

Skirtle told Molly of the changes she had seen at Roxbury House. When she arrived, along with the children, coal fires provided cheap, copious warmth; but coal will coat a house with soot. Skirtle only mentioned this once, and the earl switched to wood fires.

He had a forest of a thousand trees, and was planting a thousand more each year; they would not run short. The problem was to stop the servants clearing away the fireplaces. Servants trained on coal fires liked to clear them every morning, but a wood fire needs that ashen base; Skirtle and Roxbury both would flit around the house of a morning, springing on poor backward servants who disobeyed the new regime.

Still, wood ash wafted out, and she was constantly marshalling her troops to clean carpets, polish sideboards, and rejuvenate paintings. Consequently, Roxbury replaced the wood fires with his centralised heating core. A great furnace was built into the crags beneath the house. Hot air circulated under the basement's terracotta tiles and, via a lattice of pipes, up through the house, with smoke filtered through strategic flues. This furnace also heated three boilers, whence water was driven up through the house by hydraulic pressure. The Turkish baths were ready at any hour; from the taps issued hot and cold water. It was the most advanced system in the world, perfect for the frozen wastes of the north, as Molly called them.

Thus Roxbury, with his house; thus Roxbury, with his servants. It spoke of his obsession with developments, yet was a miraculous gift to all who used the house. His children took it for granted, until they returned to school and found themselves once again shivering at night in their beds.

The next episodes of Molly's tale she did commit to paper, but she never posted. Ruth got them from her on our visit, sensing something was awry. To maintain the order of the narrative, I place them here.

ABOUT LOVE [MOLLY]

Dear Miss V,
"I'll teach you a thing or two about love," said Wilfred. Can you imagine it? I shall write down as much as I can of my tangle with him, but whether I'll post it I know not.

It was two nights before you and Watchman visited.

We dined together, the earl, Wilfred and yours truly. The wine flowed. I tried to set aside my aversion to Wilfred Marquis of Burnfoot. He was an arrogant flapdoodle, and a hectoring Tory; but I ought to make allowances. An officer in the Dragoon Guards fresh returned from the sub-continent to resume laying about Oxford must have some sense.

Then, in my cups, I made a halfwit comment about love. Why, why did I say it? I keep my thoughts to myself. I reflect those around me, bolster their self-esteem with senseless quips: that's how I duck them arrows of fortune. It's a good method, but doesn't always work.

Port was served after dinner. The earl opened the dining room French windows. Out we stepped on the balcony, where Lady Elodie's roses are blooming in the wrought-iron trellises.

With the earl there, I felt safe enough. I was fascinated to see father and son together. Throughout Wilfred's stay, I've barely seen them exchange a word. Peggy had teased that Lodestar was usurping the boys' birthrights. Why should that be?

Father and son had little to say to each other. The earl's curiosity and warmth were in Wilfred transformed to brooding and belligerence.

I broke the silence. "How far does the Roxbury land extend?"

Wilfred threw his arms wide. "As far as one can see."

Roxy shook his head. "We only tend these slopes, the gorge, and the slate quarry. Those far hills are let to farmers, to be worked as they should be."

"Father is soft. Lets the blighters have 'em for laughable rates."

"I would rather see the land usefully tilled. We get the use of the rainwater. That is what matters."

"For your wild experiments," Wilfred huffed. "Electrocuting eels."

"Those eels were already electric, Wilfy." Roxbury sighed. "That's why they didn't survive the journey."

"Parakeets, then. Monkeys." Wilfred looked from Molly to Roxbury, as if he was plotting something. "I'll bet your young drawing mistress is against vivisection. I'll bet she's in league with journalists, plotting to expose your cruel experiments."

Roxbury looked tired. "Wilfred—"

"I'm in league with no journalists," I said. I felt the pang of guilt, knowing I was in league with Watchman.

"Aren't you curious?" Wilfred turned to me, eel-like. "Do you know what goes on in our scientists' quarter?"

I paused. I dislike a barefaced lie, but often try a misdirection; I would like nothing more than to be invited around the scientific quarter, but I fear seeming too curious. I angled for a wider tour. "I'm interested in the whole estate. The Walled Garden, for instance," I said. "And the east wing."

A bloomer. Nobody spoke. The heating system gurgled in the room behind us. The river rumbled through the gorge below the east turret, the waterwheel whirring: *chak-ke-ta chak-ke-ta*.

"Do you know," said the earl, "I've something I'd forgotten to do." And off he went.

Leaving me alone with the son of the household. Indecorously alone. I ought to have followed the earl and turned in, but I was thrown. I stayed rooted to the spot.

To fill the silence, I resorted to my stupid comment. "A strangely loveless household."

I grew up poor, amid beastliness and cruelty, but I knew love, even there; not maternal, but brotherly, companionable, and loyal. Here at Roxbury, people are pitched together like a glasshouse, the framework of panes held by frail stanchions, individually fragile, easily warped, but together sturdy against the buffeting rains. I was just muttering to myself, without meaning nothing.

Wilfred heard me. "I'll teach you a thing or two about love."

I ducked away from his grasp and made my escape.

In the menagerie, an animal screamed.

I've revelled in my melancholic tours; at least, I revelled in them until today and Wilfred.

I've discovered the reservoir, where I reflect; the gorge, whose torrents delight the soul; and the Pump House, below the dam, where I descend from the Shepherd's Refuge. I contemplate from on high the Iron Bridge and the glasshouses glimmering in the sun, where Jem toils among the fruit trees amid the cries of his wayward animals; I imagine the whirr of machines within, flashes of electrical experiments, inventions for the good of mankind—or at least the profit of Roxbury Industries.

I always enjoyed my solitude in London. There one can be always alone, whatever the crowd. One can vanish away, befriend and betray, and never be seen again in the vast multitudes I was brung up among. Here in the country, neither solitude nor security. House riddled with servants, grounds stuffed with scientists, toing and froing with their productions for the earl to approve, everyone hither and thithering wildly.

Out of doors, I have found my peace. Why did I stray near the Iron Bridge?

"Why, fair maiden. So alone?" Wilfred stood in country clothes, shoddily styled, on the far bank. "You resemble the sorrowful virgins of Rossetti's daubings. Not going to do an Ophelia on us, are you?"

This allusion doubtless carried some ribald undertone I missed. "Not I, sir."

"No need to 'sir' me, young lady." To my dismay, he strolled over the Iron Bridge towards me. Something in that idle saunter disturbed me. "Call me Wilfred. My friends call me Wolfie."

How strange is our society. When I was an urchin, there was no question of impropriety, whosoever I consorted with, or eavesdropped on, or cleared up after. Even as a servant girl, there would be nothing unusual in my being alone with the young man of the household (nothing unusual; I do not say no risk). Now I am thrust into another class, by dint of my drawing, everything is wrong. Wilfred should not approach me so; I should not allow him to approach. This swarm of social mores pricks my conscience.

In London, I could slip away from any situation; I knew the alleyways better than any copper, better than any flash gent. To be frank, I backed myself to repel an unwanted advance. Our gang was never bested, not by 'Dilly Boys nor Rude Boys, nor even those mucksnipe Clapham Crabs on forays northward. But the Burnfoot gorge is a different venue to the Blackfriars shoreline, and my drawing mistress's heels no match for the boots I grew up in.

"I can see you are a lover," said he, "of nature."

"I'm fond of Roxbury." I looked about for my escape. "Roxbury House, I mean."

"I have viewed your paintings. Romantic." He ran his finger along the balustrade, smiling, as if he had a secret at his disposal. "One might say, passionate."

"I had you down less as fanatical of art," I said, backing away along the river bank, "and more as a gun-toting nabob."

He mistook this for a compliment, and mistook my walking away as an invitation to walk with me: his gentlemanly sensitivities were so undeveloped. He fixed me with his arrogant eye. "I like a bit of art. I done life drawing, y'know, out in India." Pronounced to rhyme with "ginger". "Willing models, I tell you."

I looked around for a sure exit. The trees around us were dark. I drew my scarf tighter against this first chill of autumn.

"Ain't you done a spot of modelling yourself?"

"No fear." Was he teasing? "I mean, I shouldn't think it appropriate."

"Only I saw a drawing of Nico's which made me think he must have studied you quite intimately." Catching me up, he saw the disgust this thought invoked. "I pity those who wash the socks at Harrow. Of course, a boy of Nico's age will indulge in forbidden imaginings." He made a gesture with his hand. "Imaginings which, to those a little older, may in some pre-Raphaelite dell become real—"

One moment spouting bilge, the next tugging me to him for a kiss—and no notion of my disgust. Agh! His Piccadilly weepers against my cheek; that stink of cheroots. I am not one for intimate greetings at the best of times, but I gave up hope of absenting myself politely.

I ran.

THE WALLED GARDEN, PART THE FIRST [MOLLY]

Through the trees, and I found myself trapped between the river and the Walled Garden. Skirtle has told me this was Lady Elodie's preserve. I had no wish to intrude on her memory. Was Wilfred pursuing me? I stumbled along the walls, scraping my hands on the stones.

There: tall gates, padlocked shut. Trapped again.

I heard him coming.

But the padlock—belated discovery—was loose. I pushed one of the doors, pulled the other, creating the slimmest of gaps. Despite all my grand dinners of late, I squeezed myself through. Only my blasted dress held me, caught by the buttons; then my stupid bonnet. Still he was coming. I tore and squashed, clothes, head, shoulders lowered, hands protecting my chest.

I burst through. I pushed the gates to.

What a changed atmosphere. Within those walls, it was already wintry. Different from the rest of the grounds. Poppies and wild roses overran the forgotten flowerbeds. Purple-headed flowers swayed on their rigid stems, shrugging off fluffy white seeds as I crouched back from the gateway, listening. He would never get his bulk through.

Muttering. A wry chuckle. He stomped away.

I tiptoed through the tangle of flowers. The chill went down the back of my dress. I felt—what did I feel? That I was trespassing. That I was not alone?

I looked up at the house. Strange. Most of it could not be seen above the walls. But the turret of the east wing had a clear view down upon me. I found myself staring up at the windows again, willing the curtains to move again, wondering what business Patience Tarn had to be there—

Thud. My knee banged against a stone, upright among the flowers. What was this? Glory be, a gravestone? How I hate graveyards. And Wilfred had surely retreated. I emerged into a clearing, a copse I'd never found before, like a witches' assembly, circled by bare trunks, with spindly branches reaching into the sky. Nothing like the lush trees that covered the rest of the rockery. In the middle, a wooden bench upon a patch of lush green. I gazed around, as the horror of the Walled Garden receded from my bones. I dusted off my hands, sighed, and stretched the tension from my neck.

Wilfred leapt from the shadows. Whoosh! Like an electrified badger, bristles and toothy roar. He pinned me upon the bench. I struggled to free myself, but he had not wasted his time in the army; he proved stronger than he looked. His hands on my arms, his fingers pinning down my hair. I had the ghastly feeling he had used this place before. How often have I heard tell of servants' ruination by posh boys who think they are entitled to favours, as they expect hot dinners and fresh sheets. I have read such romances of Holywell Street publishers; I've read Skittles's autobiography, which sweetens the tale of her seduction to make the pills palatable.

Wilfred dragged me, struggling, to the centre of the grassy circle. I could see in his eyes that hunger that sometimes comes over men at the theatre, or the opera, or strolling the Haymarket when the lamplight gilds the flesh. So fast it happened, quicker than they lift your purse at Covent Garden. I felt in his grasp he was about to throw me to the ground. The sequel to that I could imagine.

Failing to free myself, I yielded to his tugging. I let him think he was the stronger; indeed, he was. Worst of all, he had been enjoying my resistance. But I have other strengths.

"Why, sir!" I exclaimed, like a Shakespearean orator in Regent's Park. A scream might lead to scandal, or be mistaken for a sick animal. The greenhouses were not far off. I might be heard. I might be. "How strong you are. You have the advantage—oh, but look!"

One of my talents is the conjurer's art of making his

audience pay attention to the wrong thing: we call it misdirection. He had pinned one of my arms; with the other, I pointed through the trees at the far bank, where I hoped for a rescuer to appear. Simultaneously, as he turned to look, I slapped his hairy cheek as hard as I could.

He turned upon me like some deranged beast, at the very moment that I brought my elbow down on his forearm. Not enough to break it, but the impact freed his hold on me.

He lurched forward at me in the nick of time to meet my elbow coming up, right into his eye socket, with a satisfying crunch.

Before his howl of pain, I had already scrambled aside. I clambered through the trees, down the bank toward the Iron Bridge and the greenhouses.

"Guttersnipe slattern!" he wailed, like a foul-mouthed ninny, and started after me.

Damnable clothing. Had I but worn the rags of my childhood, instead of this dreadful crinoline, I would have been clean away from the beast. As it was, he was after me. He scrambled down the slope without hesitation. I could hear the panting in my ear, sure my ruination was at hand—when I ran slap into someone.

"Molly!" Jem rushed out from the glasshouse. He had heard my shouts, and Wilfred's caterwaul. He held my shoulders to stop me from collapsing. "Miss Molly, I mean. Art thou all reet, miss?"

I looked back to see Wilfred draw to a stop on the bridge behind me. "Jem. Yes. Quite all right, Jem. We were just…" I looked round.

Wilfred was glaring at us.

I straightened my skirts. I put my hand to my hair, finding it disarrayed; the fibbing gigglemug had hurt my arm with his grabbing. To feel safe, I took hold of Jem's hands, affecting an intimacy beyond what we shared. "Wilfred was just... showing me around, Jem."

In Wilfred's eyes I saw, for the tiniest moment, the vengeance he was already planning. He turned, face blotchy red, and marched off up to the house.

Shillibeer's Guide to Funereal Households

The width of the hatband depends upon the relationship.

Worn by the husband for the wife, hatbands are seven inches wide. By fathers for sons, five inches; sons for fathers, the same. For other relationships, the hatband width varies from two and a half to four inches.

One should wear mourning apparel as soon as possible, not waiting until the funeral. Deep mourning is worn by the widower or widow for a year. Occasionally, half mourning is worn by widow or widower for six months longer.

Choose envelopes and notepaper edged with a deep border of black. Friends too should employ black-edged paper and envelopes, but the black border narrow.

Present the relations and friends of the deceased persons with memorial cards, stating name, age, date of death, where interred, and an apposite verse of Scripture. Although, among the poor, females attend the funeral, this custom is by no means to be recommended, since they destroy the solemnity of the ceremony with sobs or fainting.

In many cases—especially in the summer—the corpse is retained too long. This is injurious to health. Funerals in winter should take place within one week after death, and in summer shorter. We caution against giving spirits and liquors to the undertaker. Tea better suits the proper performance of funereal duties.

HARMONIOUS DIALOGUE ON A TRAIN [LAWLESS]

The dining car of our train to the frozen north (as Molly styled it) was quiet.

Ruth and I enjoyed one of those wonderful exchanges that happens rarely in a lifetime. It was a renaissance of our tearoom meetings, with the pot already brewing, but with a new intensity and directness. Anyone who has been in love will know what I mean: when you feel so close that everything they say sparks revelation.

Ruth took from her bag a file of Molly's letters. "To prepare. Make the most of our trip."

I'd read them, of course, for the most part. Ruth deciphered Molly's brief messages to me, then read the letter first, but never censored anything. Not until now, however, with our new intimacy, did she disclose her deeper interpretations.

"The word 'intelligence', Campbell, means 'reading between'," said Ruth. "It's Latin: 'inter-legens'. And I have been reading between the lines of Molly's texts."

She had been reading with insight that amazed me, and made me love her more.

First, knowing that Roxbury himself was my focal point, she showed me how much more of the earl Molly had told than I had understood. That he used to run his own business, Roxbury Industries, travelling exhaustively to every outpost, but had now handed all the wider responsibilities over to Lodestar.

"That is telling of something." Ruth, frowning, looked out the window. The suburban hamlets were giving way to open fields. "A withdrawal."

From his pinched cheek and white complexion, Molly was emphasising that this withdrawal was a symptom of something more; having worked with every type of visage, Molly would not comment on appearance unless she thought it a malaise.

This fresh interpretation took me aback. In my knowledge,

the earl had been an outspoken member of the House of Lords, dedicated to progress, unafraid of conflict, and eager to aid country and empire. Was he really loafing all day in his gardens, barely seeing even his children?

"What has happened to him?" said I.

"Think, Campbell."

I looked blankly at her.

Ruth sighed. "Who is missing from the family picture?"

"Oh, his wife, you mean?" I gazed out at the passing fields. "Yes, I suppose, if you were to die suddenly, I would—"

"You would get straight back to your detecting." Ruth smiled. "I have no doubt."

I was indignant. "As the earl has returned to his experiments. But I might do it with a new recklessness, in my grief for you."

"Ah, yes? With no thought for convention or colleagues?" Ruth was warming to this declaration of devotion. "You're normally so conventional and collegiate."

I made no attempt to rebuff her irony. "When did she die?"

"Odd that we don't know, isn't it?" Ruth crinkled her nose, and delved into her travelling bag. "I scanned the births and deaths in the periodicals—"

"British Museum Library, reference section? Strictly no borrowing, you told me."

She ignored my dig. "It took me a deal of searching. The briefest of obituaries. January 1862."

Roxbury
Lady Elodie Margaret née Loth.
5 January
Lamented by her family.

I frowned. "It doesn't actually say she's dead."

"It's in the obituaries." She rolled her eyes. "Have you never read obituaries?"

I shrugged off my gaffe. "Two and a half years gone."

"Yet she is never mentioned."

"It's a while now."

"To have lost your wife? Your mother? Your ladyship employer?" Ruth shook her head. "No, Campbell. Whatever our discomfort in this modern age with death, with mourning dress fripperies and public grief shamed, this is not right. That the children not mention her to Molly, ever?"

"A little strange, I grant." I glanced at the magazine page. The notice of Lady Roxbury's passing was dwarfed by overblown obituaries of forgotten generals, actors and governmental hangers-on, alongside lurid notices of death by misadventure.

"A little? They call themselves orphans, when Roxbury is still at hand."

"Norphans Practickly." I chuckled. "But it is a brief notice, for such an eminent lady."

Ruth leant forward. "You have no idea. Why, she was a force in the reform movement. My aunt admired her terrifically. Without her agitations, there would barely be a single course available to women in London's universities."

"Might it speak of some quarrel, that the notice is small?"

"It might. But I heard they were a devoted couple." She narrowed her eyes, "There is something more to this."

We would keep our ears open for mention of the earl's wife. But we must not draw attention to our interest, if there was something untoward within the family. More usefully, we might refocus Molly's detective faculties. She was tight with Skirtle. No gossip could escape her.

MOLLY'S AMATORY CAREER [LAWLESS]

"And this Lodestar." Ruth poured the tea. "What are we to make of him?"

"An impressive young man." I shrugged. "If Roxbury is yielding the keys of power to anyone, he is an ideal heir: energetic, sharp, charming—"

"Charming, yes." She sniffed. "Everyone finds him so charming."

"Where's the harm in that? A business must charm its fellows, mustn't it? An engineer has to talk to low and high. Draw plans at the top, build them from the bottom."

"I only hope Molly does not find him too charming." She gave me a look. "Reading between the lines, you know."

I had no sense, from the pages of her letters, that Molly was infatuated with Lodestar. On his first arrival, his shining eye and mop of hair caught her notice; less so, when he dropped off Wilfred, languid and ironical.

"But Wilfred," I said, "has taken a shine to her."

"Bravo. Outstanding deduction, Sergeant." Ruth clapped. "That was explicit. But have you noticed that young Nico also likes her, despite receiving scant encouragement?"

I frowned. "She likes Jem the stable boy."

"Liked. At the outset, maybe. But he is taken."

Our interpretative game continued. It seemed unkind to make sport of Molly's burgeoning amatory influence. To be honest, I had barely ever thought of her as a girl. When I first knew her, she was a smudge-nosed tyke among the Euston Square Worms gang, of indeterminate sex, buttoned up to the gills in a waistcoat too large, coat too small, and boots she stomped so continually in that she wore them through. As her own troupe of miscreants emerged, the Oddbody Theatricals, she became recognisably female, I suppose, but with the sexless aura of an abbess, chaperoning her charges through the hazards of London, without a thought for her own person. To find her in that East End brothel, with those blockheads dead at her feet, was a double shock: that she'd contrived the mutual murders surprised me less than her role of fatal seductress.

"And Birtle?" Ruth sipped her tea. "What do you make of him?"

I had no idea. I confessed, I was a touch nervous of him. In Molly's accounts, he lurked and watched, clearing up after visitors and giving newcomers a frosty welcome.

"Exactly. What does he get up to the rest of the time? Why so hostile to our Moll?"

"Hostile?" I was missing the obvious, again. "Perhaps he has a chip on the shoulder. Perhaps he sees through her."

"There is nothing to see through, Campbell, you outdated prig."

"She's masquerading as a prim and proper drawing mistress."

"Prim, no. But proper she is, and a drawing mistress. When will you realise that, in this day and age, one is not tied to the social milieu one has come from. To be a drawing mistress, one must simply teach drawing."

"And have manners enough not to shock. And speech decent for mixed company."

Ruth's jaw twitched. "Similar, to be a policeman."

"Or a librarian."

"No. Librarians are scrutinised. Constantly. Wherever a woman is liable to speak to men, unchaperoned, on topics outwith her control, there will arise situations—" She sighed. "Now you're just winding me up."

It was a glorious autumnal day. The train raced northwards, afternoon sunshine dappling the carriage with golden light, making my fiancée crinkle her eyes and shade her brow intermittently, with that lovely gesture when she swept a stray lock from her eyes. It was so easy to love her: that pale face, framed by those jet-black locks, and the voice.

"Campbell, did you hear?"

I had been dreaming; and I loved to hear her use my given

name, instead of Sergeant Lawless.

She shook her head. "Campbell, this French business. How concerned should we be?"

THESE EUROPEAN WARS [LAWLESS]

No explosions for weeks now, through the summer lull. But the threat was the sticking point.

Jeffcoat and I had caught nobody. None of the warning letters had led to anything, yet, and we had gone through mountains of them. I had brought the latest pile with me to scan on the train.

"Dear Sir," they all began, "I'm worried about my neighbours. They're planning an outrage..." There followed incoherent bleatings on how oddly the foreigners next door behaved, kept themselves to themselves, and had habits that seemed, well, not British. This clearly amounted to a plot against queen and country. They would not rest until the police had raided the house and deported the whole sorry crowd, clearing their street of malign European threat.

Then there were what we liked to call the French letters:

Dear Sir,

I am French and I live in [insert small town somewhere in England].

For many years, I have lived here peaceably. With these late rumours, my neighbours have observed me with suspicion. Last night, our windows were broken, today my children abused in the street.

Our opinion of your open-minded nation is forever tarnished.

Cordially yours,
Benoît and Renée LeClerc

Our call for informants was encouraging bigots, xenophobes, panic mongers and war hawks, no doubt. If the dangers were real, nonetheless, then we must protect the nation. If only we were sure our labours amounted to something. Now that Ruth and I were engaged, I could confide in her more fully. The relief of unburdening myself was immense.

"Fifty years of peace," she said, "since Waterloo, in our quadrant of the continent." For Ruth was a peace-lover and a friend to Europe, and assumed all right-thinking people were the same. "What on earth do these activists want?"

"They want, my love, to turn back time."

THE PORTSMOUTH PAPERS [LAWLESS]

Does everybody not see how we have prospered in peace? Thus ran Ruth's argument: we punished the French enough with the Treaty of Paris and Napoleon banished. That they have recovered much of their former glory—and conquering habits, as Signor Garibaldi reminded us—need not concern us, as long as they do not trifle with Her Majesty's imperial business. A strong France makes for a stable Europe. A stable Europe helps us all.

Not me, shouts the working man in Chatham, whose shipbuilding was dwindled to nothing in peacetime, until the Crimea broke our reverie.

Not me, says the Sheffield steel man, whose forks and spoons are less profitable than knives.

Not me, the City banker, for whom foreign excitements make a killing, as the struggling burghers of London pour their pennies into Sardinian railways or Kentuckian kerosene, only to find the enterprise gone up in smoke; but I have fresh opportunities to offer, ever more chances for instant prosperity.

Not me, says the politician who has learned that only his outrageous claims make the headlines, viz: "A new Napoleon has arisen; none but I can lead the nation against this resurgent evil." (Oh how he loves his resurgent evil.)

So he goes on, our popular demagogue, with thrust and counter-thrust, point of information and point of order. Ruth thought such bombast mere conquistador babble from a bygone era.

Far from it: many Britons are ready for the new European wars that, we are told, must inevitably come, as the Frogs and Krauts and Dagos and Wops and Slavs and Turks and Arabs and Parsees and Hindoos and Chinks and Aboriginals come a-chasing the riches of our industrial revolution. And if they cannot triumph through their own innovation, they will torch our navy, the wooden wall that both defends our isle but emboldens us to demand trading rights and taxes repealed and bribes overlooked. We are British, after all: our chaps never overstep the mark while seeking fortunes abroad. They made us what we are today, these heroes. We'll defend them to the death. Beware John Bull's wrath, which you only bring upon yourselves.

Until someone stands up to us.

La Gloire was more than a warship. It was Napoleon's shot across our bows. Some called it incendiary.

Passivists (such as Ruth) cried, "Nonsense." And the threatened invasions? They never came.

Now that the Guernsey papers were deciphered and delivered post haste to the highest echelons of government and military, I boggled at our naivety. If Louis Napoleon had intended to upset us, he'd have sent *La Gloire* up the Thames to cock his nose at us; we'd have condemned his effrontery and derided his ambition.

If he was serious, though, and really aimed to humiliate Britain and displace it as the foremost empire of the world, he need do only one thing.

Destroy our navy.

Even better, capture it.

Ruth and I talked through it one more time. Was the Portsmouth Plan credible? How outrageous were the plots described in the Guernsey papers? The first dated from a bygone era: Nelson's charts of the Solent, sketches of Portsmouth dockyard, engravings of our ships, annotations of their new armada. These confirmed what Victor Hugo had recognised. This plan was a revision of that long-held French dream: to capture Portsmouth, and make it a French Gibraltar, an outpost to control our waters and quash our maritime dominion.

The British Navy had been the best in the world. *HMS Warrior* was developed as a riposte to *La Gloire*, to fight fire with firepower. Strategically, though, with half the navy deployed on the other side of the world, meddling in the American war, harrying the Far East and dealing with Indies, West Indies and Antipodes, what was left? If the French came, and unexpectedly, what ships were left to face them?

Oh, but our spies in the ports would know if the French were gathering a fleet. Wouldn't they? This was the genius of the Guernsey papers' plans. The French would never need to face us, fleet to fleet.

Picture it. Their army gathers for manoeuvres, near the coast. A militia of irregulars stands ready for the call. Boarding in secret, they sail to undefended harbours within march of Portsmouth. Overnight, they land 400,000 on the south coast. They stream overland. They overwhelm the defences to cross on to the island of Portsmouth. They take Her Majesty's dockyard with ease. They walk aboard our ships, in harbour, swatting aside any resistance, seizing at a stroke the most powerful fleet in the world.

A secondary French force marches on London. They demand surrender, threatening a fleet invasion. The call goes out to our navy abroad; but they can never retake Portsmouth Harbour, defended by a quarter of a million French troops. They cede London, keeping Portsmouth as an enclave; or, buoyed by their successes, they attempt greater domination of our country.

We could only guess. The Guernsey papers only went so far.

Thank God we had stumbled upon them. It was a stroke of luck, and timely. Before the Royal Commission reported, they heard my evidence. On the strength of these revelations, they sought Parliament's approval to resuscitate the Palmerston fortifications.

The Palmerston Forts' initial budget had been huge, beyond the Crimean crisis. The forts were begun in 1860, just, only for the government to change. The nation returned to buoyant arrogance. Defence was unnecessary, budgets slashed. The artificial island forts guarding Portsmouth Harbour, however, were already under construction mid-Solent. They told the contractor to complete them for half the price; the contractor was not best pleased.

Jeffcoat and I counselled the commission we had no alternative: apologise, we advised, revalue, and pay in full at whatever rates, on condition of urgent completion.

As Ruth and I batted these grim notions back and forth, I was buoyed up with love. What could be more romantic than protecting the security of the nation, over a first-class lunch in a first-class dining car? To share world-shaking events with one's intended, whose insight turned catastrophe to hope?

"But, Campbell." She laid her hand on my forearm; she smiled, tolerant of my spoony smile. "I have three objections to raise. Serious objections."

I paled. I thought she meant our marriage.

"To your theories, you fool." She shook her head in exasperation. "If the French intend to invade, why alert us with these ghastly bombs?"

I had no immediate answer.

"Second, this Guernsey bomber: why these papers, and no others? No passport. No pen. No personal effects."

This objection I parried. "He kept them on him."

"But the contents of the satchel were intended for delivery. To Portsmouth, perhaps?"

"To a French spy." I nodded. I must visit the docks and spread our motto of vigilance.

"Third." She frowned. "Vis-à-vis Roxbury. Surely his malaise, or withdrawal, or whatever we're worried about, has happened since his wife? It's perfectly normal."

I opened my mouth. The timing was right. "That doesn't mean it's all right."

"What more can Molly tell us, though?"

I glanced askance. Broad pasturelands flashed by. Just as the sun was fading behind the distant lines of trees, my magical mood was fading

"Can you smell smoke?" I asked her. "I can smell smoke."

"It's the documents." She held up a file stuffed with papers. "From the Antony Gibbs Shipping fire. I must work through them, but I can't seem to muster—"

"Leave it be, my love." Poor Ruth: she would never forget poor Sarah Smithereen. "It's a fruitless enterprise." To distract her, I took out the sheet where Jeffcoat and I had scribbled our own puzzle: JO TWO CHE.

"Anagram, is it?" Ruth perked up at once. I explained they were partial words, possibly something to do with a mechanism.

"Ha! Very good. And is it just for fun, or are you testing my knowledge?"

"Why?" I turned the sheet for her to see. "Have you solved it?"

"Of course. Haven't you?" Ruth's smile wavered: she had not meant to embarrass me. "Nothing important, is it?"

"Important enough." I explained in a rapid undertone

where the puzzle originated. Ruth had come on board with the Guernsey papers; the previous investigations I had not shared with her.

Her eyes lit up. "Oh, but it's—"

"Don't even think of saying it's easy."

She bit her lip, and swiftly wrote in the missing parts:

> Jo*seph*
> *Whi*TW*orth*
> *Man*CHES*ter*

I wired Jeffcoat when we changed to the branch line: we should pay a visit to Whitworth post haste.

SPLENDID DINNER [LAWLESS]

"And the thing about young Lodestar here," said the earl, urging his protégé to pour the white wine (in Birtle's absence) for me, for Ruth, for Molly and the earl, "is he gets things done. Quick too. Quicker than I ever did. Which leaves me to potter about here: gardening, experimenting, tinkering with odd inventions—"

"Inventions?" I said. "I'd thought you'd taken early retirement."

His eyes flickered mischievously between Molly and me. He knew we were acquainted, but she had played down the depth of our friendship: did he suspect our complicity? This was the closest viewing of Edward, Earl of Roxbury. We had met at the Fairchild Enquiry, where I thought him a good egg.

He himself welcomed us at the grand entrance. He chatted, showed us round, and served aperitifs concocted in his own laboratory: sloe gin labelled in his own hand, neat and scientific, diverse vintages. He escorted us to dinner himself. This was not the way Molly had painted him: kindly, but absent-minded or absent completely. My first impressions were more immediate. Perhaps we summoned hospitality he did not owe Molly, as an employee. But then Ruth is fearfully attractive; men will drop everything to attend her.

Lodestar dashed up from the glasshouses in time to join us. Again, I found him charm incarnate. Ruth regarded him with a strange eye, as if a hawk were a-scouting and we were field mice considering a leisurely stroll. I could see her antipathy; he did not.

Molly had to be called from her art room. Unusually taciturn, she barely seemed pleased to see us. She was trying, she said, to capture the view in different lights; this autumnal gloaming was her final effort. Charcoal and chalk. "I do so wish to finish it before—"

Wilfred came in. The silence was audible. At the sight of Roxbury's son and heir, his eye on the way from red to purple-black, we all reacted slightly differently. It looked the outcome of a bar-room brawl. Lodestar's mouth twisted, in an effort not to titter. I gasped.

"What the devil, Wilfy-boy?" said the earl, without fondness. "Playing with the orang-utan, were you?"

This gave us an excuse to laugh, aside from Wilfred. Molly maintained her sanguine air. Ruth worked out soon enough how his eye got blackened, but did not explain to me till later.

"Steak'll be cold," said the earl. "Bloody shame."

"Could put it on that eye," muttered Lodestar.

Wilfred spoke through clenched teeth. "I'll have Birtle heat it."

"You'll do no such thing." Roxbury continued eating. "Not when you come so late to dinner."

Wilfred Roxbury gave his father an insolent stare, more like a mewling toddler's rather than an army man's. How strange families are.

"I must dash." Lodestar checked his pocket-watch and folded his napkin. "I do apologise for my rudeness. I'd hoped to challenge you at billiards."

"No fear." I smiled. "Vanquish me with your trick shots?"

He grinned. "As you know, Sergeant, and you, Miss Villiers, the capital's summons cannot be ignored. Though you will not rush back, I hope."

Roxbury went to rise but Lodestar raised his palm.

"Please, sir, enjoy your dinner. My compliments to Skirtle, for the conception, and cook, for the execution. Both excellent, as was the wine." He paused a moment in the doorway, as if to make a declaration; but the declaration was just a knowing sweep of the room with his dark brows, which seemed to say, "Wilfred, you are a fool and a cad; the rest of you are damned fine fellows; and you, Miss Molly, I shall be back to see another day."

Molly sipped her wine, flushing. Her expression was only unguarded for the merest moment, but Ruth caught it: a look of smitten awe.

UNRULY DESIRES [LAWLESS]

After Lodestar's departure, the atmosphere grew less convivial.

I found myself preoccupied. I was mulling over my discussion with Ruth on the train: "Are the French so asinine," she had said, "as to invade?" To which I had no answer. Was the Portsmouth Plan unpracticable? The panic engendered by the threat was bad enough: perhaps they intended that uncertainty, without ever intending to invade. A politic charade: cheaper than invading; safer than invading; ruinous expense for us.

Such worries I could not voice at dinner. Nor could I tell Roxbury how his changed behaviour concerned me, and how it concerned the Home Office. I must see in what way he was changed; I must judge was his behaviour erratic. Did it, as Ruth thought, simply speak of grief?

Thus preoccupied, I noticed none of Molly's discomfort.

Wilfred made flash comments. He asked for the salt as if insulting her honour. He threw a strop when tea was served without his special mustachio cup, with its porcelain strip preventing whiskery spillage. But these are the ways of the young these days, I told myself, especially the young and privileged. I would have thought the earl's children better brought up; but he had been so involved with the nation's struggles, he could not be blamed.

"I suppose, your Lordship, sir," said Molly, "that when Miss Villiers and old Watchman here leave on Monday, I may as well go along with them."

The earl's fork stopped halfway to his mouth. He returned it plateward untouched. "Why on earth would you do that? And what's this 'Your Lordship' nonsense, Moll?"

Wilfred watched her keenly.

Ruth observed them both.

Molly scratched her head. "As my post here is fulfilled." She blinked. "You know. Tutoring your rowdy brood."

"Tosh!" The earl wiped his mouth and tossed his napkin energetically aside. "That was a sideshow. It's time for the engagement I originally required you for. Did I not make that plain?"

Molly shifted in her seat. She was rarely discomfited. Her upbringing taught her to cope with situations cavalierly, risking unruly refusals. She was a diamond uncut, sparkling by nature. But the expectations of her new social station had quite unsettled her. "Sir, I understood Miss Villiers recommended me as a drawing mistress."

"True, Molly." Ruth smiled. "But you are a girl of many talents—a woman, rather."

Molly nodded. "I scribble a passable caricature."

"Ha," said Roxbury. "You've skewered us all on your satirical pen. It's quite a portfolio. Her sketch of Wilfred here is an archetype of the louche modern gent."

I was looking between Ruth and Roxbury, for I sensed they had discussed securing Molly's place without telling me. "Your Lordship," I said, "enlighten poor Molly."

"The menagerie, old girl." He beamed at her. "Illustrate the animals. Up to it? Lear said you would be, and he should know. Chuck in the rare botanicals as backgrounds. I'll publish it privately, if you'll strike a deal over it. What do you say, old girl? You haven't business down south?"

Molly blinked again, pleasure dawning across her face.

"Quite a job." Ruth put on her bargaining face, trying to hide her pleasure. "How many days will you employ her, sir?"

"Pshaw." The earl scratched his head. "Sixty odd species, leaving aside beetles and arachnids. Say, one a week."

Ruth made quick scribbles on the back of an envelope. She gave Molly the nod.

"No," said Molly, making our hearts sink. "I'll do one a day, Roxy. I prefer to work hard."

He laughed (and lovely to hear it). "Two days per animal then. From preparatory sketch to final illustration."

I raised my glass, delighted, and the wine warmed my heart. I was delighted that the children loved her so, that the earl had taken to her, that she had pulled off the stunt of impersonating a drawing mistress—of becoming a drawing mistress. Now her gainful employment could continue. And her surveillance of the earl. I needed him more than ever. In this hour of need, we all needed Roxbury Industries to keep the ship of state safe.

Ruth wasn't done bargaining on her charge's behalf. "Holidays?"

"Four days off per month, same as all my employees."

"Sick pay?"

Wilfred wiped his mouth with his sleeve. "Have we communists in the house?"

"Now, now, Miss Villiers." Roxy tutted, totting on his fingers. "You'll want free medical treatment next. Five months, I make it."

"A hundred and fifty-eight days," said Ruth, "and a half. Takes us to Valentine's Day, or thereabouts."

"But the brats are back for Christmas." The earl nodded. "You may as well keep tutoring them. And Easter. Close to a year, near as damn it. Hoi, Birtle! Birtle, could we add Miss Molly to the permanent staff? Birtle? Where is the recalcitrant devil?"

"Occupied, sir. In the tower." Lodestar strode in to hand me a telegram. "This rattled in as I was on my way, via the pneumatic. Thought you'd want to see it."

"Not bad news, I hope." I tore it open. "I'm looking forward to my tour of the grounds." I read aloud:

```
Ship ablaze, Liverpool harbour.
Rendezvous Birkenhead Pier tomorrow 5pm?
Visit Whitworth arranged subsequent.
Jeffcoat
```

"Liverpool?" said Lodestar. "I am just returned from there. I could offer you a lift to the station, although my journey lies in the other direction."

"No, no," I said. "Thank you. You go on. If Jeffcoat says tomorrow, that will be time enough."

THE DANGERS OF CHARM [LAWLESS]

Due to Roxbury's proximity to the north west, I managed to have my tour early, before dashing to Liverpool.

I did not hear of Wilfred's saturnine departure till much later. Of how Ruth teased out of Molly the tale of Wilfred's black eye, how he kissed her, chased her, and worse. I never learned the full details; Ruth, I think, knows all. Can no man be trusted? What women face—even today, in this modern age, when we think we've tamed the savage within us—oh, it's intolerable. For all Molly's savvy and resilience, no woman five foot four can fight off a sinewy lovelorn brute fresh in from the Raj.

If I had understood at the time, I would have told Molly to give up her task. But I did not know; she did not tell; she enjoined Ruth not to tell. She dug her heels in, determined to do her duty, chuffed with the earl's approval, and—another thing I didn't see—basking in the radiance of Lodestar. Of that discussion, Ruth did tell me.

They were in the art room, tackling another puzzle map. Molly looked at Ruth. "What do you make of him?"

"Wilfred?"

She made a face. "Lodestar, I meant."

"Dangerously charming." Ruth wrinkled her nose.

Molly laughed. "Where's the danger in a little charm?"

"You, of all people, need to ask me that? I heard about your East End escapade." Ruth regretted saying this, as it made Molly look anxious. "Moll, we're on your side. I do hate it when you embroil yourself in criminality. But I know you can't resist a little excitement. That's your upbringing."

"Finely brung up I was too. But aren't you proud how I've settled to the life of a rustic drawing mistress?"

"Still with an eye for excitement, I think." Ruth stood up, moving to the window. "Lodestar has caught your eye not just because he is easy to look at. He represents modernity."

"Perhaps." Molly gestured toward the glasshouses. "There sits old Roxy in his laboratory—I do mean to secure an invitation—and he invents something. A new electrical force, say. Lodestar engages the scientists to check it, perfect it, develop it." Her fingers tap-tap-tapped their way across the map. "Within a sixmonth, there are dockers here, here and here, Bombay to Bristol to Buenos Aires, thanking the heavens for this miraculous improvement. Their jobs are swifter, their limbs safer."

"An ever-hungry beast, this industrial world. Roxbury's cranes speed up the loading of cargo. Some johnny betters them, in Singapore or Sebastopol. Johnny gets rich, someone else is impoverished. The cycle of demand and consumption accelerates."

"Not Roxy's fault."

"Nor Lodestar's." Ruth nodded. "No one's fault. But where it ends I cannot imagine."

Molly spread her hands across the world. "I've lived in the world's greatest city. But even from this rural backwater, how these coils of industry electrify the empire."

"I'm glad some happiness is finding you here, despite Wilfred and his brutishness." Ruth came over and squeezed her hand. "Of dark handsome men, though, especially thrusting fellows such as Lodestar, I bid you beware. He is an egotist. If you need something from him, flatter him. He will not resist flattery, I think. If something goes wrong, tell him that we can arrange for important people to visit. That will pique his interest, and keep you safe."

Molly bit her lip. "You think very poorly of him."

"Maybe I read him wrong. I hope so." She swallowed. "I suffered at the hands of such a man, when I was little older than you. How I wish to warn you, Molly, but you never listen to warnings. What fantasies of love I suffered. I sound like a prim old maid, but they were fantasies of lust." She blew out a sharp breath. "Oh, do what you want, you contrary child. We are not alike in background, you and I. But in temperament—"

"We've the odd thing in common, Miss V." Molly nodded. "Easy to look at, as you said, such a fellow."

"Easy to fall." Ruth sighed. "Harder to rise."

LIGHTNING TOUR [LAWLESS]

Wilfred vanished back to Oxford, without a farewell.

I toured the grounds. Ruth excused herself, to hold a pow-wow with Molly, claiming fatigue from the journey. (Not true: Ruth was always energised by travelling.)

Jem drove, with Roxbury guiding. I apologised for monopolising his time. He insisted it was a pleasure to be dragged from his usual melancholic round of duties.

We drove out through the mighty rear courtyard. The wings of the house stretched back into the hillside, their gothic archways shadowing us. All was designed for efficacy, not just for the family, but servants. At the door of the kitchens, a hatch for deliveries. Trap doors for laundry. Culverts and pipes diverting water from the gorge for various purposes: drinking, cooking, cleaning, sewerage. Not forgetting the essential hydraulics: descending from the reservoirs above, the water drove dumb waiters, centralised heating, lifts, gongs, baths, and ever more contraptions, as Roxbury devised them.

We snaked down the hillside, negotiating the hairpin bends between the Burnfoot and the rockery. I let the earl do the talking.

Admitting me to the greenhouses via the heat lock of the ingenious double doors, he pointed out rare flowers, exotic herbs which transformed hearty English fodder into Babylonian feasts. In the past, they had entertained sultans, princes and emperors. Cloves, sumach, cinnamon, kaffir lime, lemongrass, pineapple sage and bergamot.

Attending this poetic roll call of species was a scientist, snipping leaves.

Roxbury smiled, wiping his brow. "For experimentation."

We toured the quadrangle known as the scientific quarter: glasshouses, botanicals, arboretum, menagerie and laboratories. Rounded off by the curve of the Burnfoot stream, these formed an angular horseshoe, like a mirror image of the house. The glass was held by wrought-iron stanchions, a crystalline reflection of the wild woodland and watery estate. He showed me the furnace beneath temperate and tropical houses, then we got back into the gig.

"And underneath us—Jem, hold a moment—there!" Roxbury stood up in his seat. He beckoned me, peering between the rocks. "See? That curve. One of our tunnels."

"Tunnels?"

He gave me a mischievous schoolboy grin. "Tunnels to the house. The biggest for pneumatic packets: food and drink down; dirty dishes back, usually with a nice note from the scientists. And once in a while notice of a discovery."

"And the lesser tunnels?"

"Communication. We can wire out to the train station. Or up to my laboratory. If they are about to annihilate the distance from Cork to Newfoundland, I'm damned well not letting ten furlongs from the station slow down messages." Talking of these wonders, he was animated; how he could describe himself as melancholic was a mystery. "Did you see the turbine of the Pump House?"

"For electricity?" I said.

"Electricity. Unlimited amounts. Converting the river's force into energy. Pistons and gears, batteries and coils. This," he said, shaking his finger aloft, "this will be the future, mark my words. Coal and gas will do for now, for heat and light and combustion engines. But they are a tremendous waste. This river provides as much calorific potential as a coal mine at full production. Hydraulic power already does the heavy jobs once reliant on coal. Electricity will take over the rest. Even today's sunlight, if we could harness it, would run every machine in Roxbury Industries." He glanced up at the pale northern sun. "Without choking us. Without polluting the skies. Without blackening our pictures and our lungs. Hear that breeze in the treetops? Another possibility for harnessing elemental power. One day, mark me. One day."

Was he mad? Or prescient? This man, to whom the whole world came for invention and mechanisation and ordnance, the epitome of the modern industrialist, already looked beyond to a future where his machines are obsolete. He might have withdrawn from public life, but he had not given up new developments. He might be changed, but he was not lost to us.

"Coal will run out, given the rate we waste it." He tapped Jem's shoulder to set him driving again. "Even if we find reserves unimaginable today. But consumption will grow. Our working class will demand the luxury we take for granted. Then the Europeans, Slavs, Indians and Chinamen will demand it, as they should, if our world is to strive for equality. Once coal is done, in 200 years say, we scientific chaps must ensure nature's bounty is harnessed for our use."

Below the Pump House, I caught sight of walls above the greenhouses, near the Iron Bridge. I had not spotted them as we descended. "What's that? A monastic retreat?"

Roxbury looked up. His eyes closed momentarily, his lips compressed. He turned to me, as if to answer. "The Walled Garden…" He trailed off. Across his features played a series of smiles and frowns, as if assailed by memories. He touched Jem's shoulder again. "Jem will show you later, perhaps. Shall we drive on?" His voice was steady, yet I felt I had upset him.

Not wishing to let my inadvertent error sour the day, I cleared my throat to apologise.

Jem glanced round from the driving seat, away from Roxbury, so his look would not be observed, and gave the tiniest shake of the head.

"Scientists' elevenses." The earl tapped at his watch. "I'll go to work."

"And I'd best be off." I bit my lip. "No time to see the scientific quarter?"

"Oh, Lodestar deals with all that." Roxbury excused himself. "*Au revoir.*"

No chance to ask of experiments. Perhaps that's how he planned it. Any impresario guards his secrecy, and I'd heard that Roxbury Industries was more guarded than any. I glimpsed the vast trees, the vivid flowers; I heard the screech of birds and the squeals of animals. I picked up the packed lunch sent down by Skirtle, at Molly's behest. I had no chance to quiz any scientists, to assess how they felt: was Roxbury Industries flourishing, were they still at the forefront? But then many were just trainees on temporary placements.

My query about the Walled Garden remained unmentioned. My visit had been otherwise fruitful, eliciting information not mentioned in Molly's letters. I felt reassured. Roxbury was robust, and rigorous, if troubled.

Now, with the train hurtling toward Liverpool, I thought through matters he had shrugged off. How far beneath the surface lurked melancholy? How did it affect the company?

He had said, more than once, "Oh, Lodestar deals with that."

Of course, a manager cannot deal with every minute decision of the vast company. Roxbury had retreated to a wonderland of experimentation in his aqueous Arcadia. Lodestar it was who made the wider decisions, those of national consequence, of international import, and export. It was of him I must enquire further, in person and clandestinely.

BOOK IV
NORTH AND SOUTH

Terrific Explosion on the Mersey
[*Liverpool Mercury*, September 1864]

A great blast shook the Mersey last night. Upward of eleven tons of gunpowder exploded, aboard the *Florence Veigh*, a vessel passing near the Monks Ferry defences lately recommissioned. Causing enormous destruction of property, and consternation around town, this event occasioned such universal alarm as has no other in living memory.

The *Florence Veigh* was bound for Africa. The cargo included claret, sherry, and port, and gunpowder: 960 quarter-kegs of powder in the hold, more than eleven tons, beneath the captain's stateroom.

Shortly after 6pm, the steward saw a lamp extinguished outside the captain's room. As he filled the lamp, he heard a buzzer go off within. There followed a detonation, not immense, but enough to set fire to the curtains. By misfortune, his paraffin can was ignited. Horror-stricken, he dropped the can, and watched its flaming contents flow into the cabin. In a flash bed clothes, bed and furniture were ignited. The fiery stream poured unstoppable through the grating of the lazarette. Within minutes, the cargo in the afterhold was alight.

By dint of the steward's alarm, the crew were able to

flee, half-dressed and in haste, on to the steamer *Queen Bee* whose captain happened to hear the shouts and, fearing mutiny, drew alongside. As the report of a flaming vessel spread, hundreds flocked to the water's edge to witness the spectacle. Not suspecting the cargo, none were anticipating the frightful calamity.

The pandemonium of noise, as the vessel blew up, is impossible to describe. Every part of Liverpool shook. Indescribable terror gripped the town. Warehouses, offices, and private dwellings were shaken to their foundations. Locked doors were thrown wide, thousands of windows shattered. With street lamps extinguished, the alarm redoubled, jeopardising those who rushed to help.

The poor rushed forth, screaming for deliverance, helpless children dragged at their heels. Crowds ran this way and that, as flames enwrapped the vessel. The ensuing sound deafened the ear, making the earth reel. From the black hull burst a hideous inferno, illuminating the heavens. Yards, masts and rigging were hurled across the shoreline, the hull smashed into a thousand pieces.

As the smoke cleared, lurid light illumined the burning mass floating downriver with the ebb. Praise is due to the *Queen Bee* for propitiously rescuing the crew so opportunely.

The damage in Castle St is irreparable. Further description of local property follows on inside pages. But take care: Mr Owens' plate glass is shattered; Mr Archer's instruments are broken; Messrs Allison and Macfie's wine and spirits are spilt.

THE GLITTERING GUEST BOOK [RUTH]

Dearest Campbell,
I have stayed on at Roxbury, nominally to plan with Molly

a schedule for attacking her art commission. I have, of course, an eye on wider concerns. I have divined the link between Molly's taciturnity and Wilfred's black eye; I had suspected the worst.

"Don't stay," I told her. We were back at our puzzling, for one cannot leave the world uncompleted. "Don't stay, if you don't want to."

"He's gone. I ain't afraid."

I tutted. "'I'm not afraid,' you should say."

"I shouldn't."

"You're never afraid. That's the trouble. A modicum of fear can prevent unwarranted attentions." I blinked, thinking aloud. "I suppose that's what Campbell—Sergeant Lawless—is trying to do for the nation."

"I'm staying." Molly sniffed. "I'll take care with what attentions I attract, thank you very much. Old Roxy's minded to show me how things work round here. Once I'm into the menagerie and that, I'll tell what's up and what's down and what's back-to-front. Bend the scientists' ears for whispers of the latest contraptions."

"Paint them." I clapped her hands.

"The scientists?"

"The contraptions. Batteries. Generators. The turbine and waterwheel. It'll give you an insight on how they work. I'll suggest it to the earl before I—"

"Before you what?" said Roxbury. He was peeking amiably around the door. "Really, ladies, it is the most extraordinary autumn day. You must come and take the view with me."

Fifteen minutes later, we were seated by the Shepherd's Refuge, atop the hill that rises, craggy and wild, over Roxbury House. Behind us, Thimbleton Reservoir, once a bog, today a sparkling lake providing water for house and glasshouses. To our left, forested slopes overhang the house. In front, the dam and sluice. Below, the tumbling falls of Burnfoot Gorge descend past the Pump House toward the Frog Stone and the Iron Bridge. Beyond, the sweep of the valley.

"One of England's finer views." I sighed. "I shall be sorry to leave."

"Don't," said Roxbury. "You brighten up the house immeasurably."

"I shall endeavour," said Molly, "not to take that as an insult to the incumbents."

"I must go." I laughed. "My affianced fellow cannot do without my organisational help, not to mention chivvying him along about a certain wedding."

"A wedding, of course." Roxbury glanced at Moll. "Where will you hold it?"

"If only you knew someone," Moll said, "someone with a house, servants and that."

"Someone well-disposed to you," Roxbury said, "and your husband-to-be."

"With space for guests," Molly continued. "And rooms for dining and dancing and prancing and stargazing."

"Flower gardens." Roxbury gazed across the mountains. "Lawns. All that romantic bosh. Even one of those secret chapels from Reformation times."

"A priest-hole?" I've read of hapless priests hiding from Elizabeth's torturers.

"No longer quite a priest-hole," said Roxbury, "since our renovations. I had it extended into a small chapel."

I laughed. "Hidden within the house?"

He nodded, pleased with his subterfuge.

Molly noted this calmly, eyes fixed on a distant hill.

I concentrated on the same lofty peak. "And yet, what a shame if I knew someone like that, and somewhere, just as you have described; but—objection one—it was a million miles from civilisation and the devil of a job for normal southern folk to get to; objection two, Your Honour—they never, ever, ever received visitors."

Roxbury was indignant. "I'm receiving now."

"Never received normal visitors."

"Pah." Roxbury gave me a look. "We do."

"Do not," said Molly.

"We've had the Emperor of Japan," Roxbury said.

"Unlikely," said Molly.

I nodded approvingly, to stir up his indignance. "And the Sultan of Turkey."

"Anywise," said Molly, "how do you know that?"

"Yes." Roxbury frowned. "How do you know that?"

"Guest book." I shrugged. "Haven't you peeked, Molly? First thing I do when visiting a grand house. Nose through the glittering guest book. Molly, you're uncommonly good at squeezing tales out of servants, cooks and gardeners, but I'm disappointed in your reading habits."

Molly bit her lip. "But I understood, Roxy, that your parties were a thing of the past."

"Not at all," said Roxbury.

We looked at him.

"Never any stated intention, at least." His brow furrowed. "I suppose you're right. We've not entertained in recent years, not on the same scale."

"You've not entertained at all in recent years," I said gently.

Moll chimed in. "Apart from your scientists."

Roxbury's jaw worked soundlessly for a moment. He gestured down at the glasshouses. "Along with the odd apothecary. A sportsman or two. Some clever medics. Yes. I can see it looks a bit rum."

"It's no criticism, sir." I hesitated. "My Aunt Lexie has

told me of the lavish parties you were known for. Back in the days—" Back in the days when your wife ran the household, I could have added, but the notion was there in the air.

"Nobody would wish," said Molly, "to force you out of your seclusion."

"Seclusion? No, no," said he. "I'm caught up, you see, with these late developments, and I... Botanists, too. Herbalists and... Yes, I do see what you mean, now that you say it."

We looked down the valley together. In the distance, the church bell tolled the half hour.

Roxbury stood. He walked to the edge of the crag, above the falls, where the river had cut through the rock. I asked myself, was I afraid for him? For his state of mind? It was as if the loss of his wife could sweep over him, at any moment, like a tide, and he was powerless to prevent it. Reason enough to steer clear of the wrangle of parliamentary duties, business cares, city life and entertaining. How trivial it must all seem; and yet he wears no mark of mourning, as the children did. There he stood, upright and noble, assailed by emotion, as if their gentle gibes had made the tide flood anew.

At the sluicegate, the water swelled. As if set off by my ruminations, the gates within the weir, holding back the waters of Thimbleton Reservoir, opened, tugged by invisible cables. Roxbury waved us to come and watch, delight on his face. The water whooshed, swooning with unstoppable force through the exit unexpectedly offered. Below, by the Pump House, the great waterwheel clanked, wheezed, and began to turn, turn, turning ever quicker as the rivulet channelled from the falls pushed it into easy implacable motion.

* * *

"I first came here as a child, you know. Come, come, I'll show you."

The water had distracted the earl from his sad reverie. He watched it, enchanted. The merry plummet of the Burnfoot made a music so different from the engines and machines and the things you might expect an industrialist to care for. He bade us follow down the steep path, pointing out the channels that guided the rivulets into pipes, harnessing streams of water into scientific service.

"I was so delighted with the water, the fresh air, the bright grass, mosses clinging to rocks, the beauty of it all. These merry streams, performing their nimble leaps and tumbles, capering over the jagging rocks. I was fishing— poaching, I suppose—when I had the revelation. Down there, by the millhouse, lounging idly, I needed no energy, for the river was doing all the work without need for efforts on my part. I admired the old waterwheel: some fellow, long ago, watching the back-breaking labour of milling, had listened to the tumbling falls, thinking, 'If only I could exploit this power galloping away.' Any device that saves labour, from the quarry to the kitchen, gains quick renown, without need for advertising, such is man's garrulity and his sloth. Yet what a paltry part of the river's force we harness with such waterwheels. How great would be the force of these falls in their entirety."

Halfway down, by the Pump House, Roxbury ignored various of his inventions that stood about, levers and dials and cranking wheels, and led us to the piston driven so inexorably by the waterwheel.

"This was the germ of my hydraulic inventions. They made me famous, and rich. I've dallied with ships and guns. And I shall experiment with electricity until my dying day: already this turbine charges batteries which will power contraptions not yet dreamt of. But there is no doubt, my friends, that my first love was water. Still today, I have water on the brain."

I shall depart in the morning. My mind is buzzing. I regret I've not seen this secret chapel he mentioned. We might genuinely consider marrying here. For Molly, who loves nothing better than lairs and boltholes, I hope it is the beginning of the trail into the secrets of Roxbury House.

TONIC FOR THE BLOOD

DR TYBALT'S BLOOD TONIC.

THE LATEST AND BEST MEDICINE, for the blood, and for the complexion.
Bright eyes, healthy skin, a pure complexion.
The best blood purifier in the world.
Smith & Co. Chemists, Taunton.
Also for wounds and sores, bad legs, abscesses, &c.

ADVISORIES AND DENUNCIATIONS
[LETTERS TO SCOTLAND YARD]

Dear sergeants of Scotland Yard,

I read in the *Mercury* you are seeking the culprit for the *Florence Veigh* outrage. With reluctance, I must draw to your attention the families living two doors down from me.

They are French speakers, or somesuch, with upwards

of twenty people in one tenement room. As proof of their criminal involvement, I noted, on the day in question, much to-ing and fro-ing from the house. If you interview the household, and neighbours, I am confident you will find the plotters. We live within sight of the Mersey.

I am a patriot, dismayed to see those welcomed to our land repay us with such venom.

James O'Dowd, Birkenhead

Dear Sergeant Jeffcoat,

I have to inform on my shipmate from the Florence Veigh, *though it rankles with seafaring loyalties: a strange fellow, that is, I didn't know him before, but I saw him go in the captain's cabin, all shifty like, where a steward's assistant had no business to be, with a bag of a fair size, and that was as we left the dock, only half an hour before we reached Monks Ferry, when the whole thing went off like a volcano, and I have not told him I am writing to you, but, him being of no fixed abode, I shall bring him for a drink to the White Horse by Liverpool dock this evening, late enough, and you can find me, as the publican knows me, and I will gesture to him, but you will surely know him by his beret.*

Seth Salzman
Merchant seaman of Liverpool and
friend to this nation

DENIAL, DENIAL, DENIAL [LAWLESS]

Jeffcoat arrived late with news: news that had delayed his departure from London.

He and I did not spend long in Liverpool. Nobody was killed, by a miracle. But to connect this to previous blasts was hopeless: all the evidence was incinerated, the ship burnt to a cinder and mostly sunk. We interviewed the captain and the steward, but the crew were dispersed and some had already taken other ships, eager to get back to sea.

We spread the word of our campaign of vigilance, though so far it had brought us nowhere. Apart from Jeffcoat's news.

He and Ruth had been asking around London prisons and prosecutors, seeking previous arrests for attempted or suspected outrages akin to our enquiries. Ruth spotted a case against a certain Jacques the Painter, three months since, in Holloway.

Jacques the Painter. Did it ring a bell? She recognised it from some damnable *Penny Satirical* article. But whence had they got it?

Ruth uncovered the link, abstruse but convincing, by historical researches. Jack the Painter was the alias of the spy who reconnoitred for the French when they planned to invade Portsmouth in 1779. This could not be a coincidence.

With Ripon's sanction, they went straight to Holloway Prison to interview him. Jacques the Painter, as he still insisted his name was, simply laughed and refused to speak anything but French. Jeffcoat knew some French, but he didn't wish to miss a detail that could be used in evidence. He called Ruth inside and instructed her as to what to say. Jeffcoat reported to me the relish with which she delivered his threats, in her most vehement *français*.

Jacques declared himself innocent. He was being held illegally. The French ambassador would negotiate his release.

"Innocent?" Jeffcoat said. "Sitting at the pub on Westminster Bridge Road with a bag of gunpowder? That's poor proof of innocence. What was your intention?"

He was taking a cognac. That was his intention.

"With a bag of gunpowder?"

That was his own business.

"Murderous material, brought within sight of the Houses of

Parliament, contravenes the Conspiracy to Murder Act."

"What a shame," Jacques said, "your parliament declined to pass the Conspiracy to Murder Act."

This was true: it remains only a misdemeanour. "So you admit murderous intent?"

"I admit nothing of the sort."

That was Jacques the Painter, cool as a langoustine. Jeffcoat suggested that he would be waiting a long time for his ambassador to get him released. They left him to stew.

ENVIOUS TIME: WHITWORTH LIKEWISE [LAWLESS]

Denials, discoveries, suspicions.

"What's it to do with me?" Joseph P Whitworth did not get up from his desk, did not shake our hand, did not offer to help our enquiries, did not even put down his pen. "That's defamatory, that is."

"Defamatory, sir?" Jeffcoat laughed. "That's rich, coming from the man who put about the rumour that those Orsini bombs were tested on his rival's estates."

Whitworth didn't look up, but his compressed lips went white.

"Sir," I said. "I'm sorry, but at the Camden train disaster, we retrieved a piece of metal imprinted with your insignia—"

"My insignia?"

"Your company's, sir."

"Circumstantial. I'm not having it." He pointed his pen at Jeffcoat, as I had been so conciliatory. A blob of ink squirted on to his desk. "Who've you said this to?"

"To Scotland Yard's commissioner, sir," said Jeffcoat. "And to the Home Office."

Whitworth finally looked up. "If it's in the papers, I'll sue your blasted behinds."

"Mr Whitworth, sir." I stepped in front of Jeffcoat, before his temper got to the boil. "Nobody's accusing you of anything. Nobody's defaming your company."

He stopped jabbing his pen at us, and regarded me sourly.

I went on. "All we're saying is that you have many, many men with mechanical knowledge, explosives knowledge, some of whom may have connections with foreign governments, may have been bribed, or turned politically; and if you could see your way to helping our enquiries, for example, giving access to records and letting us question—"

"You're wasting my time. You wasted my time, back in '58, and you're wanting to waste it again."

Silence.

"We are pursuing several enquiries—" I began.

"The bloody fire on the bloody Mersey?" He grew red-faced. "You flipping London lunatics. You're mad as hops, you lot. Liverpool, Manchester. Manchester, Liverpool. Not the same, you know. 'Ooh, it's up north. Ooh, it's so chilly.' Just because we're northern."

I refrained from out-northerning Whitworth, but he had lost my sympathy.

"Can you not get your heads around it?" He banged his desk. "Liverpool in't owt to do with me—"

"You sell machinery in Liverpool." Jeffcoat clenched his teeth.

"A lot of machinery, Mr Whitworth," I said. "Do you not?"

"I sell machinery in Nantucket, and I sell machinery in Nanking. I don't see you blaming me for bombs there, eh? Eh? I don't see the bloody Yanks or the blasted Chinks come knocking, saying, 'Ooh, Mr Whitworth, your machinery's been found at an explosion,' do I? Do I?"

Deadlock.

"You're barking up the wrong bush, Sergeant Whatsyername. You're barking in the wilderness. And that were nowt to do with me, by the way, those bombs in Paris.

That was proven, that was established."

"I'm confident, sir," I said, "that it will be established equally quickly in this case, if only we get a little cooperation on both sides."

Silence, again.

Clunk. Jeffcoat set down on the desk, clumsily, the shard of metal with the telltale lettering. "You might like to establish that, while we're at it."

Whitworth's face screwed up, as if at a dreadful stink. "Get out," he said. "Get out!"

We stood our ground.

"Bloody well get your backsides out of here and don't come back while I'm here," he said, brandishing it like Jupiter's thunderbolt, "unless you want this rammed up—" Just as we were on the point of fleeing for safety, a tremendous change came over him. He picked up the shard and weighed it in his hand. "Oh, now." He stopped shaking the shard and drew it close, a look of wonder spreading over his features. "You know what this is? This, this is off my first machine. I made this imprint myself, I did. Oh, I'll put this in my museum of artefacts. Where did you say you found it?"

Jeffcoat and I looked at each other. "On Camden Road platform," said I.

"Blown up," said he.

"Damn clever bugger to blow anything up with this. This was on a lathe. My mark on the first lathes I ever made, after Babbage's engine. Early thirties, I'd reckon: 1833? So, whoever it is you're after, whoever's used my work to ill ends, was either intoxicated by the quality of my workmanship, or wanted to incriminate me." He shook the piece at us. "Envious bastards. This'd be the cheapest old scrap they could find with any old name on it."

* * *

JACQUES THE SECOND [LAWLESS]

We went back to Liverpool. We'd grown used to ignoring informant letters: a sorry state of affairs, but you'd be amazed how quick people are to shop in their dear neighbours as international activists.

Seth Salzman's offer to present us with the Mersey bomber was less than convincing, but I persuaded Jeffcoat that we must attend. At the worst, we'd have a drink, stay the night and claim the expense back from Ripon's department.

We found the man in the beret, as promised, at the bar of the White Horse. His look of terror when we laid a hand on each shoulder was enough to tell us we'd been hasty in our judgement. Once we introduced ourselves and got him into a private room, he couldn't stop talking. As soon as he told us his name, the thing was sure. He called himself Jacques the Painter.

Jacques the Second—let us call him Mersey Jacques—was a babbler. He told us everything, before we'd asked.

Down on his luck. A fellow told him of the ship sailing. Gave him the cash. Gave him the bag. Showed him how to set it. The fellow said it was a jape: he was a friend of the captain, and this was a birthday surprise.

Up it went. Eleven tons of gunpowder.

He was beside himself at admitting it. He denied nothing. He came with us, compliant, protesting he was a fool, not an activist. He had the money still, or most of it. He described, poorly, what had been in the bag: three balls of medium weight, the size of an egg, but round. All he had to do was balance them on the captain's table. That was all.

What material?

Not wood, not metal, not rubber: something in between.

Could he tell us who had told him to do it?

He described him as best he could. "Bizarre bloke."

Jeffcoat huffed. "Bizarre like what?"

"He speak funny. Foreign like."

"French?"

"Couldn't say, like. French foreign? Might've been. Tak, tak, tak. Yes, maybe, yes. Dunno. Might not've. Couldn't say, like."

"Hold on." Jeffcoat looked at me. He laid his hand on the fellow's shoulder. "I don't understand. Aren't you French?"

"No, no," said Mersey Jacques. "I'm Polish."

"But your name?"

He told us his real name, but we couldn't even pronounce it, and he, an illiterate sailor, couldn't write it. "The man say, he say, if anything go wrong, I give name 'Jacques the Painter'. Tak, tak, tak. He call hisself Diderot." Jacques wrung his hands, suppressing a sob. "I never imagine it so."

We took him to London. It wasn't necessary to handcuff him, but we did it anyway.

THE ORIGINAL JACK [LAWLESS]

Could all the explosions, fires, and disasters be orchestrated by the French? What did that mean? Was it a directive concocted in a secret Parisian military department, sending agents? Or rogue enclaves of émigrés, dedicated to subvert our proud nation?

It was in Liverpool Jeffcoat and I began to understand the results of our labours: French families held at customs, refused entry to Britain, and ready to be deported. Some protested they were not immigrants, but lived here; others intended travelling on to America.

The officials pooh-poohed this. "Trying to get in the back door," they called it. Jack the Painter, according to Ruth's researches, was an unbalanced misfit. Incensed by some slight, he offered to spy for the French. His information underpinned the Portsmouth Plan of 1779, which nearly came to fruition.

Such informing wasn't enough for Jack. Sympathising with the American Revolution, Jack took direct action to hurt the tyrannical British. He laid gunpowder though the immense new rope house, soaked hemp in turpentine, and lit it. The fire was quickly doused, and the police caught Jack before he fled, on a French passport. In court, he confessed to laying fires in Plymouth and Bristol as well. He was hanged on the mizzen mast of *HMS Arethusa*, shouting to the crowd of 20,000 that no vigilance would save them.

TREASURE HOUSE [MOLLY]

Watchman,
Thanks for intervention on my behalf.
Kept me from cadging my way to the pudding house.
I owe you favours of a fair footing.
Roxy likewise cheered by your chummery.
Molly

Dear Miss V,
How can I describe the treasure palace of Roxbury? (The house, more than the man, though I am puzzling out the man too.) How little I showed you on your visit, too occupied with my woes. A balamy bluff, I know, (by which I mean abject apology); but there it is.

I begin to explore as much as I dare, without risking Birtle's opprobrium. Whenever I've chanced upon a servant heading down a corridor, I chat with them. It costs me nothing to be civil and they're a warm bunch.

Only the east wing remains dourly shut. More than once, I've plucked up the courage to ask Birtle:

"Who is in the east wing, Birtle? Is there something there? Someone?"

Each and every time, the question has died on my lips at the sight of his dour visage, always watching me, always suspecting me. The east wing remains dourly shut, as it had been, Skirtle informed me, "since her ladyship." I will yet dare to find a way in.

The house itself has a labyrinthine complexity. Even to treat of the basement floor is impossible, for the basement at the back is the first floor at the front (that is the basement at the front is two floors below it). Therein:

Butler's pantry, butler's rooms, butler's library.

Servants' quarters, buzzers ranged above the great flagstones.

Cabinets for crockery and crystal for functions.

Distressed wallpaper, statuettes, umbrella stand, hat stand carved with mythological beasts; stand for dibber, strake and divers garden implements for the rambling gent, for stoning, fruiting, husking, trimming edges, weeding, &c. All this in the back porch, not at the back but at the front, hidden by the east turret's steps; here the upper gardener may leave his lawn mower, rather than heave it uphill from the glasshouses.

Medicine cabinets, gaming tables. Gun room, sun room. Turkish bath, massage room, male changing, female changing, cold bath, tepid bath, hot bath, sudatorium, showers, and water closets. In the walls, stupendous boilers. The pipes curl upward like sinews disappearing into the walls. Roxy hid these within the walls, I thought; I begin to believe he has secreted a whole chapel.

The grounds at least you have seen for yourself. Here

I lose myself amid this wild nature which only months ago gave me the scarpering spooks. More of the grounds another time, as I shall explore them further, chaperoned or alone.

MAN OVERBOARD [LAWLESS]

On the train back from Roxbury House, alone, searching the SS *Great Britain*'s records for 1858-59, Ruth found Lodestar's name.

So many fruitless hours she had spent looking through these lists. Hours I thought wasted, and I was paying her. I was paying her as a translator, via the Yard, and for code-cracking through Ripon. Corpse-hunting sounded too romantic for the accounts men.

Besides, the body on the SS *Great Britain* was not unusual, now that I was working for Ripon. These were times when everyone wanted to come to London. Fugitives were caught daily, arriving at our ports, stowed on ferries, ships, yachts, hidden in carts and cases and coffins, would you believe it; fugitives from more Polish rebellions, more Irish famines, Italian vendettas, and war-torn America.

Yet there it was.

> *BOARDED CAPE TOWN*
> *7 December 1858*
> *Mr Nathaniel C. Lodestar*
> *(accompanied by his man, Zephaniah)*

She wrote to meet her at the Rising Sun.

I was rushed and in a mood after my northern interrogations with Jeffcoat. We were under pressure to deliver convictions. Catching the two Jacques was something. But our investigations were about as clear as Thames water. I was sure the threat was real: real enough to justify the forts. Jeffcoat was less convinced: his hours interviewing Jacques the First persuaded him it could easily be one madman after another, each inspiring the next, with no coherent plan, barely able to write their own name.

Ruth abruptly presented me with papers from Antony Gibbs Shipping, calling for tea as I stared at them.

"And what of it? We knew Lodestar came from Africa." I mashed the tea, brusquely, and poured, too soon. "What's the surprise?"

She looked down at the tea, as if I had slapped her.

I breathed in. "I'm sorry."

"Quite a coincidence, don't you think?"

"I suppose. What has it to do with our investigation?"

"A missing man." Ruth stared. "The ship's passenger lists have accounted for births, deaths, fugitives and stowaways. This is the first missing person."

"Missing?" I sipped the half-drawn tea, cursing my impatience. "How is he missing?"

"What attention to detail our detective force exhibits." She tapped further down the passenger list. I had not got to the second sheet.

DISEMBARKED LONDON
31 January 1859
Mr Nathaniel C. Lodestar

"Only eight weeks? Let's consider it for our honeymoon."

She rolled her eyes and waited.

I looked back and forth between the two entries. Picked up at the Cape; eight weeks later he arrives, but now it's just him. "What happened to the valet? Are you thinking…"

She smiled her sweet detecting smile. "Worth asking, wouldn't you say?"

I breathed in, my eyes wide. "Excuse me, Mr Lodestar, did your man die, by any chance, and you wrapped him up and chucked him overboard?"

"Yes. You have Numpty's sketch of the basket."

"I'm asking him to admit to a crime."

"Are you? I'm not so sure." She gave me a look that told me she was quite sure. "If the man died of consumption, he died. It's accepted colonial practice to wrap the deceased in sail cloth and weigh it down with cannonballs."

"Colonial practice is all very well, but here we report deaths to the captain and the ship's doctor."

"But it wasn't here. It was at sea somewhere."

"It was a British ship."

"He may be appalled, or ashamed, or he may not care a jot. The fact that he botched it doesn't make the crime any worse."

"And the basket may clinch it." The tea tasted better. "I'd love to rule out foul play against our mystery immigrant. At least we'd have one mystery solved."

FRUITFUL DAYS [LAWLESS]

Over those weeks, before the exeat weekend party was fixed, Molly bided her time. She sowed seeds, cultivated the soil, and waited for her labours to bear fruit. Her friendship with Roxbury blossomed quickly under her natural warmth. Her picture of how the earl and his family came to this strange pass gradually came into sharp colour. I shall tell it through her account, and her reports of the earl's tales, allowing myself occasional interpolations: a story that could have lasted a thousand and one nights.

The September sun baked the hillsides. With the children gone, it became clear why Skirtle and Birtle took such care to avoid each other. No longer inhibited, they argued like cat and dog. Molly overheard them, time and again, in the hall, in the corridor, in his pantry, in her scullery; over what remained obscure to her.

Molly took to exploring, from reservoirs down to arboretum, painting all the while. She painted so often, her paints ran low. The earl had said to order whatever she needed, via Birtle. Reluctant to ask that old curmudgeon for anything, she had an idea. She set up her easel above the rockery of a morning, early enough to stop the earl as he headed out.

He glanced over her shoulder and admired her initial sketch.

"I'd like to mix my own colours, Roxy, as I'm running low on supplies. I wonder if I might collect a few things from round the estate."

"What will you need, young Molly?" he said, charmed.

"For the whites, I'll want bones. Bones of hens and fish. Whitened in the fire, I grind them to powder and thicken with lime. For the colours, figs and plums; hazels, blackcurrants, willow twigs and sunflowers. Cobalt and charcoal. Sulphur. Eggs to brighten the colours; beeswax to dull them. For the brushes, pig bristles and horse hair." Molly knew how to make a few colours, more or less, from perusing old Lear's travel diaries; the rest she was bluffing. She thought it would pique his interest. "Can I acquire those items, do you think?"

"You can." He frowned. "Certainly you can."

"I sense a 'but' approaching."

"You can get them. All of them," he said. "But you'll be needing your own studio."

They went down to the arboretum. They found Jem checking the fruit trees in the glasshouse. Aside from the raised beds, citrus and exotic fruits and summer berries stood in great planters, rotating ever so slowly. As the Burnfoot Stream passed by, water driven through a side channel turned the planters slowly back and forth, by a system of rails and cogs, to maximise the sunlight.

The glasshouse was so hot, Jem had stripped off his waistcoat. He was sweating right through his shirt; to his charms, Molly was still not immune. Seeing them, Jem rearranged his clothing, but the earl reassured him.

"At ease, young man, when working." He frowned. "Is that a rat?"

Jem broke off his proud stance, alarmed. He scooped up the misbegotten little hare. "Patagonian mara, sir. Little one. Been poorly. Feeding it up."

"Eating our fruit, no doubt."

"No, no, sir. Nibbling off the insects. Does a grand job."

The earl led on through the foliage, shading his eyes. "What power there is in that sun. The day will come, Molly, when this country renounces fuels and relies instead on these two great benisons of nature, water and sun."

Molly laughed. "The great engineer wishes away the power that supplies his own trade. How will your ships sail? How will you smelt your steel? And your household comforts, the heating, the lamplight?"

"You'll see." He smiled. On, through the botanicals. "Coal will run out. A few decades in this country. We'll doubtless find more, and other fuels to exhaust, as we've dug up guano islands and peat bogs." He led her beneath the mighty spruces around which the glasshouses were constructed, wiping his brow. Noticing Molly's perspiration, he offered her a handkerchief. "As a youth, I stood by the Burnfoot Gorge and calculated the energy that passes through it. Harness this power, and it would outdo 10,000 tons of coal a day."

Across the glasshouse quadrangle, they entered the scientists' cloister. He showed her to a well-lit room. A broad desk, littered with drawing materials, filing cabinets, and an architect's easel, which he adjusted to her height. "Let's call this your studio."

Molly looked around in wonder. At last, she thought. The inner sanctum.

"Our very own telegram station next door. Lodestar next but one. Comes and goes. Doubt he'll bother you."

"I'm quite sure he won't." She studied the awards that covered the wall. "Is this... This is your office."

He dismissed her concern. "I don't use it these days. I do all my thinking up in the tower of power." He pointed up to the house: his central tower was visible above the trees. "Come. I've one of your ingredients we can fetch straight away."

Out the rear door of the cloister, past the Frog Stone, and they soon came to the Pump House, above the Burnfoot weir. The old waterwheel turned slowly, powered by a channel of the Burnfoot. On the platform, the turbine, its industrial piston pumping back and forth. Inside were contraptions. She barely noticed the musty smell, the dirty flagstones, the ropes, broken chairs, and odour of chemicals that stuck in the throat. What she noticed was levers by the door, affixed on the walls; the bureau, with regulating and fuse boxes and telegraphic box; the stack of great wooden boxes panelled with glass sides.

"Nice tanks," said Molly. "The fish died, did they?"

"Fish? Oh ho. Tremendous." Roxbury found this hilarious. "Rather painful for your fish, though."

"All right, clever clogs. What animals are they intended for?"

Roxbury struggled to stop laughing. "They are batteries. The liquid isn't water, but chemicals. Sulphuric acid, for example. I happen to have powdered sulphur for you here. You must promise to let me mix it up, lest it corrode your paintings—and your fingers."

He explained how the batteries stored power from the movement, back and forth, back and forth, of the turbine piston. At the end of the row of batteries, a pipe, rubber wound around copper wire, led away to house and glasshouses, powering telegram, servants' buzzers and scientists' equipment. His explanation of the various batteries was bewitching, with copper coils and Leyden jars and Siemens batteries and faradisation, and his infinite electrostatic influence machine. As the village church tolled, he led me out by the turbine to survey his domain.

"If my friend Swan is to be believed, he will illuminate our lamps within a year or two, without need for filthy candles, or whale oil or gas or this newfangled paraffin. You cannot imagine the hours of cleaning it will save Skirtle, besides the wasteful consumption of oil. My trusty old influence machine creates a healthy voltage, but this turbine can generate upwards of a thousand watts." He turned to her kindly, his face golden in the sunlight. "You must come up to my study in the house. I'll show you more of this new power and what it promises."

"New power, eh?" She looked at him with fresh eyes. "You, Roxy, sound like a magus of old."

ADVICE FROM A FENIAN: OUTRAGE FAILED [LAWLESS]

"It's a setup. Whitworth? Hardly." The Irish republican, O'Leary, spoke calmly, though he seemed weary of answering for crimes he'd nothing to do with. "An obvious ploy. I know it. You know it. Whitworth knows it. Someone buys up his old stock, bashes it around, sticks the insignia on their infernal contraption, and boom. Literally boom. You jump for joy. Press latches on to it. Whitworth's up in arms. His contractors get the shakes. Someone else cashes in. Though why you come knocking at my door, I can't imagine." He sniffed. "By the way, if you've told the papers we did it, we'll sue yous."

Jeffcoat and I had left Manchester disgruntled. Whitworth's rebuttal chastened us. No mincing of words. It was a slur and a slight, he was convinced of it.

We talked back and forth with O'Leary. "Let's say it is the French. Why would they collaborate in slurring Whitworth?"

"Damage Whitworth, damage Roxbury for that matter, you damage the country. What better way to soften you up for invasion, if that's a threat as real as you make out?"

Word had got out about the Guernsey papers. How could it not? With the millions to be lavished on the Palmerston forts, the brick factories at full capacity, the experts in damming and pumping and sea defences. It didn't take a genius to blow the whistle on it.

On the train south, with our Merseyside prisoner handcuffed between us, we read horrible news in the paper. Violence in South London against French families. They'd lived there for years, indeed fled from persecution at home. Now they'd been shouted at, followed home, their windows broken.

This was the kind of nation we lived in, and Jeffcoat and I were making it worse. Indeed, if the bombs continued, this would only be the beginning of John Bull's comeback. All due to our report of Frenchy complots and Froggy conniving.

We decided to rein in our message of vigilance, and give out a different story. "See, share, secure" was all very well, but it had driven people monomaniacal. Misdirect the public, that was the ticket, misdirect them for their own good.

"Not in our interest, though." O'Leary had come in without complaint when we called him. He was used to the Fenians being to blame. "Why on earth would we be after blowing up Liverpool, and killing our own, now? Idiocy. No point in it. Mess with Liverpool's trade? Might as well ask us to stop breathing. Would I shoot my Uncle Michael in the foot? Sure, there's more Kerry butter comes through Liverpool than is eaten in all Ireland."

"You might do it," said Jeffcoat, "to unsettle the nation."

O'Leary sighed. "These folk, whoever they are, they're just after scaring people witless. Where's the use of it, though? They'll forget soon enough. No coherence to the plan. Not our style. Not at all."

"Fear." Jeffcoat crossed his arms on the desk. "That's what you fellows like."

"You fellows! I like that. As if we're all the same." O'Leary shook his head. "The brotherhood wants society reorganised, not thrown into chaos. We're patriots. Which is more than you can say for the eejit cowards who've done this to Liverpool. Makes my blood boil."

"Patriots? You lot?" Jeffcoat said. "Killing Londoners left, right and centre?"

"And you English never killed an Irishman, did you now? Nor steal our land and livelihood? Let two million die or go to the devil across the seas?"

Jeffcoat had no answer for the Irishman. He walked away.

O'Leary was calm; these were words well considered. "We're patriotic enough to demand our own country back."

"These bombers may be patriots and all." I enjoyed their puzzlement: it broke the tension. "But French patriots."

O'Leary looked at me, then at Jeffcoat. "That's really the talk now, is it? I thought it just rumour and whisperings. Since when have the French the spunk to be bombing ships?"

"Why?" I sat forward. "Would you not credit their explosive abilities?"

"Pah." O'Leary wiped his nose. "Listen, if you've no beef with my lot, I'll—"

"Don't be going yet," I said. "We'd value your opinion."

"You're joking me." He looked at me through narrowed eyes.

I was sincere. Who better to advise us on clandestine subterfuges than a secret bomber himself? We asked O'Leary all the questions we'd been asking the two Jacques; but he had answers for us. How one would go about preparing a bomb. Whom would one ask? Where would one test it?

"Simple enough. Anyone can make an explosive. Anyone with a grain of chemistry and a particle of metalwork. The trouble is knowing when it will explode. There's many an activist blown himself to smithereens since '48 and Comrade Marx's insurrections. There's your mining companies, who overstep their knowledge and balls up their blasting."

Here was O'Leary's genius. We should go and ask the men who did this all the time. Men who blasted cuttings for railways, who built harbours and bridges and causeways and embankments. Somewhere between the chief engineer and the lowly navvy lay the knowledge that informed "safe" explosions. In this climate, though, the merest enquiry about making or purchasing explosives, for use outside their company, ought to arouse suspicion, especially if one were not local. If we asked the companies around the country who specialised in developing explosives, someone would talk.

"My guess, now, you've your disaffected workers, underpaid, over-abused. Likely enough they'll have taken a notion to make a killing and revenge themselves on the powers-that-be, selling a few blasters to the highest bidder. Even if the paymaster be the mortal enemies of the crown. Why would they give a fig?"

"Where would you start to look," I said, "if you were looking?"

He laughed. "Now I couldn't possibly say, could I, and give away such people?"

"You won't be betraying a soul. You're no friend to the French, nor to the people who did this. Eejits, you called them, unsettling us just when we need stability."

"True enough." He grinned brilliantly, shaking his head in wonder. "If you'd told me I'd be after giving detective hints to my old foes, Jeffcoat and Lawless, I'd have said you were addle-brained."

He took a piece of paper and began to write.

RIDICULOUS [LAWLESS]

"Blimming ridiculous!" Bertie put his feet up on my desk and sipped his scotch. "Louis? Louis invading England? You've got to be joshing me."

It is not often that the heir to the throne pays a call on Scotland Yard (aside from the odd divorce investigation). I had admitted Prince Albert Edward of Saxe-Coburg and Gotha, known to friends as Bertie, despite the fact Jeffcoat and I were working on the case.

Cases rather. Threats and outrages surfacing around the country: a Yorkshire coal mine explosion (natural causes); collapse of Gloucestershire bridges (flooded). Every little disaster was attributed to French extremists subverting the nation's structures to bring down the government.

Bertie made light of these investigations. "Oh, yes, I can see Louis ordering deathly blasts in Huddersfield. Oh, what pleasure that will give him. Rubbing his hands to think of the impact on the navy. Ridiculous. The only invasion Louis is interested in is the dessert trolley at Claridge's. Do you know how that man loves an English apple crumble, with Devonshire cream? Do you? Treacle sponge he adores. Are we worth invading for that?"

"With due respect, sir, Napoleon's sweet tooth doesn't preclude militaristic intentions."

"With due respect, Watchman, when people say 'with due respect' they are about to show one not one whit of respect."

Bertie tousled his hair. "Watchman, you know as well as I that Louis holds old England in high esteem."

"High enough to covet it?"

"Damn and blast, they've converted you to their warmongering." He was sitting in front of my desk. Jeffcoat and I were thus obliged to stand, of course.

I looked uncomfortably at the papers strewn across the desk: our latest notions. O'Leary's suggestion that the bombers would have received payments from this shadowy Diderot. Some he might pay face-to-face, as with Mersey Jacques; but in this modern age, he was equally likely to pay straight into their banks. To find suspects, therefore, we contacted all the banks: they must identify transfers between French and English accounts, with political groups or engineering companies of especial interest.

I started surreptitiously stacking the papers.

"Oh, for goodness' sake, Watchman, there's no need to hide things from me. I may be a tittle-tattle where private affairs are concerned, but in matters of national interest, I'm surer than EM Grace fielding at point. Safe as the Bank of England vaults."

"How safe are they, sir," I said, "in the current climate?"

"Come along." He opened his palms wide. "My mother may think me an idiot and keep the parliamentary papers from me. You know I am competent and wish to stay apprised of national concerns. How else will I be fit to be king, one day?" He sighed; his mother showed no signs of kicking the bucket. "I've read the commission's report. I've read your deputation. I won't criticise your words: you're doing your duty, in reporting the attacks. But I'd say you've exceeded your duty in ascribing them to the Frenchies."

I glanced at Jeffcoat. Mention of the Guernsey papers was made in several documents on my desk. If Bertie did not already know of them, well, as he was a friend to Louis Napoleon, we mustn't—

"I know all about your blasted Guernsey papers, don't worry. And bloody Victor Hugo prejudicing you against Louis. Hugo's bitter, of course. Louis didn't like *Les Misérables*. Truth be told, Hugo could go back to Paris any day. It suits his novelist's egotism to be in exile. And what success he's had here, far from the distractions of Paris. Hard to get a page scribbled in Paris, eh?" He winked. "I can't promise you there are no French involved. Renegades in the ranks. Who knows? They've always accepted recruits from anywhere on the globe. But the idea that it is Louis' plot to invade…"

Jeffcoat bit his lip. He took a file marked *A French Gibraltar*. He opened up the maps we had found among the Guernsey papers. We showed Bertie the landing plans, the arrows arcing from the Normandy coast to the myriad coves of Sussex and Hampshire; the arrows overland of the force's route into Portsmouth, swarming over their paltry Hilsea Lines.

"Even if it's not the French, sir." Jeffcoat tapped at the page. "Look into the future. Some other power: Russians. Prussians. Turks."

"Americans," I chimed in.

Jeffcoat blew out. "Arabs."

"Japanese. Nothing is impossible," I said in earnest. "These defences will not be wasted."

Jeffcoat took up my cause, for which I was grateful, as I knew he seriously doubted it. "Portsmouth Harbour has served the empire for centuries, and it can for centuries more. Should it ever be taken, this ring of forts we're constructing will rain down such a thunderstorm of shells as to destroy the place. Any foreign army stealing our navy, annihilated."

Bertie grinned. "And Portsmouth with it?"

"Dockyard." Jeffcoat nodded. "Old town. Gosport."

"No great loss." Bertie sighed. "Though Dickens keeps his tart down that way. I'll warn him—"

"No," I said. "Sir!"

"Only joshing." Bertie put his finger to his lips. "Your secrets are safe with me. Ta for the snifter. Believe me about old Louis, though. Take the heat off the French. My mother's such a Kraut-lover. We don't want beastly European wars again, do we, just because Bismarck and these metal-helmeted foreigners tread on each other's toes."

Off he went. Bertie clearly thought he alone could defuse European tensions. The Schleswig-Holstein cock-up had swelled his political ideas. I'd never expected him to show an interest in diplomacy, much less an aptitude for it.

I turned to Jeffcoat. "He does know Louis Napoleon."

"And would screwy Louis mention his plan to annex our navy over cigars?" Jeffcoat tucked the papers safely in the drawer, and locked it. "If only we knew what the emperor really thought."

My eyes widened. "If we knew someone who really had his ear. Pillow talk."

Jeffcoat looked at me. We were both thinking of London's most famous courtesan, Catherine Walters, or Anonyma, currently residing in Paris, and a damned good friend of mine. We said it simultaneously: "Skittles."

ENQUIRIES AND VIGILANCE [LAWLESS]

We were floundering, interviews to no avail, interrogations rebuffed.

Jacques the First was on remand in Holloway Prison. Jeffcoat kept popping up, taking Ruth to try and loosen his tongue. She dressed inconspicuously, enjoying the cut-and-thrust intrigue.

Jacques I admitted nothing. Ruth told him we knew what he was planning. He said he'd be delighted if she would tell him. She told him he had no hope of clemency in the current climate: he might be shipped to Ireland (where Conspiracy to

Murder was treasonous); or hanged here. If he gave evidence against his paymaster, we would secure a pardon.

Jacques I laughed like a hyena.

Jeffcoat asked him what amused him so.

His answer was rapid and poorly articulated, but Ruth thought he said something like: "If you only knew who it was, you would laugh as much."

I paid a visit to Portsmouth, to ensure the dockyard authorities remained vigilant. Bombs in London, bombs in Liverpool; how long before they were targeted? Vigilance, vigilance.

The dock master had heard tell of Jack the Painter of old. He gave me a cheery tour of the fateful rope house that survived that fire. It was immense, a place of industry and cooperation, the longest building I've ever seen. He took me up the lookout tower to show me the forts popping up in the middle of the Solent. The day I visited was bright and crisp; in the storms of winter, I could imagine few places grimmer. Would the day ever come when their guns would be used in anger? I pictured the flash of artillery, the booms delayed, erupting from all directions, terror as the shells pounded their target. Such a concentration of skill and technology centuries old, yet one day of mayhem from our forts would eradicate it all.

I decided I deserved a drink before departing. Ellie at the Fortitude Tap had news. Her husband had won a prize: hardest worker on his shift. I peered at her swelling belly. Oh, that too: she was expecting a fifteenth. She made me laugh.

I stopped in at Petersfield on the way north to share an exquisitely awkward dinner with Ruth and her dreaded Aunt Lexie.

Ruth had insisted I visit, as Aunt Lexie was something of an expert on Lady Elodie Loth. It was interesting; it was fascinating; Lexie knew things that Molly had never mentioned, of Lady Elodie's choral talents, her patronage of photographers, and her struggles to have degrees for women recognised by the university. I was glad, too, to reconfirm with Ruth's family my status as her betrothed, and to discuss our wedding, whenever it might come.

The uncomfortable thing was that I had once been rather fonder of Alexandra—that is, Aunt Lexie—than I should have been, and Ruth knew nothing about it.

We contrived not to be alone together, Alexandra and I. When Ruth excused herself, after dinner, we were left sitting together, looking at each other, without saying a word. Her face was pale and beautiful, her hair tied neatly up, but I recalled seeing it, many times, lustrous and splayed upon a pillow.

By the time Ruth came back, Alexandra had begun to cry.

She had the perfect reason, quick to her lips. "I'm so happy, you see, Ruth, that you've found such a terrific fellow."

PAINE'S CELERY COMPOUND

Dear Sir,
    May I report my accepting treatment, with scepticism, by means of Paine's Celery Compound? After years of digestive discomfort, I only accepted this latest quack cure to keep my wife from strangling me.
May I report, with surprise, my immediate improvement?
May I report, with joy, my successful treatment? I am cured, my digestion is second to none, my wife's relief from my complaints is assured, and my fear of strangulation reduced.
    My thanks to the mysterious Mr Paine.
        Yours, no longer pained,
            Arthur Quint, Esq, Camberley, Berks

THE MENAGERIE, PART THE FIRST [MOLLY]

WATCHMAN,
INNER SANCTUM GAINED, MORE OR LESS.
PUMP ROOM VIEWED: ELECTRICAL WORKINGS.
GLASSHOUSE DETAILS TO FOLLOW.
MOLLY

Dear Miss V,

Roxy has introduced me to the keepers in the menagerie. Warned away from the scientists by Birtle, I had avoided it till now, though I heard the birdsong from my room. I'd been through Roxy's list of animals with Miss Ruth, planning the order, from simple to trickier. We found the list odd in comparison with the Regent's Park Zoological Gardens, which I've known since a babe. It's no triumphal display of domination; rather a remedial house for medical advances.

Parrots, parakeets, macaws, lovebirds.

Exotic spider house, with their own keeper, adept at poisons and, thus, antidotes.

Sickly-looking eels, with a KEEP AWAY notice.

Beehives, providing lavender honey for the breakfast table, to complement the summer fruit preserves.

Monkey house.

Larger mammals: zebra, capybara, Highland cow, ibex (or was it ilex?) and llama, which is a spindly Peruvian sheep, more or less.

Amphibians and lizards: salamander, gecko, chameleon, and dragon (they are surely jigging my rig, as this is make-believe).

Roxy showed me these wonders without a trace of his normal melancholic reserve. He is an energetic soul driver, canting his gospel of research through these glasshouse laboratories, Pump House, tower laboratory in the house, and in his thoughts, constantly in his thoughts. Whenever he inspects Lodestar's plans for bigger coal mines and steelworks and gas holders, he is thinking of the power that will sweep away these antiquated forces, the power he would wish to be remembered for, beyond steam and combustion and hydraulics: electricity.

THE MENAGERIE, PART THE SECOND [MOLLY]

"Time to kill the birds," said Roxy. "I'll have Jem do as little harm to their plumage as he humanly can."

We were examining the aviary birds. When he dropped this madness into the conversation, I stared at him like a loon. "What? No. No animals need be harmed."

"I'll have 'em brought to your studio." He at least had the decency to look sad about it. "You'll want to capture them as fresh as you can."

"I'll paint them here, in their cages. Alive."

Roxy was funny enough about letting me in certain parts of the scientific quarter. What have they to hide? Old industrialist habits, I suspect, for his patents have often been copied. He spouted some flam about men with inappropriate manners and women's place being elsewhere. I didn't give a stuff for appropriacy, I told him, or I'd be long gone.

"Molly, my dear, they won't hold still." The macaw was preening itself. The earl smiled and extracted Edward Lear's book of coloured lithographs from his bag. Leafing through, he compared the bird to its portrait. "Look at the detail. Fabulous colour. How will you do it?"

"I can't see Lear having birds killed." I frowned at the picture. "Look at those eyes. That's a live macaw, if ever I saw one."

Roxy frowned. "Tell you what. Let's invite the fellow himself and ask him."

I stared. Ever since you spoke of his illustrious guest book, I've joshed him about his reclusive behaviour. He was depriving me of the real country house experience. All those celebrated visitors I'd heard so much about. Not to mention eligible bachelors.

"I suppose we could have a few people up." He gulped. "When the Norphans are back for exeat. Show the world we're still alive and kicking, eh? Lear, if he hasn't fled the country for winter yet." He looked around the aviary, warming to the theme. "A photographer or two, to advise you about lighting."

"Miss Ruth knows Julia Cameron. And Dodgson, a maths fellow at Oxford."

"And I know some painters, or rather my wife knew them." He pursed his lips and nodded abruptly, before he could change his mind. "We'll have a party."

NOT A BAD FELLOW [LAWLESS]

Lodestar was hard to track down. Everywhere I went, they had seen him; wherever I went, he had been. I wired Roxbury to seek his right-hand-man's whereabouts. On a tour of the south, he replied, in London's banking sector, arranging finance for the Palmerston forts.

In each of the banks, there was someone who knew him well. At Coutts and Co, I was directed to Joshua Postwood, who proved keen to boast of their special acquaintance.

"Oh, yes. We go out for lunch whenever Lodestar comes," said Joshua. "Good lunch too. Fantastic raconteur. The things he's seen. The procreating rituals of hippopotami—"

"Have you seen him recently?"

"Yesterday. He'll be round a few of the banks. Investments." He tapped the side of his nose. "Terrific fun."

Four more banks, two gentlemen's clubs, and finally a Fleet Street restaurateur advised me to check his favourite coffee house.

I found him sharing a pot of Colombian with Bracebridge Hemyng. I knew Hemyng slightly: one of Wilkie Collins's crowd, he wrote for the *Penny Satirical*, that out-priced imitation of *Punch*. He sat scribbling while we talked.

Lodestar welcomed me as an old friend, calling for fresh coffee before I could even sit down. "Business, my friend, or pleasure?" he said. "If it's business, Hemyng can listen in, and his alias Jack Harkaway can pay."

"Nothing serious." Some instinct made me reluctant to chase the journalist away. I felt myself vulnerable to Lodestar's charm, and was glad of a witness to our talk. "How did you come to Britain?"

"To make my fortune, I suppose." He gave me an insouciant look. "Back to the old country."

"I meant, by what means did you travel here?"

"By ship, of course. Why?"

"SS *Great Britain*, was it?"

Lodestar's smile was not easily read, but if his journalist friend was not there, he might have been less amenable. "Yes. That sounds right. Why?"

"Your man." I looked at him pleasantly.

"My man?"

"Yes, your valet, Zephaniah. Whatever became of him?" I blinked. "He was recorded as boarding with you at Cape Town."

"Yes, of course. Zephaniah. That's right."

"You don't retain him any longer?"

"No, no." Lodestar sipped his coffee, looking at me directly, as a native-born Englander never would. "He skipped off."

"The ship's register, on arrival in London, makes no mention of him."

"No. No, it wouldn't." Lodestar glanced at his friend. "This must be tedious for you, Hemyng."

The fellow shrugged. "Was that the ship with the arsenic wallpaper? We've done a job on that already. I'm off to the Hounds. See you later, for a trouncing at billiards."

Lodestar waved him off, then leaned forward.

I drank my coffee, waiting.

He bit his lip. "It's just a tad embarrassing. Yes, Zephaniah. He skipped off somewhere."

I sipped again, letting him stew a moment. "No record of his disembarking, though."

"Oh, servants, though." He tilted his head. "They don't always take notice."

"The records are very thorough. Where exactly did he skip off?"

"I wouldn't know for sure. Up the Atlantic coast somewhere. Spain? France? I didn't know where I was half the time; I was ill, you see."

"You were ill?" I nodded slowly. "I gathered Zephaniah had been ill."

"Did you? Yes. Well. Useless on the voyage. Barely saw him."

"Was he not in your rooms?"

"No. Rather, he had been. Kipping in the anteroom. I packed him off to the servants' quarters, where he'd get a decent berth."

"And he sneaked off ship, did he?"

"I imagined so. With some crowd of slackers, at Cadiz or Dieppe. A tad workshy. Got a better offer, I suppose."

"Galling for you."

"To be frank, his African manners wouldn't have gone down well here in London."

I frowned. Simpson had described the body as Caucasian.

"These natives, you know." He rubbed his nose. "I've managed better without him. I'm capable enough, and free-spirited. It was my father insisted a gentleman shouldn't travel without one."

"Your father? Was he not dead before you sailed?"

"Before, yes; but not long before. He knew Roxbury from Oxford."

"Rugby football. Great social milieu." I frowned. "Same age?"

"My father was older. His studies were interrupted, because of Waterloo. Went back later to get his degree. Home Office preferred it."

"And your father suggested trying Roxbury?"

"He wrote me several letters of introduction. But he always said Roxbury was the one. There's no one like him in the whole empire, you know. It's a privilege to be on his team. And a pleasure."

"His right-hand man, the girls call you."

His smile showed that he liked the title. "Sergeant, if that's all—"

"Not quite." With a heavy heart, I took Numpty's sketch of the African basket from my satchel. I turned it to show him. "I'm wondering if we may have found your man."

Lodestar was moved; whatever Simpson had thought, Lodestar recognised the basket. He did not go pale—his complexion was too swarthy for that—but he took up the drawing, mumbling under his breath, words I did not hear, or did not understand.

"I'm sorry?"

"Nothing." He recollected himself, blinking. "Zeph. Zephaniah. Was this—but has he…? He hasn't done something wrong, has he? Where did you find this?"

"I'm dreadfully sorry. I must inform you that he's dead." I

placed my hand on his arm. "He's buried in the police graveyard."

"What? Where?"

"Here. In London."

"No." He clutched his coffee cup. "I imagined he ended up in France somewhere."

"He was found dead, in a lifeboat."

"In a lifeboat?" He tightened his grip. "What the devil?"

I explained the circumstances, and how he had ended in an unmarked grave. "We can't rule out foul play, but he was malnourished. Tubercular."

"He was never robust."

"Is the basket something you recognise?"

"Basket? No, no, it's one of their rituals. He brought it with him in case of—in case something happened. This woven mask, it's part of the tribal funeral. So, Zeph, farewell." Lodestar placed his fingers on the drawing, then drew them to his lips. "Could you let me know where he is buried? He was not a bad fellow. I was fond of him."

DISCOVERIES [MOLLY]

WATCHMAN,
PREPARING TO PAINT.
EARWIGGING HARD.
MOLLY

Dear Miss V,

With the children away, I work at my illustrations every day, but I know my limits. Inveterate peeker that I am, I am gradually exploring parts of the house I had not found.

The second floor was receiving its autumn clean. The music room and the ballroom had lain under dustsheets through the summer. Servants folded away the sheets and set about their tasks, with resin cleansers, alpaca dusters, and contraptions depositing dirt into a bag by means of electrical charge.

I contrived to be walking past whenever doors were opened. I enjoyed seeing the decor of each room, stylishly coherent, each with differing views, each a different atmosphere, suited to different moments: a card game on a rainy morning, a stolen moment over cocktails at sunset. The servants never bothered about my inquisitiveness. After all, who doesn't want to poke their nose into the corners of such a house?

JACQUES THE THIRD [LAWLESS]

Jeffcoat spotted the third Jacques. He was standing opposite Scotland Yard, watching coppers leave, noting it all down: times, exits, lamps illuminated and extinguished. Jeffcoat walked round the block the long way, in order to come up behind him.

The fellow didn't run, but he tossed away his bag. When we got it out of the ditch, we found money, copper wire and diagrams of inexplicable arrows and dots.

Jeffcoat cuffed him first, asked his name after.

Jacques.

Ridiculous to have three suspects with the same name. Or claiming their name was the same. To distinguish them, in our minds and our notes, we denoted them: Jacques I (Jacques the First), Jacques II (Mersey Jacques), Jacques III (London Jacques).

O'Leary's advice gave us direction.

We hushed our noise about popular vigilance. We commandeered extra men to watch French activist strongholds:

de Beauvoir Town, Bethnal Green, New Cross. We asked Ripon
if we could intercept their post, but that had caused political
furore with past activists, and he blocked the idea. About their
telegram messages, however, he made no mention; it cost us
little to commandeer copies from their local offices.

I got pally with some bankers, as O'Leary suggested. They
weren't keen on sharing records, naturally enough. I seduced
them with the idea that tracking down any one single bomber
would make their bank heroic in the nation's eyes. Links
between Frenchmen and military or industrial companies;
clients who gave their name as Jacques LePeintre, Jacques
Dessinier or plain Jacques the Painter.

Our luck was turning, I was going to make sure of it.

THE THREE JACQUES [LAWLESS]

We interviewed the three Jacques separately.

Jacques the First still found it funny. Jeffcoat added a little
more information about hanging, which Ruth delivered with
relish: the type of gallows, the short drop, death by strangulation,
and the timescale before the victim loses consciousness.

He was unmoved.

Jeffcoat told him he was to be moved to the Clerkenwell
House of Detention, to be jailed with other political prisoners,
awaiting the trial.

Jacques the First, finally, stopped laughing.

Mersey Jacques was miserable. We kept him in a solitary cell.
He called himself Yatsek now, but still couldn't spell it. Try as
he might, he could add nothing to his confession.

Jacques the Third, that is London Jacques, was altogether more
intriguing. He had been caught in the act, but he wouldn't

explain what the diagrams represented, why he had wire, or who had paid him.

Jeffcoat and I were so impressed by Ruth's vitriol, we asked her to give London Jacques the same spiel: gallows, drop, strangulation.

He protested, somewhat hesitantly, then looked to Ruth to translate for him.

She stared at him, her eyes dark. "His father, he says, was a shepherd and his mother was a sheep."

"Hold on," Jacques said, half-rising. "That's not what I said."

Ruth tapped her papers tidy and stood up. "You won't be needing my translating services. As you can hear, this Jacques the Painter is not French either."

We had to make them talk. We had to convince them their situation was severe. They were our surest way to the source of the panic that was souring the country. If we could prove the French military were behind it, diplomatic measures could be taken; if it was renegades, we might isolate them, even ask the French for help identifying them and tracking them down.

I asked two journalist friends to mock up articles: sensationalist pieces on the treason act; the police catching other bombers; the rare but potent sentence for treason. The editorial opined that the government would be delighted to hang a few blasted Frogs to show they were in sympathy with the popular intolerance toward foreigners. A public witch-hunt: string up the ringleaders, and Palmerston would soar to a fresh majority.

We printed the mock articles privately. We deposited them around Clerkenwell and Holloway, for prisoners to gossip over.

One article must have been brought out by a visitor or a guard; it was reprinted verbatim in the cheaper weekend rags. After these persuasions, London Jacques believed that we had the ear of government and could exonerate him; but he still was resisting. He must have been paid so much it was worth serving time. But no payment is worth dying for.

As our fictional threat gained notoriety, Jeffcoat upped the stakes. The governor of Clerkenwell, with Ripon leaning on him, was happy to collude. On the day Jacques the First was to arrive at Clerkenwell, they would be erecting gallows in the recreation square.

ELECTRO-APPLIANCES
[THE ILLUSTRATED LONDON NEWS]

Dr Pulvermacher's apparatus has untold effects. Read for yourself in Mrs HM Barker's letter to *The Illustrated London News*: "Life-promoting restoration, efficacious, conveniently self-applicable. I may attest to being restored to health without shocks or unpleasant sensation."

Further endorsements available on request. Reliable evidence of self-applicable Electro-Generators is given in the pamphlet *Nature's Chief Restorer of Impaired Vitality*:

rheumatism, gout, neuralgia, deafness, toothache, paralysis, liver complaints, cramps, spasms, nervous debility, functional maladies

To ensure against the extortions of the quack fraternity, patients should peruse Pulvermacher's *A Sincere Voice of Warning Against Quacks &c.*
Price of Galvanic Appliance, according to electric power, from 2s and upwards.

THE ELECTRICAL ROXBURY [MOLLY]

WATCHMAN,
SEEKING SECRET CHAPEL. FRUSTRATED.
ROXBURY FASCINATING CHAP, THOUGH.
MOLLY

Miss V,
As it forms one narrative, I shall keep these sheaves for you to read when you visit.

He was of artisan stock, Roxbury told me. His shoemaker grandfather made a life comfortable enough to start his son in business. He thrived in the developing cities of the north. Roxbury had an elder brother, a rebel dreamer who went to fight in the South American revolutions, to throw off the dire Spaniards. He taught Chileans to rear sheep and Argentinians to raise cattle, sending his fortune home to his grateful family while Edward was still in his studies, before dying in a rearguard action at Montevideo.

Young Edward kept himself to himself as a child. He loved their trips to Yorkshire where the brooks and rills and burns and rivulets fascinated him, winding through dale and dell, vale and moor. To please his father, he studied to be a lawyer, but gave over all his time to experimentation.

"As a child," he said, "I loved rubbing amber on my shirt. I would watch in awe as the tiny fibres of cotton were pulled towards it. I rubbed pieces of glass smoothed by the sea upon my trousers, then held them by the window, watching the dust rise magically from the sill. Thunder scared me; lightning thrilled me. Storms remain a fascination. I spent my schooldays persuading the science teacher to show us his turbine. He was a churl, forever coiling wires during our lessons. He would turn the handle to generate current through the coil. At last, once we quit our tasks, he would amaze us by generating a spark between two electrodes. To me, this seemed godlike. Persuaded I was in earnest as a student, he gave me monographs on the subject of electricity. I was astonished to learn that my childhood games with amber replicated experiments of the Ancient Greeks. That's why William Gilbert, in 1600, chose the Greek word for amber to describe this force: elektron."

I loved the image of the earl as a troublesome pupil caring more for the properties of fluff than his studies; for I was just such a pupil in my ragged school at King's Cross, dilatory but obsessive.

"In my youth," he said, "travelling shows exhibited electrostatic influence machines. It was wonderful. Your hair standing on end. Medics made claims, as they do today, for electrical waistcoats and corsets. Electrical socks, I ask you. There may be truth in it. Our nervous system is undoubtedly electrical. Since Galvani, we scientists have sought the role of electricity in our musculature. In Yorkshire, there is an asylum for the infirm of mind and body, where Doctor Jackson treats malaises with voltaic shocks. He sends reports, and I provide him with batteries."

When his tale became strange like this, the earl would often recollect himself and clam up. It might be days before I got him to bring his thousand-and-one nights closer up to date. With the children away and winter approaching, the earl seemed ready to articulate a lifetime of thoughts. I was a willing listener. For I knew, from *Revelations of a Lady Detective*, that the pattern I sought lay hidden in such narrative threads, if only I could discern it.

"Around the house, I have cables which summon Birtle and Skirtle from their lairs, Jem to the station, and the horses to be saddled. These nerves of the household alert the sinews to action, bringing to life this remarkable body, with its rugged facade, and mysterious processes in its innards. Once they were cables, pulling flags and bells. Today, they are wires, transmitting charge, like the telegraph, working buzzers, dials and the annunciator Birtle so despises. What are nerves anyway? Galvani showed us they are electrical wires, jolting his dismembered frogs' legs as if still embodied. Such magic can electricity work, young Molly. What are thoughts? What memories? Mustn't they be patterns firing inside the brain, electric messages ignited by sound and light and feeling? And if these patterns become stuck? How, through memory and desire, do we relight them? We do not know, any more than we can predict when thunderclouds will discharge to the receptive earth."

Roxbury's electrical demonstrations caught the public imagination. His explications, spiced with self-deprecating wit, charmed audiences popular and scientific. He was elected to the Royal Society at the age of thirty-three.

His hydraulic experiments landed him a position with an industrial giant. With their capital, he developed his Roxbury machines, hydraulic cranes that sold two in the first year, twenty the second and two hundred the third. Every dockside in the world nowadays boasts several. His accumulator used a tower of water instead of a reservoir to generate force; for what is so implacable as water?

He met Miss Elodie Loth at the opera in 1842, the daughter of a brick magnate. She was entranced with the scenery: gothic towers, crags, and waterfalls. She loved the wild romance of the scene; he the hydraulic potential.

They struck a deal soon enough. A handsomer couple there never was. She was as brilliant as he. She studied, and wrote, and knew the artists of London, as well as scientists. He grew busier, establishing Roxbury Industries. They absorbed the Loth Brickworks when her father died. She campaigned for women's rights; it was thanks to her that women's education was promoted through Bedford College.

She had a son, and another, and the two girls. It pained her to be so often absent, but such was the style of grand families. They entertained in London, working their socks off, attending events to further their work. But the summer season turned Roxbury into a house as great as the mansions of the south. He was knighted in the Crimean War for rescuing the sorry British ordnance. He had never given warfare a moment's thought; to him it was an engineering problem. Just as he revelled in calculating the pounds per square inch a reservoir exerts on a crane, so he relished maximising the force of gunpowder propelling a mortar.

After the war, the report damned political vacillations and military incompetence; but it shone in its praise of Roxbury Industries. He was ennobled with an earldom.

Then the Orsini affair—where the earl's retelling of his tale became broken. Scandal and shame beset him. The French were enraged; the British parliament apologised—they were, after all, our allies now—and all government contracts with Roxbury Industries were rescinded.

Roxbury was shocked. Friends were sympathetic. No manager can keep an eye on every worker, and one renegade does not subvert a whole company. Nor was the sympathy for Louis Napoleon III strong. Yet the newspapers harped on about immigrants and cheap labour and how profitable industries must be accountable for deaths they caused, however improbably or unknowingly. (Deaths in the Crimea caused by Roxbury's shells they never complained about.) Roxbury withdrew. He and his wife spent time back here, at Roxbury House. Despite the furore, all was well with the world, the way he told it. For they fell in love all over again. Revelling in the free time, they explored the woods and hills, enjoying the glories of the natural world, and getting to know their children.

Indeed, Lady Elodie expressed the regret that they should have spent more care on their children's upbringing. But Wilfred went off the rails, got into fights, failed exams and infuriated teachers. The army scholarship was the only way to get him into Oxford; that required a tour of duty to India to quell the natives' disquiet, and thence to China.

She found herself wishing they could begin again. Do it all differently. And—

And that is where the earl lost his thread. He spoke no more. By that stage, it was time for the exeat party. By the bye, I have been seeking the secret chapel.

TOWARD THE SECRET CHAPEL [MOLLY]

It is always wise to be on friendly terms with housekeepers. Finding Skirtle in the lower drawing room, I seized my chance. "Skirtle, show me the secret chapel, won't you?"

Her eyes lingered involuntarily upon the bookcases. "A nosy ninny like you'll have no trouble finding it for yourself."

She looked over my shoulder. Nobody else was about. She closed the door quietly: the revelation was imminent. "It's from the times of the Romish persuasion, you know. When the earl bought the old ruin, Mad Wifey's, it was tiny, barely a room, but intact. In building this house, the earl decided to make something of it. It's the centre of the house, hidden, where all his systems are conjunctivised: buzzers, wires, heat pipes and all. He extended the shabby hideaway and redecorated it into a lovely little chapel, right between the two wings of the house." She gave me a look. "If you do find it, lass, don't let anyone see you go in. Or come out. We've a fair turnover of staff. Many of the servants know nothing of it. Us who are in the know, through long service, like to keep it to ourselves."

I smiled at this advice. "How will I be sure nobody is outside the door?"

"You'll see." She raised a finger aloft. "Ask the angels in heaven."

"If you don't want me to find it, Skirtle, why don't you lock it?"

"Oh, no, we'd never lock it." She was insistent. "The earl wouldn't want that."

I took from her answer the sense that, though she couldn't bring herself to admit it, part of her wanted me to find it.

I sat about, sketching, while she finished her tasks, thinking she might give the game away. But these tasks became extended, and before I knew it lunch was called and I had done nothing to the purpose.

I gave up for the day. That evening, late, I returned to the drawing room. The bookcase beckoned. Beneath a silvered glass mirror sat shelf after shelf of historical fictions. But, as for a way to get in, there was no secret door.

BAZ AND BERTIE [LAWLESS]

WATCHMAN
MARLBORO HSE.
PRONTO.
BAZ ENRAGED.
BERTIE

At least he signed it Bertie. If he were really angry, he would have signed off Albert Edward of Saxe-Coburg and Gotha, Prince of Wales, Earl of Chester et cetera, et cetera, and blast the profligate telegraphy rates if the Privy Purse was paying.

I'd left Ruth to confirm guests and arrangements for our weekend at Roxbury House, to rendezvous with Kitty and Peggy's leave-out weekends. She discussed suggestions with the earl. Molly would benefit from artistic advice, so they persuaded Edward Lear, poet and ornithological painter, to come. The photographer mathematician from Oxford would rendezvous with him at Crewe. Two of the more scandalous pre-Raphaelite painters had accepted the invitation, but Lear warned us not to count on them: Saturday mornings found these fellows in no state to travel after their Friday night debauches. Besides, one was bedding the other's wife. Ah, for the life of an artist.

"Watchman!" Bertie barely looked up from his billiards shot. "Hadn't expected you to be prompt, you recalcitrant Scot. The thing is—" He effected some ricochet and pointed at Bazalgette smugly. He proceeded to stalk around the table as if the balls were grouse on a shoot. "Thing is, Baz here would like a word about your follies. They're causing bother, only he's too polite to meddle in government business."

Sir Joseph Bazalgette, chief engineer of the London Metropolitan Board of Works, sighed. I knew him slightly, as we'd both had occasion to employ the same urchin gangs, for work undercover and work underground, while he was tirelessly reforming London's least glamorous network, its sewerage. He knew as well as I Bertie's tendency to melodramatise. Now that the prince was taking an interest in parliamentary affairs, there was no denying the justice of the causes he had espoused. For this, I respected him. He was spoilt, privileged, lazy, self-indulgent, hypocritical, adulterous and cocky; but he cared. He also felt himself a Londoner, in a way his parents never had. He might gallivant on country estates in every county of the four kingdoms, in the louchest European nightspots, but he was not blind to common suffering.

Cholera had decimated London over and over since it arrived from the orient in the thirties. Tens of thousands died of it. My mother in Edinburgh died of it. Bertie's father died of something similar: typhus or typhoid fever, or some other strain the doctors invented on his deathbed. So he was sympathetic to Bazalgette's cause: clean London, eradicate disease. When people realise that cholera is a preventable disease, Dickens wrote, you will see a shake in this kingdom worse than Samson pulling down the Temple. With this threat, and Disraeli's nose offended by the Thames, Parliament finally acceded to Bazalgette's requests a few years back. Money was granted. He was rebuilding the sewers, and finally the shadow of cholera was receding. Bazalgette had worked swiftly and decisively, his massive new sewers intercepting sewers to north and south of the river, with the country's best bricks given to this imperial cause.

Builders complained; but Parliament had spoken. Bazalgette got the bricks he wanted.

Until the Palmerston fortifications. Besides the sea defences, the ring of land forts around Portsmouth required tens of thousands of bricks each. In bygone days, bricks were made locally, using whatever local clay fired near the construction. Since the advent of trains, mass manufacture elsewhere was cheap and outperformed local bricks. Bazalgette spent an age finding waterproof bricks, which came from Portland in Dorset. Rub the brick of any Portsmouth house and it wears away, nothing more than caked sand. Rub the bricks of Fort Widley, Fort Nelson, or Fort Southwick and you will hurt your finger. Bazalgette begged extra funding to buy these superior bricks, so his sewers might serve the city for a century.

The forts mid-Solent were being built using techniques pioneered by Bazalgette on the Thames embankments. Of course, they wanted those same waterproof bricks. The parliamentary committee on cholera had secured them for the sewers. The Royal Commission had now stolen them for the forts. Given the choice between its citizens' health and blowing the hell out of Jean Le Frog, we chose war.

After three rubbers of billiards, I had somehow agreed to Bazalgette's plea: that I go and negotiate with the Solent fort engineers. Why a policeman, not an architect or engineer? Precisely because, as a policeman, I was outside the circles of engineer, contractor, builder. Nobody could accuse me of distorting evidence or taking bribes.

"Blimey." I took a shot, poorly. "Were such accusations afoot?"

Bazalgette sighed. He took out an article claiming he was in league with brick manufacturers, extorting government funds for their mutual profit:

We are told we shall die horribly, unless a billion bricks are conjured out of thin air, at the nation's expense. All this to counteract a nebulous bacterium, which chiefly threatens the feckless unemployed. They invent public works at astronomical cost, throwing London into confusion for no reason but the amusement of our "friends" across the Channel.

I read it, open-mouthed. That shameful rag, the *Satirical*, peddling lies at a penny a copy, its front page luring the reader with hints of scandals, salacious actresses' anecdotes, and politicians' waistlines insulted.

Bertie patted Bazalgette's shoulder and turned to crack the brandy. Early in the day, but we clinked a toast.

"I'm tempted to give up the sewerage." Bazalgette looked maudlin. "They did the same to Roxbury over those stupid bombs. I'll move to Buenos Aires. They appreciate engineers."

"Nonsense," said Bertie. "Nonsense."

"You know Roxbury, of course?" I asked Bazalgette. "What do you make of him?"

"Brilliant." Bazalgette sipped his cognac. "Monomaniacal. Haven't seen him in an age."

"Baz hasn't time to waste chatting, Watchman," Bertie said, "nor bargaining with military contractors. Pop down to Portsmouth, be a good chap. Look at their plans. On my royal request, demand they revaluate their brick usage. Baz has it all worked out."

"No doubt both projects are viable," said Bazalgette, "with a bit of sense."

"Solve the delays. Profit everyone. Get the job done." Bertie beamed to think of his admirable intervention. "We all win."

Neither did I have the time. Jeffcoat was moving Jacques the First from Holloway to Clerkenwell Prisons. We hoped for a confession. Then we'd act swiftly to catch these monsters. I said nothing of all that. "I'll do it, sir," I said, "as a favour to you."

"I'll owe you in spades, Watchman—" He broke off to stare: his man intruded suddenly, bowing in apology. "What is it, you damnable whig?"

"The sergeant will wish to know at once."

Bertie said, "What, dash it all?"

"Clerkenwell Prison." Where I dropped Jeffcoat not an hour ago, along with Ruth. "A bomb, sir. A fearful bomb."

BOOK V
INTO THE SECRET CHAPEL

Lives lost in shameful attack
[*Kensington Globe*, 1 November 1864]

Two explosions threw London into panic yesterday, East End and West End equally.

At Clerkenwell Prison, despite police surveillance during transfer of prisoners, a blast around three o'clock breached the wall. Windows were shattered to a radius of two miles, as far as Threadneedle Street. Confusion reigned.

The second explosion, almost immediate, threw Whitehall into consternation. The Scotland Yard inspectors had set a watch to the north-east side of the Yard, by the Criminal Investigation Department, considered a likely spot for Fenians or other activists. Two policemen were stationed outside the urinal, two reserve men within. Yet here the explosion originated.

The front of the building was blown out, up to the second floor. The constable on duty was severely injured. The broad frontage of the Rising Sun public house was wrecked. Two carriages were waiting: one was destroyed, the driver taken to hospital; the other had a wheel wrenched off and fell sideways. As the driver was blown off his box, the flying masonry would surely have killed him had not the coach by chance intervened.

The din was heard as far as Battersea Park, with the noise and the screams of those hurt dismal as they ran.

Detectives have been engaged to watch all the capital's penitentiaries in recent months. At Clerkenwell, several roughs—of the class representing Fenianism—were seen loitering in a pub on the prison's outskirts. Since a political prisoner was to be moved, attention was paid to these suspicious bystanders. The governor, informed of their presence, warned against moving the prisoner. The police resorted to a subterfuge: they gave out false information. A police entourage escorted him in a full hour before the time published.

Realising their stratagem stymied, the ruffians emerged from the pub, brandishing cues. They hurled billiard balls at a costermonger's barrow that was propped against the prison wall. The barrow tipped to reveal a barrel, doubtless stashed long in advance of the detectives' surveillance. The police sprang after them, but somehow a strange detonation lit the fuse. The ruffians decamped, just before the barrel full of gunpowder exploded.

A slice of the prison wall went down. The warders, not demoralised, strove to prevent escapes. Indignation raged, as it was learned how many lives were sacrificed. At least eight people were killed, and many inoffensive persons injured, including a tiny girl.

There was method in these murders, for the second blast followed within minutes, preventing the dispatch of officers from Scotland Yard to the first.

The explosions' perpetrators are uncertain. The *Globe* has ascertained from policing sources that leading Fenians have been recently questioned. If the republicans have struck again, they will not go unpunished. This may be the weight that tips public sympathy against independence for Ireland.

"You ain't patriots," called a local, as the ruffians dispersed. Most evaded the police, who were thrown in confusion by the blast.

More would have been killed if the prisoners were in the exercise yard, as they should normally be at that hour, though men were working in the yard, it is rumoured, on gallows for the political prisoners, a construction obliterated in the blast.

ESCAPE WITH OUR LIVES [LAWLESS]

Jeffcoat was injured. His leg. How my heart pounded. How our plans had imploded.

"Nothing serious," Jeffcoat grunted. Typical of him to pass it off; it looked nasty enough. He snorted, looking back at the destruction. "They want me to go to the infirmary."

"And Ruth?" I looked at him imploringly.

He looked back at me and gestured that he knew nothing.

Terrorism works. That's the secret no government can admit. It puts a cause into the headlines; it forces negotiations. This sparked hysteria across the capital. It was felt from Wapping to Rickmansworth; they said twenty babies in the womb were killed by the blast. Wild talk quickly spread, but a new scapegoat to blame: that attacks were planned across the city by the Fenians freed in the attack; despite all our vigilance, they were out for revenge.

Ripon, ever an opportunist, seized the chance to establish an official Secret Service Department. The government waved the money through, and the accounts would be passed at Ripon's discretion. The service would gather intelligence, warn of foreign interference, and anticipate further attacks. This department, of course, already existed—Jeffcoat and I were among its first incumbents—but now we had money and political resolve.

The *Globe*'s insinuations about Fenians were lies. We didn't deny it; it suited us to take the spotlight off the French menace.

O'Leary never forgave me. He must have been seen coming in; this reluctant collusion was punished through public opinion.

Only prisoners were killed, though guards, policemen and bystanders were injured. The line about babies in the womb was bunk. London Jacques was among the dead; Mersey Jacques was injured. Of Jacques the First, there was no sign.

Jeffcoat escaped severe injury by a hairbreadth; when we looked at the destruction to the wall beside him, it was hard to see how he had not been killed.

"If I ain't injured, then I shall go." Jeffcoat roundly cursed the nurses trying to calm him. I had never seen him so angry.

The nurse told him to bloody well sit down while she bloody well finished his bandages: his injuries might not be not life-threatening, but a pustulating sore could be.

"Well, get on with it." The exhaustion of the day swept over his features. "Watchman, I don't know what to— Give me a minute, and I'll come in with you."

I bade him lie back, and he gave in. I went searching, seeking, panicked. The wall that collapsed had been mostly moved, and everyone rescued, except for five poor souls who lay dead. On into the prison, I felt sure of our appraisal. It must be the French, trying to spring the three Jacques—or to kill them—before they could blab. Someone somewhere knew more than they ought; but was it the man dead under the rubble? Or was it Jacques the First?

My panic was rising. There was nothing to be done. I hurried back to ask Jeffcoat what happened before the blast. He thought back to the moment.

He was crossing the courtyard, Jacques the First walking

ahead, staring at the gallows. Ruth was beside him, brought along by Jeffcoat to translate for the one genuine Frenchman. What happened next, he could not recall.

"Leave the poor man alone, Campbell—I mean, Sergeant." Ruth was standing there. Just standing there unconcerned.

I threw my arms around her. She had dust in her hair and on her hands.

She was shaken, but she scoffed at my concern. "We found something among Jacques the First's possessions, as we were signing him in. Deposit slips. Bank bonds. Should have been spotted when they took him in at Holloway. I was just asking him about them, when—" As she gestured at the rubble, the enormity of the danger hit her. She tottered, and I swept her up in my arms.

THE SECRET CHAPEL [MOLLY]

WATCHMAN,
SECRET CHAPEL:
FOUND.
MOLLY

Dear Miss V,
The little chapel had become filled with wonder for me. Staring at that bookcase, searching for the abracadabra, I longed for that dreamlike escape.

I was lounging around in the lower drawing room after lunch, reading on the divan. I half-thought Skirtle might inadvertently reveal the secret door. When Patience Tarn appeared, it occurred to me: I should ask her where the chapel is, if I could make myself understood. If she was scandalised, she couldn't tell, for she cannot write.

Patience walked, with her ungainly grace, up to the

bookcase. She glanced around, more from habit than expecting to be watched; but I was still as a statue, and she didn't spot me. She reached out to the Walter Scotts on the shelf. She leaned upon them with a rhythmic sort of a sway. And she disappeared through the wall.

I blinked. I sat up. I looked, I listened.

She was gone.

I ran up to the bookcase and stared. I peered and felt and scratched and stared some more. And finally, there, imperceptible between *Marmion* and *The Bride of Lammermoor*, were the hinges.

The thing I realise about Patience Tarn is, of course, she reminds me of my little friend Pixie, sadly missed. But even more than that, she reminds me of me. Me in a different world.

I was an unwanted child—orphaned or abandoned, I shall never know. My brother said he'd tell me the whole tale when I was older, but he's gone and all.

Patience Tarn, I have the feeling, was another unwanted child, with no voice and no hearing. But here was a place she fitted in, even if she had been taken on as a kindness. Here she was loved, or at least needed.

I did not attempt to go in while Patience was there. Instead I went off about my business. Perhaps Patience was religious. Just as likely, Skirtle had her cleaning the chapel, as she couldn't give the secret away.

I popped down to the servants' quarters mid-afternoon, and asked casually if anyone had seen Patience. They'd seen her at lunchtime, they said; they only ever saw her around lunchtime, and she ate as if she were starved. I made the strange discovery that Patience didn't have a room in the servants' quarters. Where, then? I couldn't ask Skirtle; she would think me snooping.

Back in the drawing room, I watched and waited in case she was still to come out. Scouring the room, I felt a wave of affection sweep through me. All the games we'd played in this room: "When I embark on Auntie Mildred's ship"; teaching Kitty the tricks of caricature to belittle her brothers.

I stood at the bookcases. I glanced around, as Patience had done, checking that nobody—nobody—was around. As I pushed at the dead centre of the Walter Scotts, the casement gave way before me.

The chapel was a wonder. It was warm, warmer than the rest of the house. The room was still, with the occasional gurgle of heat pipes. Tiny, but perfect, a wood-panelled cabinet. Pale shafts of light entered from ingenious skylights. The pew ends bore carved animals. Here I sat, finding peace on a bare wooden pew for that stolen half hour: a welcome escape, for one not given to seeking spiritual repose. The altar a simple wooden table. Above it, no painting, no idol, just a simple wooden panel.

When I came back to my senses, I thought I'd get back. But Skirtle's warning came to me. "Don't let anyone see you go in. Or come out."

Standing at the panel where I had entered, I opened my mouth to protest: how could I be sure nobody was outside? I looked down and I looked up. Carved into the lintel were two angels. "Ask the angels," Skirtle had said. Sure enough, between them, the angels held a mirror up to a long thin window I was sure I'd never noticed on the other side; must be disguised within the bookcase.

In that distorted reflection, I could see the whole drawing room. Marvellous contrivance. I shook my head in wonder, and returned to the ebb and flow of Roxbury life.

APPLE PICKING [LAWLESS]

Watchman,
Beyond secret chapel.
Have found cache of documents.
Molly

Dear Miss V,

The apples are falling off the trees. Both the exotics in the glasshouses and the wild varieties of the orchard have had a bumper year, even here in the frozen north.

I barely mention the servants, but there's a goodly number, as you know. Skirtle tells me it's nothing compared to other great houses: Lord Derby had twenty-four just to serve him dinner. Of course, the earl reduces the load on his staff in many ways: no coal fires; lifts provided; hot water pumped round the house; hydraulic knife-sharpener, dish cauldron, dough tumbler, shoe-polisher. Still, the bustle of servants about the house is endless.

All at once, this afternoon, the house went silent. Everyone was called to the harvest. All the servants went to the orchard to pick or the glasshouse to load. The pneumatic packets save the backbreaking walk uphill, sending five hundredweight of apples up to the under pantry. There they are sorted and assigned either for the kitchen (apple pie, apple crumble, apple turnover, apple cake, apple Charlotte), the saucery (apple sauce, jam, chutneys, pickles and relishes as sweetener), or for fodder (sweetening pigs for the Christmas hams given to all on the Roxbury estate, and all in the town).

Everyone went out to the apples. Everyone except Birtle. And me. And Patience Tarn.

* * *

When everyone was called out, after lunch, I lurked around the servants' corridor, waiting to see if Patience would go. Skirtle even decided she'd pop down. "It's my only chance to nosy round the glasshouses," she said.

I made my excuses. I was behind with the lizards and must finish the chameleon. I watched from the art room window, as they all trooped down the hill. Half an hour later, I heard Patience drift through the entrance hall and into the lower drawing room. I rushed to the bannisters. I could picture her, vanishing through the bookcase. I planned to wait a little, then go in after her. It would be awkward, no doubt; and I didn't wish to scare the girl. But perhaps she could show me something I didn't know about the chapel. After all, Skirtle had mentioned it being the central point of the house.

I painted on, perhaps fifteen minutes, when I heard a servant's buzzer in the hallway. No surprise normally, except that there was nobody in the house. Back at my bannisters, I saw Birtle cross into the drawing room, taking a lamp. Descending as silently as I could, I caught the faint clunk, as he too went through Walter Scott's portal.

Well, well. Birtle pursuing Patience into the chapel. Or had she rung for him to follow?

I listened, eagle-eared, at the door. No sound of voices. But then Patience could not speak, nor hear Birtle if he spoke to her. Why would she summon him?

I stared at the bookcase, growing agitated. My mind could only conjure clandestine purposes: she might be murdering him while everyone was out. Or a lovers' tryst. I could go back to my work and think no more about it. Or I could follow my instinct. Open the door and go in, casual as you like. I would find them there, and excuse myself. Make my apology: I was simply coming for my own meditations; I had permission from Skirtle—but I would learn what they were about. I might even be the heroine of the hour.

I pushed at the hinges, thrilling at that give between the volumes. I awaited Birtle's exclamation of surprise and annoyance and Patience's mortification—

They were not there.

ANOTHER WAY [MOLLY]

There was another way out. I'd never seen Patience emerge. That was why: she simply passed through.

I scoured the little chapel's walls. It was so small, but I knew there were hidden interstices where the wires and pipes intertwined.

Devil take Birtle. I never thought he would be able to vanish under my nose.

I looked up above the altar, where most churches place the sacrificed Jesus, pained and gazing askance. I imagined him there. I considered a prayer. I'm sure he's heard a lot of rot. I pictured a priest, centuries past, hiding from his persecutors. If he needed an escape in the middle of his service, he would be at the altar. Every chapel faces east. The way out must give on to the east wing. Behind the altar table, two wooden steps led up to the panel on the wall. No handle, no hinge, but this must be it: the door through which both Patience and Birtle had vanished.

Soundlessly, I stepped up, glanced back over the pews and pushed.

I entered timidly. I was scared, I who have seen thefts, murder and derailment.

The fear of being unmasked, I suppose. When I was a street urchin and a copper clasped your arm, I thought,

"Fair cop, Watchman, I done it, and you know I done it, and what else did you expect of me?" Here, I have masqueraded as a drawing mistress of middling repute. I pictured Birtle's eyes. I could hear his triumphant tone. "Got you, you draggletailed scamp!" He thought me a thief from the start. Then I would be shamed before the earl, the lovely earl, and Skirtle who trusted me. And I'd be letting Watchman down, and you, Miss V.

Dark. Stillness. Nothing. They are not there: I would feel it. But I can smell books.

My eyes grow accustomed to the dark. A line betrays a shuttered window. Dare I open them? I haven't a lamp, though I can smell the paraffin from Birtle's. I find the catch and daylight streams in.

Books. Magazines. Papers, files, folders arranged on an old bureau. A trunk. I gaze in awe at the books, row upon row upon row. Popular novels, poetry, plays and women's literature, as they like to dismiss it, on lovely oak bookshelves: Austin, Behn, Braddon, Eliot, Gaskell, Radcliffe, Sappho and many more. The library behind the chapel.

Lady Elodie's library.

BANK DUTIES [LAWLESS]

The papers recovered from London Jacques' apartment contained nothing overtly incriminating. There were, however, bank slips: notation of bonds deposited at Overend and Gurney on his behalf. These might well lead to Jacques' master, the one paying him and the others, coordinating their plans and providing the means to do their worst.

Overend and Gurney were the prodigies of the banking world. From a parochial concern, they had exploded into prominence, exploiting the relaxation of bond regulations. Their latest bonds, backing African investments, sold out within hours of issue. The consequent clamour drew letters to newspapers about the disorderly queues. There were questions in the house.

I fought past the queues and demanded an interview. We found Jacques' account. He had indeed received bonds from an unnamed account.

I gripped the counter. "Tell me: who?"

Quite impossible.

"Don't dither. Scotland Yard requires that information with the utmost urgency."

The banker apologised, but, really, there would be no way of tracing the payment now that the bond was transferred.

He had to be ignorant, or lying. An untraceable payment, when banks made so much of their transparent bookkeeping? Perhaps he was equivocating, to protect their anonymity. "What about the teller who made the transaction? It's only a month ago. They might remember something."

The fellow obfuscated for all he was worth, rather than try to help.

"I'd like an appointment to see the head of the firm." I said. "Kindly speak to your manager. Obstructing enquiries will land him, and you, in serious bother."

He showed me out nervously, saying he would be in equal trouble if he didn't sell any more bonds by lunchtime.

OBFUSCATIONS [LAWLESS]

I retreated to Ripon. He wrote a letter, on Home Office stationery, requiring the bank to release the information in the national interest, whatever their normal practices of confidentiality.

Ripon had unwelcome news. He was telling Jeffcoat to take time off to recover from his injury. Jeffcoat had flown off the handle when he told him. No wonder. He was raging about it all: the blasts, Jacques who was dead, and Jacques who'd escaped, our impotence in catching them.

"I'm sending him to New York," said Ripon. "Tidy up loose ends in the Muller case." Muller had committed murder on the Metropolitan Line; he then fled to New York, only to be apprehended as he stepped off his ship.

I stared. "Surely someone else can go. He's in no fit state."

"Jeffcoat will benefit from a little jolly." Ripon looked at me. "Make him sit around for a week. The Muller paperwork will make him feel useful. Another week at sea should calm him down, before the bugger's back at work."

I felt disgusted with Ripon's intrusion, when we had suffered so much and were so near a breakthrough. But by the time I'd reached the Yard, I knew it was the right thing. Jeffcoat was resignedly packing; he was quietly furious, but that only proved Ripon's point.

Ripon's letter in hand, I rubbed my hands at the prospect of slicing aside the bank's bureaucracy. I arrived the next morning to find the queue around the block. I nearly got myself lynched, fighting my way past the queue.

The manager was unavailable; he was off sick, due to acute strain of work. Off, for tiredness? A likely story. Is that how people behave in private companies?

The under-manager politely looked up the file. He worked out who the teller must have been, but warned that they were unlikely to remember any transaction from a month ago, considering how many they processed.

He was right. The teller shook their head. As they looked in the file relating to the account, I saw an envelope peeking out with an insignia on it:

"What's that?" I exclaimed in disgust. "That envelope you're hiding: is that where the payment originated?"

Yes, but then payments were often made through gentlemen's clubs, with valets sent to make deposits. Besides, young Mr Overend was a member of the Hounds Club, so it could equally have been given to him to drop in on someone else's behalf.

The bank enquiry would get me no further.

THE LIBRARY BEHIND THE CHAPEL [MOLLY]

I determined not to linger. Birtle might return any moment. Yet sometimes butlers have roundabout routes, to keep out of the way. Yes, he had gone on. Somewhere here, there was a door. The door that led to another part of the house. Here.

I had done a little homework, sketching up a plan of the building. I viewed it from the rockery in front; I viewed it from the crag behind. In sketching the ground floor plan, I realised that the chapel lies central in the house, just alongside Birtle's pantry with Skirtle's rooms above. From their vantage points, Birtle and Skirtle may spring out, anywhere around the house, resolving troubles. Ingenious design. This door must give on to the whole series of rooms out on the east wing, the part of the house I had never seen. Ever so softly, I tried the handle.

Locked.

No! Skirtle said they never locked the doors: the earl wouldn't want that. But this door wouldn't budge. If not locked, then blocked somehow. Rather than simply go back through the door by which I had entered, I might as well explore. I did what you would have done.

I sat at the bureau. I opened a file.

Lists, diagnoses, prescriptions. Handwritten, printed, and torn from magazines. Advertisements. Contraptions. Medicines. Diets. Scientific papers.

I lost track of time, captivated, leafing through page after page of mysterious notes. By the time I rubbed my eyes and remembered where I was, time had passed. One hour, several hours: I had no idea. It was getting dark. If I could not go on, I must go back through the secret chapel. I looked for the door I had come in by.

I could not see it.

There was no handle anywhere. There was no sign of a frame. In the dark, when I entered, I hadn't noticed where I'd come in.

I scoured the panels. I felt a fool for getting myself into a situation I could not get out of. I pushed at the borders. I found an edge. That must be it: a minuscule gap between the panel and the floor. I tried to claw it apart. No way to prise it open.

I was rattled. What could I do? There was nothing else: I went back to leafing through the documents in the gathering gloom.

THE EAST WING [MOLLY]

"What in God's name do you think you are doing?" Skirtle appeared in the middle of the wall adjacent to the panel I'd clawed around.

I snapped shut the file I'd been peeking at. Our mutual astonishment was such that she didn't register the way I had passed the time, trapped in this forgotten library.

"I been worried sick over you. You're not in your room. You haven't done your work. I thought you'd fallen down the gorge and drownded yourself."

"Drown myself? No fear." I gestured unconvincingly. "I found my way in. Couldn't find my way back out."

"The house has been up to high doh about you."

"Go where you please, you said. Nobody's stopping you."

She grabbed me and pulled me back out into the chapel. "I made some excuse. It was Birtle who thought to look here."

"Birtle?" I was alarmed. "Why? Was he afraid I would discover your secret?"

"Whatever do you mean by that?"

I had spent the lonely hours in a kind of trance. Now I asked myself what this meant about the house. Patience came through these secret doorways. Birtle passed through. He did not pause. He went straight on, as if to business. What business so important should he have in the east wing which I had always been told was shut?

The curtain twitching on my first arrival. Someone peeking from the turret window. I pictured a wild face, a fixed gaze. But in the dark library, I knew my imagination was coming alive, fired up by such strange lists of medicines, prescriptions and doctors.

Nonsense, really. I had been reading too many wild romances. Although I hadn't been dreaming that first day. Here, in the forgotten library behind the chapel I began to wonder: how much of the inner life of Roxbury House has remained hidden from me?

"Skirtle. Wait." My mind was racing, over and over the things that didn't make sense. You noticed that Skirtle and

Birtle were inattentive to the running of the house. As if they had some other agenda. Other duties. In a part of the house that remained closed to the rest of us. "Tell me. Birtle's in the east wing, isn't he? Patience Tarn too."

She shooed me out, back through the chapel and out into the drawing room. After my inadvertent incarceration, it seemed a vast acreage.

I breathed, and breathed again, feeling the oppression of that inner room fading, but also its magic. I began to doubt my convictions. "Come, now, Skirtle, we're friends. Don't equivocate."

"I'll excavate you, body and soul, if you don't get out of it." She dusted me back into the hallway, towards Birtle's quarters. "Hush, and move, young miss."

At the door of Birtle's rooms, I stood my ground. "There's someone in the east wing."

"He'll just be getting it ready." She hesitated. "For the visitors."

"You don't put visitors there. Not for years. I've read the guest book. It was Lady Elodie's rooms. I've seen her books. Don't—"

"Hush." Skirtle clapped her hand over my mouth. She spoke, rapidly, with a gravity I'd never seen in her before. "Are you hushed?" She took her hand away, glancing about to see that none of the servants were about to hear my querulous chatter, but of course none of the servants came here but Patience. "You'd better come and talk to Birtle."

PRYING AND SECRETS [LAWLESS]

We all fear we'll be found out. It's inevitable: however able and qualified we are, we await discovery. I certainly do.

The public expects detectives to have superhuman powers, as they do in the penny dreadfuls. If they guessed how many crimes, dire and murderous, go unpunished in the morass of humanity that is London today, they would stage a revolution.

Bertie, the Prince of Wales, fears it. His father filled him with a sense of inadequacy. He always feels second-rate, though he charms the whole of Europe, rich and poor, into loving him. Even his dear mama, the queen, felt foolish beside that self-important intellect.

No doubt even Roxbury feels out of his depth sometimes.

BIRTLE'S RECOLLECTIONS [MOLLY]

Once inside Birtle's pantry, Skirtle thrust me so firmly into the chair that I was stuck like a plum in a pudding. She thought of locking the door, I believe, but her injunction to stay put was enough. I had no wish to be thrown out. With you, Miss Ruth, and the visitors due in a few days, I would kick myself if I put another foot wrong. I was just beginning to unfurl the mystery within the doors of Roxbury House.

Skirtle tugged a lever, sounding out a faraway buzzer in a peculiar rhythm, to summon Birtle back. Satisfied by an answering buzz, she turned tail and stormed out.

What kind of a talking to would I get? Skirtle's reaction to my explorations was strong enough. How great would be Birtle's wrath? He disliked me enough. Mightn't this be the pretext he'd been looking for to turn the earl against me?

I was seized with the strangest fear. They're going to do away with me, I thought. My heart began pounding. That's why the servants change so frequently, and the scientists. If anyone gets a sniff of their methodology, they're done for. They're a double act. They're going to do me in. That's why Skirtle has vacated, because she's fond of me and can't bear to watch him do it.

Opposite the door, behind Birtle's desk, was a closet. Only now, as it creaked open, did I realise it was not a closet after all. It was the butler's escape: a passage into the east wing, access to rooms, staircase and towers without all the faffing around at the Walter Scotts. Birtle could go there; doubtless Skirtle, from her rooms, had the same access.

Birtle ambled in, dishevelled, expecting to see Skirtle, no doubt. He shut the door carefully behind him, with not a trace of his customary ill humour, and turned to me.

"Christ Jesus on an omnibus." He leapt like a startled goat. My fears subsided, for he seemed quite afraid of me. "Who brought you in here? Don't tell me. Skirtle, wasn't it? Without my say-so."

The bell must have told him she was calling. Blimey, how I wanted to flee. But where? I could not stop Skirtle reporting my snooping. Nor could I unsee the books and the files and all her Ladyship's accoutrements. What he was going to say I could not imagine. As little as he could, surely. I would be dismissed. Reduced ignominiously to my former standing, all these efforts at ladylike tutorship cast into the dustheap. I would be warned against blabbing on pain of incarceration or transportation or worse.

Birtle collected himself. He sat steadily down opposite me, as he had that first morning, but no trace of disdain. "Oh, Molly." He had never before said my name so warmly. He looked at me steadily and swept stray locks of hair from his brow. "For such an inquisitive soul, it's a wonder to us, to Skirtle and to me, that you haven't stuck your nose into the east wing before."

"You told me not to."

"We didn't think you'd obey us."

"You told me it was closed up."

"It is." He hesitated. "Mostly."

I sat forward. "Closed up, with someone inside?"

He sighed. "You have heard, from the earl, no doubt, the story of his marriage."

I gulped. "Up to a point."

Birtle started his story at the point that Roxy and Lady Elodie retreated, stung by the government's betrayal, after he saved the day in the Crimea. "That showed him what politicians are: creatures of popularity, not sense. Like dogs, they come when their master calls them, panting to do his bidding, however stupid. Like dogs, they hang their heads when told off, for a moment. Any attempt to reason with them will fail, for their desire to please is not intelligence, but loyalty and need. The earl washed his hands of Parliament and retreated to this pleasure dome of Roxbury House. Here we are."

He buzzed a familiar pattern, and we waited in silence.

"That much you already know." Birtle took a tin from his desk. He tugged it open. It was not a gun; it was not my contract to be ripped up. It was biscuits. A moment later, the tea arrived via the dumb waiter. "Let me venture beyond."

Lady Roxbury, on her husband's withdrawal, was faced with a choice. She could persist in her London adventures, supporting women's education and charitable foundations and scientific lectures, or she could retreat with him. For many marriages, aristocratic ones most of all, such moments break the pledge of faith; the marriage was but a brief season of warmth now stilled to coldness.

But Lady Elodie loved the earl; and the earl loved her. Retreating to this frosty paradise, they came to a new understanding. Were there challenges enough to occupy them? Why, certainly, with his experiments and her gardens, with her books and his glasshouses, with visitors from the cultural world and the disposition to enjoy the haven they had created. And they fell deeper in love, all over again.

They had been a fine couple back in their twenties, well-matched and engaging. Now, either side of forty, they had business and public service behind them. The children were off to boarding school. So began their fresh romance. The earl and his Lady Elodie walked through the woods, by the gorge, around the reservoirs. He told her of his dreams: to harness the water's inner force; to master electricity.

On her side, it was no indulgence to share his fascination, for she was one of the first women inducted into the Royal Society. She kept her garden and her roses; she kept reading and studying. The earl put into place his wires and pipes and communication networks: buzzers, telegraph, and pneumatic rail down to the glasshouses, and cables to the Pump House, where the water's tumult was channelled into power.

The west wing comprised the usual drawing rooms and galleries, with gaming room, billiard room and children's quarters to appeal to everyday visitors. Roxbury established his magician's lair in the central tower. Skirtle, meanwhile, oversaw Lady Roxbury's development of the east wing into a palatial retreat for artists and like-minded thinkers, to stimulate mind and body with a visit to this palace of the North, walking in arboretum and menagerie, musing by the Burnfoot Gorge and reflecting at Thimbleton Reservoir. Lady Elodie's idea included these magical portals that connected east with west wing: through the Lady's Library and through the chapel, for the literary and philosophic of mind; through housekeeper and butler's quarters; and through Roxy's magic tower. She thought it hilarious that the ladies' library be secret, a comment on how women have long been discouraged from reading.

I'm kicking myself to hear there were other ways in, though it would have been hard to find them. There had been more ways too, each with an illusory door or a secret mirrored entrance, through the servants' quarters and kitchens and Turkish baths—but the earl had them closed up during the recent renovations, a kind of admission that the dream was over.

Where did it go wrong?

Lady Elodie had one regret, one forgotten dream, which she voiced to the earl. That she had not brought up her own children. They had handed them to Skirtle and the nannies for their upbringing.

One might suppose an aristocratic lady has no real idea of the travails of motherhood, but Lady Elodie worked to reform workhouses. She set up charities to help struggling parents keep their children. She read the research: socio-medical scholars pointed to loss of parents as by far the greatest factor in the capital's deadly cycle of homelessness, alcoholism, violence and criminality. She befriended the reformers, the journalist, Mayhew, and the doctor, Acton. She walked the streets with the Red Lion Society. Even mothers debased by drink and driven mad by opium wailed to see their children taken from them. And yet the aristocracy cannot wait to pack their little ones off and out of their hair; and the middle classes fight for the pennies to afford the same strange separation. Why, she asked herself, why had she given birth four times only to yield the privilege of motherhood to servants? Couldn't she have done it differently? Could she yet? She was advancing in her thirties, but it was not too late.

They were not blessed with another child. A year went

by. She became concerned. The anxiety began to chip at their idyll. The earl was understanding, but after a while began to feel his patience strained. They had so much; they were so blessed. Could this one lack taint all? Her Ladyship grew fixated on the idea.

Her eldest Wilfred had suffered from her absence, she saw it now. Wasn't this the reason he was such a thoroughly disagreeable child? Antagonistic to adults, distrusted by teachers, and unpopular with schoolmates, he derailed his academic studies with perverse behaviours. It took strenuous string-pulling to secure him a university place.

The next three? She knew them a little better, and they had each other for company, but their joke of being Norphans made her wildly sad, silly though it was. Why not another? Why not a chance to redeem their errors?

Lady Elodie prevailed upon the earl to have her checked by prominent medics. Thus began the procession of experts through the household: gynaecologists, obstetricians, impregnation experts, antenatal surgeons. These doctors said there was no reason. They must just accept it. She might have reluctant follicles, she might have ovarian cysts, or uterine debility. There was nothing to rectify it; and nothing could be worse for her than worry. She should simply accept it.

She did not accept it.

They toured the clinics of London. On and on into the more diverse reaches of the medical world.

Acupuncturists gave Indian head massages; alienists assessed her psyche blocked by previous births; phrenologists pronounced her occipital lobes incompatible with childbirth (though she had proved them wrong four times over). Homoeopathists prescribed poisons to provoke her uterus; naturalists prescribed rainwater filtered through pumice

(4s 6d a flagon); ramblers advised ten-league walks. She visited nutritionists, dietitians, philanthropists, philologists, vegetarians, temperancers, tea-drinkers, druggists, pharmacopoeists and every type of quack upon the earth.

Scientific Roxbury accepted all this with no more resistance than a pained expression. He wanted her happy; she could not be happy without another child in her arms. All failed. He took advice with a doctor friend. Why not adopt a child?

Roxbury was persuaded of the good sense of this solution; Lady Elodie accepted it. She travelled the length and breadth of the country, visiting orphanages. She could not bring herself to choose one over all the others: unfair that one should be selected from the thousands to receive not only the privileges, but the love she longed to bestow, while the others stayed behind, unloved.

She decided to adopt two. That was the only way to lessen her angst. She was agonising whether it was right to keep their names or to change them, when she fell pregnant.

THE LADY IN THE TURRET [MOLLY]

"Pregnant?" My breath went short. I stood up, so taken up was I with the romance of the story as Birtle told me it. I stared at him, puzzled how he could fail to share my joy in the news. Except it was not news. Or rather it was old news, and any rejoicing long over. For where was the fifth child? Where was Lady Elodie? "It didn't…" I didn't like to say it. "The child…"

"The child died. Yes." Birtle glanced down. In that glance, I saw that everything I had thought of him was false: I had thought that he was unfeeling, that he cared little for the Roxburys and less for their children. All of that was damnably wrong. I do not believe he could have been more distraught had it been his own child. "And her ladyship. Her ladyship fell ill."

A tender tap at his door. Skirtle entered, with familiar ease, before he answered. She gauged with a glance how our conversation had gone. I had been so sure these two couldn't stand each other. And here they were, in cahoots over these secrets.

"I was just mentioning," Birtle looked at Skirtle, "how her ladyship took ill."

"Oh, she did. After the bairn? Oh, ill something terrible."

"And to explain all our comings and goings?" Birtle wafted his hand towards the hidden door, gesturing to all the secrets tied therein. "Her sister."

"Oh. Yes." Skirtle turned to me, wide-eyed. "Her sister!"

"Her sister came up." Birtle elaborated. "From Dorset. To look after her. Seeing as how her ladyship was poorly, in body and mind. And his Lordship..."

"The state he was in." Skirtle rescued him. "And decisions about her safety, which only he should be making, but were left to us, so as—"

"Her sister," Birtle prompted. "Her sister was the one we called upon to help."

"Not with nursing duties, mind. We were fit for that. But there were things we couldn't decide. It takes an educated person, to deal with the 'pothecaries."

"Pharmacological decisions."

"Like I said." Skirtle glared at him. "Them potionaries, all for giving her this, and herbalisationists for that. Then the brain doctor—"

"Neurologist."

"He's warning of this. The mesmerist is claiming that. The alienist is prescribing the other. Oh!" She threw up her hands, as if to give up mid juggle and let the clubs fall on her head. "Terrible, it was."

"Then she was gone, and the sister fell poorly—"

Skirtle scowled at his interrupting, then light dawned, as she remembered their sham. "Oh, the sister!"

"Skirtle." I looked from one to the other. "Birtle. Please. There is no sister, is there?"

"No, Moll." Skirtle reached over and patted Birtle's arm tenderly. She saw that he had grown melancholy in the telling, and took it upon herself to ease his. "Her ladyship was took terrible poorly. When the boy was taken. Proper poorly. Body and mind." Skirtle blinked, and I saw how utterly devoted she was to the unlucky couple; she maintained her decorum long enough to give me this account, pointing emphatically at Birtle's secret door. "And there she is, in her tower, still today, and cannot be cured."

I sat silent, my lips working soundlessly, but unable to reply. What I wouldn't have given to be there, just a few years ago, to see the glorious summer of the marriage, before this blight ended it so precipitously. I confess, after Birtle's tale of romance and its expectations of happiness, I felt these losses—the death, and her illness—as if they were my friends and not phantasmal memories. I felt I did know her ladyship: I knew her gardens, her roses; I knew her husband's gentle manner, and her children who were no doubt like her, the girls with their plump cheeks and wicked smiles.

What need for Birtle's pretending? A tale to tell inquisitive servants, I suppose. Bad enough that she should be incurable; but to have people prying and judging and giving advice, worse. If the earl had decided, rather than suffer the world's sympathy, he would pretend she is dead, then let him.

But I had divined the sadder truth. "Is she very ill?"

"Terribly ill," said Skirtle.

Birtle sighed. "Not so ill."

"Bedridden, mostly."

He glared. "Not at death's door."

"And Patience Tarn," I said, "is employed to tend her."

"She is." Skirtle nodded. "And discreet. Though our time gets taken up, when we should be keeping the house. Patience has to buzz for help, for my lady has fits." She put her hands on her hips. "If you've been thinking us negligenting our duties."

"I haven't. Not for a moment." Exactly what you had noticed, Miss Ruth, and now it was explained. "Can she walk? Do you never take her out? Why shut her away from the world?"

"Molly," said Skirtle, her eyes soft. She seemed relieved their confession was made. "She lies abed, mostly, as if sleeping, but deeper than sleep. Patience has the devil of a time to get her to take water. She washes her. Rubs her limbs, to keep them strong. But every so often, she does awake, or seem to. She wakes, and straightaway takes a kind of a fit. That's when we have to be ready, lest we should lose her."

"And the doctors—"

"Oh, pet, you should have seen the doctors the earl tried. After the frauds and quacksalvers we'd had to get her pregnant. That's why we manage without them. I was sick of them. The earl was sick of them, and blaming hisself, poor man. As if it were his fault."

"But the fits?"

"We can stop them, though." Skirtle looked glum. "You'll see. She comes around, finally."

"But she won't speak. Won't move." Birtle bit his lip. "Not of her own volition."

"Until you take her to the window." Skirtle beamed. "When she looks down over the roses and the trees and the Walled Garden, sometimes she is calmed." She glanced at Birtle. "Sometimes calmed, sometimes driven wild."

He looked at me. "Then Patience feeds her. You can imagine, she is wasting away."

"Can she never be cured? Must you tend her forever? Shouldn't you send her away?"

"Oh, look at you, dear girl." Skirtle ruffled my hair, which I hated. "Full of concern for folk you know nothing of."

"I live with their shadow." I recalled the guest book, in which Ruth had noted so many medics and scientists. I had read, in the Lady's Library, prescriptions and doctors' reports, analyses and diagnoses. Even the earl's experiments—were they part of her treatment? A search for new treatments? All Roxbury's riches could not save his little child, nor cure his wife. "And the child's grave is hereabouts, I suppose?"

Skirtle nodded. "The Walled Garden."

Birtle gave her a stare.

Though I'd found my way in when fleeing from Wilfred, I had resolved not to trespass upon the family griefs. Now I threw out that resolution, and resolved instead that I ought to, out of respect to the dead, much as I hate graveyards.

LIES AND EXAGGERATIONS, PART THE FOURTH [LAWLESS]

Why didn't Molly explore the Walled Garden sooner?

Molly never liked cemeteries. Many folk willingly stroll through graveyards. Not Moll. She never had relatives to visit, neither grandparents, nor parents. Too many of her friends ended up there. She has lived through London's worst cholera years. Through the fifties and sixties, 30,000 died of it. She was determined not to be one of them.

She did go, in the end, with Ruth, and find just the one grave.

Why didn't Molly unearth the sad story of the dead child sooner, and of the wife?

Molly had no interest in history, outside of Shakespeare plays. I'd given her no direction to concern herself with delving into family history. Puzzled enough by the present, she was unconcerned with the past. Roxbury's household personnel were either sworn to secrecy or newly employed.

Yet she did hint of it, in despatches, and I did not notice, amid the mountain of information. The family's personal secrets didn't seem relevant to me. Molly kept quietly at her researches, until Ruth visited and told me how much she had learnt.

SKITTLES IN PARIS [LAWLESS]

"Louis has some odd notions." Skittles' eyes widened at the recollection.

I called in to Bertie's pad, Marlborough House, to hear her report.

She seemed to think it the most natural thing to pass on information about the French. Her report of the emperor was worth more than any diplomat's: she not only knew more powerful men, but they had no reason to lie to her. "Many odd notions, true, but he's not a fruitcake. He loves old Blighty as much as you and I. More than you, you Scots interloper."

Good deeds come back to haunt you. On her first arrival in London, some five years ago, I helped young Catherine Walters, before she gained fame as Skittles, or Anonyma, viz popular publications *Anonyma: or, Fair but Frail*, *The Pretty Horsebreakers*, and *Skittles in Paris*. Her meteoric rise, bar a few hiccoughs, had seen her bed dukes, ministers and royalty, allegedly.

As thanks for my introducing her to the Prince of Wales, back when he was young and wayward, she had given evidence in my last case. She risked disgrace and recriminations to clinch those convictions; and I loved her for her wild passions and honest scorn.

"You see?" Bertie looked up from the card table. It was he had introduced her to Louis Napoleon III of France. "Louis loves Blighty."

"You keep out of this," said I. "You're contaminating the evidence."

"Calling me contaminated, Sergeant?" Skittles raised an eyebrow. "Some girls would take that amiss."

"Come off it, Skittles." I shook my head. "Leave the prince to his gaming. Tell me more on a stroll through the gardens."

Skittles, freed from Bertie's earwigging, talked more of Paris. "They've noted the English outrage at these explosions.

They feel righteous, as we have long sneered at continental volatility. Oh, their assassinations! Oh, their Orsini bombs! Maybe this will make us hold our tongues."

"And are these outrages not perpetrated by the French?"

She turned to me wrinkling her nose. Really, she grew more handsome with each passing year. If her time in Paris had taught her anything, it was a gorgeous restraint: her make-up, her crimson jacket, the rose delicately woven into the hair. "Louis is rather put out that we impute such underhand tricks to him." She imitated his outraged squeak. "'And against our friends— England? Against Austria, maybe. But against the house of dear old Bertie? No, no, no.' He also said we must think him a bloody moron." She smiled. "Would he alert us to the plan by exploding every dockyard, if he was planning an invasion?"

"Invasion? Did he mention that?"

"No invasions, silly. Though Louis said he wouldn't put it past Le Mouchard of the Sûreté to suggest they are plotting, simply to waste English time and money."

I stopped dead. What if the whole Portsmouth Plan was an elaborate charade, to ignite panic in our heads? Skittles was not an agent, not officially, not unofficially, but her chitchat with powerful men was more reliable than any spy's. "Skittles, you are a wonder."

"What do you want now? You only compliment me when you want something, Watchman."

I laughed. We were back at Skittles' pad in Kensington. "Your pillow talk is worth a hundred spies. This Le Mouchard you speak of: any chance of information straight from the horse's mouth?"

"Horse's mouth is right, if you've seen him." She made a face. "For queen and country, I may be able to help. Thought you'd want to know more. I've already pencilled him in for next week."

* * *

TRUNK OF LOST DREAMS [MOLLY]

Dear Miss V,

Last night I slept ill. The wildness of the woods ventures up to the house. I retraced my time here, moments when Birtle and Skirtle absented themselves or were called away. I thought of meals prepared on trays for I knew not whom. I had ascribed it to the scientists; no better place to hide one secret than among many.

I crept from my bed. As I stood gazing, a light stirred in the turret of the east wing.

A shape. A figure at the window. She worried at her hair, swaying. Someone reached around to draw the curtain closed. Lit from behind, her face could not be seen. And then—what?—was she pulling at the window? To open it?

The person behind was trying to restrain her, but they were not quick enough. She had it unhasped; she reached outside. Oh, what a yearning was in that reach. If the window were wide enough, if she had the strength to squeeze through and fly down, she would. But where? What lies down there, amid the wild rockery?

She was calmed, and pulled back inside. Patience Tarn, always vigilant. I saw no more.

In the Lady's Library, a small notebook in the earl's handwriting, tucked in among the memorabilia hidden inside this trunk of lost dreams.

I thumbed through the assessments and diagnoses, doctor's reports, their prescriptions and proscriptions:

Extract of nutmeg root, taken four times daily in the week before the menstrual courses, shall ensure the implantation of the fertilised egg. Supplement, if you will, with applications of witch-hazel gel, unadulterated by soaps or lathers of any kind.

And a price list. It was not all such nonsense. There were appraisals from bona fide medics too, but their tenor was much bleaker. I could understand why the hapless couple looked for encouragement elsewhere.

I have stolen away as often as I can to the Lady's Library behind the chapel. The door Birtle had gone through remained blocked, but I still harboured hopes of finding my way through into the forbidden east wing.

I did not wish to be derelict of my duties. Watchman requires that Roxbury Industries remain hale and patriotic. My job was to discover how the earl was faring now.

I had the explanation for the earl's despondency. He could not let go. I could make a case, aside from general nosiness, for delving into the papers hidden here. Birtle's evasions concealed a sadder truth. Why keep Lady Elodie hidden? It was a continual reminder of their loss: his double loss. Why not send her for treatment elsewhere?

How I longed to discover something to redeem them. I could not find her diaries, though I learned that she did keep one. For I have found his, and I have taken his own words as permission to read them. You will see, from the sections I've transcribed, that the earl was seeking a confidante.

DIARIES [ROXBURY]

Dare I read it? [wrote the earl, soon after her illness began]
Her diary. Pages upon pages upon pages of Elodie's notes unread, of her dreams and fears and plans.
Dare I read even one page? Dangers await: where none before

has read, there can be no security. She may have said she hates me, or wishes we had never married. I would not believe it, not really, yet she may have written anything, in a moment of spite.

She may have written nonsense to make me doubt her sanity. She was always strange. Those last torturous weeks twisted our souls.

What if she writes of lives I never knew, of other loves, in the distant past? Will these slings fell me, unsteady as I am? The servants think I am unhinged already; the estate count me unfeeling; my family think me restless and indolent. But I am frayed; and tugging on the loose threads will unravel me.

I shall ask someone else to read—the children? Not fair. Nor Birtle, nor Skirtle, nor Lodestar. It must be someone discreet, but less tied to our world. Someone to trust with all our secret sorrows, who cannot be slain by them.

My own diary is an assemblage of fripperies:

What must I do today?

Payments to chase?

Whom to chastise? Whom to congratulate, on the estate, or in the business?

Engagements planned? Can they be cancelled? How will I get through to evening? This was not my style of old, but only since I lost my darling. My darling, Elodie.

These, her diaries, are so full of heart-wrung thoughts. Have I ever written thus? Not even as a student, when we all wished to be Byron, a wastrel, or Keats, consumptive, or Shelley, brilliant and doomed. My verses were full of posture concerning the barmaid at the Wheatsheaf; a feigned obsession, for in fact I dreamed of my tutor's wife. My own true thoughts I never write.

Yet here are Elodie's. I shall not read them now, while grief is sharp. There glimmers through these dungeon bars a ray of light: that I may spend the weary hours of my life reading her thoughts, and I will feel her still with me, feel her absence less keenly.

DARING TO READ [MOLLY]

"Dare I read a page?" he wrote. Who should he ask? Someone discreet, to trust with their sorrows. Thus wrote the earl.

I took it as an invitation. I searched for Elodie's diary. It was not in the trunk of lost dreams. There were toys for the child, little shoes, muslins, and the aroma of years gone by. But for now, I could not find it.

I escaped back through the secret chapel. There was no time. The visitors were upon us. I, for my part in persuading the earl to receive them, must play my role in entertaining them and making sure the days went smooth and brightly.

I will spend the weekend in an agony of waiting to get back to the trunk of lost dreams.

BOOK VI
SHINING HOURS

THREE SOURCES OF ENERGY [ROXBURY]

From a speech delivered to the Literary and Philosophical Society of Newcastle-upon-Tyne:

> We have first the direct heating of the sun's rays, which we have not yet succeeded in applying to motive purposes. Secondly, we have water power, wind power, and tidal power, depending upon influences lying outside of our planet. And, thirdly, we have chemical attraction or affinity, in the preserved sunbeams stored up under our feet as coal. Beyond these, there is nothing worth naming.

EXEAT PARTY [RUTH]

Dearest Campbell,

P IS FOR PARROT

WHO ALWAYS TALKS BACK.

Mr Lear sketched the bird, as he extemporised a rhyming alphabet for Kitty at the breakfast table. He spotted Skirtle hovering near, and looked in horror beneath his drawing.

"Mrs Skirtle, my dear, have I marked your lovely

tablecloth? Alack! I shall take it down to the river and scrub it, and do penance working in the fields while it dries, before ironing it flat and replacing it in time for dinner. Will you thus forgive me?"

Skirtle blushed and flapped her hands before her cheeks in rebuttal of his stupidities. She used to read poems from his *Book of Nonsense* to Kitty at bedtime. The two of them were in awe of having a poet here at Roxbury House— albeit a nonsensical poet.

Kitty giggled. She poked him to go on to Q.

Q is for Quigley

A duck who says Quack.

Roxbury absently dabbed his mouth with his handkerchief. He had welcomed us warmly the evening before, but his mind was on something else. "Feed the body," he said, as if checking off a list to himself. "Now feed the mind." With that, he disappeared down to the glasshouses, and we saw nothing of him till dinner.

I engaged Dodgson in conversation, but he was watching Lear and Kitty with an envious fascination. Molly and I were cast on to each other's company. On my earlier visit, we dissembled that we were not so well acquainted. Now we gave vent to our frivolous side. I quipped about her work ethic, breaking her fast so late.

She retorted by abusing my thinness of face. "Are you determined to marry in a restraining corset? I hear they only asphyxiate a few ladies per year."

Such candour, regarding undergarments, discomfited the reverend. Had I erred in securing an invite for an Oxford mathematician? He was recommended by the dean of Christchurch as a good egg, a photographer and popular with children. He chaperoned Kitty up, meeting her on her train at High Wycombe. When Birtle brought the papers, Dodgson pounced upon *The Times* as if it was a life jacket, turning straight to the chess page.

"Mister Wilfred," announced Birtle, "has cabled."

Beside me, Molly stiffened.

"He will not be joining us for the weekend, due to unforeseen... engagements."

Just as well. From that moment, Molly recovered her usual ebullience. Nico and Peggy were too busy to return—school debates, school sports.

The party assembled had no proclivity for hunting or riding or shooting or boozing, so we went about our respective business. Molly took Mr Lear down to the menagerie for instruction in the complex art of illustrating birds. Lear hugely enjoyed seeing his painting case sent down the pneumatical railway.

Kitty and I tagged along. The talk was technical and the parrots impassive. Molly, I realised, was not bluffing: she was an artist; and she was an art teacher. (She did not know that the children had gone to their father to ask him to re-engage her for future holidays.) When I thought of the snub-nosed smudge of a girl I'd met through Campbell's work underground, I was filled with pride. She was grown up: grown-up enough for Wilfred to take an interest in her.

"Who," asked Lear pleasantly, "is to hold the bird for us? Yes, indeed. How else to study the intricate colourings and feathers?"

Molly was flabbergasted and delighted. "The earl was all for having it strung up."

"The old-fashioned way." Lear opened his case and set out his palette. "Not necessary. Not necessary at all."

"It is as if," said I, "you are setting out on one of your painting tours."

He smiled. "I have painted from Jeddah to Jaipur, you know. Though I've made my name and money from oil paintings, I enjoy the sketching tours ten times more. Ah, the pleasures of friendships on those reckless jaunts."

A thought struck me. "Have you been to Mozambique?" I asked.

"In Africa, no further than the pyramids."

Molly looked at me quizzically.

"I just wondered if Mr Lear might know Lodestar."

"Certainly. I knew him before his African days. Last saw him in Alexandria."

I frowned. "Lodestar Senior, you mean, of course. The diplomat."

"Diplomat! I like that. Old Chichester Lodestar was about as diplomatic as a rhinoceros. But that is how the Home Office likes 'em in the equatorial regions. Vindictive and intransigent."

"How highly you think of your friend."

Lear blanched. "I hope I have not misspoken. He was an old goat. The wife suffered most, I suppose. They had a little boy: Chesty they called him."

Molly paused in setting up the easels. "That must be our Lodestar."

"Likely," said Lear unconcerned. "I've been away."

I nodded. "I believe it is. Head of Roxbury Industries."

Lear examined his paints. "Golly, I wouldn't have had him down as the engineering sort. He was a delicate young thing; but it was a long time ago."

"You must meet him again." Molly's enthusiasm for Lodestar was shining. "We shall ask the earl to summon him."

"You will do no such thing, Molly." I must dissuade Molly from pursuing this fancy. "He is a busy man."

"He won't remember me." Lear smiled. "He was a little sprout. Though I fancy I drew him an alphabet at a banquet in Alexandria."

I frowned again. A delicate thing: hard to imagine anyone describing Lodestar thus, at any age. People change, I suppose, and toughen up. I could see in Kitty's manners how school would iron out the child into a brittle young woman, ready to be presented to society and make a dull marriage. Oh dear! Her mother was such a defender of women's freedoms.

Kitty and I went back up to the house, just as Jem arrived for parrot-holding duties; Molly, I saw, paid him no regard whatsoever.

The parrot's neck had a bare patch on it. Lear was teaching Jem how to hold the bird still without distressing it or distorting its shape, when he spotted the blemishes.

"My goodness. What have you been doing with this bird?"

Feathers had been plucked, tiny plumes removed or burnt. Not a problem for the painting: there were feathers and colour enough. But Lear and Molly were bemused.

"It's them scientists," said Jem, in a sheepish mumble.

Molly looked at him.

Lear tugged at his beard and patted Molly's shoulder.

All at once, it dawned on Molly that the menagerie was no longer an assemblage of wounded beasts, as Lady Elodie had wished it. It had become, whether by Roxbury's will or Lodestar's agency, an adjunct to the scientific establishment. The scientists must be allowed—encouraged, even—to experiment upon the living creatures.

Lear was unshocked. He cut his teeth painting birds in the Regent's Park Zoo, an unapologetically scientific establishment, dedicated to preserving species, but also to understanding animals, their physiologies and maladies. While that was often possible with live animals, there must be experimenting: research, dissections, and vivisection. He talked companionably to Molly of all this, as they painted.

She steeled herself. She refrained from making a scene. She got the most out of her lessons with Lear, persuading him back in the afternoon. He was a jovial fellow, but a hard worker, and a wonderful teacher. How swiftly she improved with two days of lessons from the old eccentric.

Dodgson was still reading the paper.

I might have thought Kitty would be jealous, after Mr Lear's breakfast entertainment. But she latched on to Dodgson, demanded he tell her a story. He promptly put down his paper and began an imaginative tale, rather wild, which she illustrated as they went.

I left them to it, and went on a ramble up to the reservoir. I was seeking perspective, in this final year before we are to wed.

I believe that is when Dodgson suggested going up to the schoolroom where Kitty had her dressing-up box. The lighting was good. Dodgson had his photographic equipment sent up in the lift. There they remained till dinner, giggling and chattering.

EXEAT EXTRA [RUTH]

On the Saturday, all was glowing.

Before dinner, the reverend and his little model joined me at the puzzle. They loved maps, adorned with drawings, information and nomenclature. This latest was another world map: the colours suggested the aridity of deserts, tropical fecundity, and sickly pallor in the steppes and plains. The whole picture was redeemed by the rosy glow of pink, outposts of progress from Dublin to Durban. The illustrator had taken the opportunity to add contemporary life: sheep on South Georgia, bright fruits in Queensland; weapons to denote wars.

"I've got it," Kitty piped up. "It's all the places that Fa sells his smelly guns."

The reverend and I looked at each other. Ought we to chastise her for an observation that was palpably true, if disloyal?

Kitty sensed our discomfort. "It's all right. That's what Mama used to call them."

"Did she?" I said. In all Molly's reports, the children had never breathed a word about their departed mother. "I thought you were Norphans."

"Oh, that." Kitty studied a gap in Central Africa. "That's just Nico's silly moping. That is what happens when you become a solitary old fool."

Reverend Dodgson smiled at the thought that her brother was old and maudlin.

"Kitty," I said, "do you miss your mother? You do remember her?"

"Yes." She hunched over the Atlantic, her brows crossed with hilarious concentration. "Pass Tegucigalpa, would you?"

I watched her. "I was a great admirer of hers—not that I knew her—her work, I mean, for the furtherance of women's rights."

"Yes." Kitty sighed wearily. "I suppose I was an admirer too."

"No more?" Dodgson teased.

"We have frantically busy lives," Kitty remarked, as if she were a cabinet minister and the puzzle an affair of state. "Our paths crossed, and pleasantly. She took a great interest in my schooling. But beyond that..." She drifted off, engrossed in her task.

Dodgson and I glanced at each other, entranced by her maturity in speaking of the dead.

Just for a moment, Kitty stared out of the window and murmured with an intensity quite different to her feigned unconcern. "Of course, I should like to see her again."

My heart broke for her. I reached out to squeeze her shoulder.

The blasted reverend piped up: "You will, my child. You surely will."

Do-gooding busybody. I could have kicked him, at the very moment the girl was acknowledging the depth of her loss, that he should force on her a platitude of religiosity.

Kitty ignored him, raising her brows as if to consider his claim, then turning back to the important job in hand.

PARTY PIECES [RUTH]

The earl was elated when he returned from his experiments. Something to do with his new battery cells: glass containers, framed with wood, that hold electrical charge.

By dinnertime, the earl seemed preoccupied again.

I mentioned Lodestar and how Mr Lear fancied he had met him, as a child, years ago.

"Excellent fellow." Roxbury chomped on his steak. "Great improvement on his father."

Lear smiled, evidently relieved. "I suspect we are like-minded in that direction."

Kitty and I conspired to draw the earl out of himself, for that was the impulse behind the weekend. After dinner, we demanded the visitors do party pieces. Lear happily began declaiming, somewhat waffly, through his beard, from *Journals of a Landscape Painter in Albania*. Not at all what we had wanted, and we shouted him down.

"A limerick," cried Kitty. "You are such a big published writer of nonsense, but I'll wager you won't outdo our Molly."

"There will be no wagering," said the earl, amused, "unless by the gentlemen."

"Ha." I snorted. "You see what we're up against, ladies?"

Lear nodded. "If I must, I shall take on such a giant of poetry as young Molly; but I do it regretfully." He nodded sagely. "I believe that poetry is never competitive. And also that she will win."

The two wags got into their stride, extemporising pithy verses on topics of the weekend.

Lear began with the parrot, beaten by stick and eating a carrot.

Molly described a menagerie with animals most curmudgeonly.

I attempted a reservoir from which to see afar.

Dodgson made a hash of it, not grasping the verse scheme, though rhyming neatly, with photographs of tame giraffes, where sharks and sparks drew belly laughs.

The earl was enthused. So enthused he joined in, though he got stuck after his first line, and we leapt in to help:

[*Roxbury*] A gent long obsessed with electrics...

[*Molly*] Drove his creatures amply apoplectic.

[*Kitty*] His experiments wild

[*yours truly*] Left them gravid with child.

[*Lear*] Bless that old Inca god of obstetrics.

We laughed until we were exhausted.

Dodgson offered to read from his latest mathematical treatise. We took it that he was joking (though he wasn't), but he brought down instead his latest daguerreotype prints: a boys' cricket team; cheery skeletons of man and monkey; the dean's children in mythological poses.

"What's extraordinary," said Roxbury, "is the movement captured by the still image."

Dodgson spoke of the process today allowing shorter exposures, so people need no longer pose so rigidly, afraid of blurring their gift to posterity.

"Not what I mean, old fellow," Roxbury said. "There's an inexplicable vitality in the concatenation of light and dark chemicals reacted upon paper."

"Wonderful, yes." Dodgson saw his moment. "I hope you don't mind my photographing Kitty?"

Kitty clapped for joy, revelling in the attention.

BOTTLED LIGHTNING [RUTH]

After the singsong, we adjourned, by Roxbury's invitation, to his laboratory, which he preferred to call the Experimental Room. The servants called it the magician's lair, and Molly had never yet seen it.

The tower stood at the midpoint of the house between the two turrets, the one Molly's room, the other where Molly had, perhaps, seen someone at the window, about which she had a theory she was reluctant to share.

He introduced the equipment, bit by bit, as if they were friends; I suppose they were, during these years of his retreat.

While he set up his show, we curious souls dispersed around the room, which seemed equipped for alchemical wizardry. Dodgson gravitated toward the statue of white marble, Undine, representing Paracelsus's elemental water spirit. Molly circled the room like a cat checking for unsuspected dangers: each corner held stacked glass containers, framed with wood and filled with liquid. Of differing sizes and complex interconnections, these constituted a history of the battery: Leyden jars, Daniell cell and Siemens units. All held electrical charge. The earl warned Molly to be wary of shocks should she touch them in a particular way.

"How exactly?" I asked.

"To complete a circuit." He frowned. "It's a rather complex science. Few understand it quickly."

"Mr Lodestar?"

"Lodestar regards electricity as witchcraft." He shook his head, smiling. "The very notion of 'action at a distance'— the basic enquiry of science—remains a mystery to him."

I glanced at the framed monograph of Roxbury's speech to the Newcastle Literary and Philosophical Society. He spoke of the "great conquests of science" that lay before us, the challenge of generating motive power through electricity more cheaply than our current fuels, to fulfil humanity's ever-increasing demand.

Lear meanwhile was fascinated by a large mechanical contraption. "An influence machine, I do believe. I saw a sideshow with this when I was young. A chap got it cheap off Benjamin Franklin." Roxbury showed him the foot pedal, and Lear set it rotating until it thrummed. Pleased with the speed, he grabbed hold of the rod: at once, the hair on his balding pate leapt to attention; at once, his beard attempted an escape from his chin.

We applauded, laughing.

"My infinite influence machine I've had to move," said Roxbury, "over to the Pump House, it was so large. But these batteries, charged by the Burnfoot Stream, are enough for the experiment I wish to show you."

As if by magic, Birtle appeared—summoned, I think, by buzzer—carrying two wine glasses and a phial of water.

Roxbury set the glasses on his table. He held up the phial to the lamp, examining it minutely.

"Distilled, sir, as always." Birtle revelled in his role: magician's accomplice.

Roxbury filled the glasses halfway each. He took a thread—an ordinary thread, he assured us—and coiled it into one of the glasses, leaving just enough to reach the short distance, perhaps half an inch, between the rims.

Roxbury had an ease in explaining abstruse science lucidly. I came away convinced I could explain the latest technical advances to any dunce. (When I come to test my theorem, Campbell, you may prove too duncelike.)

"The thread: silk. The distance: four tenths of an inch. The electromotive force?" He smiled, inserting a copper wire into each glass, noticeably more at ease here in his own domain than at dinner. "Let us say, a considerable voltage."

Birtle dimmed the lamps: a routine once well-practised.

"Observe." Even as the earl spoke, the thread was coated with water. As if by a snake charmer's enchantment, the coil began to unwind, gradually depositing itself, less neatly, into the second glass.

We drew near, like disciples inspecting a miracle. "I'll be dashed," said Lear.

Dodgson rubbed at his eyes. "I'll be double dashed and dod-busted."

The final end of the thread rose from the first glass and travelled across the tenuous water bridge into the second glass. The water continued to travel, for several seconds, through thin air, unsupported.

I gasped, as a spark of blue leapt through the air. The water fell back.

I blinked, the blue lightning still on my retina. We had witnessed something remarkable. Dodgson wanted explanations. Molly and I wanted more.

In the sequel, with the string fixed at one end, the water emptied from one glass into the other.

In the finale, after the thread had finished its journey, he made water pass through mid-air—for several minutes—with no diminution of the water in either glass.

"It is beautiful, Your Lordship." I clapped my hands in excitement. "And what use can such magic be put to?"

"My dear lady, thank goodness you are here to ask the apposite question." Roxbury took my hands in his, gratefully. "I don't for the life of me know."

"Could a person be the conduit?" said Lear. "We see so many crackpot remedies in the newspapers. Darwin, you know, is always wrapping himself in galvanic belts."

"I believe so. I soon hope to make an advance." Roxbury looked exalted with hope for a moment; then he gave way to exhaustion, as if recalling how such everyday civility cost him. "I must retire. I am unaccustomed to entertaining. Will you excuse me?"

RETURN TO THE WALLED GARDEN [RUTH]

In the night, I dreamt of magical resurrections, of people long dead or lost to me as if they were dead. I dreamt of laboratory experiments: the lights extinguished, blue sparks emanating from the influence machine. Lear and Dodgson extemporising alphabets on either side of the table, on which Molly slept in a gravy boat. The earl meanwhile wrapped himself in chains and asked me to connect him to the electrical current.

"Feed the body," he said jovially, "feed the mind."

* * *

Molly took time for a Sunday walk with me, before Lear and I were whisked off to catch our connection. She told me of the library, the trunk, the documents; how Skirtle found her, and Birtle was kind, after all his stares. She told me the sad tale of love rekindled and joy destroyed. And in the turret, mad or sleeping, the lady.

"Lady Elodie?" I could hardly believe it. I stared up at that crenellated tower hanging over us, as we descended the path around the rockery. No visions of wild-haired women were afforded to me.

As I contemplated the place, I felt the earl revealed to me. The house, calm and reasoned in exterior, but alive to the torrent of unknown forces. No namby-pamby fountains for Roxbury; no ornamental grottos. What need, when nature gives you such a setting? The falls roared down the Burnfoot Gorge. With clouds massing above, how much energy must that torrent generate through his turbines?

Molly spoke only of her researches, self-contained to the point of evasion.

"But how are you," I said, "in yourself?"

"Fine, fine."

I knew her better than that. "Come along. Don't play Molly mysterious with me. I know you, and I see your lively eye, and I wonder on whom it alights." It was a new stage of our friendship for me to recognise that she was grown up and full of dreams and passions, and an easy target for the roving eye that so many men have. Down beyond the Iron Bridge, Jem the stable boy was heading for the glasshouses. "Can I see the object of your passion?"

"Him? He has a sweetheart, Dotty, a dairymaid down the valley."

"The earl is fond of you."

"Don't be a daft-pated duckling." She stopped short. "But his sons—"

"Both?"

Molly sighed. "Nico is just a boy, and a dreamer. The elder one, well." She gave an involuntary shudder.

I recalled Wilfred's blackened eye, but we did not speak of it.

Molly's demeanour changed. "Look. Here is the Walled Garden. It's the one part of the grounds I avoid."

I smiled at her evasion. "And why is that?"

"Private reasons." She coughed. "Lady Elodie's garden. Gone wild now."

"I thought you hadn't ventured?"

Molly leaned toward me, pointing at the solid wooden gates, paint peeling. "He's buried there." Her face darkened. "The child that died."

"There's no shame in paying respects to the dead."

Molly was pale. "Spoil our jolly walk."

"I love a ramble through a cemetery."

"An overgrown garden, with a grave?"

I had forgotten she was afraid of graveyards. I took her hand. We squeezed through the gap in the gates. Herbs, wildflowers, familiar and exotic, witch hazel, allium, and hogsbane, with its mawkish scent.

Dark and rough-hewn, the stone slab was free of moss, beginning to weather.

JONATHAN ROXBURY

DECEMBER 1861

IN OUR ARMS SO BRIEF,

IN OUR HEARTS FOREVER

* * *

THE MENAGERIE, PART THE THIRD [RUTH]

Our visit will be remembered by the staff, of course, for the two screams that ended the weekend's idyll. One led to Dodgson's summary departure. The second revealed the goings-on in the scientific quarter.

This latter scream came from Jem. He was combing the hair of his beloved orang-utan, when he found a neat row of stitches forward of her left ear.

The first scream was Skirtle's. She brought tea and biscuits up to the makeshift photography studio, only to find Kitty in what she considered inappropriate attire. Dodgson was taking his photographs without apparent prurience, yet Birtle persuaded him that he should leave ahead of schedule.

Not exactly sent home in disgrace, Dodgson was undoubtedly an odd fish, too fond of Kitty's whimsical declarations. The sad thing was that Kitty did look fetching in dirtied face and rags. She reminded me terribly of Molly when we first met her. It was not how an earl's daughter was usually posed; but perhaps Dodgson was ahead of photographic fashions.

LEAR AND LODESTAR [RUTH]

I have had the pleasure of travelling south with Mr Lear. I enjoined him to publish more of his limericks, as they gave us such pleasure. He pshawed and harrumphed: it was such an effort getting subscribers for his paintings, he hardly had the stomach for selling *Nonsense*; but I assured him that his *Nonsense* kept us adults sane, and lit our children's imagination, so thank God for him.

I also asked if I might send you to speak to him. For

someone who had known Lodestar Senior seemed to me an invaluable referee for this young man who had risen so swiftly to such a prominent position.

I have also decided I should write to the Lodestar estate in Africa.

ROXBURY'S MAXIMS [FRAMED IN THE MAGICIAN'S LAIR]

The greater the power, the more dangerous the abuse. (**Burke**)

Everything is interaction and reciprocal. (**Von Humboldt**)

Power should act and not talk. (**Goethe**)

Power does not consist in striking with force or with frequency, but in striking true. (**Balzac**)

A hair or two will show where a lion is hidden. (**Dickens**)

You cannot turn back time, but you may convert it into energy. (**Roxbury, Notes on Electricity**)

MARGINALIA [MOLLY]

Dear Miss V,

Since your weekend here, I have become more dedicated in my searches. Please pass on what you think useful. My daily letters are noticed. I worry that the coded notes may rouse suspicion: hence no bulletin for Watchman this time. I shall send what I can, when I can.

First, I spent time with the trunk of lost dreams. I began to find annotations, scribbled by Lady Elodie herself, in the margins of her books, so I knew her hand. Thrilling, to touch the page where she scribbled. Her literary thoughts ("Rochester—rotter"). Reminders to herself ("fish Friday—lamb Saturday?"). Her own name ("Elodie

Margaret Loth, Elodie Roxbury, Lady Elodie").

I determined to ask Birtle if I might not see her. He would refuse, of course, but at least it would mean I had asked, before I snuck in without permission.

Then I found Lady Elodie's diary.

It was on her bookshelves, betwixt Christina Rossetti and Menella Smedley. The scrap of memoir by the earl had put me on the lookout for it. It looked like a bound volume, but the spine was named by hand in beautiful script:

ELODIE ROXBURY
JOURNAL

I leafed through Lady Elodie's writings, astonished. At the end, I found notes in a script wilder than hers, and read these first.

They were by the earl, after her passing.

SHE IS GONE [ROXBURY]

Pen to paper. Words words words. Work work work. My heart leaps in my chest, rattling uselessly against its cage. No escape. No release. Our dream of sunlit valleys will never be. Again and again, the realisation: that will never be.

She is gone.

She is here.

She is gone.

In trying to write usefully, panic takes me. Useful? What use? What use can there be in writing these sufferings? What use to keep living?

I shall take my pencil, return to my laboratory, and approach my work again, without hope and without despair, as every scientist must do. Observe. Draw. Not for the relief promised by Ruskin and his artists. But an engineer is no pure scientist; he is a bridge between the worlds of science, art and life. Unless he has this equal stake in those three realms, what use is he? What use am I who can girdle the world entire with power, but cannot save her? End it all. Disconnect the cables. But there is no cliff, no reservoir that offers the release I need. I cannot vanish away.

Write again. Work again. Work until this foolishness dissolves. How can we exist and not be together?

Work. Work. Work. Not just doodles of imaginary nothings. Coherence. Construction. All the projects I daydreamed of. All the projects I promised her. The rail she wanted for the children's safety on the Iron Bridge. The rockery. Lay the copper conductor to the turbine at the gorge—the Pump House, I shall call it. Test the reservoirs' capacities. Calculate motive forces. Experiment with the waterwheel, resistance, momentum, and charging the battery jars.

Visit that asylum in West Yorkshire. Jackson has dissected brains of epileptics in York to understand the neurological damage. He has seen Fritsch and Hitzig applying shocks to dog brains, mapping the brain areas. Now he wants to try the electrical treatments, like Charcot. But I will bet their batteries are twenty years old. Hospitals.

Read more. Try again. Go back to the wine glass. Read up on developments since I first published. When the consensus is overwhelming that it is better to try than remain forever in stasis—horrid paralysis—try again. Rely on the uncertain tenets of these new sciences.

Risk all.

GATHERING SPEED [LAWLESS]

As Molly shared these revelations with Ruth, I journeyed around the country. My panic to hold shut the doors of invasion seemed overwrought. I saw at every port Frenchmen and Frenchwomen detained, their papers checked and double-checked; ever more were sent back where they came from. I wondered if Jeffcoat, on his voyage, would recover not just from his wound, but from the shock of his close call.

The rains began. It rained on the moors, it rained on the dales. In London, floods. In Teddington, floods. At the children's schools, floods. Intemperate seasons that left us fed up with tempests, and in a temper.

Molly shortened her drawing sessions with the shortening daylight, to study the secrets of the Lady's Library. I pelted round, gathering scraps of hints of murmurs about who might have anti-British sentiments or French sympathies or unexpected extra income. Ruth collated this information.

All this happened simultaneously. It is a frustration to write of it piecemeal. Indeed, I feel foolish when it is all set out thus, because I feel I should have seen it, and sooner, the thread that would wind through the labyrinth to the dark heart of the monster terrorising us.

I went back to Portsmouth to harangue the contractor for the forts on Bazalgette's behalf; I owed that much to Bertie. This tiresome man listened to my suggestions, as if I were a schoolchild proposing a half-holiday. I thought he would dismiss me without consideration.

Instead he put this proposal to me. "How many bricks can they make per week? How many does Bazalgette want? Can we get these extra bricks—of lower quality—at lower cost? Get those figures. Meet me here, with Lodestar, to make sure his company is willing to parcel out their bricks thus."

"It's not his company," I said. But I wired Lodestar, and we fixed the meeting for a fortnight's time. I sent the queries to Bazalgette, then I set all thought of bricks aside.

I bought a drink for Ellie at the Fortitude Tap, to cheer her up, and stomped back to the station through the rain.

Before he sailed, Jeffcoat and I had reported our suspicions to Ripon. He wanted more information, always more. About the explosions that had happened, the damage, how executed, what proofs, what connections, what links to the French. We told him of the bank's obstructiveness and the bonds from a gentlemen's club. We told how Jacques I had escaped, while the Jacques ready to talk, Jacques III, was killed at Clerkenwell; but then he was not French.

Ripon looked troubled. "This gentlemen's club. Have you asked there? I notice how the banks' stocks have fluctuated in the wake of each attack." He rubbed his beard. "I'd be interested to know who was throwing money around in the bar on those dates."

Difficult to check, I thought. "Why, sir?"

"Widen our list of suspects." Ripon pursed his lips. "The Frenchies aren't the only people who benefit from instability."

INVESTIGATING THE ZOOLOGICAL RESEARCH [MOLLY]

Miss V,

I have rationed my reading hours. Although Birtle and Skirtle knew that I visited Lady Elodie's library, I deemed it imprudent to let on that I was delving into the trunk. I judged how long I could risk staying and staring and flicking through these pages. The earl's endnotes, fragmentary and incoherent, provided a window on to his soul, till now opaque. But I dared not remove the volume:

it would have felt like a robbing a tomb—even if my terror of being branded a thief has abated, since Birtle's softening toward me.

I'm inquisitive, me. (My brother would have chosen a less polite word.)

After the parrot with Lear, I was looking for a chance to investigate the zoological research. Early morning, waking from slumbers, a scratch at the window made me leap to my feet. That was a distress signal, back in London among the Oddbodies. I leapt up; but it was just a bare branch, drawn across the antique panes by the wind. A carpet of grey whooshed over the bright morning: in these northerly wastes, winter can leap out at any moment. I spotted the earl tiptoeing across the gravel, making his way toward the glasshouses.

Nothing attracts my nosiness more than secretiveness. It was quick work to dress in dark clothes. The rains had swollen the stream in the night. I could hear the turbine whirring up at the Pump House; it is not usually engaged at this hour.

I flitted from bush to bush, following Roxy down to the glasshouses. He passed through the double door, greeted by a muzzy-headed scientist. I did not approach the same door, but passed along the great glass walls, checking for prying eyes. I might have been spotted from the house, but the morning was dull and my clothes dark. I snuck round the glasshouses towards the zoological end, with the animals arranged by genus, species and whatnot.

A cry. I stopped in my tracks. It sounded barely human.

Or rather nearly human. The old orang-utan, Jem's friend, is grown lethargic of late. They have treated her with massage, with herbs, with drugs, not knowing whether it is senility or a tumour causing her despondency. Most recently, they have tried galvanic belts, and succeeded in rousing her from slumber. What now?

I crouched at her window. When I gathered the courage to peek, I saw what made her scream: electrocuting belts, attached around her head; incisions at her temples, where wires emerged from under the skin.

The scientist gave a signal. Charged by the turbine, the belt shot electric charge through her head. A convulsion, and they had to hold down her arms to stop her removing the blasted thing from her ears.

She relapsed, blinking, and allowed the earl to squeeze her in a comforting embrace. For all her cries, for all her pain, there was no doubt, she was awake: awake, and more alert than she had been for many weeks.

Why this furtive experiment, at such an early hour? Because Jem could not bear to see them do it to her.

FRIENDS IN HIGH PLACES [*PENNY SATIRICAL*]

These late attacks on structures of national importance are a menace, and the perpetrators must feel the weight of Her Majesty's justice.

As violent attacks go, however, with respect to the injured, they are fiascos. Their success has been in the disproportionate scale of the terror they provoke. Consider.

Erith: ten dead, windows broken, sea wall repaired in the nick of time.

Camden: train derailed, windows broken, inconvenience, donkey exploded.

Florence Veigh: inferno, none killed, windows broken.

Clerkenwell and Scotland Yard: prisoners killed, windows broken, police narked.

Why, it's almost as if they are just upsetting people—aside from glaziers, who love them*. Who would stand to gain from that?

"The Irish, of course," say our redoubtable organs of misinformation, the newspapers.

The Detective Police Force murmurs tacit agreement.

"The French, of course!" mutters public opinion, fuelled by egotist demagogues peddling anti-European sentiments as old as the Domesday Book. Detectives emerge from the War Office demanding that Palmerston's coastal follies go ahead, the costliest defenceworks on our island since Hadrian's Wall.

"Nobody stands to gain," lament the right-minded. With people afraid, nobody trades, nobody dines out, nobody spends. We all lose.

Or do we?

(* Has Scotland Yard investigated the possibility of glazier activism?)

Your memorious *Penny Satirical* recalls an outbreak of supernatural sightings in the thirties. Remember? Ah, those distant days, when the gullible populace was so bereft of trustworthy information they believed in werewolves and vampyres.

Not at all, we reply, these were intelligent and educated people. And yet they saw Spring-Heeled Jack, that venerable larkster who sometimes robbed, sometimes leapt, sometimes groped, but above all scared the living daylights out of people.

Or so we were told. That is, trusted news organs reported what they had seen.

We are also told, by a little birdy, that the Hellfire Club placed bets on Spring-Heeled Jack's antics, raking in quite a sum over the course of two years, until the bookmakers suspected the newsmen were in cahoots.

Imagine! Selective reporting of the truth? Journalists paid off for reports with no basis in fact? Never: not in British papers. That is the preserve of despotic regimes, like Russia and France.

It was rumoured that two prominent Hellfire members, who cannot be named, profited by investing in the troubled areas. What a wheeze. Now, like Jack of old, up leaps Spring-Heeled Jacques. Down go prices. Investors buy up property sold in panic at rock-bottom prices. Nothing immoral about it.

Apart from the murderous explosions, that is.

Property in Erith, Camden, Clerkenwell and Birkenhead can be found on pp. 9, 12, 13 and 24-28.

AFRICAN SKIES [LAWLESS]

Ruth was so troubled by Lear's offhand comment about Lodestar and his delicate constitution as a child that, with my endorsement, she wrote to the Lodestar estate in Africa, including return postage, begging further details of the father's death and son's departure, with any family portraits they might have, which she would return.

She meanwhile kept an eye on bonds, which surprised me, for she despised them as a form of gambling, disapproving because it fanned the ruinous dream of unearned success. Its legitimisation, in the Stock Exchange, Ruth considered the lowest achievement of the civilised world. The City of London, renowned throughout the free world, she reviled.

Ruth had tried to explain her concerns to me. It was not until she presented the whole theory, alongside letters from Overend and Gurney (refusing to be drawn on certain payments and investment), that I gave it credence.

* * *

An explosion.

Local businesses suffer. The damaged property is a minor issue. People avoid the area. Despite the manifold fact that there is never an attack in the same place twice, people avoid it, because they have short memories.

Businesses fold. The bank presses for repayment of loans. Properties are repossessed.

Investors snap up low-priced shops and flats. Prices recover. Instant profit. (Their bank, by the way, also does nicely. It pays inflated dividends on their bonds, attracting waves of people to bank with them.)

Who are these profiteers? The bank declines to divulge, citing age-old confidentiality, a central tenet of the City's eminence.

The register of property was a labyrinthine archive, but Ruth's labours found a handful of names investing in several of the areas where explosions had taken place. These men were all members—why did this not surprise me?—of one particular London club. It was a club I have visited, and taken coffee next door to, though policemen are not generally welcomed. Besides being Lodestar's club, it was popular with bankers, such as Overend, and journalists, such as Hemyng.

Ruth tapped at the table. "Nothing to prove forethought."

"Nothing to suggest they've conspired to commit crimes," I said.

"They may just be opportunists, acting on an after-dinner whim. But if you could only persuade a Frenchman in custody to admit that he was paid not by his own government, but by local swells, then our Spring-Heeled Jacques I, II and III begin to look suspicious."

I sighed. "We kept it out of the papers: London Jacques is dead. Mersey Jacques—he was a fool from the start."

"And Jacques the First?"

"Escaped." I cast my eyes down.

Ruth sat back, dismayed. "Get a wanted poster out. We need him."

A good idea. I reached for her hand. "Brilliant work, my love. But you're such an honest soul. How did you come up with this most twisted of theories?"

She took out a recent edition of the *Penny Satirical.* "I didn't. Some witty johnny dashed it off for a joke—only it isn't so funny now."

I jabbed at the by-line: "Harkaway? That's Collins's bloody Etonian friend. I've seen him, drinking with Lodestar." I clicked my fingers. "Bracebridge Hemyng."

"How do you know?"

"I know how he signs his bills, when he doesn't want to pay them." I checked my watch. "I also know where he's drinking right now."

FEMALE REMEDIES

The weak made strong!

Dr Kilmer's FEMALE REMEDY: the great blood purifier
and system regulator. Don't neglect early symptoms.
If you have: Bright's Disease, dropsy, rheumatism,
diabetes, or gout, every dose goes right to the spot. The
only herbal alternative and depurative ever discovered,
specially adapted to a run-down female constitution.
All genuine products have Dr Kilmer's likeness on
outside and inside wrappers. Study carefully the
directions for use in *Guide to Health*, published by Dr
Kilmer & Co.

Price: £1 extra large, large 10s. Costs nothing to try it:
use contents of first bottle according to directions. If you do not receive
benefit, return empty to chemist and price will be refunded as per our
instructions to them.

TO LOVE [MOLLY]

It was just before I read Lady Elodie's diary that I chanced
to be walking back with Roxy from the glasshouses one
day. He was weary, but with an excitable air.

"Whom have you been drawing today?"

"Monkey," I said. "I tell a lie. Orang-utan."

Our companionable style encompassed many registers,
but it seemed that my answer provoked unease. He went
to speak, a couple of times, but hesitated. We wound our
passing way up the hill by a different route every day. Today
we were at the copse of witch hazels. These, I had learned,

were planted by Lady Elodie, and reminded the earl of her.

"She was not an easy woman to love, all the time," he volunteered out of the blue. He looked down to the gorge, as if into the past. "Yet our marriage was a revelation."

I was electrified to hear him speak of her at last. We walked by a circuitous path, he stopping occasionally to tidy the edging of the grass, I to pick sloes.

"Her grace, her poise," he said, "her voice all tumbled me into a passion for her. And anyone spending time with her couldn't help but be fascinated by her thoughts. The world she envisioned, she wanted now: a world where men do not withdraw to drawing rooms, nor clubs, nor night houses; where women ride bicycles, wear trousers, become ambassadors, spies, veterinarians, train drivers, engineers and prime ministers. Why not? If we may be queens or chimney sweeps, she would say, are we not qualified for every level of labour in between?" He smiled, as we turned upward, and glanced at the turret.

"Women may be librarians, after all." I'd intended to let his thoughts flow as far as they might flow, but I thought of you, Miss V, and could not stay silent. "Accountants, artists. Put those talents together. Why could we not be architects too?"

He frowned indulgently. "To build anything, one must get dirty hands and muddy boots. Travel in inclement conditions. Speak with navvies."

"Heaven forfend. You will not let me be a vet or a surgeon for the same reasons?"

"Let us not, young lady, proceed to the conclusion of those thoughts." He smiled. "She always delved into these revolutionary realms, in conversation with my friends."

I grinned. "Who doubtless took it as wild fantasies."

"Some were sympathetic, some amused. Others condescending. A few outraged. One of my hearty school chums told me I'd best watch out or they'd take her off to Bedlam."

I looked at him: it was not a joke.

"She would not be restrained; she went at her beliefs full-tilt. I could not tell her to restrain her imagination. What could I do?"

"She inspired many," I said. "Our friend Miss Villiers venerates her."

He nodded, pleased. "What I could do was move here. Far from the city, and the hundred-mouthed rumour that breeds malice there. In the country, one can express ideas as mad as a coot over dessert and one is merely eccentric. The same opinions loosed over dinner at Manor House would set these new secret policemen on your trail. Ah, Elodie, my wild-hearted rebel."

He caught his breath and leaned for a moment against a rock.

We were closing in on the house, but I wanted our talk to go on and on. It was as if I had been seeking Lady Elodie, parched for word of her. Now that he was offering a fulsome draught, I would drink as long and deep as I could.

"But she kept up her London life?" I said.

"We both did. Our children suffered from our absence. But this place became our rock, to return and gather strength. This stopped us from overwork, driving ourselves to distraction." He sighed as we gained the crest in front of the house. "This place holds a fondness for me. Since childhood holidays with my parents. Revelatory moments, as a convalescent student. Finally, buying the old ruin and building it up. I wasn't sure how Elodie would take the transition; but I was a fool. A robust soul, she. The day after we arrived, I could not find her at dinner time. My heart fluttered with a panic. Not that she was unstable, but you could not be sure of her moods, hour by hour, sentence by sentence."

He led me across the gravel, through the carriage arch. Inside the gardener's porch, we sat down and stretched out our legs.

"I need not have worried. She was weeding. Weeding the Walled Garden."

Where their boy was buried, but not she. How I wanted to ask about her, to go up and see this woman so striking; but he was in a reverie of memory that I could not disturb.

"She fell in love with the wild flowers. She planted the flowering herbs and the succulents, exploiting the soils and the rocky slope. She planned the orchard and the greenhouses, the vegetables, and these trees that have thriven so gloriously. A landscape that you artists enjoy capturing." He paused. "And then, all that nonsense."

The Paris bombs. "If it is difficult to speak of—"

"On the contrary." He tugged off his boots. "It is easy to speak of the vicissitudes of government. Public opinion! No sooner was I a pariah—reviled then forgotten—than I was begged back for sake of queen and country. The marvellous thing was," he said, fixing me with a delightful smile, "I think it cured us. Cured us of that fixation with the busy world; freed us to return and seek that simple life we promised ourselves when first married."

Reinvigorated, he beckoned me with a mischievous glance to sneak through the kitchen with him; we were always peckish coming back from work, and if we ordered something through Skirtle, it caused faff. Whereas if we just snuck in and divided a pie between us...

He watched the larder door. I grabbed the pie—game

pie, top-notch—and we retreated together. One of the undercooks, at the sink, gave us a friendly nod. He did not see Roxy slyly grab a knife, nor me a saucer. We were away, into the lift, up toward his tower workshop.

Skirtle, of course, happened to be coming out of her pantry as we rose into view. We smiled at her.

"What is it?" she said. "What mischief are yous up to now?"

Roxy blinked, with the innocent eyes of guilt. "Nothing, dear Skirtle."

She narrowed her gaze. Our spoils were hidden behind our backs. There was no way she could know what we had taken.

"That game pie," she said, "was meant for your lunch tomorrow."

We brought our thievings out into the open. "I shall go without tomorrow," said Roxbury, with a stoical sniff, "for we must have it now."

"Away with you." Skirtle advanced with her duster, as we vanished from view above her.

She was not really angry. She told me later how delighted she was to see him at his old antics, like when he and her ladyship were working on the gardens. She couldn't remember how long it was since he had the appetite and the devilment to be stealing from the pantry. As far as Skirtle was concerned, I brought out the best in the old earl and she was grateful to me.

Up in his laboratory, he set down the pie on the saucer and sliced it into quarters. Typical engineer. As we nibbled, crumbs tumbling, I took the risk of reminding him of his train of thought. "And your wife too returned here with pleasure?"

"She recovered the bloom of her youth. She exerted

herself. Managed the household with reckless decorum. Skirtle and she were in cahoots over everything. Birtle came over from her father's house. He always looked on her with paternal indulgence: this was nothing like the peaceful retirement he planned for himself. She handled everything charmingly—visits, workmen, children— renovating the old buildings, the wild inheritance of the grounds. To plan the glasshouses we got Paxton, the Crystal Palace man. The millhouse I resurrected as a Pump House, providing hydraulic power for the house and electricity for the scientific quarter. How modern her thinking, yet such a natural country lass, the finest lady for these old valley estates. But then…"

We finished the pie.

He noticed the crumbs we had spread over the desk, strewn across papers and formulae and calculations. He fought the urge to sweep the desk clear, of crumbs and papers and pens and instruments. He shook his head, barely perceptibly. On his lips were muttered words: "I must, I must," he repeated, like a child memorising his homework.

"But then, sir, she became—?"

"Do you find this sunlight melancholic, Molly?" he remarked, as if he were making small talk at Ascot races. "I find it melancholic. Don't mistake me. I love the hazy afternoons when the chill invigorates you to be done with work and retreat to the warmth. But I miss the long evenings of summer." He wiped his brow. "That golden time, shadows stretching on the lawn, when eternity greets you with a glass of good wine on the verandah. And the stars, so late, near to midnight in these climes, so bright, away from the city."

Outside the clouds swept aside the last of the light. The rain started up upon the trees in the gorge. Soon it would sweep over the house, to pound against the windows all through the night.

Roxy squinted out at the clouds, as if they were guests arrived too early.

"She was with child, sir," I prompted, as gently as I could.

"Ah." He looked surprised. "You know about all that."

"I found her library, sir, behind the chapel. I bullied Birtle into telling some secrets. Not all, I think."

"Not all," he echoed. "Well, she was with child, it's true, and then… she was no longer."

No longer—with child? Or she *was* no longer?

"Dear sweet boy," he said, barely audible. "She got her way, as in everything. She became with child. She grew happier and happier, with each passing week, and weak, and ill, and round like a ball." He leaned heavily on the arm of his chair, attempting to rise. "It is so strange to speak of it all."

I moved to help but he waved me away.

Gathering himself, he stood and leaned against the window frame. His mouth opened and closed. I poured him a drink of water, then on second thoughts poured a whisky too. He spoke now to himself, as if transported back to the past, to his wife's bedside. "Dear sweet boy. I held your tiny hand between my thumb and forefinger. Knuckles, perfect, a work of art. Little mouth, such shallow breaths; so short a time, she could not bear it. Such blossomed hopes, so early withered." He looked around at me, as if surprised to find me there.

I handed him the drink, which he took and drank down, as a man returning from the desert. "Sir," I said. "You do not have to speak of this."

"No, Molly, I must talk of it, or I am doomed." He breathed in. "Or we are doomed."

OLD BOYS' NETWORK [LAWLESS]

"Bracebridge Hemyng, old chap," I said. "Thought you'd be down at the rugger."

The young journalist was slouching around in a rather louche public house, attached to his favourite brothel. Looking up, he answered in all seriousness. "I'm devastated not to be there, old chap. But the leg, you see?"

I did see. His leg was in plaster. "Rugger accident?"

"Not bloody likely. Here, you going to buy me a drink or what?"

I laughed and called for refreshment. Hemyng was an ebullient soul. Brilliant writer, I was told, but unreliable. "It wasn't someone taking revenge for your revelations, was it?" I tossed on to the table the issue of the *Penny Satirical* Ruth had given me, in time for a slovenly barmaid to plonk two tumblers of brandy on it.

Hemyng looked rattled.

"What's wrong, old chap?" I said. There was something about his Etonian style that I couldn't help imitating. "You look like someone's got you by the tallywags."

"Not at all." He took up his glass and sank it, dragging his tone back to jollity with an effort. One thing about these public schoolboys, they know how to hide their feelings, and when to. "Silly article. Upset the old guard. Exposing a bygone ruse for a cheap laugh."

"Oh." I rubbed my chin. "That's you Eton fellows all over. No sooner have I caught on than you've lost me again."

"Nonsense," he said. But my flattery had piqued him. "How do you mean?"

"I'd just begun to believe your conspiracy in earnest. Now you're saying it was just for a laugh. I don't know. Sounded awfully convincing."

"The best satire has that kernel of credibility." He studied his glass.

I called for another brandy. "Tell me everything, or I'll roast your limbs in hellfire."

My ever so subtle mention of the club's name frightened him; I put on my scariest visage, but he was more scared of someone else. His broken leg, I was fairly sure, was a reminder not to blab.

"I couldn't possibly."

I checked that nobody was watching our dark corner, then grabbed the young layabout by the throat.

"What I mean to say is—" He tugged uselessly at my hands. "Look, let me go. I'll tell you, if you won't let on."

He rubbed at his throat as I released him from my grasp, and reached for his drink like a dying man reaching for courage. "Overheard a few chaps discussing the old Spring-Heeled scam. How it might be effected in the modern world. Take advantage of Johnny foreigner and our continual immigration whinges. That's all."

I grabbed his pint from him. "Names?"

He made a face. "Not a clue, old man."

I looked at him severely: the rogue was lying. "If there's one more bombing, you shall have blood on your hands, young man. I thought you were for reform and the breaking of the aristocracy's games with capital."

I thrust my brandy in front of him, spilling most of it over his suede coat, and walked away, ignoring his whingeing.

9.23 CLUB [LAWLESS]

My circle of drinking chums formerly met every week. Age was diminishing our abilities, however: Henry Mayhew had an unspecified injury to his back, and was neither allowed to play badminton nor to spend a sixpence on drink; Dickens was in semi-disgrace, having lied to his wife about his mistress; but Collins, well, Wilkie Collins could still be relied upon.

"The only thing I have heard about the Hellfire Club," he said, sipping porter through his prodigious beard, "is that members are forbidden to speak of it."

"Does that mean," I bega., "Hold on. Are you...? If you were—"

"I couldn't possibly say." Collins clinked his glass against mine. "Follow the logic. Ask until you're blue in the face: nobody will breathe a word. If, however, you went on the assumption that it exists and profits thusly, you ought to seek those who profited."

"It won't prove anything."

"No." His eyes gleamed, piglike, in the dark tavern. "But it'll give you satisfaction, if you keep an eye on them, when they slip up."

A PECULIAR VISITOR [LAWLESS]

A wizened old fellow was waiting to see me when I got back to the Yard. His face was scored with wrinkles, as if he had been left out in the rain too long. There was a light in his eyes that spoke of honesty or being a simpleton.

I had no time for time-wasters. "What is it you want?"

"To talk." His voice was soft and weather-beaten, wrapped in a sailor's brogue. He hesitated, shifting from foot to foot. "The ship. I heard you found that body after all."

I looked at him. I had not expected to hear more of the SS *Great Britain* corpse.

"I said it weren't a sound notion, and it ought to be reported to the captain." Jedediah Longthrop was an oddball and a misfit. He was a lowly cleaner aboard the *Great Britain*. And he knew something about our body. "He insisted it were the honourable thing. Otherwise we'd be getting the ship's owners in trouble."

"Slow down, Mr Longthrop." I thrust the fellow into a seat. I had called for tea. Not your standard way to deal with a suspected criminal. I tried Jeffcoat's style: he had the touch when dealing with recalcitrant witnesses. "Or may I call you Jed? Yes? Take the weight off your feet. You look like you've been hard at work."

Jed flexed his hands, as if to shake off the toil. "Refitting the ship."

"You've been on the ship this whole time?"

He straightened with pride. "Since it were built, sir."

"My, my." I poured the tea, watching our witness intently, until I judged the moment right. "What do you know about the body, Jed?"

Jed stiffened. "They told me down the dock as you'd found it in the lifeboat."

"Why should that concern you, Jed?"

He looked at me in distress. "He'd died already. The gentleman said it were the ship. He been poisoned. So as it were best just roll him overboard."

It took half an hour of such garbled declarations to get the picture. Five or six years ago, Jed was called into a cabin by a young gentleman. His valet had died in the cabin; he looked consumptive, but the gent insisted it was the ship's fault: the mephitic air in the lower decks had done for him, along with the dreadful food.

"I told him I'd get the ship's doctor, but it were too late for that, said he. The best thing for it was to throw him overboard, and the less said the better. He was a scrawny fellow, from abroad. No family, no friends. Wouldn't be missed."

They wrapped the body in bedsheets and a tarpaulin. In the dead of night, they dragged him up on deck. Jed fetched some kentledge to weigh the body down. The gent kept watch while

Jed pulled him to the side of the ship. They piled the stones into a basket and wrapped it all tight. "I couldn't do it. He said there was someone coming. So he pushed him off and we both of us cleared off. When I saw him the next day, he gave me a florin, and reminded me how much trouble there'd be if anyone knew of it. And I never said not one word to anyone more about it." He recalled the crew complaining of a smell, back at the time, but nobody could find where it came from. "I never knew he fell in the lifeboat. The boats hung off the side of the deck, see. I thought he was long gone to Davy Jones's locker. I wish he was."

As to the gentleman's name, he could not help us.

"Jed, come along." I leaned towards him. "You must have thought it was worth remembering."

"That's it exactly, though, sir. I didn't want to remember." All he could tell us was that it was a young fellow, spoke English with an accent. "He scared me so witless, I've prayed and prayed I won't ever see him again. You won't make me, will you?"

Poor Jed. I had no doubt he was telling the truth, though I would bet our Lodestar greased his palm with more than a florin to help him forget. I took his details, of course. The burial at sea may have taken place in the Atlantic, beyond our jurisdiction, but it was still unlawful: the death should have been reported, as he knew well. But there had been no murder. Nothing further to be done.

LADY ELODIE'S JOURNAL, PART THE FIRST [MOLLY]

Only then did I start reading her parts of the diary, after Roxy had spoken of her that night, as if to give me true permission.

He was a man changed: removed from energetic business

to these reclusive experiments. On our walks, he began to speak of her more, to point out the roses she loved, the outcrop amid the rockery where she would stand, midway between house and Iron Bridge, to look back at the turret she loved.

I laid aside all the other documents: doctor's prescriptions; recipes for cravings; concoctions for baby; speculative treatments; advertisements for curative contraptions.

I turned at last to her diary. I treasured that volume, tucked away alphabetically under Roxbury, as if she placed her story among these romantic tales and scientific expositions. I read these pages in a flurry, electrified by Roxy's recent revelations, troubled that I was still missing something, a key to the household that would finally open the doors.

BOOK VII
A LADY'S DIARY

WHEN YOU ARE AWAY [ELODIE, DIARY ENTRY, EARLY IN MARRIAGE]

Sometimes, when you are away, I imagine that you are dead.

I hear the dire news. I lock myself away. How I would sit at the rain-soaked window, gazing out at the blurry undergrowth. How I would descend to the breakfast table in a half-daze, neither rested nor wakeful, push the toast back and forth, sighing every ten minutes, not heeding the hours flitting by on the grandfather clock, which I so loved to see you wind every Sunday with diligent care. At your writing desk, replying to sevenfold parliamentarians before breakfast. How you could write sentences at that hour amazed me, with my dangling modifiers and bungled metaphors, which made you laugh and then hide your laughter for fear of hurting my feelings.

I am no academic, no deep thinker like you, yet you cherished my foolish observations, collecting them in your little notebook as if I were a deep thinker in my own way: how I notice midwinter, so as to remember that summer would return; how I unpack my summer wardrobe so promptly every spring, watching for moths;

how I list the birthdays of our godchildren and the presents we distribute around the estate; that I know all your employees and their wives, when you did not; and my ledger on their homes, which had privies, which mud floors, which larders, so that a portion of your profits might improve the lot of these old workhorses; and how, if they disdained such modernisations, I would visit unannounced and persuade them that the next generation expected them and what a pity to see them fly the coop just for the sake of a house with its own privy.

When you are away, I sweep the house and grounds, finding in each spot its particular memory: here we walked hand in hand and saw the swallows arrive that first spring in the north, flocking on the trees' branches barely beginning to sprout; here you proposed; here, when you did not expect, I kissed you, within view of the house, not caring if the servants saw, because I loved you, I simply loved you and that was enough.

Why are those days past? We were in the summer of our love: how grew the skies so dark, how fell the leaves? Too soon, too soon you have fled to the breezes of the underworld.

Until I hear a door shut. You?

But (in this game I play with myself) you are dead.

And then, my heart brightening with expectation, you appear, thoughts elsewhere, brow furrowed, and your glance makes me gleeful: a walk, down to the arboretum? And I take your hand, as I have learnt to without babbling of inconsequential nothings, waiting for your brow to unfurl and your thoughts to return from distant battlefields, from brickworks and clay pits, engines and castellations. The cloud shifts. Sunlight through the rains illumines the keeper's pool, and a fish leaps. You clutch my arm, and point, and yes, I have seen it, for once, and yes, you are back, and not dead, and with me, and our story still has time to mend. I tell of Tennyson's new poem, and you ask me to recite; and we speak of the game keeper's new pups; the draper's bill is in, but the payment from Japan is arrived, so we need not go without dinner tonight (your constant joke).

So many matters of the estate that we shared. I hope my efforts ease your burdens.

Still my deathly fancy saddens me. For these happy days are rarer than they should be. We are both fools, wrapped in our own affairs, too quick to hurt, too brusque in manners, caring too much for our worldly station and too little for love, and family, and each other. Yet I love you, and one day you will be gone, and I wish to meet that day unabashed, and say, he is gone, but—glory be—how I loved him; and how he loved me.

LADY ELODIE'S JOURNAL, PART THE SECOND [MOLLY]

Lady Elodie's diary was not all so highly strung and feverish. Much of it was workaday: talks and dinners, correspondence listed, chores achieved; but every so often, when she returned from charitable campaigns, when Roxbury was away, her poetic nature flooded.

She was a woman who wanted the world. At times, she got it; and I loved her for that dogged lyricism, her argumentative romantic style. I ached that she was gone, or rather incapacitated, and their love sundered.

Romantic teenage fool I am. But so many stories of love spoiled or foiled or embroiled one hears. To find one so true, although strained to the point of breaking, was a redemption.

Soon enough, I found Lady Elodie's discovery that she was, again, pregnant.

My love today is bursting for Roxbury. And——dare I write——for the little one. I have felt stirrings. Changes. Today Edward's doctor, blasted automaton though he is, confirmed it. "Lady Roxbury," quoth he, with an unprecedented smile, "you are expecting." Many things have I expected in these fierce years of marriage, but nothing has prepared me for the thrill of electricity that jolted through my being.

Reading these fragmented entries, the Lady Elodie's longing for the child to come was redoubled in my own longing for these fragments to be made whole; I felt I knew her, but still she eluded me, as if, turning another page or the next, she would suddenly appear fully-fledged, sat here before me in this Lady's Library of longing, hidden behind the chapel.

And yet Lady Elodie suffered doubts. Grave doubts. She feared she was old for giving birth, and older still for bringing up a child. The anxiety welled and ebbed through the pages. I wanted to reach out and say it was a needless panic, to tell her that for any child to have a mother at all is better than none at all, and she would be… She would have been a wonderful mother.

My fervour wore away as I remembered the fruitlessness of it all, and thought of the Norphans Practickly and their wayward habits. I rooted and rooted for a happy ending; I knew what finale must come.

Did these morbid reading lists tell all I needed to know? Between the accounts of Skirtle, Birtle and Roxy, and Lady Elodie's own annotations and marginalia, the sad tale was coming clear: a longed-for pregnancy, an ill-starred birth, and loss. Then illness, fading of causes I could not understand. How it ended I yet must discover.

Her local library card listed volumes taken out 1860–62:

Fertility, and How to Improve It
The Approaching Disaster
Remedies for Catastrophic Pregnancy
Hysterical Problems, Mind and Body
Post-partum Melancholia, and other Maladies
Epilepsy, St Vitus' Dance, the Falling Sickness
Convulsions and Their After-Effects
Sleepwalking and Night Terrors
Melancholia Numinosa
The Lunacy and County Asylums Act
Reaching the Unreachable
Lethargy and Ataraxy: New Treatments and Stimulations

REVELATIONS [ELODIE]

Today my love for him is fraught. (I am sure it is "him".)

I woke, sick, filling the chamber pot with acrid distillations. They make me eat. I'd rather not. Nor drink. No breakfast. I can barely rise. Edward's doting indulges my worst habits. I do not wish my sloth to be indulged. I am no paragon of self-denial, as so many wives aim to be. Self-denial I shall never achieve. If nuns and monks claim godliness in self-denial, they are misled; surely any loving god would offer the surer way to enlightenment through acknowledging desires, indulging and redeeming. That is the only path, I think, certainly the human path.

I am avoiding the nub of the problem.

I am afraid.

Something strange is happening. To me. In me, I dare not tell Edward. He will consign me to "lie in", and I have no intention of "lying in" yet. The fatigue is fatiguing, the sickness is sickening; but these I could cope with. What troubles me is this confounded confusion of senses.

Today Birtle brought the coffee up. "Morning, madam," says he, and something in the way his lips move makes me think of beef stock—no, not think—I'd swear I tasted beef stock. The glorious coffee smell was quite displaced by the odour of beef. How can that be?

"Father, Son, and Holy Spirit," said the minister.

I could smell lardy bun with golden syrup, and wished I had not dragged my weary limbs to church.

I stared about to see who was eating. Nobody was, everybody at their prayers, but my senses buzzing with an onslaught of tastes, smells, colours, textures, replacements. I stared at the minister's face for a full minute and saw his cheeks turn to pastry, lightly baked; then the choir (all six) had pastry faces: sopranos uncooked, tenors flaking, the altos nicely browned.

I made an excuse during the second psalm and stumbled home to bed.

INITIAL DIAGNOSIS [BY A DOCTOR BROUGHT BACK FROM FRANCE]

Patient describes an aura——firstly psychic, became somatic: a prodrome, as I term it.

Hears voices, single or several, chattering.

Sensation of embrace, kiss on right cheek.

Hallucinations, but she knows them for tricks, e.g. window panes tinted: colours reflect on visitors' faces.

Visions: black & dirty rats. Scenes from novels she has read. Coming & going rapidly in daytime; at night, played out slow.

None of their British doctors have done anything for her.

We may rule out everything they have suggested. They are obsessed with finding new-fangled diagnoses. Myalgia, encephalitis, dementia praecox, arthritis. Yet there is no physical evidence, no inflammation. Patient showed no loss of cognitive abilities, neither impairment of memory nor aphasia, apraxia, agnosia, and disturbed planning.

In the Salpêtrière Hospital, Paris, we are known for breakthroughs in the realm of hysteria and female diagnoses, viz my own tract, Maladies of the Spirit, treating of magnetism, morphinism and grand delirium.

I am more convinced by immunological disorder, consonant with epileptoid and synaesthetic reports. Either way, hypnosis serviceable.

Successfully hypnotised. Several muscles contracted in order to shake off debility. I was unable to release the muscles that constricted her vocal tract. Frustrating. Even when brought out of the hypnosis, tongue and larynx remained frozen, rendering her unable to speak.

A hysterico-epileptic of the most pronounced type. This leaves her vulnerable to the stresses of ordinary life, and, I believe, unfit for giving birth. I stayed with her, but was unable to discuss with Roxbury while he was called to national business. I eventually released her tongue, but larynx remained contracted. (I was obliged to administer chloroform to relax the larynx and enable her vocal chords to function.)

When he came back, all was well.

* * *

THE JUMBLE OF PERCEPTIONS [MOLLY]

Lady Elodie recorded the swift ebbing and flowing of this strange sensual equivalence, for which she discovered the name: synaesthesia. The interconnection of senses, mingling experiences with words and objects not apparently connected.

She described in minute detail how Kitty's sandals made her think of butterscotch. Birtle's hair tasted of meringue: not that she tasted it; the sight of it tasted of meringue.

DESCENT [ELODIE]

I am become uncommonly odd; I must touch only cotton, or I desire on a sudden to stroke silk. I taste words like leather, jam and fireworks. Numbers, colours, sounds, tastes, all are commingling. I had to stop talking to Birtle because the lemon kept dripping over the meringue.

Edward told me of our glasshouse extensions—to distract me, I think, from my obsessive talk which scares him rather—and that there will be 8008 panes (and the number glows pink in my mind) with 7734 stanchion frame pieces (a fiery red). As he sketches out the new scientific quarter, it lurks in my mind like vast hellish innards, plants and animals tasting of brimstone and sulphur, as if serving a banquet to spite me for my hunger.

If the savour of the inventory is so strong, how will the greenhouse itself taste?

Edward is building it for me. Really, he is occupying himself, while he feels so powerless. I am glad. At least he has set aside business a while, and is near. (Lodestar does lighten his cares, though the business redoubles).

I am afraid. This joyful season so long wished for; now it is here, I feel bizarre. I even feel alone. Though Edward is on hand, his doctors ever investigating me, I feel a blackness whirling around me.

WOMEN'S DIAGNOSES [CUTTINGS IN THE LADY'S LIBRARY]

ADMISSIONS TO YORKSHIRE'S WEST RIDING LUNATIC ASYLUM, 1863–64:

2 YEARS' SNUFF EATING

BAD COMPANY

BLOODY FLUX

BRAIN FEVER

CHRONIC MANIA

CONSECUTIVE DEMENTIA

DERANGED MASTURBATION

DESERTION BY HUSBAND

DISSIPATION OF NERVES

DISSOLUTE HABITS

DOMESTIC AFFLICTION

EGOTISM

EPILEPTIC FITS

EXPOSURE AND QUACKERY

FEEBLENESS OF INTELLECT

FEMALE DISEASE

HEREDITARY PREDISPOSITION

INTEMPERANCE AND BUSINESS TROUBLE

JEALOUSY AND RELIGION

GATHERING IN THE HEAD

GRIEF

GUNSHOT WOUND

HARD STUDY

ILL-TREATMENT BY HUSBAND

NOVEL READING
NYMPHOMANIA
OPIUM HABIT
OVERSTUDY OF RELIGION
PARENTS WERE COUSINS
PERIODICAL FITS
POLITICAL EXCITEMENT
SCARLATINA
SEDUCTION AND DISAPPOINTMENT
UTERINE DERANGEMENT
VICIOUS VICES

WHAT SHE DID NOT WRITE [MOLLY]

What Lady Elodie did not write of were the fits. It took me time to understand, but she marked in her diary a large angry asterisk—*—and usually wrote no more on that day. It was only in the catalogue of doctors' notes, prescriptions, diagnoses and fits, talking of the Falling Sickness and St Vitus' Dance, that I could now discern patterns, as they attempted to give her something to stop the fits without harming the unborn child.

She sometimes wrote in the lines before the—*—of an overwhelming feeling of wellbeing, a shining certainty that all would be fine and exalted at the end.

But I have often heard, from those who have fits, that an exaltation seizes them in the minutes before the fit begins.

BLESSED [ELODIE]

My heart hurts, [she wrote, one day recovering from a sedation]. My heart hurts to think of him. The doctor says—but the doctor is an idiot—that there may be something wrong. The heart beats irregularly; sometimes it scarcely beats at all. This bodes ill, he says.

How can something so blessed bode so ill? I chide him. Check me again and give me something. But he will not, for fear of setting me off again.

Edward insists I must not worry. "We are blessed," he repeats, as if to convince himself. But I hear his muttered conversations at the door, and I am afraid. I have been so lucky, to be loved, and wooed, and wed, and spoiled, and blessed with our children, and wealth, and health— till now. But now the doctor—hard to write—the doctor casts all into jeopardy. I will not write thus.

I shall write instead to you, my dear child, my child unimaginable, so long hoped for, my child in danger. I shall not give up, however they affright me, however I must fight them, I shall not give you up. I will cherish you—ah, but why must I write of your end, before you are even begun?

And then the diary went silent, for days, up to the due date for the birth, and beyond, with only —*—s to mark the passing of time, and doctor's receipts.

GAPS IN THE RECORD [MOLLY]

Roxbury later filled me in on the gap in the diary. How could she write of it in those terrible days, terrible weeks?

"I knew birth could be hard, could be painful," he said. "I did not know it could be a bloodbath. The yellow bedroom looked like the Colosseum by the time they'd got him out, and I was fearful first for her. The doctors wielded their knives, the midwives their forceps; we had them all lined up, forewarned of trouble. They would not let me in to be with her, fearful how I would react to the carnage. She screamed and begged for them to let me in, because she did not trust them to look after the boy. She thought their diagnoses had prejudiced me against him, and was afraid they would decide she could not have him. How much blood she lost. Pints. I cannot speak of it: the instruments they used, her fearful pallor when finally they let me see her.

"The wind was howling against the turret, just as it is now. The candles sputtered, and she would not sleep; she kept asking and asking to see him. And I did not know how to say nay: we brought him, but he was deadly ill. They said he might not last the night, as they had warned, and would not reach a week. They prescribed ten contradictory ways to cure him or save him or give him a tenth of the life we wished him to have, and all these required her to leave him in their care and try and recover. It was awful. She suffered the same fits as before, yet it was also a kind of fit that took her, a withdrawing fit that stole her away inside herself."

The next diagnostic passages confirmed this mystification, as doctors from far and wide were called to tend her. *Melancholia numinosa*, one called it. Another, post-partum depression. Still a third, *aphasia electa*, with concomitant *peregrinationes nocturnae*. But none of these was sufficient to explain her symptomology.

He told me how they tried everything to revive her to normal spirits: pills, leeches, massage (Chinese, Swedish, Indian head), rubbing, prodding, stimulation of prescribed areas, warmth, cool, bedpans, ice, Turkish bath, hair brushing, sinus tapping, gland stimulation, coffee, opium, stroking, scratching, music, noise, silence, flashing lights, and electricity.

He waved his hand, with a sort of a half-nod, and I could trouble him no further. Seventy-three contradictory treatments. No wonder he was grown tired of it. Anyone would throw up their hands and give up.

But how did it end? He did not tell, and there were yet more entries in the diary, her diary, after the birth, and sorely broken.

AFTER THE BIRTH [ELODIE]

Into my pen, I cannot heave my heart. The trees blow against the window.

Soon enough the rain will drench them, then the snow.

It seems so desperately long since I wrote of those dark clouds obscuring the days of expectancy. The journal has sat moribund here, while up in the yellow room we tussled with life and death. I cannot begin.

Movement inside. The doctor's warnings. Edward's fears, and mine.

I cannot write today. Why such things happen is unfathomable. Poor Skirtle, she had to be strong, when I was weak. The little life that struggled to find breath in the room. He was here, and here, and then gone, still gone. Forever gone. Never to return. I cannot write of it. I wish to hide from the world and never to expose these woes.

His little hands. Holding so briefly the tiny fingers. The tiniest of fingernails, so miniature in form. Perfect spine. A few short breaths, and taken away, I cannot dwell on it. I cannot write. My chest aches, and I am dying here in my tower.

* * *

CLARITY, OPACITY [ELODIE]

Clearer than this the doctors cannot be. They told us something was wrong. I am ill. My fits, unexplained and unpredictable. My pains, not simply childbirth. The doctors tell me the baby has problems—as if he were in debt or misbehaving. And yet he comes out, bawling, though they said he would be dead. He bawled, dear little heart!

Problems with his breathing; problems with his heart.

Can they perform an operation? The wonders of modern medicine, and so forth. Edward has brought the finest surgeons in the land.

They could operate, they say, but it is a congenital defect; better to leave him in Skirtle's arms for now. There he may die peacefully.

There he may die? And my arms: whom may I hold in my arms? I ask to hold him, I want to suckle him. The juddering fit comes upon me, and they press the zones to relieve it. When I come to myself, there is another doctor, another surgeon, who explains that he can open up little Jonathan's chest, like a cage, or like an oyster, to see if he cannot repair the hole in his heart.

"Will he not bleed to death?"

The surgeon says that he may.

"Are you certain there is a hole in his heart?"

As certain as he can be.

"So you are not."

I look to Edward, and we shake our heads. Skirtle and I take turns holding him, lulling him, but we cannot quiet him, that dreadful sound wheezing from his lungs.

I come round again from a fit. I wonder if I may have dreamt the latest surgeon. Edward is still trying. Everything. Anything. One surgeon believes iron lungs help congenital breathing difficulties. Within hours Edward has one made at the works, and brought for our use. But his wails are fading. Edward insists we let the doctors put him in the contraption. I am destitute; Skirtle too, but she has to comfort me.

So we watch him die, unheld, uncomforted. I cannot hate them for it, cannot hate Edward. But I feel myself unhinged. My body is rebelling. My brain whirls into a gyre from which I never shall cease spinning.

My only relief from this lifeless deathlike existence are the fits. Seizures that freeze the heart. Sometimes I feel death near. They still me, restrain me, try to keep the fragile mechanism sound, ticking from one bald hour to the next, from day to benighted day.

How long until I yield? Despair sits beside my bed. I am spent, I'm shattered. Apothecary, cannot you relieve me?

HAIL AND FAREWELL [MOLLY]

I devoured her heartfelt jottings with my heart swelling, and I wished I could reach back and redeem their loss.

I went again down to the Walled Garden. This time, I stumbled to his grave with trembling awe. The sorry family tale ran through my sundered mind. I felt drained, and drawn to him, this tiny frame: all the king's horses and all the earl's quacks could not put him back together again. His little heart beating, beating, beating; and stopped.

I have known many little souls who have faded and failed in the hard London winters, with the cholera and consumption and all; but oh, to think of Lady Elodie's wish granted, then snatched away. He lived, and she dandled him in her arms, as she had dreamed, as he struggled to cry.

And those fool doctors took him from her and did not let her see him and told her he was dead. And the fit took her again. No wonder it did. A relief. A release. She had written one last time in the book, when she knew that he was dead and was beginning to understand the bleak truth, and was becoming unhinged by it, and lost to the world of woes.

JONATHAN IS DEAD [ELODIE]

Jonathan is dead. Call for tea. Skirtle makes a lovely pot. But I shall take it with lemon. I don't wish to see milk.

His little fingers.

Call for my boots. I shall go for a walk. Can I get up? I am still bleeding. Where is the value in living? I cannot read, I cannot listen to moralising sermons. He lived, at least. All that we could do, we did. Didn't we? He lived. That cannot be said of every little soul who vanishes away. He lived, and I held him, and he shall not be forgot.

I shall walk to the Walled Garden. What is the racket down by the arboretum? What are they doing, there in the glasshouses, when I am trying to rest? No rest, now he is gone. Watchfulness: something was not right. His heart, his windpipe. They squeezed the breath into him at first. Is that so unusual? How were they sure something was amiss? Was there nothing wrong, really? They talk rot, these medics. Why did we believe them? Fiddle-faddling with facts and figures. Diagnoses. Agh, these diabolical diagnoses.

How does that square with your medical oaths, tell me, coming to tell me that he will not live, when he was palpably alive in my arms? And taking him... How can that accord with the tender ministrations of their duty? He was here; now is gone. Is he yet in the ground? I must see him. I should not like to see him put in the ground before

I am. I would keep him here, with me, until such time as I can no longer.

Already I can no longer. I am indistinct. I am vague with doubt. And guilt. Someone is to blame. A child is not alive one hour and dead the next without reason. I do not accept it.

I will not. I feel the shuddering aura approach. Where is he? Bring him back to me.

SECONDARY DIAGNOSIS [FRENCH DOCTOR]

Notes: patient in a state of catalepsy. As if I had placed her under hypnosis—no different—but I have not. Patient alternates between lethargic and cataleptic states. Continues to have tonic & clonic seizures. Has communicated with nobody since attack.

The attack:
Pain, intense, right leg: the boule hystérique radiating from the right ovary, rising through digestive tract, suffocating her, like an apple at the base of the neck.
Ears ringing, eyes pressured, heart palpitating, temples hammering.
Tongue curled up in mouth, contracted. Vision foggy, hands clenched.
Head jerked to the right—and she was gone.
Thus the onset of the hysterical attack.

Diagnosis now sure: hysterico-epileptic.
Hysterico-epileptoid origin of the fits proven, as they are arrested by hysterogenic pressure. This is her type. It is a chronic state, a disease for life. The cataleptic state is a kind of brain fog. Her body has gone limp and numb, but her eyes are open and she appears sentient.
No evidence of intellection.

I touch the skin near her neck lightly, just above the sternocleidomastoid, and she twists her neck, afflicted with torticollis; I rub the other side, and she untwists. There is no sense of volition. She can be shaped, like a wax model. If the flexors of the forearm are rubbed, they become rigid; I cannot overcome this flexion by force, but only by rubbing the corresponding extensors. Any number of muscles may be contracted: biceps, pectorals, whatever, producing contractions as severe as seen in hemiplegia; but they may be resolved simply by exciting in turn the antagonistic muscles.

She cannot answer questions; neither distressed nor at rest. To prove her anaesthesia, I pierced her skin with a needle. Roxbury was disquieted, yet it caused her no apparent pain.

Too far, during these experiments. Whatever experiments we attempted, she relapsed into lethargic sleep. When tried to wake her, unable. Splashed her with water. Tried ovarian compression, faradisation——nothing worked.

Next morning, after twenty-two hours of sleep, her body was limp.

Her pulse was 28–32; her breathing slowed to three to six breaths per minute; temperature was below 98 degrees; face cyanotic, suggesting extreme danger to life.

We pressed on her hysterogenic zones and brought her back to consciousness. This "attack of artificial sleep", like that caused by narcotics, scared the earl so much that he wishes me to desist from these experiments.

She thus remains in this cataleptic state, malleable, feedable, but desperately absent.

BRUSH WITH DEATH [MOLLY]

After the narrow brush with death, Roxbury dismissed the Frenchman, I read in the diagnostic notes. He resigned himself to her state, though continually seeking other avenues.

At last, he met John Hughlings Jackson, who had already mapped out many of the disorders of the brain through posthumous dissections of patients he had known well.

As his knowledge of the brain increased, and which areas governed which faculties, he was becoming increasingly interested in the stimulation of the brain by electricity. He believed that, just as Galvani had made frogs' legs jerk with the correct positioning and voltage, so we might shift the sluggish faculties, if only we could be precise both in our knowledge of the brain and our control of electricity. Jackson had nearly arrived at the neurological knowledge; it was by great good fortune that he met Roxbury, who had nearly achieved the necessary mastery of electricity.

When he closed her eyes, though, she relapsed into lethargy. This sleep, of indeterminate length, could last days. She could be awoken at any time by shining a bright light in her eyes, or banging a gong. This returned her to the cataleptic state, in which she was manageable, but not present.

THE TURRET OF THE EAST WING [MOLLY]

Down at the Walled Garden, I looked up at the house.

In the turret, a movement. My mind swirled with Lady Elodie's words. In my mind, I conjured her up, at the window, pulling back the heavy floral curtain. A solemn heart-shaped face, blinking at the day's brightness, seeing, but unseeing, the gaze directed inwards at her forlorn self, isolated in that high tower above the Burnfoot gorge, above the bustling activity of the house, of the glasshouses and menagerie, where scientists busied themselves with opaque researches.

I walked back to the house, the rain driving against my coat and scarf, my mind tumbling through the past weeks. The earl's melancholy; Birtle and Skirtle's complicity; I could no longer bear to be excluded.

I tore unannounced into Birtle's quarters.

He looked at me, and I believe he understood my crisis.

"Lady Elodie?" I beseeched him. "I must— Will you not let me—?"

"I'll take you up to see her." He stood. He put his hand kindly on my shoulder. "Now that you're one of the family."

GYRE [LAWLESS]

In the week before I met up with Lodestar on No Man's Land Fort, things changed. Perhaps I had been naive, rather than foolish; we had certainly not been lazy. Things only now began to make sense, things I would never have connected.

I made discoveries about Lodestar's style, in business and pleasure, that tallied with Ruth's concerns.

Bracebridge Hemyng had clammed up that day. But I caught up with him again, tight as a boiled owl, at the old Coach and Horses. I provided him with more neck-oil, to ease his leg pain, and he never suspected he was being worked for information.

Hemyng spoke of the incessant gambling in the Hounds Club. Lodestar liked to hang around the flash set, never drinking, always listening. I took down the names surreptitiously. I'd brought a betting pencil specially, so Hemyng would think I was just planning my afternoon's bets. Each man he named, peers and parliamentarians among them, had accounts at Overend and Gurney. They had profited in the wake of the outrages from buying up cheap property in Erith, Camden, et cetera.

Useless to name them here: I could garner no proof of their involvement, beyond their clairvoyant profiteering.

Lodestar himself never bet.

"Hadn't the capital for it." Hemyng took a hefty pinch of snuff. "Not that that prevented him accruing debts."

I refused his proffered snuff tin. "How did Lodestar catch these fellows' interest?"

"Information." Hemyng winked. "He was the information man. A fascinating aura of otherness about him. He knows some rum coves with their ear to the ground."

"Meaning?"

"As if he knew of the attacks before they happened. It was uncanny."

"That's one word for it. Hemyng, you wouldn't suspect he had a hand in orchestrating them?"

"Lodestar? No fear. A greater patriot you couldn't meet. A bigot for John Bull, if ever there was one. A xenophobe. A Francophobe!"

"You didn't find it odd for an incomer to be so patriotic?"

"Not at all. These sons of empire are more vehement in admiring the homeland's greatness. And overlooking its flaws. And his old pa had a beef with Napoleon. Injury at Waterloo. Buy us a drink, won't you?"

I executed the same squeeze on Overend and one or two others from the Hounds Club. Nobody spilled the whole stratagem. Nobody mentioned Hellfire. But two spoke of recent investments in property, and Overend had recently opened a profitable branch on Guernsey.

Lodestar Senior was by no means injured in the Napoleonic Wars, as he was a child at the time; but he may have spun that yarn to his young sons, avid for tales of Europe at war. He had brought them up on a diet of French plots. Could that be where the Guernsey papers originate, with a disaffected Home Office renegade, obsessed by Waterloo?

Ruth's researches dug up further anomalies about Lodestar Senior. He was never consul to Mozambique and the Interior, as Overend believed. On the contrary, he had covert instructions to penetrate the Portuguese Zambesi, dealing with tribes in Nyasaland and Bechuanaland, with a view to future absorption in the empire. Lodestar Senior was a hard man, whom the Home Office was happy to risk, if not glad to see the back of. (He may have called his farm a British protectorate, but that was personal fancy, not by royal decree.) Another thing Lodestar had omitted to tell was that his father was effectively exiled from Britain after serious misdemeanours. Ruth discovered, back in the thirties, a coterie within the Hounds Club rejoicing in the name of "Hellfire Hounds". I went into Ripon's files to investigate this banishment, but the documents were incomplete. A dead end.

I sped around the country, speaking to foremen and contractors who dealt with Lodestar frequently. He was universally known for getting the job done, with minimum fuss. That sounds complimentary, at first. Once they realised we were not company men, though, they were inclined to give a rounder view.

Take the harbour master in Portsmouth, for example, where I visited to prepare the details for my meeting on behalf of Bazalgette. He liked Lodestar, but there was a twinkle to the eye that invited further questions. "There was that one time." He glanced down at the mudflats underlying the pier. Lodestar, it turned out, had a habit of throwing workers off their cranes and into the mud, as a warning against complaints. This gave the mudlarks a laugh, but it was not smart practice. "I told him off for it. I said, there's no use getting the cranesmen in a strop. He'd broke one bloke's ankle." The man whistled. "The look he gave me. Let's just say, I backed down. Looked like he would skin me alive."

FRUITLESS [LAWLESS]

All our efforts to prove the blasts connected proved fruitless. Enquiries, interviews. Each outrage had been meticulously planned and yet rather carelessly executed. No trace was found of the perpetrators, or their bosses, yet the outcome was ineffective.

Ripon called me in. He coughed uncomfortably. "Do you think, Lawless, that you may have overstated the French threat to the parliamentary committee?"

"You've changed your tune." I stared at him. "Sir."

"No, no." He held up a finger. "Not fair, old man. I had no tune. I simply asked you to investigate."

I stared at him. Ripon had whipped up the French panic from the first day we met him. "We found convincing evidence of malevolent French interference."

Ripon looked smug. "The Guernsey papers."

"Yes, sir. So where's the overstatement?" I said. "The alleged overstatement, sir."

He chuckled. "As word gets out about those papers, well, you must have heard the rumours. The press is saying that these are antique plans. All this fuss. Over old threats. And the French have neither the capacity nor the will to do anything of the sort now."

"That could be true, sir." I shrugged. "But that's what the French would want us to think. My trust in the press's intentions is shaky. I'm down to Portsmouth this week, to negotiate a deal on bricks. I'll see what they think."

Ripon put his head in his hands. Whether justified or not, these forts were in danger of ending his cabinet career, and he wouldn't hesitate to blame Jeffcoat and me for the whole scheme.

"Before you go," he said, "forgot to mention. Your Jacques the First, the real Frenchman. One of our plain-clothes saw him boarding a train at King's Cross."

* * *

SKITTLES AT HOME [LAWLESS]

Skittles was at home, and welcomed me warmly. She did enjoy the investigative tasks I set her, and she had made quick work of getting on top of the French secret service.

"I can absolutely guarantee you." She poured: a beautiful brew. Her many admirers competed over having cases of tea delivered to her. "It is not the French."

"Bloody hell." I had a thirst, after my scorching from Ripon. "You can't absolutely guarantee it."

She took up the half-lemon and squeezed it into her cup, with a thoughtful look. "The head of the Sûreté has a fetish. Le Mouchard likes to extract information with a tiny bit of torture. In turn, I have discovered, he doesn't mind a playful tying up himself. I took the chance to interrogate him. All in fun, you understand. I made him beg. And I am good at distinguishing what is said in love play and what in earnest. This was in earnest. He knows nothing about it. She squeezed the lemon dry and tossed it aside. "Not a thing."

NEWS FROM AFRICA [LAWLESS]

That same week, Ruth heard back from Africa. She came in at once. A peculiar letter, somewhat hysterical in tone. We pored over it. The estate had fallen on hard times, since the departure of Lodestar Senior from this vale of woe. They wrote of his son and heir, Nathan Chichester Lodestar, of his childhood illnesses and continuing frailty, of his decision despite poor health to set out for the Cape and the steamer to Britain, accompanied only by his father's valet Zephaniah. They had heard nothing since, beyond the curtest of cards, saying he had arrived in London, he was winding up his father's sorry affairs, and they should hear no further from him.

"And here." Ruth, with the satisfaction of a lawyer delivering the clinching point, laid a photograph in front of me. "Dated 1857. A year or more before our man sailed for Britain."

Lodestar Senior was a beguiling dragon, by the looks of it, surrounded by native servants, mostly female.

That was not the most striking thing. The thing that changed everything was his son, seated next to him. Nothing like Roxbury's vivacious swarthy right-hand man, he was spindly as a rake, with fair hair and piercing eyes, and teeth prominent like a rabbit's.

"The only thing we know for certain about 'Nathan Lodestar'," said Ruth, "is that his name is not Nathan Lodestar."

MOLLY AT THE BEDSIDE [MOLLY]

Lady Elodie lay still, a picture of poetry. Clouds scuttered darkly past the window of the turret: the gorge fell away beneath us, sparkling and forbidding. I approached her, dumbstruck. Her body was at rest, and yet the face showed a lack of ease. The restful repose to which we dedicate ourselves in the haven of our bedchambers was denied to her. Had she not been through enough? She twitched imperceptibly, and I leapt back, stumbling into Birtle.

He patted my shoulder, to sit me down. I watched, awestruck, as this magical nymph lay there, pale and wan, but alive. Drawn features, pinched white cheeks. Yet in her limbs a statuesque grace.

Again she twitched, and I imagined that in her dreams she was running, on a beach somewhere, the cells of her brain struggling to throw a ball, and to catch it, millions of nerves sending messages back and forth, to the faraway parts of the body, striving to alert them to stir the body, to wake it from these dreams and tell it that all was working and alive.

I turned and looked at Birtle. Their obsessive behaviour and strange absences: it all made sense now.

He stared at her, noting the twitches. I began to understand Skirtle's account of her phases of somnolence and waking.

"Is she all right?" I said.

He stood, dampened a cloth in the glass of water on the bedside table, and dabbed at her brow. "She is… unrestful these last days."

It seemed wrong to speak of her like that, in front of her. And now that I write of her phases, nearer to consciousness, and further from it, I wonder if there are the patterns in this wakefulness.

When we came away, he told me more: how Patience tends and bathes her. She sometimes manages to rouse her, stand her up, sit her on the end of the bed, bring her to the window, open the windows, try to get her to breathe the air of Roxbury.

Every so often she does wake, or seem to wake. Then she feeds her, tentatively, soft fruits and drinks and whatever she can manage, though she never speaks, never ever speaks. Skirtle used to tell Roxbury whenever she was awake, but it made him so wild with grief, she desisted. He visits still, but he has not seen that still she stirs sometimes, and the fit comes upon her, and then they are able to rouse her from her stupor.

"Does he not try to rescue her?"

"He tried." Birtle shook his head. "Oh, Molly, he has tried. He tried so many, many things, Miss Moll."

"But he has given up?"

Birtle, hesitantly, melancholically, nodded.

I thought for a moment. I thought of the glasshouses, the parrot, the monkey. Has he given up? Has the earl given up?

Not likely.

LODESTAR'S PENULTIMATE VISIT [MOLLY]

WATCHMAN,
LODESTAR NOT ALL HE PURPORTS TO BE.
DETAILS TO FOLLOW.
TAKE CARE.
MOLL

Dear Miss V,
Lodestar's latest visit has set my head spinning.

I was late to breakfast. I was on the window seat, sketching the view, as the rains hammered down. Up span his phaeton, mud splashing in its wake. He leapt down, throwing down the reins before Birtle could put up his umbrella. Into the house he strode, throwing off his wet things, shouting for coffee and clothes.

He breezed into the breakfast room. He seemed tired, yet always that roguish energy within him. Unaware of me, he slumped on a chair, loosening his collar. His shirt clung to his shoulders, sodden. For a man of business, he was muscular. All the business dinners he attended, and still he kept the sculptural physique. He began peeling off his shirt.

I thought it time to pipe up. "Why, Mr Lodestar, the roads must be miserable today."

He gave me an insolent glance, and pulled off his shirt anyway. "Not at all, with the destination so… delectable."

He ran his tongue deliberately around his lips.

He expected me to avert my eyes. He did not know that I grew up in mixed lodgings, where the sexes mingle indecorously without wasting effort. As a young lady, more or less, I knew he shouldn't bare his torso in my presence. To remonstrate, though, would accomplish nothing; Jem has told of Lodestar's angers, when provoked or contradicted. Besides, it was not my way to comment on dress.

"Beautiful indeed, sir." I turned deliberately back to my drawing. "If only I could capture it."

He threw down the wet shirt and looked for the coffee pot, which sat by me.

"It should still be warm." I brought a cup to the table near him and returned demurely to my window.

He reached out, amused by watching me not watching him. He took a lingering sip, craning his neck to see my work. "Captured beauty I never find as attractive as beauty wild and loose."

I turned to the window, ashamed of my blushes. Turncoat flesh.

The maid came in, with dry clothes. Upon seeing him half-clad, she shrieked. She dropped the bundle, scooped it up again, all but threw it at him and fled. The atmosphere was rarefied, as if sparks were flying between us. I stared out the window, affecting a casual tone. "What brings you to Roxbury in this inclement season?"

He looked at me impudently. "Hellfire!" he declared.

I stared. He had pulled on a dry shirt, so this was no indecency. His eyes were big and wide beneath those dark brows. He thought his oath would shock me. Ha: he is a squeaking rantallion in oath-making, compared to my Oddbody friends.

"I am perfecting new explosives. Testing for the

Portsmouth Forts. I'm to meet your detective there, what's his name?"

"Lawless. Not my detective. Miss Ruth's."

His look suggested untoward thoughts. "I thought you were well acquainted."

"I am well acquainted, sir, with much of London's society, as are you." I wondered why he was trying to rile me; perhaps it was just habitual, now that he'd noticed me, sitting in the window, framed by the thunderous skies. "And how are your scientists progressing?"

"Not my scientists. Roxbury's." Touché. He drank down the coffee I had poured, something carnivorous in his manner. "Progress for me is progress for the nation. Which also entails progress for the earl and his private endeavours. It's a satisfactory establishment."

"And yet its one fault is that it is not yours." I don't know what provoked me into such provocation: his arrogant air, I suppose. I turned back to drawing. "Galling to receive the plaudits, but not the profits."

By luck, the serving maid returned with fresh coffee to distract him from my insults. As she set it down, timidly, she gave a yelp: sure enough, Mr Lodestar had removed his trousers and was reaching for the dry pair. The maid's shock amused him. He made a grab for her behind, as she fled in a panic.

I stared at him.

He continued to dress, deliberate and unhurried.

This disregard for decency no longer surprised me. Until now, I had seen him ever charming, if offhand.

Something told me this was the real Lodestar, unobserved; or rather observed by those who could not report his behaviour and be believed. If the maid told, or if I told, we would be suspected of encouraging him, flirting, or worse. His indecency would brand us loose-moralled.

Lodestar's behaviour galled me, but also thrilled. It made me want to beguile him. Yes, to cast a noose around his vanity and draw it tight. What would impress this fast gent in his swift phaeton? He might scoff at my humble station, or yours, Miss Ruth; but there are people he'd consider worthy of notice, and we know them. What could impress him more than royalty?

"The sergeant will be back here soon enough." I gathered my things, nonchalant. "Miss Villiers and he have plans for a very important visitor. I'm sure you know all about it."

He did not, of course. As you know, I was making it up.

I felt no guilt at inventing this diversion, Miss Ruth. I've felt Lodestar's grandiosity growing with every visit. I am drawn to him, but I do not trust him. He will stop at nothing to get what he wants. If we stand in his way, he will not hesitate to clear us aside. I cannot flee: I cannot desert my commission, nor leave Roxbury and Elodie under his influence. But his strength is flawed. He desires the world's approval—oh, how he longs for it. He loves the company of the powerful, and needs to feel their equal.

Hence my plan, improvised in that moment (which, I pray, you will help me fulfil).

He was, for a moment, on the back foot.

I made for the door, but he interposed his frame.

"Explain yourself, little one," he purred, "won't you? Miss Molly, isn't it?"

No doubt he was a powerful specimen. He had noticed me finally. But I have spent these last weeks caged with pythons and jaguars, and I have emerged unscathed. I would not have him dominate me, nor presume upon my favours. I looked up at him. The dark bristles on his chin contrasted with the crisp linen collar. He smelt of rain. I shook myself, debating whether I'd have more chance kicking him in his privates, or insulting them.

"Sir?" Birtle appeared in the doorway, thank God. He reached out and took my hand, kindly, for the maid must have warned him I should be fetched to safety. "The earl will see you now, if your apparel is to your satisfaction."

"Birtle?" Lodestar stepped aside, disgruntled. "Right. New developments, eh?"

Birtle retreated to the stairs, satisfied that he had saved my honour, at least for now.

"Miss Molly." Lodestar lingered at the door, adjusting his belt, and lingered over my name. "One moment. You are the one sending letters, is it true?"

"Yes." I edged out the doorway, stony-faced.

"Daily. Encoded letters."

"Yes." I faced him. "Why?"

He ran his tongue around his lips. "Don't." He swept past, with a lingering look, up the stairs towards the tower.

Miss Ruth, here is my suggestion, and I hope you will agree to facilitate it. We must pretend that the Prince of Wales is going to visit. This will keep Lodestar at bay. Though amoral and reckless, he is a royalist and a narcissist.

For an introduction to royalty, he would sacrifice much. If we are the key to that introduction, it will tether him to decency, for the time being, and keep us safe, for the time being.

I shall tell Roxy the ruse, without explaining why; neither he nor I will answer if Lodestar asks of it, beyond the vaguest hints.

Nerve Stimulation [*British Medical Journal*]

Stimulation therapy offers a new treatment for epilepsy. It involves a stimulator connected to the left vagus nerve in the neck, generating electrical pulses within the body.

Dr Hughlings Jackson has long studied faints, vagal attacks, megrims, and cataplexy. Building upon the advances of Fritsch and Hitzig, who provoked seizures by stimulating dogs' brains, Jackson has understood epilepsy on a pathological and anatomical basis, identifying the localised cortical lesions that cause epileptic convulsions.

Based on his study of convulsions, the doctor sends a regular, electrical stimulation through the vagal nerve. This appears to calm the irregular electrical brain activity that leads to seizures. "Epilepsy," says the doctor, "is occasional, sudden, excessive, rapid and local discharges of grey matter."

Nerve stimulation therapy offers hope of treatment for those whose seizures are not controlled with medication. How treatment varies from one person to another is still a point of research, but the doctor hopes to treat paralysis arising from both from hysterical causes and from diseases of the spine, corpus striatum and brain hemispheres.

INTERCEPTED [MOLLY]

Miss V,
Knowing my postbag no longer safe, I am encoding this whole missive.

This afternoon, I heard him intercept a Frenchman at the door.

I was already shaken to think how I had misjudged Lodestar, though you warned me off him, I know, I know.

I consider myself a reasonable judge of character. It's an imperative of business in London to hope for the best of people, but expect the worst. This visit has changed my estimation of Lodestar: from magnetic man of business to cocksure flash gent, shining his eyes to attract you toward his dark continent, where ships were wrecked upriver.

All this you must pass on to Watchman, but with careful forethought, I pray. Our continual question was the solidity of Roxbury. The earl's mysteries I have fathomed.

But in Roxbury Industries, Lodestar runs the show, and runs it as he ran his father's estate in Africa, with impunity. Never a doubt in his decisions, nor hesitation in stealing ideas. This brings confidence in his decisions, and a desire to please him; it has brought out the best from Jem to the scientists to mighty Birtle.

Lodestar has, however, no compunction in punishing. Ask of his transgressions—intemperate outbursts— to gain a rounded picture of this fellow so embroiled with our Roxburys. Jem says he almost killed a stable boy for giving him the wrong horses for the phaeton; except they weren't the wrong horses; Lodestar just drove them so recklessly. Blaming others for our faults is not a trait I admire (though essential for bankers and politicians). It is one thing to sack employees for misdeeds; it is another to terrorise them. Another still to presume on the innocence of maids. But he is a peacock, ever seeking admiration, which speaks of pride. Flash gents are always vulnerable, in my experience: to overconfidence, to seduction, to blackmail.

This morning, I felt the threat of his insolence; I resent his intrusion upon our correspondence. When I escaped, I decided: I must be smart, and slippery, in order to exact my revenge. I pined for him those many weeks. Did my heart turn so quickly? I saw that something in his eyes and recoiled. My addled senses recovered their girlish wits.

It was pure luck I overheard his rendezvous. I'd gone to the secret chapel to ponder my plan, when I heard a fracas at the front door. I peered out through the angel glass.

Lodestar was giving some fellow a roasting. "You don't saunter up to a house like this and ring the doorbell. Get in." He threw him into the lower drawing room, and cornered him behind the door like a fugitive. "Don't let anybody see you."

By God, he was a fugitive. They spoke a potpourri of French and English: "Flee prison", "lucky to live", "once more", "Shepherd's Refuge…" That was all I could make out. It was enough. Lodestar bundled him out the side entrance.

I emerged, tentatively, and went straight to my sketchbook. Enclosed, my sketch of the Frenchman. Though of Watchman's investigations I know little, a Frenchman discussing escape seems worthy of mention: perhaps they will recognise him.

I hope this encoding does not hamper you. I shall ask Jem to post this for me when he goes to see his sweetheart, Dotty. Lodestar cannot have bought off the whole post office.

BOOK VIII
TO BRING HER BACK

A DREAM [LAWLESS]

I met with Edward Lear, at Ruth's behest, because he not only knew Lodestar Senior, but had met the young Nathaniel Chichester Lodestar long years ago.

Lear was about to set off for the Mediterranean. "I'm surprised how active this young Lodestar is. Can it really be Chesty? He was such a sickly boy. Angelic but pale."

"Pale?" I was astonished. "I'd say our Lodestar has a touch of the tar brush."

Lear frowned. "Then your Miss Villiers is right."

The one thing we knew about our Nathan Lodestar was that his name was not Nathan Lodestar.

The night before the final rendezvous, I had dreadful dreams.

Ellie's pub was pounded by bombs, from all around the city. Out of the pub, one by one, ran her fourteen children, each trying to extinguish the blazing clothes of the one in front. I knew them all: Molly, Kitty and Peggy and Nico, Jeffcoat and Ripon and Lodestar, Jacques I, II and III, Skirtle and Birtle and Roxbury. The cobbles were strewn with wires, crisscrossed, and melting. I was too slow: too late to roll it into the rope house and save the empire.

Last of all, out came Ellie, pregnant, except that she wasn't Ellie. She was Lady Elodie, come alive just to see her whole brood burning up in the conflagration.

"It's my home," she said. She poured me a pint of Long's Southsea Stout, with a look of reproach. She turned back to the Fortitude Tap, adorned with Roxbury's turrets, ablaze with thunderous clouds. The last I saw, her maternity dress fell to the ground, burnt to a cinder.

ELECTRICAL ECCENTRICALS
[PUNCH, OR THE LONDON CHARIVARI, 1844]

Those attending Edward Roxbury's public display of his electrical experiments may expect more than entertainment, more than edification.

Those afflicted by torpidity will sit on Leyden jars attached to Roxbury's hydro-electric machinery. A series of shocks will excite the liver to resume its proper duties.

The immense powers of this wondrous machine shall proceed to solidify nitrogen gas and albumen into animal fibre. Mr Roxbury will thus make beefsteaks out of cheap glue and birds' eggs, cook them to the audience's taste, and telegram your review directly to the moon.

INFILTRATION [MOLLY]

Miss V,

I have missed a few days. Our plans are advancing.

Roxy and I have brought the latest equipment up from the menagerie by pneumatic package. We are trying it daily, increasing the voltaic faradisation under Roxy's expertise, positioned according to his doctor friend's guidelines. You may think me wishful, but I believe the patient is beginning to show signs of responding.

Bertie himself? You are a marvel. That you hope to make my plan real is beyond marvellous.

I am on the point of uncovering the secrets you sent me here to discover, and not where we expected to find them. Don't tell Watchman. No, do tell him to be on guard, but don't tell him how I've got the information. I'm not proud of my methods; but more, I don't wish him to doubt my loyalty. I think you will understand. I dearly hope so.

The morning after my last letter, I was in the menagerie painting the Patagonian hare. Lodestar passed by with no comment, but only a dirty look. I sauntered along to his office. He took this as flirtation. I knew he would.

It was a grand office, with leather sofas and a billiard table.

"Fancy a game?" I challenged him. It took little to persuade him I was spoony-eyed over him. Soon enough, we were on first-name terms again.

Between paintings, I've toddled along to his office, bringing him fruits and sweetmeats.

He has thrown caution to the wind. Such are the pitfalls of arrogance, for he believes me devoted to him. In these cavalier moments, he has shared secret details, of Roxbury Industries, of the scientific quarter, and his personal investments on the side.

He sent me to leave provisions outside the Shepherd's Refuge daily. We said nothing of it; I did not see the French fugitive, but he will likely be there to apprehend, when you come.

Lodestar was fiddling continually with the telegraphic buzzers. They please and frustrate him in equal measure. The magic of it enthrals him; but, like a spoilt child, he has not the discipline to fathom the principles of circuitry.

He was always busy with explosive tests in the quarry. I can but guess of their purpose. Yet I could always persuade him to relax by playing billiards. There was a trick shot he swindled me with. He balanced three balls against the bottom cushion in a triangle: one atop two. He demanded I bet with him.

"Do you think I can hit that top one with the cue ball? Do you? Do you?"

I laid down my money.

He knocked the cue ball lightly, with no effort to make it leap into midair, as was surely required. It rebounded gently off the bottom cushion, returning towards the balls. At the moment it was to hit the lower balls—losing the bet—he leaned back and gave the table a deliberate kick.

The lower two balls parted, like the Red Sea.

The upper one fell, just in time for the cue ball to hit its mark.

"Amazing," I said, "what a man may do with his cue, when wielded with ingenuity."

Today I found the baize scorched right down the middle of the table. He wasn't amused.

"What happened?" I laughed. "Mixed your cue ball with your detonator?"

"Something like that." He stomped off to take out his anger on the scientists.

I took the chance to rootle around in his desk. I found his work diary. He has recorded his meetings over the last months. My, he does get around. He's visited all the big cities and ports, which I know from maps—many appointments also marked with women's names.

* * *

Besides my efforts with Lodestar, I have been absorbed in Lady Elodie's diaries.

Birtle and Skirtle have been particularly absent from the house. Not because of Bertie's putative visit: we haven't mentioned that to them. No, they are preparing up in the east wing, or the invalid's lair, as I now think of it. The lady's turret. Now I know the sorry tale, I am helping wherever I can.

NO MAN'S LAND [LAWLESS]

The fog was thick when I reached the Portsmouth docks. The brackish tide stifled the aroma of biscuits and breweries. A foghorn sounded, so close I nearly jumped out of my skin: the ferry, no doubt, invisible, though it was yards from shore. My feet were chilled in my boots as I arrived at the Fortitude Tap, but it was unaccountably shut.

Dark waters swirled beneath the jetty: the buildings set round the harbour floated like islands. I had been chasing around the country, while Ruth made arrangements with Molly, and I felt unsure of my footing. I pulled my jacket tight around me, as the sunlight struggled to find its way through.

How carefully I must play my hand today. Lodestar did not know that I knew him for an impostor. While he did not, I was no threat.

But I suspected him of greater crimes. I had been duped, I was sure, about the source of the blasts: Skittles and Hemyng had assured me of that. But this was not the time to wring my hands over it. How deeply Lodestar was involved, I could not be sure. To find out, I must win his trust. I must flatter him, hint at colluding, even profiting from his wiles, thus tempting him to confide. Showing that I knew his secret might earn his respect, might bring danger.

Brilliant sunlight lifted my gaze, sweeping across the harbour. A shout resounded: a fellow turned at the dockyard gate, bound for the other end of the empire, to see his full-bosomed lass bid him goodbye from an alley, where they had made the most of their farewell. The wooden railings steamed in the pale morning. The gentry of the town appeared, all at once, to take the sea air. They strolled along the front, perambulators and parasols, as if it were summer: a hardy lot, these coast people. A lady dandled her child in her arms. I gazed on them enviously. Might that be Ruth and me, in a year or two? Strange kind of world to bring children into: a world I have made less safe with my warmongering, when I thought to make it safer.

"Ho, there, my friend." Lodestar saluted me from the tugboat, as it drew in. "Not a bad day for visiting imaginary islands, eh?"

The pilot glared at the skies. Clouds were amassing, flecked with orange streaks, across the waters. The sea was restive, as if monsters crouched beneath, waiting to eat us. I observed the boat uneasily, still lost in my thoughts.

Lodestar reached out a hand. "Ready to view our miracle forts, Lawless?"

"Thank you." I meant it, as I gripped his hand, but my mind was swirling. This man, so engaging and magnetic: has he not duped me from the first? I know he has, because he is not Nathan Lodestar. Does that discredit all his charms?

The pilot gesticulated towards the cloud banks, insistent. True enough, though the sea glittered out by the sand spits—our destination—the next swathe of mist was already descending over the Isle of Wight.

Lodestar lost his patience. He rounded on the fellow, snarling in an undertone.

The pilot was unhappy to have his command usurped.

Lodestar grasped him by the coat. "If you're refusing to

pilot us, I can take the wheel myself." He lifted him up as if to dangle him off the side.

The pilot made a swift concession.

"Good." Lodestar set him down, back at the wheel, all grace and charm again, now he had got his way.

I was thrilled and scared by turns as we pulled clear of the harbourmouth. The buildings receded, the noises of the town fell away. Yet the sea jumbled sounds from near and far: the waves, shouts from the pebbles, foghorns of distant cargo ships.

The sun blazed on the bulwarks of the first fort, Spitbank.

What an outlandish venture. Men, small as ants, busied themselves on the scaffolding that rose, glinting, out of the sparkling waves: like a house in a dream. Daring sailboats flitted around it, white canvas swelling in the wind. Beyond, the low inclines of the island were indistinguishable amid rafts of mist and cloud.

Our destination, No Man's Land Fort, remained a ghostly outline.

My view of the case was about as clear. Bertie may not have convinced me of Louis Napoleon's good intentions, but Skittles had. The French would love to see us squander our budget on these absurd forts: never to be attacked, obsolete within the decade. That her fellow in the Sûreté puzzled over our invasion panic was more convincing than any number of denials.

If not the French, who? Who else would gain? Hemyng's theory, of dastardly profiteering, seemed a satirical exaggeration. Would a clubful of toffs incite murder for the sake of an investment wheeze? The risk was not commensurate with the gain. If caught, it was incitement to violence. It was treason. They might be chancers, but they were no fools.

Ruth's latest research showed how many of Lodestar's chums

in the Hounds, besides dabbling in property, were investing in Roxbury Industries—but that proved nothing. Roxbury's stock was higher than ever, under Lodestar's guidance.

Lodestar clapped me on the back. Inspecting my pasty expression, he called out above the wind. "Don't you like our glamorous form of transport?"

I attempted a laugh. "Not quite the SS *Great Britain*."

"Quite a trip," he said, "for a colonial boy."

I bit my lip. I must conclude Bazalgette's business, and get back to dry land, before I confronted him as an impostor.

"There's something about you," said Lodestar, "something not very English. Your colleague, now, what's his name?"

"Jeffcoat?" I had never introduced him to Jeffcoat.

"That's the fellow. You're leagues ahead of him."

As Lodestar inspected me for assent, a bank of cloud as dense as I had ever seen blocked out the sun. We were drawing near No Man's Land Fort, pulling into the shadow of the incipient walls. The air went chill.

Yet his words flattered me, for I never like to be taken for English. "And you?" I said. "Do you consider yourself an Englishman?"

"I am a colonial child of England. The fecund empire, eh? My allegiance is fiercer than any dull Londoner."

Toot! A vast horn nearly made me jump from the deck. The fog had pulled over the Solent, tucking it under a thick blanket. Out of it loomed the huge outline of the ferry, right beside us, like a grand hotel threatening to topple on to us. The pilot's expression showed what he thought of the whole outing.

"You've got a certain something, Sergeant." Lodestar patted my shoulder, as if he were romancing me. "Remember me, if ever you're looking for a job in the wider world, beyond your sleuthing."

* * *

His attentions intensified as we landed at No Man's Land Fort, and continued till the end of our meeting. I was magnetically attracted to him, but I could not work him out: all I knew was that I must stick close by him.

"How amazing that you have risen so fast." I flattered him in turn, as we entered the gun bays. "Never mind letters of introduction and friends of your father. To come all that way, and no inheritance."

He grinned. "How nice that you've taken an interest." The thought that I'd enquired about his finances didn't rattle him at all.

Roxbury's monumental artillery gun was already installed. I examined it in awe. The greatest beneficiaries of our war panic, it struck me, were of course the gunmakers. When the government seesawed between Whitworth and Roxbury, trusting the loyalty of one but design of the other, both sets of shareholders profited.

The crux of our meeting came soon enough. Their engineer stated his determination not to budge.

I put forward Bazalgette's point of view, with figures to support it.

Lodestar had given me to understand that he would be sympathetic. Not at all. "Your fool politicians have delayed our work, over and again. They should be ashamed," he sneered. "My boys could have finished this in the spring. Because of their prevarications, we're working in this." He meant the fog. Minute by minute, it crept closer, threatening to envelop the whole fort. "They'll have blood on their hands. Remind me, why on earth would we want to help your fellow Bazalgette?"

I smiled. I had misjudged his tricksy business groundwork. But I was willing to deploy my own firepower, keeping the heavy artillery in reserve. "Because you ought to, Mr Lodestar, as a good upstanding Briton."

He quivered, as if suppressing a jolt of electricity.

"For the good standing of your company. For the health of London, Mr Lodestar." My repetition of his name seemed to cause him unease. His identity I would not question, but I could play on his loyalty, and his thirst for recognition. This trump card I kept till last, pointing between us to suggest our link with Bertie. "And our beloved royals."

He looked me in the eye, weighing whether I really had the connections to make surrender worthwhile. "I shouldn't like to offend them."

I smiled. "Especially when they're taking such an interest in Roxbury."

He made his decision. "You're right, my friend. You sort out the deal, and I can save my country twice over." He turned to his engineers, dazzling us with his smile. "That's settled. We'll go through the details on the way back."

We shook hands, and concluded the meeting. I laughed uncertainly, enjoying my victory. It was the first time I had seen a trace of respect in his eyes.

Freezing rain drove into our faces. The pilot set off at a crawl. I joined Lodestar on the bridge. How easy it would be to fall in—or to be pushed.

I turned away from the blasts of the rain to remind him about finalising the details.

"Bricks, bricks, bricks." He dismissed my concerns. "Enough business for now. I'm just the engineer overseeing."

I bit my lip. But my reference to Bertie still had his attention: he was fascinated to know more.

"Look! That's where the French would attack." He pointed out the channels and the sandbanks, just as I had seen on the Guernsey papers. "And that is where the French will founder. We will blast them out of the water. If they come overland, they will be blasted to buggery from these forts, and enslaved like old Napoleon's armies."

"You imagine it very fully."

"Engineers are prophets. We must imagine disasters and successes."

"You believe the French would invade?"

"Of course. I know you agree. The French would love us to think it's a game."

"Our hatred of foreigners," I said, "must be fanned."

"Sergeant." He gestured to the low grey skyline of the town, battered by the rains. "We unite against oppressors. This country is happy when it is united against a common foe. The tribes in Nyasa are the same, with the English to hate."

We Scots, I thought, are no different.

"Louis Napoleon does us a service. He has revivified England's enemy. Employment booms. Unions are beaten down. Industry's coffers filled. The government plans real strategies, rather than their usual pandering to an electorate of dunces."

"Are you not a democrat?"

"Deep down, nobody is. We all know we are fools. Let someone trustworthy take the decisions. Protect us from our own greed and narrow-mindedness."

Someone trustworthy? I looked at him reproachfully. "Who could that be?"

He laughed. "Ridiculous, I grant you." Growing impatient with the pilot's caution, Lodestar pushed him aside, gripping the wheel to speed us onward, careless of what lay hidden in the fog.

NEWS IN THE PORT [LAWLESS]

There were wires waiting for me back at port. I had given the address of the Fortitude Tap to Ruth and the Yard. We stood aside as a group of Russians staggered out, brandishing their rum, with a priest leading their shanty.

Lodestar took on a local at billiards, while I went straight to the bar. Ellie was distraught: her husband had lost his job in the docks, with all the money diverted to the forts. I sympathised, briefly, but couldn't hide how glad I was of the drink after that voyage.

I skimmed through the three wires, as Lodestar showed off his trick shots. I had to swallow hard in order not to gasp out loud. I learned three things. First, from Jeffcoat. I hadn't expected him back so soon, but there it was.

Hemyng had fled. When Jeffcoat leaned on him—and persuasive methods he had—Hemyng hinted that the Hellfire Hounds were indeed afoot again, but would not say who was leading them, for fear he'd be killed.

Ruth sent on news from Molly.

SHE SAW LODESTAR WITH A FRENCHMAN:
JACQUES I, I'M SURE.

Some leap of logic. For Lodestar to be implicated with the Hounds was one thing; for him to be hobnobbing with terrorists, another. Ruth's discoveries of Lodestar Senior's antics and equivocations came back to me; only what exactly was the connection with our "Lodestar"?

Another garbled claim from Molly:

LODESTAR HAD BEEN TO EACH BLAST LOCATION,
EXCEPT GUERNSEY.

If that was significant, it would imply terrible crimes behind all the Hellfire Hounds, their property speculation, and their profits; more likely, it was coincidence.

My mind was spinning. Each strand was inconclusive; their profiteering was immoral, but surely not so diabolically conniving.

"I head north." I put his drink on the table. "I have business with Roxbury."

He paused in his shot, eyeing the wires in my hand. "Do tell." What magic Molly's idea was working—for he longed to know more.

I tapped the side of my nose. "You'll hear, soon enough." I was prodding at his aspirations, his *nouveau riche* egotism. "Oh, I almost forgot. There's a wire for you." I sat down, attempting nonchalance, as he perused it.

This proved the *coup de grâce*. I saw those bright eyes twitch, though he recovered himself at once. "Shall we share a compartment to London?"

It was from Roxbury. Molly had arranged that he would summon Lodestar, adverting to a possible royal visit.

How Lodestar liked to be centre of attention. His job was constructed around that tenet. If someone more important than he was to visit, he couldn't bear not knowing about it. And the royals—well, really!—what could be better?

From his travelling bag, he took out his notebook, a dog-eared affair, and tucked the wire into it. He narrowed his eyes and scored through his appointments for the next day. I needed him to stick with me; it was this clinched it. He would come all the way to Roxbury House alongside me.

WATERLOO TRAIN [LAWLESS]

On the train from Portsmouth and Southsea, I bribed the guard to keep our compartment free, and I let him see me do it. I could have asked him to lock us in—as we do with prisoners in transit—but I wanted to play a subtler game. The only one of his crimes I had proof of was his imposture. I knew what he had done with the real Lodestar's body, and that was a crime too. But of greater crimes, yet no proof, nor any certainty. And nothing would do as well as a confession.

I sat back and took a deep breath. "Who are you?"

"Lodestar." He grinned. "You know me, Sergeant."

"Can we not be frank, after all your games?"

"I'm Lodestar." No sense of shame, no sense of fear. The train plunged into a cutting, and made his features appear satanically dark.

"But you're not." I stared at him, fascinated; I had found his broad grin so charming, but was it delusional?

I took out Numpty's drawing of the basket we'd found filled with stones. Beside it, I placed the pale daguerreotype: in the glaring African sun, the old goat, Lodestar Senior, sits like an emperor among his harem of servant women, with a boy or two among them. Seated beside him—the names of the whites were written at the bottom—that pale willowy youth with the prominent teeth whom Jeffcoat and I found in that boat, a discarded skeleton, all those months ago.

"You are not Nathaniel Chichester Lodestar. It was he met his end on the SS *Great Britain*, not Zephaniah. You put the mask in the tarpaulin with his body, and weighed it down, to take him to the bottom."

"But it didn't go to the bottom."

"No."

He pushed his hand through his hair, and looked at me sideways. "I haven't done anything wrong, have I?"

"Apart from improper disposal of a corpse?"

He opened his mouth to deny it, but thought better of it. "Well done, Sergeant." He snatched the photo up to the light, examining it minutely. His eyes widened, seemingly in pleasure, rather than shock. The gentle hills of Hampshire rolled past: green copper spire, deer leaping; a brook, a rill, a pensive bridge. "I knew this day would come, but I had not imagined it thus."

"You don't seem surprised."

"I thought I might be discovered one day."

"So who are you? You've passed yourself off as Nathan

Lodestar. You've taken his identity. Tried to take his inheritance."

"Oh, your lawyers." He rolled his eyes. "Rules and edicts. I had a certificate, I had papers. I am effectively Nathan Lodestar. You Britons, why must everything be a problem?"

"Your problem." I found his nonchalance unnerving. "Impersonating the deceased. False inheritance claim. How did you come by his papers?"

"He had them. He was coming to claim the inheritance."

"When he died, did you buy them from his man Zephaniah? How livid you must have been when you discovered the estate debt-ridden." I was missing something. "How long had you known Chichester Lodestar?"

"How long? Why, all his life." He tapped at the picture. "I'm his brother."

I looked closer and gasped.

"See?" In the photograph, behind Lodestar Senior and Nathaniel Chichester Lodestar Junior, among the Negro women stood a lanky half-caste boy. Only the names of the whites were inked at the bottom, but there was something familiar about his cocksure expression. Beside the half-caste boy stood an imposing Negress, her hand on his father's shoulder, her lover. "And there is my mother."

Now I looked close, it was certainly he, younger and willowy, and darker in the face, but still he. "You are Zephaniah."

"Zephaniah Chichester Lodestar, mark you." He laughed again.

For a man whose world has been upended, he was ebullient. His imposture we could prove; that was a crime. But he had not gained from it. He had made his own way. Gained respect, and friends. He had supporters who would argue for clemency. I must bide my time: entrap him for the greater crimes we suspected him of? I would flatter him, admire his ingenuity, keep him talking. Off his guard, he might tell all. How much of a risk could that be?

He was enjoying my obvious discomfort. "Such a shame. If I could remain Lodestar, I might marry her. Your Molly. If you unmask me, I will just have to bed her and drop her."

I should have guessed that he would not take a blow without striking back.

"Polite society has these pitfalls, compared to colonial life. Advantages too, don't mistake me: the clothes, the status; beds, instead of mud floors; not being beaten, or worse. That's how my mother died, when I was still a youth." He smiled a broad smile. "No, no sympathy, please. I was old enough for her to fill me with conceit. She told how father loved her, despite appearances. She whispered how I could be great, greater than his legitimate son. Father loved her, you know. I am sure of it. When he spoke of her, he spoke with true affection. It was my African blood that made him love me, more than his real boy. Poor sickly Chesty! A sickly child. Hateful to his father. Useless companion. Couldn't run, couldn't throw. Such a weakling. He only had to survive the journey from Cape Town to London, and he couldn't."

I gave him a moment. "How did he die, the real Nathaniel Chichester Lodestar?"

"Chesty? You want to know how Chesty died?"

Nothing would surprise me now. "Did you kill him?"

"Not at all." He sat back, laughing. "I was trying to keep him alive."

I found his consternation strangely credible. "I doubt it."

"Yes! I wanted him to get to London, collect the inheritance, and then die."

"So how did he end up in the bottom of a lifeboat?"

"Should have been the bottom of the ocean." He shook his head. He was weighing the loss in sharing his confidences. He adjudged there might be gain in it. "He was sick the day we left home; and the trip to the Cape was not easy. Aboard the ship, he took straight to his bed. Nobody knew us from Nyasaland. I presented myself as Nathan Lodestar from the outset. Why not? I put it about that he was my servant and he had fever, and must be quarantined."

"Drop of poison in his medicine?"

"No need. His own medicine did for him, but he would insist on taking it." He pressed his fingers to his eyes. "Father always hated Chesty's mewling. Father took nothing for his own pain, when his stomach was eaten away, bar a little opium. I took to wearing Chesty's clothes: rather skinny and long in the leg, but they served. He didn't even notice. I didn't let it spoil the voyage. I enjoyed the pleasures of ship life. Stood me in good stead for the Hounds. I played dice, cards and billiards. Nobody knew me. I reinvented myself."

He had sat and watched the real Lodestar die, sick and neglected, in order to steal his identity. "And you let him die."

"I hoped he'd last the trip."

"You never planned to push him overboard."

"Come now." He shrugged. "What benefit in keeping his body for burial at home? What would they have done, pickle him in aspic?"

"Therefore you just got rid of him?" I glanced at the two pictures. "Pushed him overboard in the night, with the scout's help."

"What point in explaining everything? It was the easiest thing in the world. Nobody lost by it, but myself."

And the daguerreotype. "Mr Lear knew you weren't Nathaniel Chichester."

"The painter? Chesty talked about him. He had a cartoon alphabet he cherished."

"Your brother's keeper." I shook my head. "Easy to step into his shoes. Culpable, still."

"Hold, now. I am the surviving heir. That is exoneration enough. Alongside my character references." He was truly unashamed. "And, as you keep telling us, Roxbury's work is vital to the nation."

I shook my head, impressed. "Have you no fear of me broadcasting this?"

"I've been a better son to my father than Chesty ever was. I have been a son to Roxbury too, when he needed one, and the idiot Wilfred was off chasing women and money. Do you grudge me what I have done? Try me, if you dare. I have no fear. If you succeed—and you won't—I've had a better life than if I'd stayed in Africa. Father's money I couldn't give two hoots about. It was Chesty's place in the world I wanted. Illegitimate half-caste boys are denied that. But father brought me up British. To seem Father's rightful heir, I simply had to play the white boy, burnt by hours in the colonial sun. Credible, is it not? Though my mother was black, I am pale enough to pass for a European born under the skies of Empire."

WHAT DO WE REALLY KNOW ABOUT LODESTAR? [RUTH'S LETTER, DELIVERED TO WATERLOO STATION]

NOT TO BE READ IN PUBLIC

(THE FOLLOWING ENCODED)

Campbell, my dearest love,

I fear for your safety. Below is what I have gleaned from researches at Somerset House and, with Jeffcoat's help, the Home Office.

What if Lodestar is Diderot? If he is, being an arrogant beggar, let's tempt him. Molly says he has Jacques I in hiding at the Shepherd's Refuge. They are practising blasts. What if they are behind the devilments you have been investigating?

Bring him to our favoured table chez Great Northern. I have a scheme cooked up with Bertie. Disparage the prince all you can; discourage any thought of them meeting. That is your role, and see that you stick to it. A bang on the table will seal it.

Stick with him. If you get the chance, set his watch slow: five minutes should be enough. Molly will be at the Pump House at midnight, watching the turbine.

Tread carefully. Take care of that impetuous head of yours.

Your devoted
Ruth

STATIONS OF THE JOURNEY [LAWLESS]

Arriving at Waterloo, I stuck close to him.

At the wire desk, I found the letter from Ruth, alongside the following telegram:

> Bertie plan afoot.
>
> Lodestar may be master of the Jacques?
>
> Persuade him to Roxbury.
>
> Will trail you there.
>
> Jeffcoat

I was relieved he was back; and that he and Ruth had worked together to anticipate these dark conclusions. When Ripon sent him to New York he took it as a rap on the knuckles; I knew it was to let him heal.

Lodestar had wires too. Roxbury chasing him to come north forthwith, as royal plans were developing nicely.

The second wire he kept hidden from me. From Jacques the First? A rendezvous in the hills behind the house?

"Join me in a cab, will you?" he said. He had considered skipping off, I am sure, after our dialogue in the train. Not now. Oh no, not any more. "Our plans are intertwined after all."

* * *

LAWLESS, LODESTAR, LONDON [LAWLESS]

At King's Cross, we made two rendezvous, to Lodestar's detriment.

In the corner of the ticket office lurked a couple of blokes. Lodestar didn't notice them, as they looked out through the window, spying on us. Jeffcoat! God man. His coat sleeves disguised the handcuffs that attached him to the prisoner: Mersey Jacques. Jacques could confirm it. If we had any lingering doubt, he could attest that Lodestar was the mysterious man who paid him: Lodestar it was who blew up the *Florence Veigh*.

This was our best evidence yet. Was it enough to convict him? Lodestar conjured up the blast, but he lit no fuse. Mersey Jacques was a stupid mule; and my prey was slippery. Lodestar could deny it flat. He could claim Mersey Jacques mistook his intention; the goods were given, in good faith, to be delivered to Africa; and there was Jacques contriving to blow it all up. Why should we slander Lodestar's name, for outrages others had wrought, and those in error?

We stepped into the Great Northern Hotel to await our train. I led him, head racing, towards the booths at the back, where people could lurk with some anonymity.

"Ho, there." Lodestar stopped me with an outstretched arm. "Isn't that the Prince of Wales?"

I was truly astonished. But it took me only a moment to convert my surprise according to Ruth's directions. "Oh, not Bertie?" I cringed. "And who's that fellow he's with? Not Victor Hugo. Talk the hind legs off a donkey."

"An exploded donkey?" Lodestar's joke fell flat, though he thought it tremendous. He was as excited as a schoolgirl on jubilee day. "And the woman?"

"Some floozy of Bertie's." I craned my neck. "Might have known: Skittles."

"The famous Skittles?" He was agog. "Ask them over. We could invite them to come north—"

I tugged him into a booth, as if embarrassed at his ingenuousness. "Don't let's bother him. Ideas above his station, that boy has, and so indiscreet."

"Above his station?" Lodestar whistled silently.

"He hates commoners." I leaned close and whispered, "He's also a dreadful bore."

"Not what I've heard. Not what I've heard at all." Lodestar raised an eyebrow in thought. "I'll invite him to see the Roxbury works."

"He hates engineering. Prince Albert used to torture him with it."

"Introduce us, won't you?"

"I couldn't bear his spoiling our trip." I had surprised him with my unpatriotic outburst. "I wish our bomber would blow him up."

Lodestar narrowed his eyes in dismissal. "Pah. You don't really know him at all."

I banged the table, in exasperation, ready to go and prove my claim.

Upon the signal, Bertie pushed back his chair and walked over, bringing his colleagues. Lodestar shrank back into the darkness. He might be an amoral scoundrel, unobservant of social boundaries, but a prince still cowed him. Let me describe the scene as he saw it.

I reluctantly stood up.

Bertie leapt to embrace me, as if I were a long-lost friend: it was an act, but he threw himself into it. "Lawless, old chum, you scrumptious periwinkle. You know Monsieur Hugo?"

"What pleasure, *Monsieur Chien de Garde*, to re-encounter." The great novelist gripped my hand, managing both to quote from *Les Misérables* and to translate my nickname, Watchman (or near enough).

Skittles emerged from behind Hugo's bulk. She grasped my hands and drew me to her for a kiss, as if I were an old flame; and a kiss from Skittles never went amiss.

Bertie burst out, "I do hope we're not interrupting."

Lodestar's eyes bulged. "Not at all," he managed, hoarsely, but I cut him off.

"Bertie old man, you are." I was thoroughly enjoying my licence to extemporise, as rudely as I wished, for Bertie always treated me rather cavalierly. "That's exactly what you're doing, as always. Interrupting important business."

"*Pardon*." Unabashed, Bertie launched into some anecdote about a bishop, a tart and a Guernsey cheese.

I let him witter on a bit, before gesturing over at poor Lodestar. What look on his face. The childlike expectancy, mixing hope and fear, not knowing whether he would secure his longed-for royal introduction.

Bertie took pity on him. "And your friend?"

"Excuse me, Bertie. I ought to present Mr Lodestar here. Roxbury's right-hand man, you know."

"Oh." Bertie's face fell, right on cue. "Oh, I do know."

Lodestar kept up his hopeful smile.

Bertie rubbed his whiskers, glancing awkwardly between us. "I say, Lawless, would you step aside with me, just a mo?"

We left Skittles regaling Hugo with Parisian gossip, Lodestar listening in envious awe.

Two minutes later, I returned to my seat.

Courtesan and novelist made their excuses, and rejoined the prince.

Lodestar stared, his egotistical dream evaporating before his eyes. "What happened? Did you explain who I am?"

I made a face.

"You argued." He was dismayed. "What did he say?"

"He knows you're behind the forts." I sighed. "Bertie knows Roxbury, and I'm sure he'd love to visit, but he's on

Bazalgette's side. He's a Londoner; of course he wants to stop cholera. I told him you're just the engineer overseeing." I tutted. "Shame. He does love a fishing weekend, especially where the cellar is as good as Roxbury's."

"Do you think—?" He blinked, eager as a puppy. "Is a royal visit possible?"

"Not without the bricks." I waggled my finger. "Sort that deal for Bazalgette. Then Bertie may come around." A neat ploy.

Lodestar looked at me. He stood up and went straight over to Bertie. He returned, moments later, beaming. "You'll never guess. I gave in on the bricks—"

"You did what?" I thought of his pose on No Man's Land Fort: it showed his need to dominate, more than anything.

He brushed aside my indignation. "I don't give a hoot for the bricks. I'll wire the idiot in the government. I told him, if he ever fancies a trip…" He gestured to the tracks, and the north.

Molly had hit on the perfect scheme. The one thing to impress Lodestar: my knowing the prince. He was a royalist, full-blooded and unrepentant. Ruth had judged the scene just right, and Bertie played his role so admirably. He owed me a favour or two, and this was payment in spades. They'd raised my stock with Lodestar. That would protect us against his wiles—for the moment.

"Tell you what, gents." Bertie reappeared. Tugging up his sleeves, he leaned on our table. "We're hopping aboard with you now. I've ordered a case of Moët."

ON A TRAIN TO THE FROZEN NORTH [LAWLESS]

Often enough have I travelled the Great Northern Railway. Never has the trip been so fraught with awkwardness and expectation.

Talk, the whole way north, badinage and chatter. We laughed, drank, and talked more. Bertie cracked a bottle at once, and Bertie always poured with a heavy hand. I feigned that I was matching them, drink for drink; but I kept swapping my full glass for Bertie's empty, so as to keep my wits.

Lodestar took no such precaution. At first, he kept his distance from Hugo, frowning at the Frenchman's pronunciation as if the words stank of garlic. He fawned over Bertie, falling over himself to show what a supporter he was of queen and country. As he began to gauge Hugo's anti-Louis stance and Bertie's lax European morals, things changed.

Another bottle, and then a third.

Hugo spoke of France in the forties: the Paris Commune. Lodestar lapped it up. Louis Napoleon's corruption. Hugo's exile. "And they threaten me. How they threaten me." He thumped the seat proudly. "Still! Whenever I criticise the *soi-disant* emperor."

"A veritable monster." Lodestar waggled his finger.

"Old Louis," I said, with a cough, "is a friend of Bertie's."

"I'm sorry." An ironic apology. Lodestar frowned at the prince, slurring slightly, "But I am a patriot, and I cannot be silent. Louis is a nasty piece of work."

We must keep him talking. The import of the messages from Ruth, Molly and Jeffcoat was just sinking in. If Lodestar had profited from the outrages, and directed his friends to profit too, what had he known about them? How deeply was he entangled? If he had information in advance about bombs, was he consorting with French extremists? But he was such a patriot: surely he would have turned them in? The more he said, the more he was likely to incriminate himself, and the more we could bear witness to any confessions he made.

I kept quiet, as far as I could—until the oysters arrived, and Hugo nudged me. "And, Monsieur Watchdog, what is afoot at Scotland Yard?"

"Victor," Bertie remonstrated. "You're only looking for plots for your next filthy romance. State secrets. He can't possibly reveal them." He turned to me, bright-eyed. "You can hint a little, though."

I laughed. He was giving me a chance to unnerve Lodestar. "I cannot say much. Let me tell you, though, that we are damnably close to solving the mystery of the blasts."

"The London hooha?"

"Not just that. Erith, Camden, the *Florence Veigh*. Everything."

"I heard some fellow got away."

"That fellow's not important." I watched Lodestar closely. "What matters is who's giving the orders. That's who we're after."

Stevenage, Peterborough. Lodestar, enjoying himself thoroughly, offered to go down to the dining car for brandy. This was my chance to snoop.

"Might have a smoke in the corridor." Bertie glanced at me in delight. "We'll watch out," he whispered, once Lodestar was out of sight. "Give you three coughs when he's coming back."

In his travelling bag, I found cash. French letters. More cash.

A patent application for a new compound of oil residues, named Parkesine, for use with brushes, umbrella handles, and billiard balls.

His notebook. Shabby, stuffed with slips of paper and calling cards, crammed with names and dates and addresses. He used it as an appointments diary. I flicked back to the dates of the outrages. Notes upon notes, densely scribbled, appointments and assignations.

Erith, in late June. But June? A week before the blast.

Suddenly I understood what Molly meant. She meant that Lodestar had been to the location of each blast before the outrage took place. (Except one; he had scribbled "Guernsey" ten days in advance of that blast, and written underneath: "Overend.")

It was beyond coincidence. Had he known about them in advance, all of them? Each place: Erith, Camden, Liverpool, Clerkenwell. He'd visited them all. Why had he been there? Could it be—I stared about in disgust—could he be responsible for them? Travelling the country, laying the groundwork for the blasts?

Molly was right to mention it. I looked closer: the fire at the docks too. And hold on: the fire at the Princess's Theatre. The blaze that Ruth still had nightmares about—damn his eyes—was commemorated thus:

Jaunt to Oxford St.
Adam and Eve Alley.
Terrific circus:
set the house ablaze.

Damn the man's arrogance. This changed everything. My plans were naive. I had imagined I might find incriminating bank accounts, to prove collusion in the Hellfire Hounds' opportunism. I never imagined he was the font of the evils. I should have arrested him there and then. Something prevented me: a kind of hubris, I suppose. Twice he had nearly killed my Ruth. And he thought himself so enchanted, so worthy of Bertie's attention, or the world's admiration.

I glanced out at Bertie in the corridor. My breath ran short. Here was the heir to the throne. I couldn't let him travel further with this monster. I turned the pages, seeing not words but the rubble at Clerkenwell, at Erith the bodies blown apart, and us trying to collect the pieces. How much had he explained of his crimes here? Would this stand as proof of his murderous orders? How many had he killed?

I would catch him red-handed. He thought himself beyond our morality. He had stepped out of his African world into ours, bringing the laws of colonial rule with him. I would trick him into confirming his crimes. His plans for the next outrage. Catch him admixing explosives. Preparing detonators.

Bertie coughed.

What else was there? Arsenical soap. Comical, to think of Lodestar desperate to "lighten his countenance", if it were not entwined with such carnage.

And there was his waistcoat, damn it, with the watch hanging out of the pocket. I set it back five minutes, as requested. It was the work of moments.

But as I did it, I realised how poorly prepared we were. It was too late to communicate the depth of the danger to Ruth, to Molly. They were relying on me to be strong, to be cunning. I must manage him myself.

Cough. Cough, cough. I could hear Bertie valiantly delaying Lodestar in the corridor. I bundled the watch into the pocket and the notebook into the travelling bag, catching a glimpse of twists of bright copper wire. Alongside it, tucked in a side pocket, a slim elegant volume: *Jacques the Fatalist*, by Diderot.

Hugo elbowed the door urgently, and Lodestar appeared round the compartment door, brandishing a bottle. Debonair and carefree, he set down four crystal glasses. Nobody would guess him the plotter of terror. "Brandy?"

Doncaster, Leeds. Hugo and Bertie welcomed the brandy with an uproar, thank goodness, for it gave me a few moments to collect myself. Lodestar was blind to my furtive glances, as he basked in the glory of his famous companions. This was company befitting him, the company he deserved for his talents and his labours.

I had been naive. I had underestimated my adversary. I knew enough now to convict him—and enough to fear for our lives, if he realised that I knew. I had seen his flashing temper in Portsmouth; I had seen his duplicitous self-satisfaction. In all my career as a detective, I have never been so dismayed. What more was Lodestar capable of? If I had so misjudged his venom, was I not underestimating his capacity for vengeance?

I must send Bertie to safety, when we changed trains.

I would proceed alone with Lodestar to Roxbury and let him implicate himself. I was scared. I would have wished to be better prepared. But I had allies: Jeffcoat, if he could get there; Ruth, though she was there for Roxbury in his hour of need; and of course trusty old Molly.

At the change for the branch line, Lodestar went to wire ahead, for Jem to pick us up.

I whispered to Bertie that he and Hugo must make an excuse.

"And miss all the fireworks? No fear."

"As they said to Guy Fawkes." I gave him such a look that he piped down. "For your own safety, you must go."

Hugo clapped his hand on Bertie's shoulder. "A night of repose, my prince."

"Really?" Bertie sighed. "Glad of it, if I'm honest. He's a blabbing spoony, if ever there was one. Wouldn't trust him to black my shoes."

I laughed: I should have guessed that two such egotists, who both charmed the world and his wife, wouldn't take to each other. "Go, sir."

"You going to be all right, old man?" Bertie whispered to me. "I've got him as sozzled as I could. As long as you get to Roxbury House in one piece. Your Miss Villiers tells me they're terribly occupied—medical high jinks—but if you can secure him there tonight, she's confident there's evidence enough to send him down for good, come the morning." He glanced at Hugo. "Come along, monsieur. We'll find some entertainment in the Railway Tavern. I'll make our excuses and bunk off."

"All set?" Lodestar approached, clapping his hands. He handed me a slip of paper. "A wire. Molly, I imagine."

WATCH-MAN,
CHINKER OF MEZZY NOCHY
ESUOHPMUP.
MOLLY

I perused it surreptitiously. Molly's best parlyaree and backslang: five to midnight at the Pump House.

Bertie put on his best repentant look. "Look, Lodestar, old chap. We've decided to stop over here."

Lodestar was crestfallen. For all his amorality, he could not contradict a prince.

"Don't worry. We'll come on tomorrow. Wouldn't do to have the servants all a-flutter." Bertie patted his shoulder and edged away, Hugo at his side. "Besides, Lawless wants to inspect your electrical rigmarole tonight, which I couldn't give two hoots over."

Hugo gestured to a young lady stood outside the tavern.

"Hush, now, Hugo." Bertie grinned. "None of your continental immorality."

"Your Highness," Lodestar began, too desperately, "I can arrange—"

"Wouldn't dream of it, old man. See you tomorrow, eh? Behave yourselves. No dastardly mischief—at least none that I wouldn't approve of."

PARKESINE: A NEW ERA

Forswear the expense of ivory, and save the elephants' pains.

A new era, a new material: buttons, combs, pens. Parkesine is malleable and transparent. It retains its moulded shape upon cooling. It is adaptable to everything from brooches and hair combs to billiard balls. Collars and cuffs can be easily cleaned.

Alexander Parkes, scientist-inventor, first demonstrated his organic compound, of nitrocellulose, at the London Exhibition of 1862.

Today we see before us a new world of inventions and products.

(Warning: upon impact, items may combust.)

TO CATCH LODESTAR [LAWLESS]

"Just the two of us." Lodestar poured two brandies.

"Yes." I smiled. "Shame Bertie couldn't come along."

"You were right, though. A dreadful bore." He waved away my apology. The change of plan dented his egotism; but he made an effort to conceal his disappointment. "I can indulge myself, showing you some of our electrical experiments."

I raised my glass and sipped at the brandy. I had to recover my bonhomie. I mustn't ignite his suspicions. I must hide what I knew.

And I must swallow my disgust at not having worked it out sooner. I was complicit in his crimes.

"Something wrong?" he said. "You look a bit green around the gills."

"No, no." The strain of the recent weeks was beginning to show, and I tugged at my collar. Had I contracted a chill in the morning fog?

"You wouldn't prefer to knock it on the head?" He smiled, like a school matron teasing a recalcitrant footballer to stir his school spirit. "Head home while you can?"

"I'll see it through, thank you very much." I rubbed my eyes, as he refilled his glass.

"A toast, my friend?" Lodestar twitched his head, a distinctly un-English gesture. He topped me up with a hefty measure. "To our provincial pasts."

I drank to that. "And to our imperial future, why not?"

"Why not?"

I would flatter him. Admire him. Persuade him I thought him a friend, even a hero. My energy was fluctuating strangely. Something about the way he proposed the toast struck me—I had better drink no more, just in case—but I would show willing. The brandy had revived my spirits. I had to keep him talking.

Once the branch line train set off, it was not too hard. What a lot we had in common: both of us immigrants to the greatest city in the world. Escaped from provincial backwaters, under tyrannical fathers, to shine our light on the bigger stage of world affairs.

Lodestar listened, drawing me to speak, even as I tried to open him up. He had that easy natural way. He could have charmed a tax inspector. It was a blessing Aunt Lexie would never meet him. He overflowed with confidence. I found myself reflecting his manic glee. If he should tire of me now, see through my plan, his vengeance would know no limit. His crimes were proof of that.

The real Nathaniel Chichester Lodestar lay buried in the police cemetery, unmarked and unmourned. Who was this Lodestar? Why, an unholy creation—and yet he really was

Lodestar. Zephaniah Lodestar, illegitimate child of the self-styled governor of Nyasaland, filled with princely entitlement by his mother, the beauty of her tribe. He thought he could do no wrong.

The air became rarefied as we rocketed into the dark night. It was as if the pressures of his duplicity were building up. When a man has dissimulated so much, unseen forces press within him. More drinks. More hours. And he began to talk.

"My father was known," he told me. "Known and feared in London society. Friend to peers and MPs. Plenty of bankers in the Hounds Club. Roxbury knew him. Lear knew him. They despatched him to darkest Africa to harness its riches. We natives had not known what we were lacking. We thought wealth grew on trees: dates and tamarind. Water fell from heaven. We knew nothing of whisky and money and debt and syphilis, until you forced these upon us, to enslave us into our ways of desire, debenture, drudgery. Bravo, brave colonisers. Alas, craven colonists."

I refrained from commenting that he had his revenge, though the image of Chichester's skeleton swam before my eyes.

"Let me tell you what it was like arriving in London." And he spoke, with candid fervour.

COLONIALS AND INVESTMENTS [LODESTAR]

Any son returning from the colonies would have barriers to surmount. People label you colonial: are you spoilt by servants? Have you fallen into depravity? Has the pipe dazed you? Dark skin entranced you?

Guilty as charged, I warrant. Yet I could sup politely, lose at cards, and stand the boys a drink. I squared the lawyer's accounts, discharging the debts of my dissolute father's. Once people stopped regarding me suspiciously, it was time to beg favours.

I was fortunate, on arrival. My finances were stated plainly by West, West, Prosser, West: no inheritance; father bankrupt; the African estate lost. Old Mr Prosser took pity on me. He lent me £10 and coached me to evade my debts, cajole cash from rich shirkers, and carve out a career. An invaluable start. I was able to reach out for helping hands. By God, I reached.

First, to the Hounds Club. I latched on to young Overend, a fool, and a rich one. Father's old friends let me buy them a drink. Their sons let slip business prospects. They left guineas as tips on dinner tables. They left wallets in their jackets.

I wrote to the earl. He liked me. He took me on. Today I manage his affairs. I am proud to say, I have expanded his business threefold. The hydraulics, the weaponry and the bricks. You cannot challenge these contributions.

As to Overend & Gurney, you seem suspicious. Well, well. You'd think unstable markets cast terror into the hearts of City gents, and they'd steer clear of such treacherous straits. Not a bit. They sniff treasure. Do you see how? I didn't.

After two hours at the bar in the Hounds Club, I felt like a virgin despoiled. What depths these gents stoop to for money. The cash in which the City bathes may look soothing. Easy pickings, we assume. *Au contraire*. These boys are constantly waiting for the sky to fall on their heads. So when a sure thing turns up…

The Hellfire Hounds make their fortune by spreading anxiety. They extract their investments. They tip off the biggest johnny they know, quietly, who runs to his broker and pulls out, whispering to the under-clerk, who whispers to a cabby, who drives the secret all the way to Cockfosters. Hey presto: panic in the market.

Our boys follow the panic from the pub. When they judge it at its low point, they sweep in. With their ready cash, they buy up the property sold in such panic. Like everything in London, it regains its overpriced valuation soon enough. There's nothing scandalous about the mountains of cash they make, because everyone in the chain benefits: at least everyone they know. Once the panic is over, all the hasty panickers look at what they have sold and wring their hands over how little they got for it.

Our boys make mountains from these non-events. They could listen for news from the colonies: corn fields, coffee plants, or nut harvests. Why bother? Wherever there is a boom, a dip will follow. They even buy the debt of the poor beggars they are robbing, and profit from that too. They even profit from debt.

LIGHTING A FIRE [IN LODESTAR'S NOTEBOOK]

It begins as I touch the wires to complete the circuit. I hear the buzzer. It sets the precarious balls a-rolling.

Boom.

As the first one explodes, just a small bang, I feel a tremendous calm. Stronger than remorse, stronger than vindication. The hand of the gods directs me. Some are exalted in life; some are destroyed. If I am the adjunct of the gods, how can I say no? The Parkesine detonators have lit the paper. The black powder will catch any moment. I have chosen the place carefully: the utmost disturbance, with no chance of discovery.

It is light enough that I can see my way down the lane, back to the busy street. There I lose myself in the emerging crowd. The flames from the theatre turn the clouds orange. I hear the cries of the parents and children, strangers and neighbours, too panicked to help each other, rushing to find a way out, screams across Oxford Street. The street is a battlefield. Whoosh—they flee headlong, trampling each other. It works so smoothly. I shall be able to employ fools to set these traps of mine. Simply set up the detonators, complete the circuit, walk away. If some go wrong, and the dunce police catch them, what matter? However they quiz them, whatever they admit, they will not be believed; for my dissembled plot is too convincing, too widespread to be the invention of one malevolent profiteer.

The dancers' pain is heard in each scream.

If they cannot fathom the fire's cause, the people will vent their anger by demanding guns and walls and ships. We feel vulnerable: defend us!

I would feel ashamed, if my cause was not right. Death I inflict here, at the heart of this city of careless souls; I thereby save the heart of the empire.

LODESTAR CONFESSIONS [LAWLESS]

I read his account of the fire.

I would not ask Lodestar about the explosions; I did not ask about the fires. When he excused himself, I simply dug out his diary and turned to August 16, the date of the fire which terrified Ruth.

I read his annotations impassively, and thrust the book away. I could doubt no more.

I stared out at the black night, a queasy darkness enveloping my brain.

Living such a life as he, you must awaken every day knowing you may be unmasked. Any moment may compromise the fiction you have so long maintained. The impersonation you have kept up. Such a slip would ruin your life. Even if you could survive that, it would throw to the devil a hundred plots you are in the midst of contriving. Your friends will not accept you letting them down, your powerful friends, to whom you have promised so much: you have promised diversion, impunity and easy wealth.

Rain on the carriage roof; rain against the window.

I felt stretched tight with anxiety. He believed he had me charmed. And I must keep him thinking that. He thought I had forgiven him his imposture, because of his efforts, because of his talent, because of his charm. He didn't know I knew everything.

I was beyond disgust, beyond fear. I simply listened,

pretended to drink his brandy, and admired his achievements. I was fascinated and sickened by him in equal measure. I would unmask him, but not here. This was not the place to push for a confession; that would make me unnecessarily endangered while I was alone and exhausted. Nausea threatened my senses, but I must prevail. In my head, I had Ruth's instruction, and Molly's promise of aid: I must go to the Pump House, where Molly would come to work the turbine.

I must get him to Roxbury House.

ALDINI'S ELECTRICAL RESURRECTIONS

Giovanni Aldini, prince of scientist showmen, brings his latest Milanese revelation to the London stage. You are invited to bring along any recently deceased pets: rodents, cats, small dogs, amphibians—none, please, more than two days old, we beg you.

Using the technique of Luigi Galvani, developed in experiments upon frogs' legs, Aldini will AMAZE and DELIGHT with demonstrations upon the recently executed.

GASP as they twitch end jerk.

GAZE as the eyes of Newgate malefactors open, the jaws quiver and the limbs shake. The mouths of the DEAD shape soundless words.

A spectacle for layman and connoisseur.

LIES AND EXAGGERATIONS, PART THE FIFTH [LAWLESS]

I had also asked myself, why didn't Molly get to know Lodestar? She reported early enough that this magnetic charmer was at the heart of Roxbury Industries. She gauged that her task was to evaluate threats to Roxbury, pressures and influences injurious to its proper functioning.

And indeed she wanted to know him. She wanted too much. A combination of shyness and pride prevented her from showing too much interest, in those first months. But Lodestar was not an easy nut to crack. He enjoyed the power of his position, where he could come and go at will, ignoring duties or questions and even the everyday courtesies that make us available to our fellow man.

He was also secretive. He was secretive from his upbringing, where he had to be a good young Englishman in his father's house, and a good young Chewa warrior in his tribe. He was fiercely secretive in business too. This made him trusted by those young investors at the Hounds Club. This secrecy endeared him to Roxbury too. Innovations in engineering can change the world, and it will not do to have any old trainee swan in and inspect the latest design for a tunnelling shield or a drilling rig, only to reproduce it for your rival. Lodestar kept a closed shop at the greenhouses. Any who broke his rules of secrecy were swiftly dismissed.

No wonder it took Molly so long to penetrate the inner sanctums. Once she started painting in the menagerie, she had licence to visit the scientific offices. But not until Lodestar's last visits was she able to snoop as she would wish. And snoop she did.

She snooped round Lodestar's office. She found a notable absence of personal information, aside from calling cards of businessmen; she wasn't to know he kept his accounts at the Hounds. She snooped round his room in the house. No memorabilia—aside from a few notes from females. If his lascivious behaviour in the breakfast room hadn't been enough, this convinced her that he bedded women in every port.

But in that final stretch, she caught Lodestar's interest. She already knew how to work the telegraph and the pneumatic rail. When he called into her office, he was amused to find her studio decorated with her caricatures of all the scientists. She went with him to his office, she played billiards, she asked about the new explosives he was developing. She also offered to accompany him to the Shepherd's Refuge.

Quite how intimately she got to know him, I never knew.

TO BRING HER BACK TO US [MOLLY]

Roxbury was sitting at Lady Elodie's bedside. The rain redoubled against the turret windows.

She was completely still, head still, pale cheeks, facing heavenward, the pillows plumped beneath her. She might have been dead, but for the way he spoke to her, sotto voce, like confiding in an old friend. He did not know I was there.

Since Birtle first took me up to see her, I came over and again, amazed to see just how often they visited her, he and Skirtle, how devoted they were. There were flowers in the room. It was always airy and light. It was the most lovely room in the house, the view commanding the whole Roxbury estate, over gorge and rockery, the forest spread out below and the Burnfoot Falls tumbling above.

In those first days, she seemed asleep. "This is the lethargic phase," Skirtle told me. "It's not exactly sleep. You'll see."

They managed to stretch her limbs, massage, and bathe her. Patience Tarn worked quietly, tirelessly, to keep her from getting bedsores. After the earl had given up on the French doctor who all but killed her, they had taken advice from Hughlings Jackson, the epileptic specialist. He had told them how to care for her in her comatose lethargy, and how they should observe her in case of epileptoid episodes. They managed to get water down her throat. Skirtle added drops from two tiny phials: artemisia and belladonna.

"Poisoning her?" I whispered.

"Wheesht." She glared at me. "It's a calmative mix. If we don't give it her... well, you'll soon enough see, I'm sure, what happens when we don't."

On the third day, I did see. Patience Tarn, normally so silent, put the bedpan away rather carelessly. It rang against the great vase in the corner, like a mesmerist's gong.

Lady Elodie opened her eyes, as if awakened from a trance.

"Patience! Quick." I waved my arms to attract the girl's attentions. "Is she awake?"

Patience came and stood beside me. She shook her head, smiling sadly. She buzzed for Skirtle.

As we waited, it became quite clear to me that Lady Elodie was just as unresponsive as in her lethargy. I lamented thus to Skirtle when she appeared.

"I often think she is just joshing us, my dear." She sighed. "And maybe one day she will stop the game. But she'll not be quite so unresponsive now. You'll see."

This was the cataleptic phase. Lady Elodie was not fully awake, but her eyes opened again just before her right side clenched with pain. Patience caught her head as she threw it back, fighting for breath, with ripples going through her upper body. Skirtle checked her heart—racing—and put a wooden spatula upon her tongue—curled up in her mouth—just as she lost consciousness completely. Patience took hold of Lady Elodie's hands, which were fearfully clenched. Skirtle watched closely, checking her forehead with the back of her hand.

As she had explained, Elodie's fit began, quivering and jerking in her bed.

Skirtle waited only a few moments. She clenched her jaw, pulled down the covers, felt around her ladyship's belly, and launched herself forward to press down with the base of her hands. A quiver, a shudder. And the fit was over.

They kept her alive.

Roxy came up and spoke to her.

I had tiptoed into the bedroom. It still felt to me, entering the east wing, that I was travelling through an impossible realm, a shadow world of the main house, and I could barely believe I was here. Her bedroom was beautifully kept. Warm, soft, spotless, with no trace of careless cobwebs that accrued in the rest of the house.

"Remember, darling," said Roxy, "when we had brought Wilfred down and packed him off to school." He spoke plainly, as if she was present; and in speaking thus, he made her present. "And when we got home, the countryside was sparkling. I don't know if you remember it as I do, darling. And you said, let's go a-wandering, and off we went, no work for once. And it all seemed radiant; the whole world was shining, and your smile seemed to me to reflect it."

He went on, reminiscing as any couple might—only she was only there in body, never moving, never responding.

I stared open-mouthed, ashamed of my trespassing. How the house was transformed. That there was a sadness about it I had felt from the first. That the children were motherless was sad, but there are many motherless children.

Yet Lady Elodie was here, alive. Not buried down in the Walled Garden with her boy, her garden nurtured with such attention, more attention than she gave her children, more attention than she had paid to herself through all those busy years. Now that she needed that attention, when everything had fallen apart, she was gone from us. Comatose. Absent. You think you know a place; then all you know turns upside down.

I liked the way he spoke to her every day. This, then, was Roxbury's absence. Not self-absorption or melancholy, not scientific boffinry (though that took up much of the rest of his time), but devotion to love, love lost, lost and frozen.

He paused, hearing my approach. He seemed to know it was me. Birtle or Skirtle would have spoken perhaps, and the children were away—

"Do the children know?"

"Yes. They were in on it." He explained to me how it had all transpired, how they have hoped for her to recover, and she had got worse; how they had thought she was at death's door, and would not be long for this world; and then the fits came again. And the doctors warned him that she might not ever recover her senses fully; she might be a pale shadow of her former ebullient self. They cooked up the scheme by accident. In the first depth of her illness, an insensitive doctor scribbled the brief obituary notice— "Just in case, to save the family's trouble"—and somehow it was posted to *The Times*. They could have complained, or retracted it; but they chose to let people believe she had died. There seemed less shame in it, and less awkwardness.

All the servants, but Birtle and Skirtle, were kept from that side of the house anyway. The aunt was brought into the plot; the grave news was spread; the funeral was real, for their boy, Jonathan. Only family in attendance, and the vicar tacitly went along with the deception. Nobody was going to gainsay Roxbury in that village: he employed nine out of ten of them, and the others relied on his lands.

He kept hold of his wife's hand. Looking over his shoulder at me, he smiled.

I came and perched on the arm of his chair. As a child, I dreamed of having parents like these—of any parents, to be honest. I felt a strange enchantment. We stayed thus a few minutes. He said no more to her.

I had nothing I could say. Did she know we were there? He seemed to feel she knew him. I must not ask. I must not undermine his belief.

"Does she understand what we say?" I said.

He bit his lip. "We don't know." He looked back at her. "We just do not know. But Skirtle is convinced that, sometimes, in the night, when none of us are around, she gets up and walks to the window."

I thought back to my first arrival all those months ago, and the time I saw Patience pull her back from the window; if he did know about these stirrings, they must try to keep it from him, to ease his sorrow.

"It may be that she even goes around the house. I cannot find it in my heart to lock any doors; I would hate, in her position, to be trammelled or feel myself watched."

In her position? How deeply he had tried to understand her suffering, to imagine himself there, trapped. "Is she frustrated, do you think?"

"I think she has been, at times." He rubbed at his cheeks, looking down at her in concern. "At first, I wondered if she was doing it on purpose. To punish herself. To punish me, for all the blasted doctors I paraded her before, hoping to save…"

He broke off. He never spoke of the fifth child. That was when he decided they had had enough of doctors. He took me through the stages of their theories about her malady. That she was perfectly compos mentis but purposely cutting herself off from the world.

"This may not be wilful, I have discovered, or conscious. There is a series of disorders in the penumbra of hysteria, from elective mutism, through unexplained aphasia, disturbance of Broca's area and other brain disorders. They can be ignited by childbirth, or by fits, which are a thunderstorm of the mind, you see. All the way to something known as akinetic mutism, ataractic palsy."

"Does it matter what it is? If we can bring her back."

"That, young lady, is it. If we could but bring her back."

When she was calmed, they would bring her the fruits of the garden. She had the apple juice and plum cider, pumpkin soup and lamb hotpot, spiced with cloves and cinnamon. Things from their own garden, water fresh from the Burnfoot Stream. All this seemed to revive her.

And they would wash and clean her, and tell her stories (though she did not reply), of the world she was missing, though they preferred not to speak of the family, as often it brought on the fit. Finally, she would be calm, but the light shone in her eyes, full of the griefs that were passing her by in this strange half-life she was living.

Gradually, the fit would steal upon her again, a trembling absence that started deep within her limbs and emanated outward, washing up and through her like a great wave washing away all their efforts to revive her and retrieve her. She would begin to shake, and they would hold her down (better than let her hurt herself) and press on her tender zones until the fit abated and she was again still, back in that fearful deathlike sleep from which none could predict when she would awake.

Skirtle and Birtle worked together, in a harmony I

would not have believed, for they were always at odds
over everything else in the house.

Roxy made his confessions to me at her bedside, and I
believe it lightened his soul.

"When she became ill, I was downcast. I was angry, I
suppose. She had suffered; but so had I. I could not believe
she would abandon me. Was she punishing me? I should
have fought her corner: demanded that we hold our child
instead of letting the useless doctors spoil even those
precious moments. But I am a man of science. I could see
no better way to save him. He could not be saved."

He made these admissions brightly, steadily, with
an undercurrent of feeling that made sense of his long
melancholy.

"Maybe one day soon they will have the medical
wherewithal to do it. Not today. I knew it. She could not
believe—understandably, after the sufferings she endured.
Ah! Why?" He sighed. "Her illness, I could not credit its
severity. How could our lives together end thus? She had
promised me her life, and I her mine: in sickness and in
health. What could I do but devote myself to her rescue?"
He closed his eyes, picturing a wretched regime of neglect.
"Third, I must gather physicians and experimenters,
to discover treatments, test their efficacy, and deliver
them, before her suffering and assiduous efforts at self-
nullification might end this fragile existence—which I
would never accept. Soon it was clear she would not fight
off our efforts to keep her hale and nourished."

We sat there, looking at her placid features. Beautiful.
It was hard to believe she was not there listening to us
peacefully. If we could but buy her soul a moment's peace,
perhaps her imagination might take flight again.

* * *

"See?" I laid my hand on his arm. "You have tried."

"I have tried. You cannot imagine how I have tried. Cannot imagine." His lips quivered. He covered his face with his hand. "Oh, Molly, excuse my agitation. Many have lost their partners. I should be as resilient as they."

"Roxy, my friend, that is different. They aren't tortured by hope."

We sat, without a word. I had grown up imagining that those with money had no troubles. But money brings its own problems. And money cannot buy everything. It cannot buy health; it cannot buy you redemption.

I contemplated my lady's face, which seemed to me, though pale and drawn, unutterably beautiful; and, stupid as it sounds, I felt for the first time the completeness of the family Roxbury. I watched her, her breathing so shallow it seemed she might fade any moment. "Should you not have doctors attending her daily?"

An anguished look passed across his face. "Doctors brought her here. Doubly so: first, by taking her baby; again, by prodding and poking her." He glanced between Lady Elodie and me. "But we have made progress."

He enumerated these late breakthroughs with a zealous fervour:

—batteries that hold charge longer, release it more steadily, regulated by capacitors with accurate gauges.

—at West Riding Asylum, hysterics with comparable pathologies: epileptic, mute, comatose, ataractic. Dr Jackson has tested electro-therapies, under Roxy's direction, and is on the point of achieving the successes they have hoped for.

—in the menagerie, they have tested the impulses on animals from tiny to large, starting with avians, but lately succeeding with mammals too, viz the lethargic orang-utan.

"We have also had failures; though the orang-utan's recovery has brought Jem joy. Jackson says it must be soon. I have waited as long as I can. No engineer risks lives unnecessarily on untested equipment. But I can wait no longer. If we cannot save her, she is not long for this world." He looked away a moment. "Patience has noted the days of her disturbance. The coincidence of the fits with the moon's phases is striking. The full moon falls on 13th November. I should dearly like to have your friends, Villiers and Lawless, with us. I regard them as lucky mascots. All will be arranged. One of us must monitor the Pump House, checking the Burnfoot flow through the sluice, the turbine reaching full power. That is the moment—that is when I must finesse the fateful dark spark."

I stared at him. This was wild talk. "You sound like an alchemical crank, Roxy."

"This one doctor I credit, Molly, and I should like you to meet him." He stood up, and rubbed his eyes. "Would you care to accompany me on a trip? I have an appointment in the West Riding of Yorkshire."

ASYLUM [MOLLY]

To the West Riding Pauper Lunatic Asylum we travelled. There we were met by an energetic doctor, Hughlings Jackson. Though employed by one of the London universities, Jackson oversaw the programme here: it promised great change. Jackson gave us tea. He was delighted to see the earl so animated.

We lost little time in visiting the doctor's coterie of patients. One had epilepsy, another lethargy, a third chronic ataraxy. Some were peaceful, some were twitching; some had nurses attending them, stretching them, massaging them, feeding them, treating them with machines and implements. The doctor led us through a corridor to a newer section of the asylum.

ROXBURY WING

I stared at the nameplate. As Roxy went to inspect the rows of batteries aligned there, the electrical equipment, and experimental tubes and phials, the doctor whispered the story to me.

Roxbury's mother had ended her days here. The old sciences were not able to save her, and Roxbury lamented her living out her last days among lunatics, shut up not just with inoffensive madmen, but with dangerous maniacs, chained and terrible to behold.

He had therefore been a staunch supporter, not just of the treatments that exist, but of the treatments that will exist, and that ought to.

Jackson wanted us to see Wide-Eyed Lou. Her real name nobody knew. She had been in the old asylum back before government reforms required records. Abandoned and adrift, she had floated in and out of consciousness for years, barely living.

"Slower and slower she became. We don't know why. We may never know. We've tried this same treatment on two patients with post-partum depression. One is so cheered, she has gone home."

"And the other?" said Roxy.

Jackson's face darkened. "But look at this." He opened the door of Lou's room. A bright-eyed granny was sitting up in bed, an eye mask pushed up to her forehead, and *Les Misérables* in her lap.

She put aside her book, and inspected us. "Oh ho, who

have we?"

"My dear old girl." Roxy strode over to her, thunderstruck. "You're back with us."

"So they tell me, young Edward."

As they chattered, Jackson prepared the apparatus. He muttered the names to himself, as a priest might intone his psalmody, or a surgeon his instruments. "Voltaic pile, Cruickshank's Trough, Stohrer's battery, Parelle's battery. Sulphate of mercury, sulphate of lead battery. Galvanic chains, Goldberger and Pulvermacher. Rheophore choices: static electricity, electrise the skin; dynamic electricity, cutaneous galvanisation; induced current, for muscular faradisation."

The earl stood by. "I'll have the portable batteries delivered, but I have high hopes for the ribbon battery's efficacy. I am trying to prevent the jars getting too powerfully charged. Using Lane's electrometer, one can avert very strong contractions, painful sensations, and exactly the general excitement contra-indicated in these cases."

"Appreciated, sir." The doctor glanced my way. "One day, you know, they will call Roxbury's place the house of electricity. Lou, are you ready?"

"As ever, Doctor," said the game old bird. "As ever."

"I shall excite the motricity of your nerves."

"That's fine, dear."

"Then the contractility of the neck muscles."

"That's not so nice, is it?"

"That's right, Lou." Jackson smiled. "Ready?"

The old lady pulled down her eye mask, the doctor started up the electrostatic influence machine I had seen in Roxy's lair, and picked up the galvanic chains.

DUCHENNE'S MAGNETO-ELECTRIC APPARATUS

Localized electrisation, and its applications to pathology and therapeutics, by Dr GB Duchenne (third edition).

The intensity of the shocks is regulated by the button and screw, C & D, which serve to bring the magnets and the armature, E & F, nearer to or more distant from each other; but a more effectual regulator is supplied by two copper cylinders, G & G, which envelop the bobbins, and, by means of the graduated rod H, can be drawn off or on to any desired extent.

However favourable the conditions under which muscular electrisation is attempted, it is imprudent to expose the patient to many discharges. Moreover, the operation is always painful, since the cutaneous excitation inseparable from the use of static electricity increases in proportion to the increase of tension.

The therapeutic effects of these apparatus are reputed, among French medical practitioners, to be beneficial in several classes of maladies, especially cases of paralysis.

SHOWDOWN [LAWLESS]

The rain was an affront. Shivers seized me, as we emerged on to the platform. No sign of Jem, with the phaeton and his favourite horses to speed us to Roxbury. Lodestar was fuming.

The stationmaster called us over. Jem had left the phaeton for us, and gone off. Something to do with the rain, he said.

Lodestar tugged me roughly out to the phaeton. The horses were restive, huddling against the station walls.

I tugged my coat around me. My head was swirling. "Are we going up to the house?"

"Didn't you say," he said with his suavest smile, "you'd like to see the Pump House? I can show you what I've been working on."

He was right, that was what I had wanted. But I couldn't get my thoughts clear: it was a risk, going alone with him, and I felt my powers of resistance at their lowest ebb. I tumbled into the vehicle, as if it were a longed-for bed.

I felt I would never be warm.

"Don't move." Lodestar stopped at the glasshouse. The horses were sweating and the wheels muddy. The last thing I remember was the road from the station, all but blocked by the rains, as if to cut the house off from civilisation. I must have fallen asleep, as Lodestar drove wildly into the storm.

What was wrong with me? My eyes stung, and my head hung heavy. I should be thinking, planning, ready for the hour ahead, but the rain battering down seemed to pierce right through me. Poor Jem, walking home in this.

Lodestar threw something on to the luggage plate and leapt back in. He swept us onward up the hill. He stopped the horses halfway up the road between house and glasshouses. I recognised the place: where you crossed to the Pump House.

I felt sick in the stomach. I'd vowed to stay close by him, to keep my discoveries to myself, and to keep him from the house, but I have misjudged my powers. We neared the gorge, to cross to the Pump House, where Ruth and Molly and Roxbury had passed an afternoon of such friendship; such bright days seemed a long time gone in this downpour. I had to gather my wits.

I stumbled. Lodestar grabbed me with one arm; the other held an animal cage. I thanked him for his help, without understanding why I needed help. I glanced back, from house to glasshouse, from me to Lodestar.

"You and I," I muttered, "are like the house and the scientific quarter, locked in a balance of magnetism and power."

He laughed at my incoherent philosophising. He dragged me onward toward the river.

I woke again. I was sick. I couldn't stand. We were in a shed. Levers at the door, affixed wires along the rough stone walls, equipment on tables and an old bureau. I could hear water rushing past. The Pump House? Yes, I had made good on my appointment. The air was musty: I wanted to go outside, into the fresh rain, but I couldn't even wipe my face.

"I don't understand." I was groggy, struggling to form my words, wretched to the pit of my stomach. It was pouring outside and I was soaked to the skin. "What's happened?"

Lodestar's silhouette appeared in the doorway, against the lights of the house, behind him, across the gorge. He walked in, peered at me, examining my face as if I were a fungus.

I shook myself, trying to wake my addled senses. My hands wouldn't move. My feet the same. "What the devil?"

A bucket, emptied of its water, rolled back and forth on the concrete floor. He had thrown it over me to wake me. A strange animal, like an outsized hare, rocked back and forth in its cage, panting disquieted. He had tied it, trussed its limbs like a Sunday joint. Only then did I realise, he had done the same to me. My hands were bound behind my back.

"What's happened?" I kicked and kicked again. I only made the chair teeter.

My feet were tied together. I looked up at him, dark against the doorway, and only now realised I was lost. How could my memory play such games with me? "What have you done to me? Please, I don't understand."

"No, my friend. *I* don't understand." He leaned in the

doorway, still exuding the suavity that first won me over to him. "What I don't understand is why you're here. You could have run off with Bertie. You could have escaped with your life. Why ever did you come?"

My heart sank. What had I revealed on the train? I'd been off guard, dismayed to find I'd been wrong all along. In trying to be vigilant, I have been complicit with murderers and terrorists. Complicit with Lodestar. My only hope was to delay, and delay long enough for help to come. I must strike at his arrogance. "To arrest you."

"Please." He laughed. "Why not arrest me in London, where a thousand idiot coppers would help you?"

"The proof of your crimes is here."

A derisive snort exploded from him. "That's what I love about this job. You never know what the evening will bring. This morning, I woke up. I ate, I shat, I fornicated. I caught a train. Just another meeting, I thought. Some fool to dominate. Then up you spring: a policeman, in place of an engineer. Oho, I thought, something is astir. You looked so sick on the boat. What a disappointment. Was there no worthy adversary they could send? If this was to be it, must it be you? Such a pushover?"

"I haven't proved a pushover."

He let the situation speak for itself.

I wriggled miserably at my bonds. "I knew more than you realised."

"True. This morning, I didn't know I'd have to kill you." He took an apple from his pocket and bit into it. "If that gives you comfort."

I felt I would vomit. He must have poisoned me. I felt so far on the way to death, I almost wished it was over. He had played his tricks and played me false; he let me think I fooled him, when my bluffing was plain as day. I had no stomach for his game. No sleeves to hide my cards up. I could only play my hand. I would tell him all I knew: how clever he has been to hoodwink us all. He will like that: how brilliantly he has outwitted us.

I breathed deep. "This morning, when I knew your secret, it was as if you noticed me for the first time. You had talked to me, sure, at your coffee house. Charmed me, flattered me; but you hoodwink fools daily. Today, when I knew you were not Lodestar, not the real Lodestar, you took note."

He looked at me without pity.

"You can't kill me. You won't kill me, with Bertie coming."

He considered this. "Doesn't matter two hoots. You're expendable. Bertie knows it. Why did he let you come on with me?"

"Why kill me here? You could have stabbed me on the train, or thrown me in the river."

"And been discovered. A touch obvious."

"If you kill me here, you'll be discovered. Bertie knows you're coming here with me."

"That evidence will do nicely. I went to bed. You insisted on snooping round the electrics. Your 'accidental' death will be a sadness to everyone."

"Molly knows."

"Thanks for your concern." He grinned. "You read my diary, you little snoop. I saw you. I could see it in your face. What do you know?"

"You set up the blasts," I said. "You paid them. Instructed them. Provided explosives."

He sat back, tickled to hear his achievements itemised. "Nobody would believe that."

"Hard to prove, I admit. But Mersey Jacques has identified you. And we'll catch Jacques the First—"

He burst out laughing. "Who?"

"All these fools you've named Jacques the Painter. Mersey Jacques, who blew up the *Florence Veigh*. Jacques the First, who was eyeing up Parliament."

"I don't remember." He shrugged. "I've paid a lot of vagabonds and idiots."

"The bloody idiot who's hiding in your Shepherd's Refuge, if that makes it clearer." However befuddled I was, I had to hold back from saying more. Lodestar was plotting with Jacques, and that would be his downfall. He did not know that Jeffcoat was back from his jaunt and ready to pounce.

"Is he?" He clapped his hands. "Is he! Fantastical."

"Why fantastical? You put him there."

"The only person I can think of who might have brought him there—oh dear, oh dear." He put his hand to his mouth, in mock horror. He was play-acting, and enjoying it. "Oh, little Molly. This doesn't look good for your friend."

"Molly?" My throat burned. "Why Molly?"

"Faithless bint. She must have an agent of the Frenchies all along. Picture it: the detective sergeant is found electrocuted, sniffing around dangerous equipment." A wave of nausea shook me, as he let that sink in. "Meanwhile, his come-hither accomplice, who has all the while been spying on Roxbury's secrets, crucial to the nation's safety, is found consorting in the hills with a French activist. Was she the mastermind of it all? These waves of terror sweeping the nation?" He clapped his hands. "Why, yes. She comes from London. Contacts in criminal circles. Inveigled her way into the country's most important company." He came close and ogled me manically, his nose in my face. "Unfortunately, she dies. I haven't decided how."

"Be quiet."

"A traitress, as well as a harlot—"

"Shut your filthy mouth."

Poison in the brandy. He has poisoned my body, addled my wits.

He was dragging my chair back upright. My cheek stung; I

barely recalled the blow. The pain in my stomach was worse, anyway. He was speaking matter-of-factly. "I don't see your objection to the charge of harlotry. From a tuppenny brothel off the Ratcliffe Highway, to my bed."

I spat at him.

This slap did not knock me over, but it balanced out the pain in my cheeks. I cried out, which gave momentary relief from the sickness in my guts.

"Behold, how gallantly he defends his little harlot." His eyes gleamed. "You're right. I did know about the Frenchman in the hut. I've informed the authorities."

"You—informed on him?"

"Responsible citizen, I am." He pulled up a chair and sat beside me, looking outwards. "Yes, I heard this rumour. Frenchy on the loose. Of course, I told Scotland Yard at once. Asked for Jeffcoat specially."

"How—how do you mean, you asked for Jeffcoat?"

"Ripon and I have an understanding. What with my important standing in this important firm." He was enjoying this tremendously, pulling the rug from under my feet. "I've told Ripon all the way, I trust your intentions, but that Jeffcoat, he's less convincing. I mean, are you confident of his loyalty? He's interviewed all those French activists; maybe they have turned his head? After all, he was always undermining the forts, wasn't he? Let's test his loyalty, I told Ripon. Send him under cover, pretend he's gone abroad, say. Then send him after this Frenchman. If he catches him, he proves himself. If he lets him go free—"

"He won't." He was playing with my head. If he had sway over Ripon, who could I trust?

"Then again, he may come to grief in the quicksands behind the Shepherd's Refuge. Killed in the line of duty, alas, and evidence emerges of his dealings with these activists."

"There is no evidence."

"I have all the evidence I want. With you dead, and a proven turncoat, who will gainsay me?" He grabbed hold of my hair, and pulled. "And if you and Jeffcoat were wrong 'uns, your doubts over the Portsmouth Plan unravel."

My head jerked forward, as he let go. "You don't know about that plan."

"Of course I do." He looked delighted. "I wrote it."

PLAY-ACTING [LAWLESS]

The rains redoubled on the slate roof above us. A filthy night. The Pump House doors lay open. Outside, the weir and the falls that drove the turbine. My stomach was in revolt, but worst were my curses for my own stupidity.

"Are you unwell, Sergeant?"

"Perfectly well." I would not give him the satisfaction of describing my pains. He had poisoned me: my eyes were dry, while body shivering. Beside me in the cage, the Patagonian hare quivered as well. "Why have you brought the animal?"

"Would you like to see?" he said, enthused. He peered out, across the gorge, to the house.

The light glowed in the turret of the east wing. He checked his watch, which reminded me: Molly knows; Molly knows I am here.

"Time enough." He nodded. "Good. Observe."

He turned to the lever by the doorway, released the catch, and drew it downward. Creak, clunk. As the gears engaged the waterwheel, the turbine began, ever so slowly, to rotate and whirr. Lodestar gazed upon his preparations. He pulled on rubber galoshes, and thick leather gloves. Hampered by the gloves, he opened the battered old bureau.

He turned to me, holding two wires. They were attached to the banks of batteries, those strange glass cases, charged by the stream. The wires were wrapped in gutta-percha rubber, with copper ends exposed: the gloves were a precaution, but a wise one. Even with the gentle roll of the waterwheel, the turbine's piston pumped relentlessly. I could envisage the electricity coursing down each wire, seeking only a conductor to join it to the other.

Lodestar's eyes were bright with devilry. He came at me, plunging the wires at my head.

I jerked away. The chair rocked, tipped over, and I fell hard, cracking my head on the stone floor behind the cage. I couldn't move, but I could see: in the dim light, right in front of my face, he thrust the wires against the hare's flanks. Sparks flared. There was an unholy wail.

Spasms ran through it. It rattled wildly around the cage. The back legs kicked, jerked, burst their knots to thump against the cage, just six inches from my eyes. The stench of burnt hair filled the room, and burned flesh. I was transfixed by the black bloody scorch that materialised between the wires. I thought the beast was dead, then it trembled again, flinching away from its torturer, before settling in the corner of the cage, limp and dying. Another stench: at the last, it fouled itself.

Lodestar leaned over towards the stricken animal, inspecting it for signs of vitality. Satisfied, he took the wires back to the bureau, wiped them off, and set them carefully in place. He was never normally tentative—I registered this uncertainty, and tucked it aside, like a sovereign for a rainy day.

"Ugh." Lodestar clicked his tongue at the stench, disgruntled. "More current, or charge, or—damn it—what does Molly call it? Potential difference."

The Patagonian hare was dead. He tugged the cage outside. He watched the waterwheel's slow insistent spin—*chak-KE-ta chak-KE-ta*—and threw the animal upon it. With an irregular thud, the wheel chopped it into the water.

He turned back inside and pulled a chair to the bureau.

Outside, I saw a shadow, rocking oddly. A hand appeared in the doorframe, and then a pair of eyes. For a moment, I thought I was saved; but it was the orang-utan. It saw us, and, judging by the mournful expression, it had watched the demise of its Patagonian friend.

Lodestar turned, sensing the presence, but the orang-utan was too quick, vanished away out of sight. At the bureau, Lodestar had opened up a telegraphic apparatus. Removing his gloves, he consulted a chart affixed to the inner panel. For upwards of a minute, he tapped laboriously at the machine, ignoring me where I lay.

The hare's stench lingered. Nausea grabbed me, and I retched on to the grimy stone.

"That should do it." He pushed the machine away. "I have signalled Molly to come and assist in our experiments. That's what you wanted, isn't it?"

My heart leapt. Molly would not let me down. And yet— "To assist?"

He span to face me. "Oh, you are more interesting than I expected. Molly is such a willing experimenter. In so many ways." He straightened his trousers.

"What did you say to—?"

"Quiet, you worm." He lunged, as if to hit me, but instead grabbed me, tugging the chair upright again.

I struggled at the ropes, but they just became tighter.

The machine began buzzing. "Ah—she replies." He sat back down and annotated the noises with ill grace. When it fell silent, he scratched at the paper, decoding, his face screwed up. "Ah. A short delay. But worth the wait in the end." He clapped the desk brusquely shut, and turned to me. "Molly's complicity must disappoint you, Sergeant?"

I looked at him. I was unwilling to give excuse for another blow by answering.

"Isn't this wonderful?" He beamed, which was more

discomfiting than his cruelty. "We have a little time. Molly is setting detonators. One in my office, just in case I have to destroy any evidence."

"But the others. The others don't know—"

"They'd better not know, or I'll have to do for them all. On second thoughts, that might be the safest path anyway. The Frenchman has laid explosives beneath the house. They'll do for your Miss Villiers and old Roxbury, just in case."

My heart was thumping, impotent in the face of this evil, so long suspected, so gravely underestimated. "You wouldn't risk the prince's life."

"Why not?" He clapped his hands. "I could save him, and become a national hero. If it should go wrong, well, you'll be blamed. And we don't want a French-lover running the country one day, do we?" He scratched his head. "Molly's leaving a little gift for our friends in the house, just in case. It's very cunning: I can set them off from here, if need be. The house is a fuel in waiting." He observed me for a moment.

I must give no satisfaction. I could believe he would sacrifice the scientific quarter to hide his misdeeds. But to set alight Roxbury House, though, was unimaginable: Skirtle, Birtle, Roxbury, his wife, and my darling Ruth.

Lodestar could read this despair in my face, despite my efforts. He took immeasurable pleasure in my suffering. "Molly's coming to release the sluice for me. Increases the power. I'll give you a taste of the same medicine as the little rodent. Ten times stronger."

FORGIVENESS [LAWLESS]

"It was clever," I said, "that you did it for financial gain." I watched him absorb the compliment. My fear galvanised me: I had nothing to lose, and that gave me a reckless freedom.

The only game I could play now was to delay him; perhaps it was the wrong game, but it was late for tactics now. "Very clever, Lodestar. Three gains. The Hellfire Hounds make a killing on property after each outrage. They consequently buy your stock, grateful for your information—which they think you get from underworld contacts. They never guess you are orchestrating the outrages yourself."

He revelled in this. "And the third?"

"Profits for Roxbury. Over and over. Britain builds your forts, for fear of its European neighbours. We buy your bricks, we order your guns. Tough life for the arms builders."

"Is this the famed English irony?"

"Scottish. A grimmer sort of irony."

He snorted. "Your case against me is weak."

"Jacques will identify you. You can deny it, of course."

"Go on. Teach me more of my defence. I won't need it, after you're dead."

"You will, if I have told others."

"Have you? Shame if you have. They are all here. I will kill them, if I have to. I can do it without leaving this Pump House."

"You're cocksure of your abilities."

He laughed. "I've learned a few things."

"Enlighten me."

He checked the watch again, tapping his foot impatiently. "To get rich, one must exploit. Exploit weakness. Make people think they're getting what they want. I make bankers rich; they've repaid me. I've made Roxbury rich; his reputation protects me. I'm tough, of course. That's what people want from a manager. Your system is a hoot. The only people who get to the top are people who stop at nothing. Braggarts and blusterers. You let these people run reputable companies. You give them knighthoods. I'm not the worst. I haven't even killed that many."

I just waited for him to finish. Don't enrage him. Flatter him. For now, flatter him.

He looked at me as if I were accusing him. "What's so wrong with a little killing? You lot have done it for years."

I pictured Ruth, that day in Clerkenwell, stepping out from the rubble, covered in dust, like a miracle. "We don't kill. Not in Britain. Not in the heart of London."

"No, in my land. In the heart of Nyasaland." He pointed at me. "You people killed my mother. You massacred my people. Not even for profit. Just to pass the time in the tropical heat. You tortured. You raped. Took our goods. Called it trading, when you were stealing. Gave us alcohol to enslave us, and told us to be grateful." He clapped. "And you send Wilfred to China to make them buy your Indian opium. That is breathtaking arrogance! I'm nothing by comparison. You trot round the world, murdering and pillaging, stirring up wars, like hornets' nests, so you can sell them guns. Peace costs: oh, such a cost. War, on the other hand—people die, oh yes, but nobody important. That's how you think of it, no? And if anybody important dies, they're a hero. A *cause célèbre*. It's been a struggle to get myself to the right side of that line. I won't mess it up now, or let you."

CHARGES [LAWLESS]

I had travelled all this way with Lodestar, making him think I liked him, even loved. The cost was high. Flattering, always flattering. That was his one weakness, that I knew. He fancied himself untrickable, and that made him vulnerable; and he believed himself in the right.

"It's the end," I murmured.

"For you, yes. You will die. So sorry." He shot me a pitying look. "Ha ha! I'm not sorry. I'm jubilant. I shall walk away to fame and riches. Best of all, I shall blame the whole thing upon you and your Jeffcoat. And Molly too if I need to. What a surprise they would have to hear she has been playing a double game; spying, yes, but all the while giving our explosives to terrorists." He shook his head, imagining it. "Cruel to traduce her, this silly girl who dotes upon me."

Silhouetted, Lodestar loomed over me, a spectre of doom.

Behind him, the lights of the east wing. My heart contracted to think of Roxbury and his Lady Elodie; it gave me a moment's relief from my pains.

"Why, Lodestar. Don't you want Roxbury as your father figure? It almost gives you a place in the English aristocracy."

He stepped into the light, his face disarmingly courteous. "Roxbury is my champion. He suffers. I do all I can to give him relief. This has required money, you cannot imagine how much, to make his companies profitable. The only reliable way is the country in crisis."

I drew deep upon my reserves of sympathy, trying to see his point of view: that he had done nothing wrong. "It has been hard for you."

"Nobody enters upon a life of deception without reason. To wake every day, knowing you must not slip; to speak even a word of your mother's language would give you away. Most are easily persuaded, but there are doubters, watching for a slip. And a slip would endanger not just me, but the Hounds. Roxbury Industries. The security of the nation. Prison or deportation are nothing, beside the exposure of the Portsmouth Plan."

"Which you invented."

"The threat is real."

"It's false witness, Lodestar, deliberate lies. That is hard to forgive."

"Forgiveness is laudable in your religion," said Lodestar. "Yet so few of you practise it. You harp on about Christian values. Who spread the false witness? You. You spread it so eagerly! It's become the gospel for this generation reared on passivism and distractions. Finally we have given them permission to hate."

"Why?" I shook my head in wonder. "You're such an able man. Why couldn't you use your talents for good?"

He stared at me, neither indignant nor concerned by these accusations, and he smiled that brilliant smile. "But I have."

DARK SPARK [LAWLESS]

Molly was whistling as she sauntered up the hill. I heard the tune long before we saw her emerge from the rain. Oh, how I'd longed for her to come. She would plead my cause. I've saved her in the past, and her friends. Could she yet save me?

"My beautiful assistant." Lodestar made eyes at her, as she appeared.

She melted into him. She had not spared me a glance.

"More beautiful," Lodestar said, "than Roxbury's assistant."

"Than Birtle?" She batted at his chest. "You know how to compliment a girl."

They were lovers.

It was impossible to think anything else. I watched this display, horror crawling through my veins. Reading between the lines, eh, Ruth? She had seen Molly's fancy for Lodestar, and she had tried to warn her off. All in vain. I had thought she was relying on me, whereas it was I needed her, and I felt heartsick, as well as sick in body.

I could see it now: I had wondered why she didn't write more of Lodestar, and this was why. She loved him.

"Molly?" I pleaded, my throat dry. She ignored me, and when I tried again, my throat constricted in a sob. She would side with him and send me to my death.

"Glad to see you've your boots on, darling," Molly said to him, as if they were an old married couple. "Fetching. Now tell me what you're after. I'll do the necessary and be off."

"You don't want to see the finale?" He was petulant. "After all you've been through together."

"Not really." She shook her head, with a tolerant air. "Main drama's over in the house. They're going to bring Lady Elodie back from the dead."

"Is this not more compelling?"

"Kill a lilly law, raise from the dead." She weighed it up. "I'll take the main house."

Her indifference to his performance stung him. The whole reason he had dragged me here was for her to admire this ridiculous melodrama, when he could so easily have shoved me from the train or dropped me in the river. "Why did you bother coming?"

"Don't be so shrewish: it's unattractive." Molly manipulated him more adeptly than I ever could. She knew him, knew his weaknesses. "You told me to come. And I'm checking the sluice."

"The sluice. That's right." Lodestar gave me a look. He had confided in me that he was ready to drop her in the soup, if he had to. That could be a wedge between them, if she learned of it. He pulled his gloves back on and looked at me, as if to carve me up. "Open the sluice, Molly. Let's fry some breakfast for the animals."

"Midnight." She put her hands on her hips. "They're doing it at midnight, you shallow-pated noddle, with the full moon."

"Open it now."

"The sluice can't be worked from here, Nathan. I've told you." She tutted. She was at ease with him, intimate enough to insult him. "You never listen. For such an achiever, you're dense. If the sluice were worked from here, any animal could flip it—any French vagabonds. Where's your watch?"

Lodestar indicated with his glove.

Molly reached into his waistcoat pocket—such a heedless intimacy—gave me an inscrutable glance, and set the watch on the bureau. "Fifteen minutes. I'll wire the house." She sat at the telegraphic box to buzz a rapid message: she needed no chart to help her, with her mastery of codes. "Remind Miss Ruth about the sluice at midnight. Want me to buzz the scientific quarter?"

"No! Not yet." Lodestar rubbed his hands together, like a child waiting for the circus to begin. "Why don't you give our friend a little shock? To warm him up, while we wait for the extra power."

Molly looked at him, glanced at me, as if I were no more than a science experiment. She attended to the switches by the bureau, adjusted a dial, then turned toward me. She was holding the gutta-percha wires circumspectly, clear of the exposed ends. No gloves for her. "Any last words, Captain Clocky? Thought not." She was close up, where he could not see. As I stared at her, overwhelmed with nausea and regret, she winked. "Never eloquent at the best of times, were you?"

She touched a wire to my right temple.

I sat upright, awaiting the jolts. She held the other wire close: I could sense it by my head. I could hear the electricity that foretold the fatal shake.

Nothing.

"What the blazes is wrong?" Lodestar stomped in, peevish.

She batted away his hand. "Don't meddle, Nathan."

"You useless baggage—" He grabbed for the wires. Somehow they caught on his clothing, one under his shirtsleeve, the other at his open collar. He gave out such an ugly wail. Back he staggered, beating away the wires. He was lit up against the night—this was the little shock he'd planned for me. It hurt him, but not badly enough. He turned upon her, blinking, intent in his eyes.

"Your own fault, you blunderbuss." Molly dropped the wires, unembarrassed, and adjusted the dial at the bureau. "Such a fuss. A little shock. He didn't moan at all—"

"You sly snake." He stared, enraged, unsure whether she had contrived to do it.

Molly looked at him impassively. "That's the thanks I get?"

"Give me those." He flailed with his gloves to pick up the wires. "I can't trust you. You told him about the Frenchman, did you?"

"I told him nothing."

Lodestar was talking himself into a fury. "Villiers knows, doubtless. And that fool Jeffcoat. But the Frenchman will do for him. And the others are ignorant, I suspect."

"They are," said Molly, "but you can't be sure. Better despatch them all."

He looked up at her with some respect. "I plan to."

"Blow up the house. That's what I'd do." She sniffed. "Clear the evidence. Start afresh."

Calm overtook him, as sudden as his rage, and as alarming. He shook off the gloves and set the wires, carefully, back in their place. He smiled at Molly's vehemence, for it made her a kindred spirit. "The package you sent up by pneumatic railway is my latest development in bombs. The detonator is not disturbed until the compartment is opened and the Parkesine balls disturbed. They roll apart. They fall. They combust. I've had the Frenchman lay black powder in the hall. That whole house is a fuel in waiting. A conflagration will destroy any evidence against me, you're right. Shall we buzz the house now? Birtle will open the pneumatic packet thing, and then we shall see some fireworks."

"No, we won't," Molly muttered.

Lodestar couldn't judge whether she were teasing or not. He narrowed his eyes and sat to work the telegraph.

"He won't get far with that." Molly spoke to me, to annoy him. "Can't make head nor tail of 'action at a distance'. Rather important for scientists."

"What the devil did you say?"

"You heard." Molly bobbed in front of him, pleased with his reaction: she knew how to belittle him, and to enrage him.

"The thing is, Nathan, Roxy's made advances recently: voltage regulation and discharge. Whereas you've swanned around showing off that whole time."

Sure enough, though he tried to remain cool, his eyes blazed up. He snatched up the wires and thrust them against her.

I cried out. That Molly should come so far, through so much grime and misery, to meet her end here, despatched by this egotistical madman. And my fault.

Nothing. The wires did nothing to her.

She didn't even flinch: she must have adjusted the power without him realising. She was playing with his spirit, teasing, tormenting him into making mistakes.

"What the hell?" Lodestar dropped the wires. His anger evaporated, he backed away from her. "You are a witch."

"If that's what you like, Nathan." She fluttered her eyelashes. "I always do whatever you like. Don't I, Nathan?"

This provocation overcame his fear of her uncanny power. He snatched her up by her jacket, like a child about to throw its doll out of the pram. Upending her in one movement, he held her upside down by the ankles. He snatched up a rope; he had her tethered within moments. "Like a rabbit." He laughed to see her helpless. "A caged rabbit."

"That didn't go so well, did it?" she said. "I was only teasing, you empty-headed jobber knot."

He growled at her. "You were siding with him."

"If this is her siding with me," I said, "I'd hate to see her hostile."

She twisted around toward me, trussed up but grinning. "Told you Lodestar wasn't the sharpest spanner in the toolkit."

He could not abide her insults. To shut them out, he swung her over his shoulder and carried her out into the night.

"Blast you to hell, you ultracrepidarian bedswerver," she said, white-faced; though he had knocked the breath out of her, her vocabulary remained unerring.

He raised her high, to throw her into the river, as he had tumbled his own brother to oblivion five long years ago. I could still see her face, as she dangled over his shoulder, on the point of being hoiked over the weir down the Burnfoot Gorge to be crushed on the rocks. She saw me, desperately trying to rise and come to her aid. She winked again, this time a little sadly.

I had never known, until that moment, how much I loved her. I loved her, like a daughter; I loved her like a sister; and I felt her sorrow at botching the job so desperately.

Out of the night reared a beast. It flew headlong at Lodestar's midriff, felling him to the platform.

Molly was flung aside.

Lodestar was hefted against the side of the turbine. Only a few inches further, and the piston, pounding with implacable regularity, would be striking him. Lodestar was winded, maybe hurt, but most of all he was shaken by this ambush.

For a moment, I thought it must be a beast: the orang-utan, avenging his friend. It was Jem. He picked himself up from the platform's edge, and advanced on Lodestar. He rounded on him, grim-faced, unappeasable as a wild animal, leaving him no escape, staring as if he were the devil.

"Jem! Well, well." Lodestar puffed. "What can it be?"

"You beetle-browed traitor," Jem said, his voice a lament. The pain in his soft young features was terrible. He was ready to tear Lodestar apart, and I hoped to God he would. "Why did you?"

Lodestar straightened up, feeling his back for damage. The piston rapped his fingers, and he flinched: how desperately close he'd come to his ruin. He laughed, in relief and disdain. "Don't you think Molly is out of your reach?"

"Jem," Molly called, "what's happened?"

"Yes, what did I do, little Jemmy?"

Jem's face crumpled. "Dotty, down the village."

"Dotty." Lodestar's eyes ranged around.

"The dairymaid. My girl." He sniffed. "We were to be married."

"Oh, Dotty, with the..." He described two circles in the air. "You'd think they'd be unforgettable; her vulgarity quite blotted her name from my memory."

Jem swung: no wild swipe, but a measured punch. Lodestar was waiting for it—he had riled him purposely—and he ducked away. Not quick enough. The stable boy was nimble as well as strong. Lodestar's nose crunched, and he cried out.

As Jem stepped in to finish the job, Lodestar grabbed at him. He snatched hold of Jem's waistcoat, maddened. Stepping deftly back, he tugged, swinging the boy's weight around. He thrust him against the turbine and into the piston which he had so narrowly evaded.

It struck against Jem's back, pounding over and over, driven by the waterwheel's spin. Jem's eyes widened. He opened his mouth, but no cry emerged.

Lodestar held the poor boy there, the piston juddering into his back, once, twice, again and again. With a cackle, Lodestar pulled Jem away from the torture, and threw him down on to the jutting ledge.

Blood darkened the boy's lower back. He dragged himself, half crawling, away from his torturer toward the edge, but he had no strength. He had saved Molly only for a moment; she lay, still bundled, at the platform's edge, where it overhung the waterwheel. So much for Jem's revenge. His strength had failed him; his nimbleness had failed him. Lodestar had bedded his girl, and carelessly. Now Lodestar stepped across, feeling at his neck, and aimed a kick at Jem's kidneys.

Jem grabbed at Lodestar's trouser legs, as if to beg for pardon.

Another kick, to the groin. Jem jack-knifed, the pain too hard to bear. Like a bottle set too near the table's edge, where all see it totter but none is quick enough to stop it falling, Jem rolled, toppling over the edge and out of sight: down, down into the gorge.

There was a cry, but we saw no more. I knew where the water ran, ever swift, over the mossy stones and down, down, down the white water of the Burnfoot Gorge to the rocks below.

Molly craned her neck. Jem had died for us, and Jem had died for us uselessly. Even she struggled to remain nonchalant. She looked over the edge, her voice cracked. "Messed that up, didn't I?"

"Molly, Molly." Lodestar stood above her, breathing heavily, but apparently unconcerned. He wiped his hands on his trousers, and tutted, as one would at a puppy. "It is a shame to kill you too. We could have struck a deal. We could have made a partnership."

"We did," she said. She couldn't bear to look at him. Any power he had had over her, he had lost: she would side with him no more. The rain redoubled.

He grinned, too cocksure to hear the loathing in her voice. "We are alike, you and I. You remind me of home."

"How nice for you," she said. "Is that why you let me live when you've killed so many?"

I groaned. Molly's diplomacy was ever unorthodox. And yet he was still talking. While he was talking, all was not lost. Indeed Lodestar was regarding her with petulant affection. "My plan was that you would live, and I would enjoy you. Why did you spoil it? Why couldn't you be sensible?"

"Just be done with it, Nathan." Molly sighed. She held out her hands, trussed in the ropes, and nodded toward the bureau and the wires. "Charge up the batteries, won't you? We don't want to be sizzling like sausages."

He hesitated. "With the influence machine?"

"You remember how." She tutted. She was coaching him on how to kill us.

He blinked. "Of course I do."

"Your circuitry was never great, was it? Check the time. The surge from the sluice'll come soon. Roxbury'll open it at midnight. Ten minutes. Why don't I show you how to harness it? Do for our friend Watchman here. Then decide whether you keep me or toast my block off."

The tower glowed, across the Burnfoot Gorge, beneath a sky brooding with destruction.

Lodestar nodded, won for a moment. But the exhilaration of his victory over Jem was ebbing. He recoiled from her, deflated, suspecting treachery. He turned back into the Pump House. "You shouldn't have betrayed me."

"A misunderstanding—" she began.

"I could have saved you, and the ones in the house. But now..." He sat at the telegraph station. His teeth clenched, as he punched out two pointed messages. He pushed the apparatus away, and turned to us triumphant. "Detonated the glasshouses. Detonated the main house."

"Molly?" I stirred from my stupefaction. My stomach was ablaze, wrists numb, arms frozen against the chair. I listened for the detonations, but heard nothing. I could already picture the house on fire, the flames licking up the walls, leaping up curtains and through windows, towards my love. "He's setting off the bombs, Molly. Molly?"

"Hush your noise," she called. She was wriggling back toward him, like a caterpillar, across the platform towards the wires. She was sodden and pathetic, trapped as surely as the hare, yet she spoke again with her habitual calm. "It's just pneumatic packets. He put detonators in my artist's case, the yellow-bellied skulker. They won't open it."

He snorted. "They will."

"I'll tell them not to open it."

"Too late. I've buzzed for Birtle to fetch it. The blast will do for him. The house will be on fire in minutes."

"Kill Birtle? That's low." Molly gave me a look, the tiniest shake of the head. She was up to something; she had some way of diverting Lodestar's messages. "You're a blustering bully, ain't you?"

A detonation sounded, and I winced. But it had come from high up on the hillside, not the house.

Lodestar rubbed his hands. "Jacques," he said in satisfaction. "The Frenchman's traps are sprung. I told him to expect a visit from Jeffcoat. Good: that's him dealt with. Now to finish the two of you."

Molly had wriggled all the way to his feet. He grabbed at her coat and pulled her upright. He would drag her out and throw her over. She would not escape him again.

"You'd kill a woman, I know." Moll shrank away in self-defence. "But you wouldn't kill your own child."

His stare softened.

"Kill your own son, would you?" She looked at him, placing her trussed hands upon her belly. "I reckon it's a son."

"Molly—!" I yelled, as if I were her father, but I broke off.

Lodestar was dumbstruck. I had never seen him at a loss before. He took hold of her shoulders and stared at her. Should he strike her or kiss her? He shook his head in wonder.

I marvelled at her tactic. It had better be a tactic.

He pulled her into an embrace. She resisted, then yielded. She smiled so winningly that he did not notice that her arms were untied. She pulled back gently from him. Holding his gaze, she reached behind her, stretching as if to entice him. Then , with sudden fervour, she clasped her hands upon either side of his neck.

He juddered, uncomprehending. He could not see the wires in her hands; he could not understand how her hands were free; his swift knots were no match for Molly.

The wires.

She held the wires firm, jolting power through him, until his legs buckled. She leaned back as she assailed him, gripping the gutta-percha to avoid shocks herself. The moment he fell to the ground, she threw down the wires. She slipped the ropes around his legs, quick as anything. She yanked, tightening the knot, and yanked again, then hurried to bind his wrists.

Coming to his senses, he struggled, but the more he struggled the more the rope tightened. "I've set up cells," he stammered, weakened. "Enough activists to keep the English afraid for a hundred years. You won't be free from terror, unless you let me go—"

"A shame," she said, snatching up the wires again, "to despatch your handsome fizzog to prison."

He writhed back. "I can testify about you. Traitress to your country. Double murderess of the Ratcliffe Highway."

How he knew of that, I could not guess, but it riled her. She brandished the wires in his face.

"Don't. Don't hurt me." He froze. "We can—"

"Captured beauty's never as attractive," she said, "as beauty on the loose. Wasn't that what you told me?"

He lashed out in sudden fury, only to strike the wires again.

"Watch yourself." She held them firm against him, as he endured the shock, worse than the first.

How he writhed to free himself from the torture. He kept wriggling, twisting, and ducking back, convinced he could grab hold of her, but she was dextrous and determined.

"There'll be fried breakfast for the python tomorrow, Nathan, if you don't give over."

"Faithless…" His voice was slurred. "Faithless fool." He tried to strike at her, but had no strength; tried to spit at her, but only drooled. He passed out.

"Who is the fool now, eh?" she said, standing over him. She dropped the wires. "Who is the faithless one?"

We stared at him, collapsed upon the platform. Then Molly hurried to untie my ropes, deft but exhausted. I thanked her. I could barely move my limbs.

"You're welcome, Watchman. You'd do the same for me, I'm sure."

"Tell me." I rubbed at my wrists. "Why did you let him tie you up?"

"Best way to put him off guard." She kept her eyes firmly on Lodestar, prostrate between us and the gorge. The waterwheel clunked: *chak-ke-ta chak-ke-ta*.

"He was ready to kill you."

"Error of judgement. We all make 'em." She took from the bureau drawer a discoloured billiard ball. She tossed it in a deliberate arc, up and over Lodestar's head. BANG: it smashed upon the platform, with a burst of flame.

"Them's what started your blasts." She watched intently. Lodestar did not stir. Satisfied, she made an adjustment to a regulator dial. She glanced from Lodestar back to the wires dropped carelessly beside him. Calmly she put on the gloves.

"Molly, wait." I tried to stand, to plead with her. "We can send him to trial. His victims—"

A gunshot from up the hillside broke into my plea. An almighty splash into the pool above us spattered the platform with cold droplets. A voice echoed down the gorge: a voice I knew. It was Jeffcoat calling down from the Shepherd's Refuge. "Got him!" he called. "I got Jacques."

With that inspiration, I pushed myself to my feet. Molly pointed up at the light, over in the house. The night was blacker than ever, the moon unseen, exerting its mysterious pressure from the tremulous clouds. I put my arm around her, and felt her soften against me.

She nodded. She threw down the wires, took off the gloves and offered me her arm. "Come along."

I gazed up at the tower. A figure was silhouetted in the turret—Ruth, I felt sure. The light in the turret flashed once, twice.

The village church tolled the hour of midnight. The swoosh

of the sluice sounded above us: the sluice gates were opened. Under cover of the noise, he stirred.

The light in the turret flashed again: once, twice, thrice. Molly was enthralled with the wonder of it: what was going to happen, up there, to her Lady Elodie? All their planning, their researches: the animals, and the experimentation; the batteries and the regulation. All was coming to a finale, and she was missing it. She had missed it, in order to save my life, because I had the fool notion I was going to catch Lodestar red-handed.

She didn't see him coming.

I turned at the last moment. He had the wires in his hand. He lunged at Molly, his feet still trussed together. He was already upon her, when I threw myself in between them. We tumbled, rolling on the platform. Our heads clashed as we writhed above the waterwheel, and he groaned, his nose crushed. He rolled on top of me, with a roar. I gripped on to his waistcoat; he still clutched the wires.

The falls swelled. The water gathered to gush through the wheel, spinning it ever faster and ever faster—*CHAK-ta CHAK-ta CHAK-ta*—speeding the piston and setting the circuits a-humming with life.

We were at the very edge. His jaw clenched, as he urged the bare wires upon me. He was too late. I was weakened, but I had the strength of fury. With the last of my energies, I pushed him off me and over the edge. The wires pulled taut beneath me. Dangling from the platform, he clung to the gutta-percha, his feet tied and useless to help him. He stared up wildly, his eyes bulging. After all the terrors he had inflicted upon me, the fear and the poison and the misery of having failed myself and having failed my dear Molly, in the terror of his eyes I could see myself. I reached out my hand. He registered the wild stupidity of my offer as he tried to pull himself back up. For a few moments, he was succeeding. The stream rushed through the waterwheel. He looked down to see it, so close beneath him, turning ever faster.

He let go of one of the wires in order to reach for my hand.

I looked into his brown, brown eyes.

But his grip on the wet rubber was not enough to hold firm. He slipped down the last inches of insulated wire, flexing his wrist to gain purchase on the gutta-percha. The bare metal was already touching his clenched hand. In panic, he reached again for my proffered hand, but he could only grab for the other wire.

The waterwheel accelerated, the piston pounding ever faster. As he clutched on to the metal end of the second wire, his eyes widened with surprise.

The electricity coursed through him. His mouth opened, but he could not scream. With a fizzling crack, he shook, like a rag doll, writhing, a barely human thing. Energy lit up his body against the dark pool below. The shock must have killed him; it must have been enough. I hope so. For as he fell, he thudded on to the waterwheel, turning with the water's unforgiving pressure, breaking his body apart.

I wrenched myself away. Molly had scrambled away to the bureau. She looked back at me, silent, clutching the regulator dials.

Lodestar was gone.

I put my arm around her. Through the black night, lightning shot from the clouds, illuminating the trees on the hillside, outlining the walls of Roxbury House. The lamps in the tower were all at once extinguished. We gazed up in awe.

Within the turret, a spark. Another spark. And the final dark transcendent spark.

BOOK IX
THE COST

RETURNED TO LIFE [RUTH]

"I'm sorry," said Elodie. "So terribly sorry to have caused you such trouble. Can anyone smell beef dripping?"

Lady Elodie was back, resurrected from that limbo so long endured by her and all those around her.

We were standing at the window, looking across at the Pump House. We had given up our efforts, convinced we had failed.

I whispered a prayer of thanks, as Molly wired that they were safe and that Birtle should on no account open the pneumatic package.

How long Elodie had been standing by us at the window, none of us knew. Skirtle took such a leap of surprise, she nearly tumbled Birtle out of the window. Elodie's voice was soft, fuzzy at the edges, persuasive, a delight to all who heard it.

Roxbury took her in his arms.

How she had been all that time, she could not quite explain.

"I was awake, aware, some of the time, a lot of the time. I wanted to say so, and ask how everyone was, but you seemed so terribly distant. The notion that you would actually hear me seemed dreadfully unlikely."

How could she live up to the promise of her diaries, to the

promise of the earl's love, now that she was back from the dead? Easily. She was more natural and approachable than the headstrong princess, frozen in time, that Molly had painted her as. More magical than I had imagined, simply by being real.

IN CONCLUSION [LAWLESS]

That winter, Lady Elodie recovered her strength and learned what she had missed of the world's woes. The children were called back from the far-flung shires: fearing the worst of this summons, they arrived despondent, but quickly gave way to joy.

"I said I should like to see you again," said Kitty, "and now we can."

Molly became like another daughter to her; and Elodie a devoted friend to Ruth and me. By the time of our wedding, in July of the summer following, we could not imagine our world without her.

If society made a scandal of her unexpected renascence, they did not notice. Nico wrote to *The Times* to announce her alive and hale.

And so they lived; and with them Birtle and Skirtle, who were in fact—as may have been plain from the start—Mr and Mrs Soutar, a couple themselves, equally devoted, married long years ago, soon after entering service and long before they were united in keeping Lady Elodie alive. Bertie visited after all (with his wife Alix), and the renewed vigour of the household persuaded Peggy to defer her plans for escape.

The Roxburys lived as happily as any couple can, or any couple I have heard of, outside of stories. She still had seizures, once in a while, but they learned to avert them. Compressing the hysterogenic regions was still effective, but bruising, and an ordeal. If she noticed the onset of the aura that preceded the fit, however, she could go to one of her husband's electrical devices, around the house and grounds, perpetually charged by the Pump House dynamo; by giving herself regulated shocks, trammelling the unruly nervous system through the musculature of the neck, she somehow rode past the seizure's approach, sensing it near, but not succumbing.

Ripon accepted Lodestar's guilt. He never forgave, though, our bamboozlement by the Guernsey papers: two of his special Home Office staff, responsible for bankrupting the military.

Lodestar's claim, that he had an understanding with Ripon, the Secretary of State for War, was never admitted. My confidence in him was broken; my confidence in all those Westminster whiddlers and whingers. Jeffcoat too lost his faith. That Ripon had colluded with Lodestar, while doubting each of us, was no sound basis for work like ours. Ripon had sent Jeffcoat to sneak up on Jacques, but told him not to tell me, lest I were a traitor and might warn the Frenchman. Consequently, the Frenchman was waiting for him.

The detonation we heard was a defence system: Parkesine balls set to go off if anyone approached his refuge. Jeffcoat fell, stunned, in the grass between the Shepherd's Refuge and the Thimbleton lake. He lay still, knowing his advantage lost; only by luck, patience and skill did he manage to shoot the Frenchman when Jacques came to find out what had tripped the detonation.

So far did they reach, Lodestar's efforts to divide us. Yet I had been the most deceived. I was the fuel in waiting, ignited by the sparks of his outrages to inflame the nation into a conflagration of bigotry. I spread the panic for him.

Six members of the Hounds Club were investigated by Scotland Yard: their accounts and investments examined, their whereabouts established for each blast. Prosecutions were brought against four, but dropped before they came to trial, on the grounds of insufficient evidence. In the police, we know what this means: you did it, and we know you did it, but we cannot prove it. Jeffcoat was furious at this cover-up. Thus were Lodestar's crimes suppressed, his associates exonerated, and our efforts belittled.

A leading article in the Tory press threw the blame at our feet, styling it a witch-hunt against these gallant investors, who risked their cash in grim localities troubled by immigrant activism. Hogwash and havering. It made me sick.

London was beyond reform. When Ruth suggested we move to Edinburgh, I leapt at the chance: she to join the Old College Library, and I the Edinburgh City Police Force.

Did Roxbury need to know the depth of Lodestar's treachery? We told him about the imposture and the inheritance.

"Suspected as much. Didn't bother me. His work was outstanding, truly outstanding. Sorry to lose him. He could get anything done, that fellow."

Anything—even start a war.

Birtle and Skirtle never accepted what Lodestar had been up to, still under his spell long after he was gone. Yet Jem's funeral was a sad affair that none could explain away: the Roxbury staff attended to a man; his girl Dotty wept quietly throughout, for she blamed herself.

Lodestar's ambition knew no bounds. Ruth and I debated and debated whether Roxbury truly accepted that Lodestar had been the mastermind of all the explosions, the duping of the nation and the wasting of millions. The company was thus responsible for terrible things. What were we to do? The wrongdoer was gone. Why force the company into disrepute? Whom would that benefit?

Yet so many lives cried out for redress. In our investigations, everything was blamed on Lodestar: every crime, terror, and depravity ascribed to him. Employees around the country admitted terrible things he'd persuaded them to do. Manipulations he had exacted upon them, forcing them—under pain of losing their livelihoods—to do his bidding.

He was undoubtedly the villain, though never brought to justice.

Except, from his point of view, he decidedly was no villain. He was asked to profit a company, and he did, with glowing success. From the company's point of view, his efforts were undeniably to the benefit of Roxbury Industries—even the crimes.

We have constructed a world where those we trusted to protect us are empowered to kill without reproach or redress.

Before I left, I made sure the Home Office had the story clear. I didn't want the Fenians blamed, after O'Leary's help. Nor the French. It was only with individual mercenaries that Lodestar had concocted his schemes, never the French government. Bertie was right all along. When Louis Napoleon finally lost the reins of power, it was to Chislehurst he would move, and the house of an Englishwoman.

So many hurt. So many dead.

Roxbury's achievements will outlive him. They changed the way we think about power. His dream of dispensing with coal remains laughable, however. Wind and sun may be clean and abundant—and one day even his beloved electricity—but what is the hurry, while we are enjoying the profits of empire?

I think in the end Roxbury did understand the truth. He stayed aloof from government. He divested himself of the armaments business; if it was not his company, it would be another. He gave talks on the ethics of technology: science without morality was a rabid, improvident animal. He set up libraries, institutions for working men, housing associations, and hospitals, in a sustained frenzy of charity that, to me, suggested he knew what his company had been responsible for.

He and Elodie left behind Roxbury House in the end, retiring to the coast, where they could watch the village cricket matches from their blustery castle windows—until she died, too young; her ordeal had taken a toll on her slight frame. But the memories remain, good and bad, etched like lightning sparks across our minds, for Roxbury, me, Ruth, and—the heroine of our story in the end—for Molly.

DRAMATIS PERSONAE

LONDON & THE SOUTH

SERGEANT CAMPBELL LAWLESS, also known as Watchman
MOLLY, street urchin, leader of Oddbody Theatricals, drawing mistress
MISS RUTH VILLIERS, former librarian
SERGEANT SOLOMON JEFFCOAT
BODY aboard SS *Great Britain*
HARBOUR MASTER, London docks
DR MALACHI SIMPSON
NUMPTY, urchin
RIPON, Secretary of State for War
LOUIS NAPOLEON III, emperor of France
O'LEARY, a prominent Irish republican
DE NESLE, Guernsey police commissioner
VICTOR HUGO, popular novelist
SPRING-HEELED JACK, legendary character from penny dreadfuls
JULIAN OVEREND, junior partner in Overend and Gurney bank
JACQUES THE PAINTER (Jacques the First)
BERTIE, Prince of Wales, son of Queen Victoria
JOSEPH BAZALGETTE, chief engineer of London Metropolitan Board of Works

ELLIE, a Portsmouth barmaid
LEXIE, Miss Villiers' dreaded aunt
JOSHUA POSTWOOD, banker
BRACEBRIDGE HEMYNG (Jack Harkaway), journalist and flâneur
JACQUES THE PAINTER (London Jacques)
SKITTLES, or **ANONYMA**, or **CATHERINE WALTERS**, courtesan
JEDEDIAH LONGTHROP, orderly on SS *Great Britain*
An engineer for the Solent forts
WILKIE COLLINS, novelist
A PILOT, Portsmouth Harbour

ROXBURY HOUSE & THE NORTH

MOLLY, drawing mistress (viz street urchin, above, the same)
JEM STABLES
BIRTLE, the butler
SKIRTLE, the housekeeper
THE NORPHANS PRACTICKLY, viz:
       Nico, Nicodemus L Roxbury
       Peggy, Margaret V Roxbury
       Kitty, Mary Catherine E Roxbury
NATHAN (NATHANIEL CHICHESTER) LODESTAR, manager of Roxbury Industries
EDWARD, Earl of Roxbury, also called Roxbury or Roxy
PATIENCE TARN, maid, deaf and dumb
WILFRED E ROXBURY, Dragoon Guard, student of Christchurch College, Oxford University
JOSEPH P WHITWORTH, industrialist
SETH SALZMAN, sailor
JACQUES THE PAINTER (Mersey Jacques)
EDWARD LEAR, poet, filthy landscape painter
REVEREND CL DODGSON, an Oxford mathematician

JONATHAN ROXBURY

A DOCTOR

ELODIE, Lady Roxbury

A maid

ZEPHANIAH, of Nyasaland

HUGHLINGS JACKSON, neurologist, visiting associate West Riding Asylum

WIDE-EYED LOU, a patient

In addition, manifold sundry servants, workmen, labourers, scientists, and Dotty, dairymaid, Jem's sweetheart in the village

ACKNOWLEDGMENTS

Thanks to Caroline and to my Dad, Leslie M^cL Sutton.

Thanks to my brother John Sutton for notes on complicity and for dreaming of Nathan Lodestar. Thanks to Nina McIlwain.

Thanks to trusty readers Tessa Ditner, Mirko Sekulic, Diana Bretherick, SJ Butler, John Lloyd, Noel Le Bon, Philip Jeays, John Waltho, Sarah Salway, Vikki Cookson, and Shomit Dutta. Thanks to Karl Bell, John Sackett, Janet Ayers, VH Leslie, Maggie Sawkins, Matt Wingett, Zella Compton, AJ Noon, Tom Harris, Christine Lawrence, Charlotte Comley; to Dallas Campbell, Lucy Holmes, Tim Lewis, Jeremy Campbell; and to the many readers of *Lawless and the Devil of Euston Square* and *Lawless and the Flowers of Sin* who have got in touch to discuss their opinions of Watchman and his errant friends.

Special thanks to Rebecca Lea Williams, director of maps (rebeccaleawilliams.com), and to Mike and William Richards.

Thanks to my wonderful agent Phil Patterson and likewise to John Waltho for pointing me towards Cragside. Thanks to Henry Toulson for the secret chapel. Thanks to Lucy Prosser.

Thanks to Jamie West, Noel Le Bon and Roddy McDevitt, launch collaborators; to Joanna West at Blackwell's Portsmouth; to Lou and all at Forbidden Planet, Shaftesbury

Avenue; to Clare Forsyth and Portsmouth Bookfest. Thanks to Andrew Powney, Greg Klerkx, Roy Leighton, Charlie and Ali Loxton, to George, Lisa, and Fiamma, to Mr Joe Black and his House of Burlesque; to the Boom and Bang Circus; to Tara and Martin Knight @southseacoffee, Farkfk and Lilou @TheTeaTray in the Sky, Kevin and Zirrinia Dean of *Southsea Lifestyle*, Portsmouth Writers' Hub, and to the Authors CC XI. Thanks to Kerry Beel and Talking Change.

And thanks to Cat Camacho, Miranda Jewess, Philippa Ward, Lydia Gittins, and all at Titan Books.

NOTE ON SOURCES

The characters are all fictional, apart from those that aren't. Many of the events are adapted from reality: the blasts, bombs and fires (except Guernsey) are firmly based on 1860s events; for narrative purposes, I have shifted the dates of the Erith blast (October 1864), Camden derailment (August 1864), Princess's Theatre fire (January 1863), the Mersey explosion (January 1864, in fact the *Lottie Sleigh*), and Clerkenwell Prison break (December 1867). Most of the electrical experiments are real, and all the advertisements, more or less. Details and links are on my website, on the Extras page for *Lawless and the House of Electricity*.

I stumbled across William Armstrong, engineer, in the writing of *Lawless and the Devil of Euston Square*, which begins with a burst hydraulic engine.

Before creating my own house of electricity, I had no idea that there was a country house genre. I wanted to recall the warmth I remembered from visits to Barraderry House, Kiltegan, and Schloss Achstetten, Baden-Württemberg; and the glow pervading novels such as JB Priestley's *Bright Day*, Nancy Mitford's *The Pursuit of Love*, Wilkie Collins' *The Moonstone*, and countless Wodehouse novels. I recommend also Mary Shelley's *Frankenstein*, Jane Austen's *Northanger*

Abbey, Wilkie Collins' *Armadale*, Evelyn Waugh's *Brideshead Revisited*, Arthur Conan Doyle's *The Hound of the Baskervilles*, Bill Bryson's delightful *At Home: A Short History of Private Life*, Judith Flanders' seminal *The Victorian House: Domestic Life from Childhood to Deathbed*, and poet Maggie Sawkins' exploration of Charcot in *The Zig Zag Woman*, and Christine Lawrence's *Caught in the Web*. I am grateful to Blake Morrison's article in *The Guardian* on country house novels: theguardian.com/books/2011/jun/11/country-house-novels-blake-morrison

Thanks to Victoria Leslie for guiding me towards *Northanger Abbey*, Daphne du Maurier's *Rebecca* and Edith Wharton's story "Afterward"; and to my dad for Kipling's story "An Habitation Enforced".

What was Elodie's disease? It may be diagnosable by modern criteria: post-partum depression, with epileptic absences or fugues. It has much in common with the *encephalitis lethargica* described in Oliver Sacks' *Awakenings*. But I urge you to consider seriously the catalepsy-lethargy-somnambulism cycle of Charcot's Saltpêtrière hysterics, dissected so brilliantly by Asti Hustvedt in *Medical Muses: Hysteria in Nineteenth-Century Paris*.

Perhaps, just as we laugh at Victorian diagnoses such as strolling congestion, drawing room anguish, dissipation of nerves and imaginary female trouble (contributory factors cited upon commitment to a Victorian asylum), we should think how today's diagnoses will be laughed at in the future. Note Jon Ronson's excellent *The Psychopath Test* for the alarmingly arbitrary origins of DSM diagnostic criteria (*Diagnostic and Statistical Manual of Mental Disorders*).

Hustvedt notes striking similarities between Victorian hysteria diagnoses and today's undifferentiated somatoform disorder, conversion disorder and psychogenic pain syndrome. As Hustvedt writes of her famous Saltpêtrière hysterics, "People have often asked me what I think these women were really suffering from... If only they had been born later, they could have been properly diagnosed and benefited from the latest treatments and pharmaceuticals."

Hustvedt posits, convincingly, that paralysis was an expression of women's disempowerment within society, just as our dysmorphia, eating disorders, depression and anxiety reflect today's narcissistically judgemental obsession with image: "Diseases do not exist outside of diagnoses."

As to Lady Elodie's malady, judge for yourself.

For her treatment, Electro-Convulsive Therapy, as it is known today, may have begun in the 1930s, but "electrical brain stimulation has been used since the 1860s" (*Encyclopedia of Behavioral Neuroscience*).

William Fiennes in *The Music Room* details the early origins of therapeutic electrical stimulation. Duchenne's *Localized electrisation, and its applications to pathology and therapeutics* (1855) was widely read and is republished as a Classic of Neurology edition. *Electro-Physiology and Electro-Therapeutics* by AC Garratt gives further details on Duchenne's procedures, including shocks administered to the brain: "Life is electro-chemistry vitalized. This greatest force of nature, viz, Electricity, which also holds such varied and powerful influences over life, health, and disease, does assuredly command our more attentive study," writes Garratt.

"The therapeutic effects of these apparatus are reputed, among French medical practitioners, to be beneficial in several classes of maladies, and especially in cases of paralysis," reports Dionysius Lardner in his 1856 *Handbook of Natural Philosophy: Electricity, Magnetism, and Acoustics*.

In the 1860s, psychiatrist Gustav Fritsch and anatomist Eduard Hitzig were applying electricity directly to dogs' brains, having removed sections of their skulls under anaesthesia, noting which areas stimulated which movements. Meanwhile, Hughlings Jackson was dissecting brains of deceased epileptic patients in London and York, matching the seizures he had detailed to the injuries, tumours, and lesions. In 1874, physician Roberts Bartholow in Cincinnati induced seizures in Mary Rafferty, whose skull was eroded by cancers. David Ferrier's 1870s work in West Riding Lunatic Asylum, stimulating brains of anaesthetised animals, identified fifteen motor centres.

Sleeping Beauty's awakening by a kiss seems magical, but so did Charcot's revival of comatose hysterics.

Thanks to Matt Wingett for lending me *Portsmouth—A French Gibraltar? (The Portsmouth Papers No. 10)*, by A. Temple Patterson. Molly's paint-mixing is inspired by Ali Smith's *How to Be Both* and influenced by Ivan Morison's series of cards, *Colours in Ivan Morison's garden*.

I acknowledge debts to "The presentation of madness in the Victorian novel" by Allan Beveridge and Edward Renvoize; BBC Radio 4 Frontiers episode "Vagus Nerve", 26 November 2014; "Handling a social threat: the fate of women beyond Victorian societal definition", Alexandra Clifton.

See also: William Stephens Hayward's *Revelations of a Lady Detective*; Lee Jackson's *Dictionary of Victorian London*; Karl Bell's extensive work on Spring-Heeled Jack; *Wayward Women: Female Offending in Victorian England*, by Lucy Williams; *Electricity and Magnetism*, Mike Clemmet; *British Fortification in the Late 19th and Early 20th Centuries*, Nick Dyer and the Palmerston Forts Society; *Spit Bank and the Spithead Forts*, Garry Mitchell; *The Moonstone*, Wilkie Collins; *Lady Audley's Secret*, Mary Elizabeth Braddon; *Edward Lear*, Angus Davidson; *Edward Lear: The Life of a Wanderer*, by Vivien Noakes; *The Wayward Muse*, by Elizabeth Hickey; *Wilkie Collins: A Life of Sensation*, by Andrew Lycett; *William Armstrong: Magician of the North*, by Henrietta Heald; *Emperor of Industry: Lord Armstrong of Cragside*, by Ken Smith; Tolstoy's *What Then Must We Do?* and equally *What Is To Be Done?* by Nikolai Chernyshevsky; Charlotte Brontë's *Jane Eyre* and Emily Brontë's *Wuthering Heights*.

ABOUT THE AUTHOR

William Sutton comes from Dunblane, Scotland. He has appeared at CrimeFest, the Edinburgh International Book Festival, CSI Portsmouth and High Down Prison. He co-produces Portsmouth's DarkFest, in which he compères *Day of the Dead* at the Square Tower; and he helps to programme Portsmouth Bookfest, including *Valentine's Day Massacre* at the Wave Maiden.

He teaches classics. He has written for radio, stage, *The Times*, *The Author*, and magazines around the world. He plays bass in the bands of songwriter Jamie West and chansonnier Philip Jeays. He played cricket for Brazil, and occasionally opens for The Authors Cricket Club. He lives in Southsea with his wife, Caroline.

william-sutton.co.uk | twitter.com/WilliamGeorgeQ
facebook.com/WilliamGeorgeQ | pinterest.com/wgq42/lawless-and-the-house-of-electricity
soundcloud.com/william-george-sutton/sets/watchman

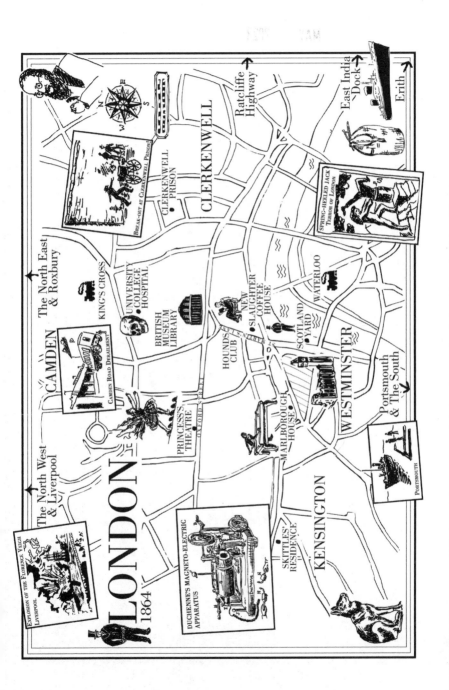

LONDON
1864

EXPLOSION OF THE FLORENCE VEIGH
LIVERPOOL

The North West
& Liverpool

The North East
& Roxbury

CAMDEN

CAMDEN ROAD DERAILMENT

KING'S CROSS

UNIVERSITY
COLLEGE
HOSPITAL

BRITISH
MUSEUM
LIBRARY

PRINCESS'S
THEATRE

OXFORD STREET

DUCHENNE'S MAGNETO-ELECTRIC
APPARATUS

SKITTLES'
RESIDENCE

KENSINGTON

HOUNDS
CLUB

NEW
SLAUGHTER
COFFEE
HOUSE

SCOTLAND
YARD

WATERLOO

MARLBOROUGH
HOUSE

WESTMINSTER

Portsmouth
& The South

PORTSMOUTH

CLERKENWELL
PRISON

CLERKENWELL

BREAK-OUT AT CLERKENWELL PRISON

Ratcliffe
Highway

SPRING-HEELED JACK
TERROR OF LONDON

East India
Dock

Erith

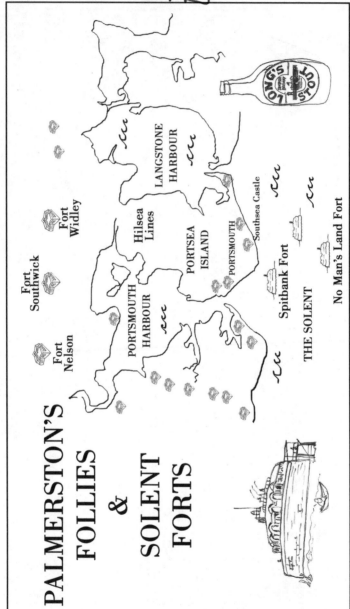

PALMERSTON'S FOLLIES & SOLENT FORTS